THE DIFFICULT YEARS OF TOSHI OZAWA

Kamaishi Heritage – Book II

Copyright © 2024 by

D. D. Davenport

ISBN 979-8-9905440-2-4 Paperback

ISBN 979-8-9905440-3-1 (eBook)

Library of Congress Control Number: 2024910962

All rights reserved. No part of this book may be used or reproduced in any manner without permission.

Version V.12302024

This Book is Dedicated

to

readers of every age and culture who push forward with integrity, in search of a better life.

This is a work of historical fiction. Three of the many characters in the story were real and living at the time of their appearance. All thoughts, conversations, and actions attributed to them are solely of my imagination. See Author's Notes following the story for more information about the story and the characters.

***

While Japanese culture refers to family name first, followed by the given name, this book refers to them in western format, given name first, followed by family or surname. Admittedly, it is an example of why Japan was reluctant to interact with foreign countries back in 1864: the fear of losing their cultural heritage. Since most readers of this book will likely be Westerners, that is the format used here.

Regarding honorifics, *san* is used at times in the story to show respect for a stranger, age, or social standing. While there are many variations of honorifics, depending on who is being addressed, only *san* is used here.

INTRODUCTION

The Difficult Years of Toshi Ozawa is Book II of the *Kamaishi Heritage* series. The series spans seventy years and three generations of the Ozawa family. While Toshi and his family and friends are characters of my imagination, the story is based on actual historical events.

Book I began the story at a small village on the northeast coast of Japan. Toshi moved to Kamaishi from Tokyo in search of a rewarding career. His future wife, Ayami moved there to escape an abusive father. It was love at first sight for the two of them, although it took time and ingenuity for them to meet.

The fledgling Kamaishi iron foundry struggled to survive, in spite of the dedicated efforts by Toshi and his uncle, Haruki.

When Toshi learned that Ayami's father consigned her younger sister to work at a silk factory, Toshi took steps to bring her home. The daring raid was successful, but not without a price.

With help from their new friend at the *Warrior Empress Emporium,* they began selling fish and rice to the very silk factory they had raided not long before.

Book II begins with one of those deliveries.

For a more enjoyable reading experience, I urge you to read each book in sequence.

Contents

SABURO KONDO	1
CHOLERA	7
OSAKI COMMITMENT	17
BANDITS	25
BODYGUARDS	33
STUBBORN AS A MULE	39
SAFELY HOME	49
CONVERSION	59
TWO VERSIONS OF THE SAME STORY	67
CHRISTIANS AT LAST	73
NIGHTTIME DREAM	79
DISASTER	89
THE FISHING FLEET	99
HAJIME	109
EMIKO	113
HELP FROM THE FOUNDRY	119
HELP FROM THE EMPRESS	133
MILK FOR THE FOUNDLING	145
AFTERMATH	149
DESIGNING THE CHURCH	153
REVELATION	161
PLEA FOR A PRIEST	167
FIRST MASS AT ST. MARY'S	177
ISAMU GROWS UP	191

A LOOK THROUGH THE MIRROR	199
ISAMU'S DREAM	203
LIFE AT THE FOUNDRY	221
FR. KATZ'S CONFESSION	231
ENGLISH LESSONS	237
TIME TO SAY GOODBYE	245
YOKOHAMA	249
NOT CHO AT THE DOCK	257
LEAVING JAPAN	269
TROUBLE AT SEA	287
LOCATING THE TARGET	297
THE NET TIGHTENS	313
OROCHI MIZUNO	319
REACHING OUT	325
THE CAPTAIN'S TEAM	339
FIRST VIEW	359
EPILOGUE	367
AUTHOR'S NOTES	381
ABOUT THE AUTHOR	385

PART ONE

The Kamaishi Trading Company

CHAPTER 1
Saburo Kondo

JULY 1882 – KAMAISHI, JAPAN

A single rider approached Kamaishi from the west. July heat bore across his head and shoulders. Sweat dripped down the back of his neck. The coal-black mare, once young and beautiful, today looked tired and worn, much like the middle-aged man who sat astride her sagging back.

Overhead, two black-eared kites drifted across the open sky, their wings outstretched to catch unseen thermals as they peered to the ground below for unsuspecting prey. A sika deer tugged gently at leaves from a nearby beech tree, then slipped to the shadows and out of sight. Beside them, Japanese white-eyes flitted among the nearby pines, their high-pitched warbles the only sound along the trail. Neither horse nor rider seemed to care.

Saburo hunched slightly in the saddle. It had been a long and difficult ride from Tokyo; almost a month since he left home, and he missed his family. He missed his regular bed, his home-cooked meals, and his neighbors. Even the one who annoyed him so with late-night parties. He would gladly trade late-night singing for long days far from home.

But Saburo had to keep going. He was behind schedule, and behind in schedule meant behind in earnings. He had not earned a commission in over two weeks. If the Kamaishi Iron Works really had closed, as rumors maintained, there would surely be workers needing a job. If a breadwinner was out of work, his family would suffer. Saburo could not replace the breadwinner's job but he could help in another way. He could put one of the children to work. Not only would it bring in a modest income, it would reduce the number of mouths to feed. Taken together, an attractive option.

In the early days, recruiting for silk factories had been easy. The job of reeling raw silk from the cocoons of silkworms was once considered something special. A mark of honor for daughters of wealthy families. But that was years ago. Since then, factories had sprung up everywhere, it seemed, and there weren't enough wealthy daughters to go around. Now, recruiters like himself had to travel the country in search of peasant daughters from desperate families.

Sometimes, in order to convince a protective father, Saburo found it necessary to embellish the truth regarding the pay, or the working conditions, but only enough to convince the protective father.

It could be argued that Saburo Kondo had killed people. That is to say, he had placed young people in positions that led to their death. He would never have killed someone intentionally. He was a family man himself. He loved his wife, and he loved his children. He liked people in general.

Perhaps if he had written a note, it might have saved others. Maybe hundreds of others, in the small village up ahead. Saburo had no way of knowing the cool, clear water of the Kasshigawa River was a common source for drinking water in the village of Kamaishi. Had he known, he might not have rinsed himself in the shaded pool just off the trail.

Even had he known he had hours to live, what good would it have done? He was too far from home to turn back now. Tokyo was days away, even on horseback. He knew not a single soul in Kamaishi. And if the small village had a physician, would it matter? The damage was done.

***

At midday, Saburo had a queasy stomach and decided not to stop for lunch. Kamaishi was only a few hours away. He pictured in his mind a cool room, an open window, a gentle breeze. If he were lucky, the room might even overlook the blue waters of the Pacific Ocean. He had heard Kamaishi was nestled on the coast, with panoramic views of the sea. When he closed his eyes, he could almost feel the breeze, sifting through an open window.

An hour later, uneasiness gave way to mild cramping. Soon after, his bowels began to tighten. Trying to keep the growing discomfort from his mind, he forced himself to think of the sleeping room, with its gentle breeze and ocean view, and pushed slowly onward.

Suddenly, with barely enough warning to jump from the horse, Saburo rushed to a nearby clump of bushes and emptied his stomach. *That came on quick,* he thought. He wondered if something had been wrong with his last meal. The more he thought about it the more he convinced himself the boiled eggs he'd eaten for breakfast had a peculiar taste. *It must have been the eggs.*

Minutes later, he needed to empty his bowels. He dashed behind the same clump of bushes, lowered his undergarment, and squatted. Feces burst from his rectum, loose and wet. *This will pass*, he convinced himself. *It must have been the eggs.*

With the episode behind him, he climbed on the black mare and resumed his course. He tried to decide if his stomach was settling. The more he thought about it, the more he convinced himself he was better. He rode on, at a quickened pace. Kamaishi should be just ahead.

An hour later, he was forced to stop a second time. Again, he vomited, though his stomach was mostly empty. Then came a cramp in his bowels, which he also emptied for the second time. It was nearly all water this time. He had not experienced diarrhea like this before, and it troubled him. For the first time, he wondered if it really was the eggs.

Pressing on, he lasted another hour before it hit again. Surely, Kamaishi was just ahead. He regretted not having traveled here before, to become familiar with the region. Then he regretted coming now.

He desperately wanted to be home with his family. It dawned on him this might be something serious. These were not familiar symptoms. This time, the third time, he was not able to dismount fast enough to spare the horse. He leaned over the side as far as he could reach and vomited sputters of bile, which landed, some on the horse and some on the ground below. But the diarrhea had no place to go except his undergarment.

Saburo was beginning to feel light-headed in addition to the eruptions from his stomach and bowel. He finally accepted that Kamaishi was too far to travel, and looked along the roadway for a place to rest. He would stop for the night. *Surely, he would feel better after a night's rest.*

It became more and more difficult to concentrate on a place to camp, as his symptoms became increasingly acute. Finally, spotting a stand of trees next to a bend in the river, he found the perfect spot. It was quiet, shaded, and hidden from passersby along the road. Saburo was not in a mood to be disturbed by strangers.

Dismounting for the fourth time in as many hours, he quickly grabbed a blanket and his satchel from the horse, then shuffled to a space behind the trees, close to the river. The water flowed slowly here, in a quiet pool of shallow water.

Though late afternoon, it was still a warm July day. The sun reflected brightly off the water and reminded him how thirsty he had become. He took several long drinks from the waterskin pouch he always carried. It tasted good. He tried to remember where he'd filled it last. Traveling as he did, one could not depend on finding a suitable stream or river from which to drink.

By the time he unsaddled his horse and set up a makeshift camp, his symptoms were more extreme. His undergarments, even his outer garments, were saturated with an excrement that felt like soup. His fingers and toes began to tingle; something new to worry about.

He waded into the shallow water and lay down on his back, letting the current wash vomit and excrement from his clothes and body. He splashed his face to rinse away the sweat and dirt. He was tired, but too restless to sleep. As he lay cleansing himself, or to be more accurate, letting the current cleanse him, he listened to the soothing sound of birds in the nearby trees;

two warblers called back and forth. *I'd like to come here again, when I'm feeling better*, he thought to himself.

Too exhausted to lift his head and look for intruders, he yielded to the cramp in his stomach, and relaxed the muscle holding back his bowel. The watery substance sent bubbles to the surface as it joined the gently flowing stream.

He laid there until the cramp subsided. Then, forcing himself from the river, he moved to the grassy bank, and laid down on his blanket. Suddenly, he was chilled. *It must have been the water*, he thought. It felt good at first, but now he was cold. He rolled to his side, facing the western sun. It felt good as it warmed his face. He drew his knees upward to his chest, trying to retain what body heat he could.

Using all his remaining strength, Saburo reached for his water pouch, and lifting it slightly above his mouth, drank the few remaining swallows. It tasted good. He wished for more, and licked his lips. *Why am I so thirsty?* he wondered.

He placed his left arm under his head for a pillow, with his right arm stretched out across the blanket in front of him. Too tired to lift his head again, he stared ahead at whatever was in his line of view. Mostly, it was his right arm. He studied it as it lay there, inches from his head. It felt like he was viewing it from a different world. *When did the skin get so loose?* he wondered. *I don't remember it sagging like that before.*

Panic struck, as it finally occurred to Saburo this was the end.

I'm going to die here alone. I won't be able to say goodbye to my family. They don't even know where I am. I'm a stranger in this land and they won't know who to report me to. I am sorry if I wronged anyone along the way. I did the best I could.

Saburo had no way of knowing whether any of the girls he recruited had died from their working conditions, but if records had been kept, Suki Ishii, Age 15, Hanamaki, Iwate Prefecture, would have been counted among them.

Five people were with her that day she died. Two of them were Kazuo Tetsuo, of the rescue team, and Emiko Matsumoto, Suki's friend and coworker at the factory. They watched helplessly as Suki took her last breath, three kilometers from the Osaki Thread Mill. She was on her way home to family and freedom. It was in April of 1881.

Hours later, Saburo Kondo remembered seeing the sun go down, and the moon come up. His mind was aware until the last breath.

CHAPTER 2
CHOLERA

JULY 1882 – KAMAISHI

The road Saburo traveled was the same route that led Haruki, Toshi, and Kazuo to and from Kitakami with their cargo of freshly smoked fish. By now, the trail had matured to the point it could safely be called a road. The Kamaishi Trading Company was able to haul their freight in a wagon, pulled by a team of mules, and the trio made a round trip every other week, thanks to their recent contract with the Osaki Silk Factory. Once or twice each month, Kazuo's recent wife, Emiko, would join the group, riding in the wagon to visit the Empress in Kitakami, and her family in Hanamaki.

By sheer coincidence, they were headed to Kitakami the morning after Saburo died. As they approached the ill-fated location, Kazuo saw a black mare just beyond the side of the road, with no saddle and no one in sight. He pulled up on his favorite horse, the blood bay, and stopped to make sure the horse was being cared for.

It was skittish at first, as Kazuo approached, but Kazuo was an experienced horseman, and knew how to gain its trust. Walking slowly toward him and speaking in a low voice, he held out a carrot as inducement for the horse to let him come near. Having accomplished that, he took the reins, still on the horse, and led him to the river to let him drink.

As he passed behind a dense clump of red barberry bushes, Kazuo caught the glimpse of a man, lying on a blanket, not far from the water. He called out to the man, but received no reply.

He took several steps toward the man and called again. Still no reply. Concerned, he bent down close for a better look. It was then he saw the emaciated face, and the blue-gray color of his skin. The man was dead.

Careful not to get too close without knowing what had happened, he first called back to Emiko and the others to stay in the wagon. Then he edged closer for a better look, still calling out, hoping for a reply.

He turned back then, and looked into the eyes of the horse. Was it possible the horse was also sick? While it did not seem likely, Kazuo could not be sure.

He looked around for belongings of the man, hoping to learn who he was or where he came from. There was a water pouch lying next to the body, but nothing more. Possibly he carried important papers on his person, but Kazuo was not inclined to look.

He walked in silence back to the wagon. "The horse's owner is lying by the river, but I didn't want to get too close. He must have died from something terrible. He looks like a skeleton, lying there. His eyes are sunken back in his head, and his skin is dark, and its hanging from his bones. I don't know what it is, and I don't want to get any closer."

Haruki climbed from the wagon and Toshi dismounted his horse, and the two slowly approached. They craned their necks as they neared the clump of bushes. Three steps later, Toshi quietly declared, "I've never seen a body so…" and his voice trailed off, color draining from his face.

"What should we do?" Kazuo asked.

Even the normally unflappable Haruki was caught off-guard. After a moment he answered, "We have to alert the authorities. I'll ride back to Kamaishi and get the physician. Kazuo, you and Emiko take the wagon and head for Kitakami. We still have to make the delivery. Toshi, maybe you should stay here and keep everyone away from the body."

"What about the horse?" Kazuo asked. "He'll need a place to stay, or at least to make sure he's fed and watered."

"I think we should let him be for now, until the physician has a chance to look at the body," Haruki replied. "What if the horse can catch whatever the man had?"

Then Emiko exclaimed. "Kazuo! Did you touch the horse? What if the horse is sick? Please don't touch him again."

"I don't think horses can get human diseases," he replied softly. "But just to be safe, I won't touch him again. At least until the physician gives his approval."

"I'll stay here with the horse and the body," Toshi said. "If the physician thinks it's safe, we can ask him to take the horse back to Kamaishi and leave it at the livery. We can worry about what to do with it when we get back from Kitakami. He obviously belongs to someone. By the time we get back, maybe they'll figure out who. Surely the man has a family."

"He probably has some kind of identification papers, but I'm not about to look for them," Kazuo said.

"Me either," replied Toshi.

"It's settled, then. Kazuo, you and Emiko take the team and go. Toshi, you stay here and keep everyone away until I get back with the physician. Kazuo, we shouldn't have any trouble catching up to you, but if not, we'll meet you tonight at the campsite."

Then Haruki rode east, and Kazuo drove the mule team west, with Emiko in the wagon beside him.

Toshi stood under a tree away from the dead man's body, trying to determine the most efficient way to keep the horse from getting either too close or too far away from him. He started almost immediately to count the minutes until Haruki's return.

Haruki let the horse gallop most of the way back to the village. He was not accustomed to riding fast and would have actually enjoyed the thrill of it, had he not been so focused on the task ahead. *What if the physician isn't home? What should I do then? Should I warn the entire village? What if it's not even contagious? It would be almost as bad to sound a false alarm, as to not warn them at all.*

It took what seemed an eternity to reach the physician's house, yet it also seemed like he'd barely left the dead man's remains, as he sped past the little church at the edge of the village. Fr. Lispard, the Jesuit missionary, had just finished his early morning mass, and was exiting through the front door when he saw his friend Haruki ride past.

He knew instinctively something was wrong, for Haruki to be in such a hurry. Instead of continuing to his own house for the breakfast of warm bread and jam he was accustomed to, he headed in the opposite direction. *Haruki was most likely headed to the physician. Something must have happened to his wife, Minako, or one of their girls,* he thought. But why would he have one of Kazuo's horses? *Did something happen to Kazuo?* He quickened his pace as he considered the possibilities.

Sure enough, the horse was standing in front of the physician's house, the reins draped across the saddle and on the ground. Haruki had already dismounted and gone inside. Fr. Lispard let himself in and walked to the small parlor, where he heard two quiet voices. He recognized them both.

"I've never seen a man so shriveled," he heard Haruki say in a voice almost quivering. "His eyes were sunken way back in his head, and his cheeks were like someone sucked out all the flesh from the inside. His color was dark, and the skin draped from his hands. He was mostly under a blanket, so I couldn't see a lot of him. But he looked like a skeleton, wrapped in skin."

"Could you see any sign of him vomiting or thrashing around before he died?" the physician asked. "And you say he was alone? Had he made camp there? Was there any remnant of food? Maybe it was something he'd eaten."

"To be honest, I didn't really look around much," Haruki replied. "Once I saw his face, I was afraid to get close. Toshi is with him now, to make sure no one gets close, and to keep the man's horse from running away. We didn't know if it was something the horse could catch, whatever it is."

"Usually, animals aren't susceptible to human diseases, but that's not always the case. I'll hitch up the buggy and follow you out there. We may as well take a shovel along. I don't want to expose the village if it's contagious." He paused. "I'm afraid it might be cholera from the sound of it." He grabbed up his bag of instruments and compounds, and headed to the livery, where he kept a horse and buggy.

"Maybe I should ride with you," Fr. Lispard interjected. "I can help dig the grave if nothing else." He looked at the physician. "I have a medical book the order provides to all missionaries. It contains a list of symptoms and remedies for all maladies likely to be encountered during the course of our work. Would you like me to bring it along?"

The physician tried not to show he was offended by the offer, but it was not lost on Haruki. Or on Fr. Lispard.

"I won't need your medical help. But you might be helpful digging the grave. Come with me to get the buggy and we'll leave from there." Then he headed out the door and down the street toward the livery barn.

Haruki, not wanting to call additional attention in the village, mounted his horse and nudged him at a walk past the church, along the route he had just traveled in haste. The physician would catch up to him soon enough. With luck, few in the village would have witnessed their short encounter.

Suddenly, he thought about Minako and their girls, Hisa, Kanae, and Saya, the youngest, and of Toshi's wife, Ayami, and their two boys, Kiyoshi and Isamu. They should be safe as long as they stayed at home up on the ridge, but they would soon be coming down to open the teahouse.

Haruki turned his horse around and, at a trot this time, headed past the physician's house and the short distance beyond, to their joint family enterprise. No one was there, so he let himself in and found one of the papers they used to keep track of sales and purchases. Writing in big scratchy letters, he left instructions.

Found dead man just outside village. Physician, Fr. Lispard and I on way to determine cause. Could be contagious and serious. Close the store immediately and keep everyone at home. Meet you there when I get back. Haruki

Then he re-locked the door, mounted his horse, and for the third time that day, headed west on the road to Kitakami. It was barely nine o'clock.

He could see the physician approaching a few hundred meters behind in the buggy, with Fr. Lispard seated alongside. Even from this distance, Haruki could see the angst on their faces. He hoped he was the only one who noticed.

***

Toshi was pacing under a tree several meters from where the body lay. A look of relief crossed his face when he saw them approach.

Haruki looked for the man's horse and was relieved to see it grazing in a stand of grass, a short distance beyond Toshi. He dismounted as the two men in the buggy climbed out. He and the priest hung back as the physician timidly walked forward, around the clump of barberry, to get his first glimpse of the corpse. He stared at it for some time, then returned to the group.

"You were right, Haruki," he began. "The man has definitely been through a traumatic death. One sure symptom of cholera is a 'rice water' stool. I'm afraid we're going to have to disturb the body and see if we can find any evidence of diarrhea. I've got a pair of gloves in my bag. Do any of you have gloves, or an old rag, or something you can use to help me examine the body?"

The three men looked at one another with anxious faces. Fr. Lispard stepped forward. "I have two *lavabo* towels in my pocket. I was taking them home to launder. I don't think our Lord would mind if I used them for an emergency like this." He pulled out the two linens. They were about thirty-five by forty-five centimeters in size.

The physician remarked without much effort to hide his impatience. "I have no idea what a *lavabo* towel is, but if it can keep germs away from your hands, then it will have to do."

Fr. Lispard smiled back at him with sincerity. "My apologies. Of course, you couldn't know what a *lavabo* is. It's simply a small bowl and urn used in preparation for communion during mass. The priest washes his fingers prior to handling the hosts, and the *lavabo* towel is used to dry them."

The physician seemed to ignore the explanation as he turned his attention to the dead man's body. He was laying on his right side, in a fetal position, with his knees pulled up toward his chest. Whether it was for warmth or from pain in his stomach, could not be determined.

"We need to straighten him out if we can, and examine his feces, if there are any. Use your 'towels' to grab both his ankles and see if you can straighten them out. I'll hang on to his shoulders so he doesn't slide away."

Looking at Toshi and Haruki, he said, "You might as well get the pick and shovel from the buggy and start digging a grave. Put it somewhere away from the river; I don't want it to contaminate the water. I imagine it's going to be rocky digging, but make it as deep as you can. We'll have to cover the rest with rocks and such."

Fr. Lispard gently wrapped one of the towels around each of the dead man's ankles, trying to avoid contact with the sagging flesh as best he could. He tugged first on the ankle closest to him, which was the man's left foot. He was aghast at how light it was, from complete dehydration. The irony was not lost on the priest. *He was using the drying towel on a man who had been completely purged of his life-sustaining water.*

Then he stooped down to take hold of the man's right ankle. Even with both feet and legs off the ground, it felt like not more than twenty kilograms. Fr. Lispard slowly pulled on his legs, by the ankles.

"Put some force in it," the physician grunted. "He's not going to break. And even if he does, he'll be none the worse for it."

Fr. Lispard applied more and more pressure until gradually, the legs began to straighten. When the dead man was finally in more or less a straight-line posture, the physician signaled it was enough. He rolled the body over on its stomach and proceeded to remove his undergarments. While still at arms-length, he studied the garment for traces of feces. It was clearly saturated with a liquid of some kind, most likely watery diarrhea.

Had Fr. Lispard brought his medical reference book along, either of them might have learned additional symptoms to look for. Unfortunately, the large bound manual was resting on a shelf, next to a window, in the small hut he referred to as home.

With nothing more to be done, the physician announced: "Let's pick him up by the blanket he was on and carry him over to the grave." Fr. Lispard grabbed both corners of the blanket on his end, while the physician did the same at the opposite end. Carefully picking their path so as not to let the body fall, they made their way to where Toshi and Haruki were busy digging a rectangular hole some twenty meters north of the river, under an aging Sycamore tree.

They placed him in the hole, still lying on the blanket. The physician removed his gloves and tossed them in the hole near the dead man's feet. Fr. Lispard looked forlornly at the ghoulish cadaver, facing upward toward a peaceful blue sky. He bent down slowly and placed the lavabo towels over the man's face. He could not bear to cover his face with rocks and dirt, the linens would preserve a tiny sliver of dignity. He stood up again, and gazing at the man one last time, heard two songbirds hidden from view. They seemed to be offering a final farewell to whoever it was that had come to an end on the floor below.

Then Toshi and Haruki gently covered the body with loose dirt, for as much as they could, and finally with rocks of different shapes and sizes. The cadaver was covered with enough dirt to keep his scent intact, then topped with an upper layer of rocks, heavy enough to prevent animals of the forest from exhuming the body. The dead man would be at peace.

The physician was busy adjusting the contents of his bag and writing sketchy notes in one of his journals. Toshi, Haruki, and the priest stood a short distance away.

Toshi looked at Fr. Lispard and asked, "What made you do that?"

Fr. Lispard looked at him with a look of surprise. "Do what?" he replied.

"What made you help the physician? Weren't you afraid of getting whatever the man had? He was a complete stranger, and you risked your life by touching him when you didn't need to. You're not even a countryman. You're from France. Why would you do that?"

Fr. Lispard looked over at the mound of rocks not far away. Then he turned back to Toshi. "Well, first of all, it wasn't for the complete stranger. It was too late for him. I did it for you, and for Haruki, and for your families. And for all my friends and parishioners here who are not strangers."

He thought for a few moments before continuing. He was not sure he had adequately conveyed his meaning. "If you truly believe in God, then it follows that you have complete trust in Him. If you have both of those things, then it's not so hard to follow Him wherever He leads you. I could fall from the roof fixing a leak tomorrow. I could drown in the sea a few years from now, or I could die from old age when I'm ninety-five.

"Since earth is only a temporary place for man, and eternity is the true goal, then it really doesn't matter how long we're here. Our Lord was only on earth for thirty-three years. I've already been here longer than that. So, I guess the answer is 'no,' I wasn't worried about catching whatever he had. And if I can help prevent others from getting what he had, then I really don't have much of a decision to make."

Toshi and Haruki simply watched his face and listened. How long they stayed that way would be difficult to say. The physician broke their spell when he said in an unnecessarily loud voice, "Do you have any idea which way the man was headed? Was he coming to Kamaishi or leaving?"

Haruki and Toshi looked at each other and shook their heads. "I don't know where he was going," Haruki answered.

"If he was on his way to Kamaishi, maybe his early death saved a lot of lives. But if he has already been there, he has probably exposed some number of people," the physician said.

"Is it cholera, then?" asked Fr. Lispard.

"I can't be sure, since he was already dead. His symptoms appear to be from cholera. But without seeing the progression, I can't be sure. Have you found anything to identify the man? Did he have any papers in his saddle bag? Surely, he must have some kind of papers. How can I notify his family if we don't know who he is?"

With that, the four of them made a search of the entire area, including the horse and saddle, which had been lying on the ground near his body. Finally, Toshi looked out in the river, and in the shallows, spotted a leather bag partly submerged, and lodged against a rock formation near the bank.

"What's that?" he exclaimed, pointing toward the brown leather skin. Then he waded out to retrieve it. The water was only up to his ankles. He reached down to pick it up and carefully carried it back to the group.

He handed it to the physician, who peered down into each of the two pockets. Then he sighed and handed it back. Whatever was there must have washed away in the current.

"It looks like we're out of luck," Fr. Lispard said quietly, "unless someone in the village recognizes his horse. If he came through Kamaishi, he would probably have boarded his horse at the livery. Maybe they'll remember something about him."

The others nodded in agreement. No one could think of other options. The man seemed to have come from nowhere.

Haruki turned to Toshi. "One of us needs to go back to Kamaishi and take care of our families. I left a note at the store to tell them all to go back home and wait. And one of us needs to catch up with Kazuo and Emiko to make the delivery to the silk factory. He looked directly at Toshi when he said that, as a reminder that neither Kazuo nor Emiko could go.

"Why don't you go with them, and I'll go back to Kamaishi," Haruki continued. "You should be able to catch up to them by nightfall without much trouble. And I'll take care of things at home. We'll take the man's horse and saddle to the livery for now...if they'll take him. They might not want him when they hear how we found him."

Toshi mounted his horse. "We'll try to get back early if we can." Then he turned his horse to the west and nudged him to a trot, waved goodbye, and rode away.

Haruki rounded up the man's horse and saddle, then led him by the reins, from his own. Fr. Lispard and the physician turned the buggy around, and the three men headed east, each man burdened with thoughts of what lay ahead.

CHAPTER 3
OSAKI COMMITMENT

JULY 1882 - KAMAISHI

When he reached the physician's house, Haruki dismounted and joined the others. "What do we do now?" he asked.

"Now we wait," the physician replied. "If we're lucky, he died before infecting anyone else, and we won't have an outbreak. If we can get by for four or five days, we should be out of the woods."

"What should I tell the livery?" Haruki asked. "Should I tell them about the owner? I'll have to give them a reason for having the horse."

"Tell them we found the horse grazing by the river and we're trying to locate the owner. Maybe they'll recognize the horse and remember something about the man. I don't think the horse can spread the disease, no matter what it was."

Haruki proceeded to the livery stable, which was toward the docks and one street over from North Front.

The physician quickly entered his house and retrieved his *Journal of Symptoms and Remedies* reference manual. Several of the chapters were worn and tattered, but the section on *Vibrio cholerae* was untouched.

On reaching the church, Fr. Lispard did the same. Reading from his reference book, he considered the implications.

Symptoms: *abrupt onset of vomiting and diarrhea, resulting in dehydration. Followed by severe and painful cramping of the legs, arms, back, and abdomen. Watery stools resemble rice water. Skin* *loses elasticity, becomes wrinkled, cold, clammy to the touch. Sometimes described as 'washerwoman's hands.' Eyes become sunken, cheeks hollow.* **Means of contraction:** *Ingested through the mouth, usually from feces-contaminated water, but occasionally from food.* **Treatment:** *prayer and rehydration. Death occurs from acute dehydration of internal organs. Ingest as much purified water or liquid as possible, as soon as possible following onset of symptoms.*

It was cholera; he knew for sure. The questions remaining were: where had he drank the water, and had he passed it on to the village? Then he thought about the waterskin he'd seen laying by the man's body and the blanket. *What had they done with the waterskin?*

No one at the livery stable remembered seeing the horse before. Haruki chose his words carefully whenever asked about the owner of the horse. It was not within his ability to lie, yet he did not want to cause needless concern. Particularly, if it turned out to be a false alarm. "The physician is looking into it," he would reply to questions about its owner.

***

As Toshi pressed onward to Kitakami, he had time alone to ponder all the events of that fateful morning. His mind would not relinquish the hideous image of the dead man on his blanket. Never had he seen such empty eye sockets, such an emaciated body, such loosely hanging skin. He could not help but wonder how painful his death must have been. *Did it happen quickly? Did he suffer? Did he know what was coming?* He tried to push the questions from his mind.

He was almost to the campsite when he caught up to the wagon. He could see them looking back periodically as he came into their view. They were noticeably anxious to learn about the fate of the dead man. As soon as he was near enough, questions from the wagon began.

"Did he have cholera?" Kazuo shouted above the noise of the mules and the wagon.

"The physician thinks so but said he wasn't sure," Toshi shouted back. He looked at Emiko, who returned his gaze with a sad and empty look.

"Did you stop to eat?" he asked, trying to change the subject.

"We grabbed a snack as we drove, but we didn't want to stop," Kazuo replied. "We should be at the campsite in less than an hour. Let's keep going and rest when we get there. You can go on ahead, if you want. Maybe you could get a fire started."

"Okay. I'll see you there."

With that, he rode on ahead to prepare their camp. He had a small fire burning and was heating water for tea when the wagon arrived.

"What about the horse?" Kazuo asked. "Did the horse get sick too?"

"No, the horse seemed normal when I left. Haruki was going to take him to the livery for safekeeping until they find out who he belongs to."

"He didn't have any identification?"

"No, we found a saddle bag floating in the river, but it was partly open. We figure any papers he might have had were washed away," Toshi replied.

The campfire slowly eroded the burden of worry from the travelers. Something about the flames brought quiet comfort to the trio. Surrounded by a forest of pines, firewood was plentiful, gathered from the nearby trees. Most was dry enough to burn quietly, but the fire snapped and popped as it worked its way through newer wood. The three of them gazed solemnly at the fire as they ate.

Toshi thought about Ayami and the boys. *What if cholera made it to the village?*

Kazuo wondered about his animals. *Could animals get cholera?*

Emiko thought about Haruki and her aunt, Minako. *Would cholera take over the village?*

Finally, half-way through his second cup of tea, Toshi started a conversation, hoping to remove cholera from their thoughts. "At times like this, I really miss coffee from the foundry director. Did you know that about him, Kazuo? I don't think he ever drank tea. He always drank coffee. It took me a few times to like it. The first time he offered me coffee, I was too afraid to tell him no. Then, after a few times, I learned to like it. I haven't had coffee since they closed the foundry."

"I heard he liked coffee, but I never had occasion to try it. What does it taste like?" Kazuo replied.

Toshi had to think about that. "Well, it's kind of hard to describe since it doesn't taste like anything else. I guess you could say it is similar to tea, but stronger. It's darker. Heavier, maybe. More…robust. Yes, I like that description. It's more robust than tea. Perfect for a night around the campfire."

As Kazuo considered the explanation, Emiko spoke up. "Why don't you add coffee to your inventory? You should find a way to import coffee and sell it in Japan. The Empress is always looking for new merchandise at the emporium. I'm sure she'd be happy to introduce coffee to her customers."

Toshi chuckled at first, and then he thought about it. "I think you might be on to something, Emiko. It could take a while to catch on, but if others are like me, they would learn to like it. Maybe not all the time, but on special occasions. I wonder how we'd go about it. Let's talk to the Empress tomorrow."

"Do you think we should go home in the morning?" Emiko finally asked. "If there's an outbreak, shouldn't we be there to help?"

"It is tempting to go back," Toshi replied. I've thought about it, too. But we can't, really. We have to get this fish and especially the rice to Osaki, or the workers will go hungry. That's something we didn't consider when we got the contract. But the girls depend on us now. If we missed a shipment, I don't know how Cho would feed them.

"Besides, there is nothing we could do in Kamaishi. We don't even know if there's a problem. Maybe the man died before he ever got to Kamaishi and wasn't able to contaminate anyone. So I don't think there's any reason to turn back. But I would be in favor of getting back a day early, if we could. Do you have any idea how we could make better time on our trip?"

Emiko was ready with an answer. "If we left at dawn tomorrow, we could get to Hanamaki and load the rice, then get back to Kitakami and spend the night with the Empress. As much as I like to spend the night with my mother, I could give it up this time. Then, if we left at dawn from the emporium, we could get to Osaki the following morning and head home from there before noon. If we traveled late, we could make it back to Kamaishi a day early. We did it with Suki. And we're all stronger now. I'm sure we could make it."

They reached the emporium in Kitakami before noon and quickly unloaded their order of fish before heading out again for Hanamaki. Toshi didn't bother to ask the Empress about how to import coffee. It would keep until they returned for the night. He did, though, tell her about their encounter with the mysterious man, and his concern that Kamaishi might erupt with the disease. They both wondered, but did not ask, whether cholera could be transmitted through their order of smoked fish.

Kunio was not expecting them until evening, but recognized the wagon drawn by four mules when it approached. It was the only such rig to be seen in the region of this farm community. He had already laid out four hundred kilos of rice, ready for shipment to Osaki. He, Kazuo, and Toshi loaded the wagon while Emiko visited with her mother in the kitchen.

Toshi and Kazuo talked with Kunio as they worked. "Your supply is running low, Kunio," Toshi said. "And we're committed to providing rice every two weeks. Would your neighbors be willing to make us the same deal as you?"

"A number of them have been hoping you would," he replied. "They're a lot more friendly now that I gave up drinking. But a few of them are giving me the cold shoulder because of the rice. They would like to have a cash buyer for their crop, too."

Toshi flinched at the mention of Kunio's drinking problem. It was only one year ago that he managed to break the spell. It happened after Suki died. Whether it was guilt from sending Emiko to the silk factory, or Suki's death, Toshi didn't know. But whatever the reason, Kunio had become a changed person.

"If you'd like my suggestion, the first person I would ask is Suki's father. He never talks about it, but I know he thinks about her every day. And I'm afraid he holds me responsible, since she went there with Emiko. Maybe it would help if you could buy rice from him."

"What if we appointed you as our official agent? You could organize the purchases. It would save us a lot of time, and since you know the farmers, you could make sure we always get the best rice."

"I would like that," Kunio replied.

Once loaded, the three of them turned the mules southward, down the same road they had just traversed. This time the wagon was filled with rice, and the mules were not happy. They felt sure they were done for the day, once they reached Kunio's farm. A few well-placed carrots helped soften their pain. Kazuo gave them extra pats on the face, then rubbed their ears for good measure.

At Kitakami once again, the Empress summoned Enji to help cover the wagon and bed down the mules for the night. The others convened in her dining room for supper, and to share their news. She poured her most expensive tea into modest cups. "I'd rather spend the money on the contents than on the container," she said as she laughed.

It gave Toshi the opportunity he had hoped for. "Have you ever tried coffee? The German director at the foundry always drank coffee. He offered it to me several times until I tried it, and after the first cup, I really liked it. I wish there was a place around here that sold it."

"Does it come from Germany?" she asked.

"No, I don't think so. I think mostly from somewhere in South America. Brazil, maybe. Wherever that is. It was actually Emiko's idea, that we import it and add to our inventory."

The Empress responded to Toshi. "Would your father know someone in Tokyo who could import it for us? Doesn't he have a factory there? Maybe he has contacts who could help. I would gladly promote it in my store if it's as good as you say. We might have to give away a lot of free samples before we get them hooked, but if the price is right, we could make a profit in the long run."

Toshi was surprised he hadn't thought of it himself. He decided to write his father a letter that very night to share his idea. Maybe his father could help. The Empress could send it for him in the morning.

As for a possible cholera outbreak, none of those present had enough knowledge of the disease to offer any guidance. They could only wait and see what happened. "On your next trip, be sure to bring medical advice with you," the Empress requested. "In the meantime, I'll find out what I can from our local physician. I'll be sure to keep it quiet, don't you worry."

For the second time in as many days, the trio left before dawn, this time headed south to Osaki with their cargo of rice and fish. They made it all the way to the river campsite by well after dark. There they made a hasty camp, bedded down the animals, ate a light supper, and went to bed.

CHAPTER 4
BANDITS

JULY 1882 – OSAKI SILK FACTORY

Toshi arrived at the factory just before nine o'clock the next morning. He tied the wagon in front of the factory and entered the front door as he usually did. The assistant was seated at her table, peering at what appeared to be a book of ledgers. She looked up with the faintest of smiles as he approached her table and smiled at her.

"Do you really travel all this way alone?" she asked.

Toshi caught himself in a nick of time. He almost told her his companions were waiting just up the road. It would have been hard to explain why they hadn't come the rest of the way.

"I wouldn't recommend traveling alone these days, particularly with the cargo you're carrying. Not to mention the cash on your return trip. There have been a number of robberies around here. A band of thugs, I should imagine. All the same, if they jumped you along the road, you wouldn't have much opportunity to protect yourself. Or your valuables."

Toshi was still on edge about the dead man from the day before. And he always thought of Suki when he rode past where she died. It took a minute for her warning to sink in.

"Bandits?" he asked, with a growing voice. "Around here? Where? Are they on the road from Kitakami?"

"They've been several places," she replied. "We never know where they're going to show up."

Then she looked back at her ledger book, as if catching her breath, and continued. "Cho-san asked to see you right away when you arrived. We weren't expecting you until later, but follow me and we'll see if he's available."

With that, she rose from her table and headed for the stairway to Cho's office. Toshi had little choice but to follow.

She tapped lightly on his door, then opened it and let the two of them in. Cho looked up with a start and then a smile. Or at least as much of a smile as Toshi had ever seen on him. "Toshi-san," he began. "I'm glad you're early. I want to introduce you to my cousin. He owns the biggest and best emporium in Osaki. And for kilometers around, as far as that goes. I took him a bit of your fish and rice last week, and he wants to add both to his inventory at the emporium. He was so anxious to get started that he wanted to travel all the way up to Kamaishi to meet with you, but I told him you were coming this week and that because it's so far up there, he should just wait and meet with you today."

He closed up the book he'd been studying so diligently and squared up several papers at the edge of his table, then stood and motioned for Toshi to follow him. In a momentary state of panic, Toshi was not sure what to do. Today of all days, he did not have extra time to ride to the village and meet Cho's cousin. Kazuo and Emiko were expecting him back at camp in three hours. They could not come looking for him, or the assistant would recognize them from the 'Ministry of Labor' episode. And Toshi dare not reveal the cause of his haste. Cho might cancel their contract if he thought the fish was contaminated.

When he considered the choices, he realized he had none. He would have to meet Cho's cousin, and hope it would only be a short diversion.

"I have an extra horse you can ride to the emporium. It's only a couple kilometers. Would you mind bringing along a packet of fish and a bag of rice? He tasted some at our house, but I know he'd be more inclined to give you an order if he knew the quality was consistent."

Toshi felt it was more of a requirement than a request, and did as he was asked. "I do need to get back on the road as soon as I can, so perhaps you could have someone unload the wagon while we're gone?" he asked. He wanted to put some of the burden on Cho for the unexpected delay. Were it not for the simmering cholera epidemic back home, he would be more than happy to meet the cousin and try to expand their struggling enterprise.

"I'll get one of the kitchen helpers to unload your wagon. That will give us plenty of time to talk business with my cousin."

As they rode to the emporium, Toshi inquired, "Your assistant said there have been some robberies recently. Do you think it's something I need to worry about?"

Cho tried to remain passive, but Toshi sensed the tightening of his features as he considered the question. "Truthfully, I don't know," replied Cho. "There have been three or four hold-ups along the road leading away from Osaki in the last couple of weeks. So far, no one has been injured, but the bandits have shown a handgun, so it's a growing concern. There are two of them, and the victims think they might be in their twenties or early thirties. They wear a mask to hide their faces, so it's hard to say for sure. If I were you, I wouldn't travel alone. The farthest holdup so far has been about six kilometers from Osaki, but who knows where they'll strike next."

Now it was Toshi's turn to tense. In addition to the cholera threat, now he had to worry about a holdup, just getting home from the silk factory. Before he had time to ponder it further, Cho announced their arrival at his cousin's emporium. They dismounted and entered the store.

Toshi compared it to that of the Empress back in Kitakami. Hers was at least twice the size, and it didn't take long to notice the shelves at her store were much more attractive and better organized. Even a man could see that. There was something about their arrangement that made hers more appealing. Nonetheless, he was here hoping to attract a customer, not criticize his store.

Cho entered the office of his cousin. "Toshi, this is my cousin, Miyu. Miyu, this is Toshi-san. He brought you a gift of fish and rice. You may judge for yourself the quality of his wares. I know you won't be disappointed."

Toshi bowed to Miyu. "Miyu-san, thank you for seeing me on short notice. Cho-san tells me you might have an interest in adding our fish and rice to your inventory. We can offer you our most favorable price, since you are related to Cho-san. And it would be convenient to deliver goods to you, on the same trips as we deliver to his very fine factory."

"Let me show you around," replied Miyu. "It's the finest emporium in all of northern Japan. You can see for yourself. Follow me. I'll put your name on the merchandise, and people from all across Japan will buy your fish and rice. I'll make you famous, if I sell your products in my emporium."

Toshi followed along as they circled each and every aisle and display counter in the store. It was obvious to Toshi that Miyu had led him through the store so as to make it look larger than it was. Toshi was astute enough, though he was certain even young Enji back at the Empress's emporium would have noticed as well, that Miyu was leading him up and down the same aisle from both directions, hoping he wouldn't notice.

At last, after what seemed an eternity, since Toshi could barely wait to get on the road again, they convened in Miyu's office.

"It is indeed a very fine emporium," exclaimed Toshi, with the sincerest expression he could manage. "We would be honored and delighted to have you display our fish and rice on your shelves. In order to be fair to Cho-san, we will offer you the same terms we have provided to him. It would certainly not be fair to him," as he turned to face Cho and bowed, "if we sold our products to you at a lesser amount. Wouldn't you agree, Cho-san?"

This put both cousins in a position of equal stature. Miyu would purchase one hundred kilos of fish to start, and if his customers liked the fish, he would increase future orders accordingly. He would start with four hundred kilos of rice, with the option of increasing future orders to meet demand.

The two men bowed to one another, and Toshi and Cho returned to their waiting horses. During the short ride home, Toshi first tried to calculate how much more weight it would add to their wagon, and how much it would slow them down on the delivery trip. Then he thought about the hold-ups.

Turning to Cho-san, he said, "I'm grateful for your wise counsel regarding the recent robberies. You would be doing me a great favor if you could withhold payment for today's shipment until our next delivery. In future, we'll not make any deliveries without an escort. I'll return in two weeks with your regular shipment, as well as the order for your cousin. And I'll speak with Haruki-san about a token of our appreciation to you as well. Good day." He bowed one last time to the factory owner and made for the wagon team, trying his best not to appear as if running away.

Toshi and Haruki normally brought five yen each, to cover expenses during the trip. Since Haruki turned back at the last minute, Toshi had not thought to ask for his share. Once in the wagon, he slipped the small purse from his pocket and counted the cash, three one-yen bills, and another fifty sen in coins. Looking around to make sure no one was watching, he removed a shoe and slipped two of the yen along the sole, before re-inserting his foot. In case of a robbery, he could pretend he only had one yen fifty sen.

A bandit would be unlikely to believe a man traveling with four mules and a wagon would have no cash at all. He might have to sacrifice something, but if he was lucky, might be able to salvage the remaining two yen.

That done, he shouted for the mules to move, and guided them north, toward the encampment and his two companions. It was already noon, and he was just now leaving the factory. When he arrived, he had expected to be well on his way back to Kitakami by this time. Kazuo and Emiko must surely be getting worried.

He tapped the rear mules on their rump with his whip, urging them to pick up the pace. It was a fragile balance, he'd learned from experience. If he pushed too hard, they revolted, and to reaffirm who was in control, slowed their pace instead. He dare not push them harder. Already they had been pressed well beyond their normal routine. He would give them extra water and carrots when they reached the camp.

Toshi was getting close enough that he began to strain his eyes toward the familiar copse of trees next to the river, hoping for a glimpse of Kazuo and Emiko. Surely they would have the gear stowed and be ready to keep moving.

Watching for them as he was, he barely noticed on the roadway just ahead, what appeared to be a man lying prostrate, his face pointing away from Toshi. He wasn't moving. Toshi's heart raced at the sight. *Surely not another dead man,* he thought. He drew the mules to a bracing halt, pulling up not more than five meters from the lifeless body.

Just as he pulled on the handle to set the brake, the body jumped up from the ground and held out his arms in the direction of Toshi. He seemed to be signaling for him not to drive away. Of course Toshi would not have been able to anyway, without running over the man. As he tried to process what the man wanted, and why he would be standing in the middle of the road, a movement on his left caught his attention.

A second man appeared, standing on a large flat rock next to the road. His face was covered with a mask, and with a jolt of terror, Toshi saw in his right hand, the unmistakable weapon. The man held a gun. And it was pointed directly at Toshi.

"Hand over your money!" the man shouted in a menacing voice. "Be quick about it if you value your life."

Toshi stole a glance at the first man, and now realized that he, too, was wearing a mask. Toshi could see both his hands and felt modest relief that neither held a gun. He turned back to the second man, his gun still aimed at Toshi's chest.

The man in the road had placed himself perfectly. When the wagon came to a stop, Toshi found himself directly opposite the second man, who, still standing on the rock, looked down at Toshi, sitting in his wagon some three meters away. Toshi had no chance to whip the mules into action and drive away.

He slowly reached down to retrieve his purse. He looked directly at the man as he was doing so. "I don't carry much money," he declared in a shaky voice. "I'm on my way home and haven't much left from the journey."

"Don't lie to me," the man bellowed. "I know who you are and where you've been. You bring supplies to the silk factory every two weeks. You're on your way home alright, but your purse is overflowing with payment for all that rice. Hand over the purse!" He shouted.

"I'm telling you the truth," replied Toshi. He tossed his purse to the man. "This is all I have. The factory transfers money through their bank." He hated to lie, even to this scoundrel, but felt justified due to the circumstance. "I promise you, I am not carrying any money for the food I delivered." That part was the truth.

The man, now obviously upset and disappointed, seemed to be pondering how to save face from what he had expected to be an easy heist. He opened the purse to look.

"You can see for yourself," Toshi implored. "There's nothing more here. All I have is an empty wagon."

"Someone's coming!" the first man shouted.

The second man looked up the road in the direction the first man was pointing. Two riders were heading toward them, closing fast.

In a moment of panic, the second man turned his focus on the approaching riders, raised his handgun in their direction, took brief aim, and pulled the trigger. The two riders slowed their horses. The man aimed a second time. Another shot fired from his gun. Then a third.

Toshi had stopped breathing without realizing it. He turned to the approaching riders and was relieved to see them still coming. The shots had missed. He watched them slow to a halt, still some distance away. When fully stopped, he realized it was Kazuo and Emiko. His heart fluttered again, with a mixture of horror and relief. He watched intently as the rider on the left seemed to bend in the saddle slightly and retrieve something from alongside his horse. He thought he could see the rider then raise it to his shoulder while looking in the direction of Toshi and the wagon.

As he watched, he saw a small puff of smoke just above the rider's horse's head. Then the sound of a small explosion. He had heard it once before, on their first trip to Kitakami. It was the sound of Kazuo's Chassepot rifle.

Next, he heard the sound of a muffled thud, like the sound of throwing a rock in a puddle of mud. A moment later, the sound of a painful cry.

"Help me, I'm dying!" shouted the second man.

"Run!" shouted the first man, back to him.

"Help me!" the second man repeated. "I can't run, you fool. Come and help me!"

When the first man scrambled his way over to the rock, and climbed up to help the second man, Toshi saw his chance. He quickly released the brake with one hand while he cracked the whip with his other. The mules seemed to somehow understand what was happening, and started with a bolt. Toshi had never seen them quite so agile. He barely had time to look back at the second man to see his injuries. He was holding his leg, and Toshi could see blotches of red on the man's clothing, and a portion of leg, which was now exposed.

From the way the man flailed around, Toshi was pretty sure he was not going to die. Or if he did, it would not be from the wound.

When Toshi reached Kazuo and Emiko, he kept on going. They turned their horses and easily kept up with him as they continued back to the campsite. Toshi wanted to keep going, but he knew the mules needed a drink and a rest.

It crossed his mind to go back for the money purse. He was pretty sure the bandits would have been too preoccupied with the injury to pick up a purse containing one yen fifty sen.

But he decided it could wait until his next trip.

CHAPTER 5
BODYGUARDS

JULY 1882 – KITAKAMI

After a short rest and time for the mules to drink at the stream, Toshi climbed back in the wagon. His arms still trembled as he grabbed the reins and released the brake. The sound of the gunshots played in his head as the wagon began to move. That was only the second handgun he had ever seen, and the first time ever, one had actually been aimed at him. He licked the dryness from his lips and planted his feet firmly on the floor. *I'm glad he is a poor shot*, he thought. If something had happened to Kazuo or Emiko, it would have been even worse.

As he rode beside the wagon on Autumn, Kazuo replayed the images in his mind as well. He kept seeing the man reach for his leg as he cried out for help. He had no trouble killing animals for food. But to shoot a man was something different. He wondered if the man would die.

For her part, Emiko tried to hide her relentless trembling, from Kazuo and Toshi. She kept thinking back to her time at the factory. Then she realized the place where they were ambushed was almost exactly the place where Suki had died. But there was something more. Something she could not put her finger on, exactly. Something about the bandits gnawed at her. Especially the one with the gun. Something about his voice, when he called out for help. She felt sorry for him none the less, and she was glad Kazuo was there to run them off. She knew he had no choice. Toshi was in danger, and the man obviously meant to harm them, or he would not have fired his gun.

Toshi said a prayer of thanks that Kazuo and Emiko arrived when they did. When the bandits realized they would only get one yen fifty sen, they might well have used the gun on him. He wondered what led to their desperate state of affairs. They seemed young and healthy. Surely there was legitimate work for them somewhere. *Even the silk factory would be an honest living.*

All three of them, whether consciously or not, scanned the horizon as they traveled on. Toshi stared at every large rock as they passed it by, and Kazuo reached for the Chassepot whenever he saw movement up ahead or in the trees along the road.

Once, when a pair of sika deer bounded across the road, he lunged for his rifle and was about to fire until he realized they were not a threat.

Toshi was so busy looking around that he missed seeing the deer entirely. Every few minutes he craned his neck to make sure no one was sneaking up from behind.

They met an assortment of horsemen along the way, as well as pedestrians. The same strangers on a different trip would hardly have caused a second look. Now, everyone seemed suspicious.

On they traveled, late into the night, using what moonlight there was to find the way. Kazuo kept his hand close to the rifle, just in case. Finally, he spoke up. "It's time to give the mules a rest. Let's stop for the night. Toshi, you and I can take turns keeping guard."

They unhitched the mules and tied them to a tree beside the river. Then Emiko laid out a few rice cakes and smoked fish at the back of the wagon.

"I'm not very hungry," Toshi said. "I keep thinking about the man with the gun."

"Me, too," Emiko replied. Her voice was raggedy when she spoke. "What if he had hit one of us? If Kazuo hadn't hit him, he might have shot all of us." Her voice ratcheted up as she spoke.

Kazuo moved over to his wife and put an arm around her shoulder. "Try not to think about that," he said, his own voice trembling lightly. "It's over now, and none of us are hurt. To hit someone from that far away with a handgun would be almost impossible, even for a good shot. So I don't think we were in much danger. Toshi is the one I worried about; he could easily have hit Toshi from that distance if he wanted to. I'm not sure he intended to use the gun. He probably just panicked when we came along."

Now Toshi began to fluster. "I don't think he could have missed me from that range," he said. "I'm just glad you came when you did. It's a good thing Cho and his assistant warned me about bandits. At least I didn't have much money." He thought about his purse. "But I still wish I had the one yen fifty sen back."

Toshi volunteered to take the first watch, and sat with his back to the trunk of a large oak tree, close to the mules. Emiko tossed him a blanket for warmth, then climbed in the back of the wagon, alongside Kazuo.

"Wake me if you hear anything, or when you get tired," Kazuo said, and resting one arm next to Emiko, the other across the Chassepot, he closed his eyes.

Toshi looked above him at the majestic oak. No moonlight penetrated through its heavy leaves. He was sitting in the dark. Across the way, in an open meadow, moon shadows danced slowly in the breeze. Sitting as quietly as he could, he slowly turned his head from side to side, scanning the horizon for anything unexpected. The wagon was ten meters away, the mules about the same, in the other direction.

An hour went by. Toshi fought to stay awake. He was tired, but it was too early to ask Kazuo to take his place. The moon was brighter now, and the shadows more pronounced. They must be coming from nearby trees, he decided. Nothing to worry about.

Then suddenly, a noise. Did it come from the wagon? Or the mules? He wasn't sure. He held his breath as he listened again, this time more intently. Nothing. Then a thump. Then a cooing sound. It came from the direction of the meadow. Just then, right above him, in the oak tree, the sound of a small branch cracking. Toshi froze at the base of the tree. Should he yell for Kazuo? It would alert the intruder if he did. He waited.

A moment later, another sound just above him. This time it was the sound of leaves, rustling in one of the branches.

Afraid to look up, for fear of giving away his hiding place, he listened. Then he took a long, deep breath, inhaling through his nose. Was there a smell? Yes, he thought so. A musty smell. Not something a bandit would smell like. Not dirty and sweaty, just musty.

Finally, building his courage, he slowly stood from the tree and as quietly as he could, stole toward the wagon. He knew Kazuo had the Chassepot lying next to him. Surely, between the two of them, they could retrieve the rifle and protect themselves.

Just as he reached the wagon, and began slowly to reach inside for the chassepot, something furry skittered down the tree. Without any light at all reaching through its dense canopy, the furry thing was only a blob. But close behind, Toshi counted three more blobs.

The family of raccoons reached the ground exactly where Toshi had been sitting, then headed toward the river, keeping clear of the mules, who were most likely asleep. The mother raccoon cooed to her young as they went.

Toshi was exhausted. His body went limp as he sighed in relief. "I'm glad Kazuo was asleep," he muttered. "He would never let me forget being afraid of a family of raccoons."

An hour later, Kazuo woke up on his own and came over to relieve Toshi. "Did you see anything or hear anything?" he asked.

"No, nothing," Toshi replied.

***

When the horizon turned a silky pink the next morning, Kazuo already had the mules hitched and ready to go. He seemed well rested, in spite of keeping guard for most of the night. Toshi, on the other hand, seemed worn and frazzled. Even after moving to the wagon, he listened for noises most of the night.

Safely back in Kitakami, the Empress listened intently as each of the travelers shared their recollection of the hold-up, but she was especially concerned about Emiko.

"From now on, you won't be traveling without an escort, and I know how to fix that. I have plenty of friends from my days as a samurai, you know. And many of them are still in need of work. There's not much demand these days for warriors. But that's exactly what you need when you're delivering your goods, or coming home with cash…especially when you're coming home with cash. Bandits could easily figure out your routine if they saw your wagon coming and going every other week. And even the dim ones would assume you had cash on the return trip."

CHAPTER 6
STUBBORN AS A MULE

JULY 1882 – RETURN TO KAMAISHI

Every delivery provided time to think. Whether rolling with the gait on horseback or lumbering along on the seat of a wagon, kilometers could only be acquired with the passage of time. On the way from Kamaishi, Osaki, or Hanamaki, thoughts usually centered around Kitakami and the Empress. Yesterday, as they traveled from Osaki, the travelers looked forward to her presence. She always had good advice.

Today, their thoughts turned to Kamaishi. With the excitement of the holdup, they'd almost forgotten the crisis they'd left behind in Kamaishi. It could no longer be ignored. Toshi shouted the mules to a trot. The horses easily followed their pace. They made camp late, twenty kilometers from home.

Surrounded by the night, light from the open fire bounced across the trunks and canopy of the two large maples that sheltered their camp. With Toshi driving the wagon and Kazuo and Emiko riding horseback, conversations throughout the day were limited. Together, around the fire, the travelers could finally share their thoughts aloud, the ones held inside throughout the day.

"Do you think Haruki and Fr. Lispard will be okay when we see them?" Emiko asked.

"I've been wondering that, too," replied Toshi. "And all of them."

"Do you think it's cholera?" Kazuo asked. "If it is, won't the whole village get it? What will we do if everyone is sick? Does anyone ever survive cholera?"

No one responded.

"I wonder if we should have stayed in Kitakami," Emiko finally wondered aloud.

All three of them had questions. None of them had answers. They gazed into the fire with such intensity that it seemed they thought the flames might provide them.

Finally, Toshi spoke up. "Tomorrow, you two go on ahead as soon as we have breakfast. I'll follow in the wagon as fast as I can, but you'll travel a lot faster without me. Go straight to Haruki's house. Everyone should be waiting for us there. I'll take the wagon to the store and find out what I can. Surely either Fr. Lispard or the physician will know what's happening. Hopefully, no one else has caught it, and we've been worrying over nothing. But if not, one of them can tell us how to protect ourselves, or how to treat it, if we need to. I'm sure Haruki is anxious for our return. I told him we'd try to come back early if we could."

It was not much of a plan, but enough to provide a focus for the three of them. Having even a rudimentary plan in place was enough to help them fall asleep. The last thing Toshi remembered was a prayer asking for strength to cope, whatever tomorrow brought.

Kazuo and Emiko helped Toshi harness the wagon and then waved goodbye, as they hurried their mounts toward Kamaishi.

"I'll see you tonight," Toshi called as they rode off. Then he tapped the mules on the rump and watched the riders slowly disappear ahead.

It was mid-afternoon when Toshi reached the spot where they'd found the dead man's body. He found himself blinking, trying to shake the images from his mind. Slowing the mules, he came to a stop and pulled the heavy lever toward him, firmly setting the brake. Cautiously, he stepped down from the wagon and approached the river's edge.

He peered behind the clump of bushes where he'd first seen the shriveled man. He released an unwilling sigh when he saw nothing there but rocky soil. Gaining confidence, he walked over to the river and gazed at the water in the afternoon light. *This is a peaceful place,* he thought to himself. *Actually, not a bad place for your final hours on earth.* Just then, a rush warbler called out to its mate. It was one of Toshi's favorite songbirds. He waited to see if the mate would answer. The bird called out a second time.

More confident now, Toshi walked slowly to the grave. It was undisturbed. He stood and stared in silence at the mound of rocks. When things were normal again, he would ask Fr. Lispard about putting a marker there. It seemed a shame for a man to die alone like that. Toshi wondered about the man's family. Maybe Haruki or the others had discovered who he was by now. He turned to walk back to the wagon just as a second warbler called out. He looked in their direction to find the two of them, sitting on opposite branches of a large black pine.

A whisp of breeze washed across his face as he listened to their song. For a few minutes, he was able to forget about the dead man, buried a few meters away. Then he walked back to the wagon and climbed up. It was time to go.

The mules, tired as they were from days of extra work, now recognized their surroundings. They were almost home. Toshi didn't need to prod them any longer. They trotted the last two kilometers into Kamaishi, and drew the wagon to its proper place behind the store. Toshi quickly unhitched the wagon from the mules, then brought them water and oats. He still had a dozen carrots which he'd saved for last.

Then he hurried around to the front of the store. The door was latched, with no one there. He read the note nailed beside the door.

Warning. Cholera Epidemic in Kamaishi. DO NOT DRINK WATER until further notice. Symptoms of Cholera are vomiting, diarrhea, and high fever. Notify the physician if you or your family have these symptoms. Cholera is transmitted by drinking contaminated water. Do not drink water until notified.

Toshi's heart sank. This was exactly what they'd feared. The man must have been in Kamaishi before he died. *What about Ayami? And the boys? And Haruki and his family? Did they come down with it?* He looked up and down the street. For the first time, he realized there was no one there. At this time of day there should be people coming from the wharf or returning home from work.

The physician would know, but he was probably too busy to answer questions. And besides, Toshi didn't care for his attitude. Fr. Lispard would also know. He left the mules and hurried toward the church.

Panting as he opened the door, he stopped long enough to let his eyes adjust to the dusky light. Quickly, he scanned the area surrounding the altar and then the benches. It was a small church with hardly any space hidden from view. Toshi scanned a second time as he wondered where else to look. The priest lived in a small hut next to the church but rarely spent much time there.

Toshi decided to approach the altar. Possibly Fr. Lispard was cleaning behind it. He looked up at the large cross holding Jesus, and something about his hideous death reminded him of the poor man beside the river. Then his foot stumbled on something in front of the altar, and he had to catch himself on the back of the nearest bench. That's when he heard a faint groan, followed by an apology.

"I'm sorry," said the voice. "I wasn't expecting any visitors at this time of day."

"Fr. Lispard?" Toshi managed to say.

"Toshi?" came the reply.

"Yes, it's me, Toshi. Are you alright? Are you ill? Why are you lying on the floor?"

Fr. Lispard pulled himself quickly up. Even though he was older than Toshi by some years, he was in good physical condition.

"I sometimes prostrate myself before the crucifix in honor of our Lord," explained Fr. Lispard. "Especially in times of exceptional need, which we seem to be in at the moment. I was asking our Lord to show us the way, in regard to the cholera. I asked him for guidance on how to bring it to an end before it takes too many of our villagers. We can hardly stand to lose many more."

Toshi stared at him. "How many have we lost?" he asked, his eyes open wide.

"Well over a hundred," he replied. "At first, we thought it would pass us by. There were no symptoms reported for two days following the discovery. Then, on the third day, a woman came to the physician and said her husband and children were sick. He went to see them and confirmed they all had symptoms of cholera. Why she herself did not get sick is a mystery, but all three of her family members died two days later. Every day since, there has been a continuing line of people coming to see the physician. Others are too sick to come, and he has to go to them, which takes a lot of his time. He's barely slept since that first day. So, you can imagine his demeanor by now." He smiled grimly at Toshi.

"What about Ayami and Haruki and our families?" asked Toshi timidly. He was almost afraid to hear the answer.

"So far, no one up on the ridge has been affected. It's only been those here in the village. The physician thinks the bad water must be somewhere down here. The odd thing is that the wife of that first family didn't get sick, while all her family did. We both asked her where they get their drinking water, and whether she drank from it as well as her family, and she said 'yes.' Maybe some people are just stronger than others. Or, she might have forgotten," he added. "She was obviously upset at the time."

"And Hisa? Haruki's oldest daughter. She lives in the village. Have you heard anything of her?"

"The physician sends me a list every morning of all the new patients. So far, Hisa has not been on the list. I have a feeling she may have gone up to stay with Haruki." He paused for a minute, then continued. "We have asked every patient or their family where they get their water, and so far, we can't identify a common source. It's very frustrating, and we know time is against us. Every day that we don't find the source results in more deaths. At the physician's request, I solicited help from my parishioners to put up notices all around the village. The only thing we can do is warn people not to use *any* water until the crisis is over. That's a hard thing to do, so I don't know how successful we will be."

"The Empress sent two kegs of water with me just in case we needed it. I'll leave one with you. You can share it with the physician. It won't be enough to make a big difference, but maybe it will help. I have to unload two bags of rice, and then I'll drop it off on my way to Haruki's."

He quickly stored the two bags at the teahouse. Then he decided to keep one. With so many people at Haruki's, they might need extra food before the crisis was over. He loaded one of the bags on one of the mules, lashed kegs of water on two of the others, closed up the store, and headed back to the church.

When Fr. Lispard greeted him at the door, Toshi said, "Here's the water. Do you need any rice?"

"Thank you for the water. We'll use it wisely. And, no, I don't need anything else…except God's help." He added.

Toshi waved goodbye as he led the mules away to Haruki's house.

Buoyed by news his family was safe from the illness, at least for now, Toshi could hardly wait to see them again. He found himself counting his steps as he walked the two hundred meters from the church to the trailhead. Only when he started up the rocky trail did he realize the mules had never climbed it before. Kazuo always took care of the animals, and he kept them at his farm west of the village.

The trail was much improved since the days when Toshi first moved up there, but it was still a daunting challenge for hooved animals. After climbing only six meters, the mules stood still. Toshi tried gentle coaxing. Then he tried rubbing their ears and necks. They looked at him with unblinking eyes and a face that clearly indicated their resolve.

The first mule carried the bag of rice. The second carried the remaining keg of water. The other two carried no load. Toshi walked back to the third mule and stroked his mane, then scratched his ears as he pleaded with him to budge. The mule looked at him and bobbed his head in appreciation. It was a sign of encouragement. But the mule didn't follow.

Toshi checked his money purse. He still had fifty sen from the trip. He'd spent the rest back in Kitakami. In desperation, he tied the lead mule to a nearby tree and ran back down to the village. Between the church and the store lived a man who sold fruit. He ran to the door and knocked rapidly several times. No one answered. He tried again. This time, a voice responded. "What do you want?"

"Do you have any apples to sell?" replied Toshi. "I'd like to buy four apples."

"How do I know you don't have cholera?" the voice replied. "Go away."

"It's me—Toshi. I don't have cholera. I just got back from Kitakami. There is no cholera there. I need apples for my mules."

"I'm sorry, we're closed. The whole village is closed because of cholera. Come back another time."

"I have to have the apples now, to get the mules home," Toshi pleaded. I'll pay you fifty sen for four apples. That's twice what they're worth."

The man didn't answer. At least he was considering the offer.

"I'll lay the fifty sen on your step. You can pick it up and leave the apples. You won't even have to come near me," he continued.

Not hearing a reply, Toshi laid all his money on the man's doorstep and backed away. He saw a shadow peek through the window and disappear.

Finally, the door opened ajar, just enough for a hand to reach out and pick up the money. Then it went back behind the door. Toshi waited. It seemed like several minutes. *Did the man just steal my money?* he wondered. *Surely, he wouldn't take my money and not leave the apples.*

Toshi started toward the door, his anger beginning to build. Just then it opened, and a hand appeared with an apple. It gently placed the apple where the money had been. It receded back into the house and then appeared a second time. It laid a second apple next to the first. Toshi stepped back, to give the hand plenty of room.

When the hand finally placed a fourth apple next to the three, Toshi started to move closer. But the hand appeared again. It added a fifth apple to the cache. "This one is for you," the voice said. "Good luck with your mules."

Toshi smiled at the man behind the door and then chuckled at himself when it occurred to him the man couldn't see it. "Thank you," was all he could think to say.

He picked up the apples and ran back, past the church, to the trail, then up the ascent, where the mules were quietly munching the few tufts of grass and weeds they could find in the rocky soil.

Toshi began with the third mule. He scratched his ears and rubbed his nose. Then he scratched him under the neck. When he felt he had the full attention of the mule, he held out the first apple and passed it directly under his nose. The mule was quick, and made a sudden attempt at stealing it, out from Toshi's hand.

Toshi barely retracted it in time to keep from having it snatched, along with a finger. At least he had the mule's attention. He untied the mule from the one in front, and started up the incline, holding the apple behind him, but far enough ahead so the mule could not grab it from his hand. The third mule followed him, but the fourth refused to budge.

Toshi untied the fourth mule from the third and tried again. This time, the third mule followed him all the way to the top of the trail, keeping a close eye on the apple the entire way. The incline from the village to the top of the ridge was almost fifteen meters. It was late in the afternoon, and Toshi was exhausted from his long day on the road. The sun was barely up when they left camp that morning.

He tied the mule to a tree at the top of the trail and held out the apple as the mule's reward. This time, the mule accepted it graciously. Toshi did not have to guard his fingers.

Now, it was back down the trail for mule number four. He untied the mule and coaxed it with the same technique as before. He scratched his ears and neck and showed him the apple. Having watched the previous mule, this one followed without a struggle, and Toshi gave him his reward at the top of the trail.

Two down and two to go, thought Toshi. *The last two should be easier now they've seen the first two get their apples.* He descended the trail for the fourth time in the last thirty minutes. He decided to take the second mule up first. The second mule carried the cask of water. Having been successful with his technique the previous two times, Toshi started again by rubbing the ears, nose, and neck of the second mule. Then he waved the apple under his nose. By now, he knew to stay alert for a sudden attempt to steal it by the mule.

The mule remained stiff-legged, with unblinking eyes and a face that radiated indignation.

Toshi pleaded and plodded. He waved the apple again. He left the second mule and went to the first. This mule carried the bag of rice. He performed his ritual with the first mule, taking extra care to wave the apple in front of the mule and then proceed upward on the trail. The first mule stood straight-legged as well. It did not move.

Finally, exasperated, Toshi untied the rice and laid it off to the side of the trail. Now the mule looked at Toshi in the eye with a look that said, "Let's try this again."

Toshi stroked his neck and scratched his ears and nose. Then he brought forth the apple and held it in front of the mule. When he began to climb the trail, the mule followed without hesitation. Afraid to stop for fear the mule would not go again, Toshi ascended the trail for the third time. At the top, he dutifully gave the mule his apple and tied him with the others.

Back down the trail, for the last mule, Toshi at least knew what was in store. He untied the water cask from the mule and laid it to the side. Then he held the apple half a meter from the mule's nose and began to climb up the trail. The mule followed close behind. At the top of the ridge, Toshi tied all four mules back together in a chain, and tied the lead mule to a tree. He checked the ropes a second time. They were almost to Haruki's house, and he did not relish having to chase down a team of recalcitrant mules at the end of an already difficult day.

For the fifth time, Toshi headed back down the trail. He picked up the cask of water. At first, he carried it with both hands, one on either end of the small barrel. After climbing several meters, his back ached so much that he had to stop. He rested a few minutes, then hoisted it to his shoulder.

Up the trail he went. He picked his footing carefully with every step upward. Afraid he would not be able to hoist it up again if he stopped to rest, he plodded step-by-step until he reached the top.

The mules stared peacefully at him as he clumsily placed the cask safely on the ground. To make matters worse, the last two mules were still munching on their apples.

Seeing their apples reminded him the man had given him an extra. "Here's one for you," he had said. Toshi sat down on the water cask and pulled the last of the apples from his pocket. Staring back at the mules, he made sure they saw him bite into his own, and slowly eat every bite.

Revived slightly from the effects of his nourishment, Toshi headed back down the trail one more time. Having already learned from the water cask, he hoisted the bag of rice over his shoulder, steadied the load, and carefully began the final ascent.

Instead of laying the rice on the ground, however, he headed straight for the lead mule, and slung the bag directly onto its back. Then he tied it in place and proceeded to do likewise for the water. He placed and tied it to the second mule. He needed them to know they might win an occasional battle, but he was still the one in charge.

CHAPTER 7
SAFELY HOME

JULY 1882 - HARUKI'S HOUSE

Kazuo's horse nibbled at the late summer vegetation in a makeshift corral beside Haruki's house. Kazuo had strung a length of rope about waist-high around a dozen of the elderly pines to contain the horses until he could take them home to a proper corral and barn. Behind the house, the sounds of muted conversations were occasionally interrupted by squeals of laughter from Kiyoshi and his little brother, Isamu. A light breeze blew across the compound from the west, causing leaves from the few scattered deciduous trees to flutter lazily to the ground.

Suddenly, Kazuo's horse raised its head and looked directly into the wind. Emiko's horse, grazing alongside, noticed his movement and did the same. Both horses stood motionless for almost a minute. A familiar scent was present in the breeze. Kazuo's horse emitted a low, mournful rumble, deep down inside his throat. Then, as it found its way from the throat, called out a loud greeting into the direction of the wind. Emiko's horse followed with a loud whinny of its own. Both horses began to move about their small confines, repeating their whinnied greetings, to visitors still unseen.

Toshi thought he heard the faint whinny of a horse when he was still a half-kilometer away, but he was so tired and exhausted he decided it must have been only wishful thinking.

He loosened his grip on the lead rope and transferred it to his other hand, his fingers numb from holding it tight.

Just as he did, the lead mule let out a piercing bray and gave Toshi a push with his nose. Before he could figure out what was happening, the other three mules began to bray almost in unison, responding to the first. Toshi turned to look at them just as the first mule pushed him off-balance and took off at a run, with the others close behind.

Toshi, now lying on the ground, could only watch them go. He watched the precious bag of rice bounce up and down on the back of the lead mule, and prayed he had tied it securely. Then he looked at the water cask, and in his mind, all he could see was a pile of wooden slats along the path, trampled by the two remaining mules.

Behind Haruki's house, on hearing first, the horse's whinnies, followed soon after by the indisputable brays of four mules, Kazuo knew immediately it had to be Toshi. "Toshi's here," he shouted to all who could hear. "Toshi's here," he repeated again.

"Papa is here," Ayami shouted to Kiyoshi. "Let's go see Papa."

The four-year-old ran to the front of the house to see his papa. Kazuo, Emiko, and all the others from behind the house followed. Haruki and Minako, who were inside the house with Saya and the rest of their family, ran out the front door to join the group.

Kiyoshi, once reaching the front of the house, found no one there. "Where Papa?" he asked, turning to his mother.

"He's coming. Watch for him. He'll be coming very soon," she replied.

Then the mules came into view. They were coming at a run, unusual in itself, but Toshi was not with them. The crowd watched the fast-approaching mules with looks of bewilderment.

"Where's Toshi?" Shouted Kazuo, above the din of the continual braying.

Kiyoshi, still first in line to greet his papa, watched the animals draw closer and closer. Surely his papa must be there somewhere. His mother had told him so. He strained his eyes as best he could, looking west into the setting sun. The entire scene was so different from what any of them expected when they ran to meet Toshi, they were dumbstruck at the sight of it.

Finally, Kiyoshi burst into tears and ran to his mother for comfort. "Where Papa?" he wailed. "You said Papa coming."

The mules were getting closer, and still they maintained their frantic pace. Haruki watched as their trampling hooves kicked up clouds of dust along the trail. Dried leaves and small twigs swirled in the dirt as they ran. Off to the side, two rabbits, munching lazily at a cluster of daisies along the path, darted off the path just in time to avoid their menacing feet.

Ayami stared with growing alarm as still they came. When they showed no sign of stopping, she reached down and grabbed Kiyoshi under the arms and pulled him close. She turned to Saya, who was holding Isamu, and shouted, "In the house! Everyone inside!"

Haruki confirmed her concerns by turning toward the house and starting for the door.

Still on a run, the mules finally veered, at the very last minute, toward the side of the house and the makeshift corral. When they arrived at the strand of rope Kazuo had tied to the trees, they simply stopped and waited. The horses quietly whinnied their hellos and went back to grazing.

Meanwhile, at the front of the house, all eyes were still on the path, watching for Toshi. "Something must have happened to him," Ayami exclaimed. "He wouldn't let the mules run loose like that."

"Kazuo, come with me!" Haruki shouted as the two of them headed up the path. They hurried in the direction the mules had come, but before they'd gone two hundred meters, they spotted a figure walking slowly toward them.

"Toshi," they shouted, "are you alright?"

Toshi managed a wave of his arm, to signal he was okay. The three men continued to converge as they walked. When Toshi got closer, Haruki gasped at the sight of him. He called back to Minako. "Get Toshi a cup of saké, he looks worse than the mules."

Only when Toshi laughed, did Haruki know he was truly all right.

Minako and Ayami scrambled to fix Toshi something to eat while Haruki and Kazuo listened, as Toshi told about his battle with the mules. They had already heard a full accounting of the bandits, but eagerly listened to Toshi's version of the event as though hearing of it for the first time.

"This has been the worst trip of my life," Toshi lamented. "I'm not sure I ever want to do it again," he continued. Just then Saya came in with tea and a sweet rice cake.

Hearing his words, Ayami darted a glance at Haruki, then back to Toshi. He was admittedly, a sorry sight. His hair was in disarray, his clothing wrinkled, torn, and dirty, but worst of all, the sparkle was gone from his eyes.

Haruki returned the look to Ayami, and then he said, "A man from the foundry came to see us while you were gone. He said when the cholera is over, they plan to re-open the plant, and he asked if we wanted our old jobs back."

Toshi looked at him in disbelief. Finally, he sputtered, "They're going to re-open it? And they want us to come back?"

"That's what the man told us," Haruki replied.

Toshi let it sink in before replying, "What about charcoal? What are they going to do about charcoal? Did they find a new place to get it?"

"They plan to use coal instead of charcoal." He didn't elaborate further.

Toshi thought about that. "Have they actually tried it? To see if coal will work with magnetite."

"The man didn't say. I asked if the German director was coming back, and he didn't know."

"Did he say if the other men have been invited back?"

"He said they have all been asked to come back. If they do, I don't know what we'll do with the boats. We may have to sell one and reorganize the schedule."

"Did you tell the man we were interested?" Toshi asked.

"I told him only that we would talk it over and consider it, but whatever you decide to do is up to you. You don't have to do what I do. I hope you know that."

The next afternoon, all three men met at the church to learn the latest cholera news. Fr. Lispard had an updated list, and now the number of dead was over two hundred. But the good news, he told them, was that the number of new cases had leveled. According to the physician, it was because of the sanctions on drinking water. He thinks the virus can live up to fourteen days, so he won't consider us out of the woods until there are no new cases for two weeks.

Several of Fr. Lispard's parishioners were included on the list of victims. He and the physician still were not able to identify a common source of the water, based on what they learned from the victims and their families. The physician, in a new state of panic, ordered additional sanctions. Several parishioners were already busy posting new warning messages throughout the village.

WARNING: Due to the current Cholera Epidemic, the following sanctions have been implemented: All public bath houses and all public laundry providers will be closed until further notice. The ban on all drinking water remains in effect. For emergency rations of drinking water consult the village physician.

"Do we dare go out on the boat?" Toshi asked, looking mostly at Fr. Lispard. "Is it safe for us to fish? Are the fish safe to eat? What if cholera is in the fish and we take it to the factory? All our work to help feed the workers would end up killing them, instead."

"I don't think it would be in the fish," Fr. Lispard replied. "If the man's horse didn't have it, fish probably wouldn't either. But I'll read my medical book again to see what it says. Why don't you check with the physician while I'm doing that... see what he thinks."

"I'll go ask him," Haruki offered. "You can wait for me here."

Ten minutes later, he returned. The priest was just closing the cover on his medical journal when Haruki walked in. "He thinks we're safe as long as we don't drink the water," Haruki said as he entered. "He thinks it is safe for us to go out."

"That's good to hear," Fr. Lispard replied. "My book isn't very clear about how it's transmitted, other than from drinking contaminated water."

"So it's safe to go down to the wharf and see if any of our friends are there?"

"That's what the physician said," Haruki replied. "Just don't drink any water."

Even though he was not a member of the fishing fleet, Kazuo went along. He wanted to know if there would be enough fish for their next shipment to Osaki.

"Do you think anyone will show up?" Toshi asked as they walked. "They might be afraid to come out until the cholera is over."

His concerns were answered when, one by one, the four fishermen assigned to that day arrived for their night's work.

News of the foundry re-opening traveled fast. The four fishermen had already spoken to several of their foundry friends who were unable to participate in the boat consortium. They were eager to get back to work, and for them, the prospect of another shutdown was irrelevant, since they were already out of work.

"Are you planning to go back?" asked one of the fishermen, looking at Haruki.

"I haven't decided yet," he replied. "We have a commitment at the silk factory to think about. If too many of us leave the boats, there won't be enough fish to provide the factory, and we'll have to buy from the other boats. And if we do that, there won't be enough profit left to make it worth the effort. Kazuo could easily continue to haul rice from Hanamaki to Osaki, but that is only half our objective."

When they were alone again, Haruki turned to Toshi and asked, "Have you decided what you're going to do?"

"Ayami and I discussed it on the way home from your house yesterday," he replied. "She said I should re-read the journal I kept while at the foundry, and we would talk about it later."

Haruki waited, expecting to hear his decision.

Instead, Toshi talked about the journal. "I didn't realize the journal was so long," he said. "I read through most of it, but then I fell asleep."

Haruki kept still.

"This morning, before I left, she asked if I'd read the journal. I told her, 'Yes, most of it.' Ayami is so smart. She always gets to the heart of it. You know what I mean?" He turned to Haruki.

Haruki nodded.

"She asked me if I'd counted the number of times I'd written in the journal about the foundry running out of fuel. I didn't actually count them, but I was surprised by how many entries there were. It was a constant concern. More than I'd remembered."

As they walked home through the village, Toshi continued. "Now that I've had a chance to rest, things look different," he said. "Seeing the men and our boats reminded me how much I like being out on the water, especially in the early morning sun. And bringing in a net filled with fish is a lot more exciting than pouring a mold full of iron. You never know what is going to be there.

"But my favorite part is the travel back and forth to Kitakami, Hanamaki, and even Osaki. There is nothing quite as nice as riding under a canopy of leaves or evergreens, and listening for the sounds of songbirds along the way. As for the bandits, from now on, we need to make sure we always have someone with us. And the Empress has arranged for that.

"The foundry is good for those who didn't find other jobs. I don't think it will last more than six months, but it could make a big difference for those who need it."

Finally, he got to his answer.

"I'm going to remain a fisherman," he said.

When Toshi and Haruki arrived at their boat on Friday, the two men from the 'Thursday' boat were waiting for them.

"We've decided that when the foundry opens again, we're going back," one of the men told them. "We don't mind fishing, but we have to make more money. With our families to support, we need more than simply food on the table," he continued. He sounded almost apologetic when he spoke.

"We understand," Haruki said. "The boats were always meant only as a means to keep food on our tables until something better came along. Were it not for our commitments to Hanamaki and Osaki, we would most likely be joining you, but as it is, we're going to keep trying to make our trading company successful."

"Have you decided what you're going to do with your share of the boat?" Toshi asked.

"That's why we're here," one of the men said. "We wondered if you would be interested in taking over our share. We would gladly turn it over to you in repayment for all you've done for us."

Haruki and Toshi looked blankly at one another. Neither felt as if they had done a lot for the two men. Finally, Haruki spoke up. "You're very kind to think of us, and even more so, for the offer. I don't feel we deserve your generosity, but if you feel that way, we'll accept, on one condition. Actually, make it two.

"First, we'll take over for your 'Thursday share,' but we might have to use it on a different day of the week. With our trips to the silk factory, we need at least five free days between our fishing trips. If you don't object to that, we can do it. But we'll keep the boat in your name. If the foundry closes again and you want to resume your share, it will be yours to take."

The two men looked at each other and smiled. Then they looked at Toshi and Haruki and smiled even bigger. "We were secretly hoping you would say that," they exclaimed. "Of course we're hoping the foundry goes on forever, but if it doesn't, it's good to know we have something to fall back on."

Then the other man interjected, "What's the other condition?"

"The other condition," Haruki replied, "is that you keep the two biggest fish from our Thursday catch. And since you'll be busy at the foundry, Toshi and I can pick them for you, and deliver to your houses."

The smiles of the two men broke into laughter at Haruki's condition. "I'm not sure I've ever known two men better than you," one of them managed to say. When Toshi looked, he saw a glisten of tears forming in both their eyes.

On some days, the boat seemed to weigh more than the two could handle. Particularly when trying to force it through breakers pounding in from a windy sea. But today, it seemed as light as an eagle's feather. It might have been simply the result of all the strenuous exercise Toshi received during his trips in the wagon, or it might have been the result of months of experience at sailing the boat. But most likely, it was the result of a buoyed conscience, of having done a quiet good thing for a friend. Both sailors left port that night without once thinking about bandits, or cholera, or cantankerous mules.

It was good to be back on the water again.

CHAPTER 8
CONVERSION

JULY 1882 – KAMAISHI

Toshi and Haruki returned to the wharf on a Sunday morning with one of their best catches ever. "It's a good thing we can sell fish in Kitakami and Osaki," remarked Toshi, as they walked toward home. "Kamaishi is like a town filled with ghosts, even for a Sunday." Then, realizing it was Sunday, he added, "Let's stop and see Fr. Lispard on our way by. He should be finished with mass by now. Maybe he'll have an update on the cholera."

"Good morning," he exclaimed, when he saw the two fishermen approaching. "Did our Lord grant you a good catch during the night?"

"Yes, he did, Father. It was one of our best nights ever. And we were just talking about how lucky we are to have customers outside Kamaishi. Hardly anyone was in the village when we came through. Does that mean the cholera has gotten worse?"

"No, happily, there have been fewer cases reported in the last two days. The physician thinks the worst is over. Of course, he believes it's because he convinced everyone to stop drinking water. I, on the other hand, know it was because God granted it so." His eyes sparkled as he laughed.

"Do you really think God intervened to spare us?" Toshi asked. He was smiling, but also serious.

"Yes, I think he did," Fr. Lispard replied. "As I've said before, it might not have been the way we expected, but I'm sure he had a hand in it. He may have been the one who convinced my parishioners to post all those signs, or he may even have been the one who convinced the physician it was cholera and to stop drinking the water. What matters now is that we seem to be winning the battle. Maybe it was meant as a warning; to treat our neighbors a little better, or to live our lives with a bit more compassion. Whatever the reason, I'm pretty sure He had a hand in it."

***

When they left and continued their way home, Toshi thought back on the conversation. Turning to Haruki, he asked, "Do you think Fr. Lispard was right? That God helped us get past the cholera outbreak."

"I suppose it's possible, looking back on it. If we hadn't found the dead man when we did cholera might have had a few more days head start. The way it was, the physician had time to study his book and be ready when the next case was discovered two days later. And I don't even want to think what would have happened if the man had made it all the way to Kamaishi before he died. A lot more people would have been exposed."

Both men were quiet the rest of the way.

At Haruki's house, he said to Toshi, "Let's get together tomorrow and make plans for the week."

"Okay, I'll see you in the morning," he replied.

***

"How was your night?" Ayami asked, when he came through the door. "Did you enjoy being back on the water after your trip to Osaki last week?"

"It was nice to have some peace and quiet. I don't think I'll complain about a boring night ever again."

"Did you have a good catch?"

"Yes, it was a good night. One of our best ever. We stopped to visit with Fr. Lispard on the way home. That's why I'm a little late."

"How is he? We haven't seen him for a while."

"He looked good; he seemed more relaxed than the last time I saw him. He said the epidemic might be getting better. The number of new cases is down, and he hopes it's coming to an end."

"I can't wait to get back to a normal life again," Ayami replied. "I didn't realize how much we took water for granted. Or how hard it is to get by without it. What's even worse is the 'not knowing.' It makes me afraid of everything when I can't actually *see* where the poison is. It's taken a toll on everyone— I can see it even in Minako and the girls. Everyone has been on edge."

"Thank God, none of us have gotten it. I've been thanking him every night before I go to sleep, for keeping us safe."

Ayami looked at him with a solemn face. "Speaking of God," she began, "I've been thinking. Isn't it about time you stopped talking to him?"

"Stopped talking to him?" Toshi repeated, with a puzzled look.

"Yes. You ask for things, and you thank him a lot, but we're 'outsiders.' Wouldn't it be better if we did the baptism and joined his church for real?"

Toshi looked at her. "Do you think we should?"

"Cholera scares me. What if we get it. You could still get it, so could I. What will happen to us if we die? Fr. Lispard says we would go to a beautiful place and live forever. That book he read from at Christmas—I liked what it said. If the stories are true, I think we should learn more about them."

Toshi's face tensed up just enough for her to see. "I'm not so sure," he said.

"Sure about the stories?"

"Not the stories. I believe the stories, I'm just not sure we should join the church."

Ayami looked at him for a minute. "Is it because of your father?"

"My father?"

"Yes, the letter from your father, back when you worked at the foundry. The one where you told him you were worried about the charcoal."

"Oh."

The one where he told you not to meddle in other people's responsibilities and to stay away from the Catholics."

"Oh," he said. "Yes, I remember."

"What happened with the charcoal?"

"I was right, we were running out of charcoal." His face softened around the edges.

"Do you remember what I told you about the letter?"

"You said if I had a choice between what my father believed and what I believed, I would be a lot happier if I was true to what I believed—or something like that."

"Is your father's letter the reason you keep putting off a decision?"

Toshi looked at his wife and his face softened further. "I suppose it is," he said.

"What about the boys—should they join too?" he asked.

"Of course, they should." She paused and gave him a look.

Toshi stood silent for a minute without looking at her. "What about Haruki and Minako?"

"They'll have to decide for themselves, but I think we should tell them we're going to talk to the priest."

"I was planning to see Haruki tomorrow. We could all go."

***

The next morning, the four of them stood at Haruki's door, the summer sun still on the rise.

Minako answered. "Good morning. What a nice surprise to see all of you. Haruki said Toshi was planning to stop by, but he didn't mention anything about you and the boys."

"I hope we aren't interrupting you," Ayami replied. "It was kind of a last-minute decision. Do you have time for us?"

"Of course, you are always welcome. Is there something special that brings you?"

"You could say that," Ayami said. "We're thinking about joining Fr. Lispard's church, and we wondered if you would be interested in going with us."

"What?" Haruki said. He came to see who was at the door. "Joining the church? When did you decide that?"

"Actually, I think it has been in Toshi's mind ever since the first day he met Fr. Lispard, but he didn't realize it until now."

Haruki looked at Toshi, standing behind Ayami and the boys. "Is that true?" he asked. "You have thought about it for a long time?"

"I guess I have," he confessed. "But it didn't seem real until yesterday. I was telling Ayami about our visit with Fr. Lispard and about the cholera, and then I remembered all the times I've asked his God for help, and all of a sudden, it just hit me—actually, more like it hit Ayami. She's the one who thought it was time to make a decision."

"We were talking about cholera," Ayami explained. "Cholera has taken a toll on the whole village. Everywhere you go, people are worried. You can see it in their faces. They don't smile, they don't laugh, they look like they're carrying the weight of the world on their shoulders. Everyone wonders who is going to be next, and what can we do if we get it—I'm too young to die. Who would take care of Toshi and the boys?"

"I know exactly what you mean," Minako replied. "It weighs us down even if we aren't sick. I'm afraid to go anywhere. They say it's from drinking the water but how can we be sure? And where is the water we're not supposed to drink? That first family that died, the mother didn't get it but the rest of them did. So how could that be if it comes from drinking water? Didn't they all drink the same water? Our girls are old enough to take care of themselves, but even so, I'm not ready to die, either. Not yet."

"When we saw Fr. Lispard yesterday, he told us the number of new cases is starting to decline, so hopefully it will be over soon," Haruki said.

"Declining does not mean over," Minako replied. "We could still catch it. Do you think mourning would be any easier for the last person to die from it than for the first? If anything, being the last probably makes it harder. You would always wonder what should have been done differently to prevent it. And who's to say cholera won't come back again, or maybe even something worse. Who knows what other evil could visit the village? It could be anything."

"How does joining the church prevent something bad happening?" Haruki asked. "I don't think cholera cares whether you are Christian, or Shinto, or Buddhist. I'm sure some of Fr. Lispard's parishioners have died, too."

"It's not whether you die," Minako replied. "It's what happens after you die. Fr. Lispard says they go to a place called heaven. But only the ones who are baptized. I don't know what happens to everyone else. He didn't say."

"What will people think if we join his church?" Haruki continued. He wasn't looking at Minako, or even at anyone in particular. "Most people are leery about Christians. Hideji might be an exception. People like him. He's a good person. But he was a good person even before he was a Christian."

Ayami spoke up. "It's not so much how you act on the outside," she said. "It's more about how you feel on the inside. Hideji is at peace with himself, I can see it when I talk to him. Fr. Lispard is at peace with himself, I see it every time we talk to him. I'm sure if he died tomorrow, he would not be worried."

Toshi shot a quick look at Haruki, but not so quick that Ayami didn't notice.

"What?" she said.

Haruki looked at Toshi first, then at Ayami. "That is exactly what Fr. Lispard told us the morning we found the dead man on our way to Kitakami. He said he might be here one year or thirty, but it didn't matter to him. It was about being ready when the time came."

"For what it's worth," Ayami said, "I told Toshi that if he had to decide between what he thinks and what others think, he will be better off following what he thinks. If other people think less of us for becoming Christian, then so be it. But it's our life and we have to live it the way we think best."

A few minutes later Kanae and Saya brought tea to everyone and sat down to join them. "What's this about?" Kanae asked. "Everyone has such somber faces."

"Toshi and Ayami are planning to join Fr. Lispard's church, and they wanted to know if we're interested. We could all learn together."

"Are we?" Kanae asked. Her cheeks began to flush. She looked over at Saya and grinned.

"Are we?" Saya echoed.

"Well, if we do, it would have to be because we wanted to learn about the Christian God," Minako quickly replied. "Not because we think his messenger is handsome." She looked sternly at both girls.

Haruki laughed. "Your mother is right," he said. "And besides, you are both too young for him. He could almost be your father. How would you like to marry me? That's what it would be like."

"As much as we love you, Papa, that would not be a good match," Kanae said. "Even so, he would certainly make our lessons more enjoyable."

"I agree," Saya added. "Count me in."

Haruki looked around the room at his family. After a while, he said, "I guess we'll go with you. Have you scheduled any time yet, for the lessons?"

"No, but we can talk to him about it tomorrow."

CHAPTER 9
TWO VERSIONS OF THE SAME STORY

JULY 1882 – RETURN TO OSAKI

"Are you sure you're ready to go back?" Haruki asked. "I will gladly go if you want me to."

"I have to go back sometime," Toshi replied. "I think I'm ready. The longer I wait the harder it will be. And besides, the Empress said she would find someone to send along for protection. Kazuo has his chassepot, and with two other men along, we should be fine."

It was soon after dawn on a Sunday morning. Toshi was seated in the wagon, four mules hitched and ready. Kazuo rode his favorite, the blood bay and tied an extra horse to the wagon just in case.

Haruki smiled when he looked at their load of fish and gave out a whistle. "This is three times what we used to sell," he said. "I wish we could find a way to fill the wagon on the trip home."

"It takes the same amount of time to drive an empty wagon as it does a full one," Toshi affirmed. "Do you think we should start bringing rice back to Kamaishi? It worked the first time, but I'm not sure it would work on a regular basis."

"We would need a place to sell it," Kazuo offered. "I don't think St. Mary's would want to help us every week. But it's something to think about."

The two men waved at Haruki and headed west. "See you in a week," Haruki shouted.

Fr. Lispard was just walking into the church for Sunday mass when the wagon passed by on the street. He waved at them as he opened the door.

"We're leaving for Osaki," Toshi yelled. "We'll see you when we get back."

"I'll be watching for you—and pray you don't get held up again."

Toshi tried to laugh, but deep inside he could not shake the image of a handgun, pointed at his chest.

When they reached Kitakami, the Empress was waiting with two of her former samurai warriors. Both were women.

"They will ride with you to Osaki and back," she told them. "If bandits think you're easy prey with two women guarding the wagon, they'll be in for a rude awakening. You probably don't want to know how many people they have killed." Then she looked at Toshi with a stern face and added, "So you probably better stay on their good side. They might forget who they're working for."

"Oh," Toshi uttered. His face started to pale. "We…"

But the Empress couldn't hold back her laugh any longer. "Toshi, you take me too serious. I was teasing. You're safe as long as they're around. Just stay close to them and you'll be fine. Now, you'd better get started. I'll see you when you get back."

The load from Kitakami to Osaki was heavy, all the remaining space in the wagon was filled with rice from Hanamaki. The mules remembered their trips from before and refused to hurry, no matter how many times Toshi threatened them with his voice, but he could not bring himself to use the whip. It was a long trip and he sympathized with them. Somehow, his agonizing trip up the ridge to Haruki's house had deepened his respect for the animals. It was well after dark when they made camp along the river, several kilometers short of the silk factory.

Anxious to deliver the order and begin their journey home, the four travelers woke early. They hitched the team and Toshi climbed in the wagon.

"I'll be okay here alone," Kazuo said. "Take the guards with you. I don't have anything of value, and I have the chassepot. I'll be okay."

Toshi waved goodbye and nudged the mules forward. By eight o'clock, Toshi and the two guards were on their way to the first stop. Toshi constantly scanned from side to side searching for unexpected movement.

When he reached the rock where he'd been held up by the bandits, he stopped the wagon. Carefully scanning the horizon in all directions he climbed up on the rock, hoping to find his purse with the one yen fifty sen. Excited to see it lying almost exactly where he'd tossed it to the second man, he picked it up and looked inside.

It was empty. The money was gone. He tucked the purse into his pocket, returned to the wagon, and tapped the mules with his whip. *The man must not have been injured too badly*, he thought, *if he took time to take my money.*

Soon after, when the door to the factory came into view, Toshi felt almost giddy with relief. He had made it half way. One more trip past the rock and the worst should be over.

Cho's assistant saw him coming, and Toshi thought he almost detected a smile on her face when he came through the door.

"Cho-san is expecting you. I'll get help from the kitchen to start unloading your wagon." Without waiting, she led Toshi up the stairs to Cho's office. After trading polite bows, Toshi was motioned to a seat.

"I'm very happy to see you, Toshi-san. I trust you had a safe and uneventful trip?"

"Yes, I'm happy to report we had a safe trip." He paused, wondering if he should burden Cho with his account of the previous trip. He finally decided it might confirm his dedication if he told Cho the story.

"My last trip was not so good," he began. "Shortly after I left here, I was tricked by a bandit into halting the wagon. Just when I stopped, a second bandit jumped out at me from the top of a rock. He had a gun and demanded my money. Fortunately, I didn't have much, thanks to your excellent forewarning. At any rate, I tried to convince him I wasn't carrying much and I tossed him my purse with what little I had, and just at that moment, two…" Toshi caught himself just in time, "…*strangers*… on horseback were coming down the road from the other direction. When they saw what was happening they must have yelled something, I was so surprised by it all, I admit I don't remember that part clearly. When the man on the rock saw them coming he must have panicked because he turned the gun on the two strangers and pulled the trigger. They slowed down, but he shot again, two more times. By that time, the riders had stopped, and one of them shot back with a rifle and hit the bandit in the leg. Maybe I should have waited to see if he needed help, but I was afraid the bandit would turn his gun on me, so I prodded the mules and took off."

Toshi watched Cho for his reaction to the story. He seemed to be listening intently, but Toshi had a gnawing feeling that Cho was thinking about something else.

"You may have noticed I'm traveling with two companions this trip, he continued. "Don't be fooled because they're women. They might not look tough, but if anyone tries to rob me when they're around, they'll be in for a big surprise. We decided to hire a guard until the roads are safe again."

Toshi tried not to stare but was hoping to glean something of Cho's state of mind regarding the hold-up.

Cho looked for the longest time out the large window of his elaborate office. Then he stood and walked over closer to it. From there, Toshi supposed he could see the two samurai women waiting patiently beside the wagon.

Finally, Cho turned and walked over to an empty chair next to Toshi. "I find your story most fascinating," he said.

Toshi held his breath. It sounded like Cho didn't believe his story at all, let alone consider it a mark of loyalty to deliver his goods on time.

"I have a nephew who used to work here," he began. "One day, while a very important inspector from the Ministry of Labor was here for an unannounced visit, I summoned my nephew to assist, and found him in an…unsavory situation. I had no choice but to sack him on the spot. Of course, my brother thinks I was mistaken, or hasty, or who knows what, but I know what I saw. And it was not the first time. I had received complaints about him for months. From the beginning, actually. He was a selfish and wicked young man."

As if to collect his breath, or his thoughts, Cho remained silent for a time.

"That day you left here, my nephew also reported an encounter with bandits. He claimed he was walking along the road north from here when he was accosted by ruffians who demanded his money and even after giving them all the money he had, they still shot him and left him for dead.

"Orochi has been a problem since he was a child. I gave him a job, hoping it would help turn his life around. There was something about his story that seemed amiss. I suspect your version is much more likely to explain the gunshot to his leg. Rest assured, I will be speaking to the authorities. They will likely want to speak with you during one of your future visits."

Toshi was at a loss for words. Cho, who had heretofore convinced Toshi that he was an arrogant, uncaring factory owner, was actually a sympathetic and caring person. Toshi wondered how many others he had misjudged over the years.

"I'm very sorry to learn about your nephew. And of course, I'll be glad to tell the authorities what I know, if they want to speak with me."

"It pains me to say this, but I'm afraid Orochi will continue to be a thug unless he is sent to prison. He can't be trusted on his own."

The two men sat quietly.

Finally, beginning to feel uncomfortable in the silence, Toshi said, "I brought ten kilos of fish and a hundred kilos of rice for introducing me to Miyu-san. Thank you for the introduction. We'll be taking his delivery to him as soon as we leave here."

When Toshi and his protectors arrived at the campsite later that afternoon, Toshi told Kazuo the story of Cho's nephew.

"He said the name was Orochi?" Kazuo asked.

"Yes, that was the name he told me."

"Emiko will be interested in his story," is all Kazuo said.

CHAPTER 10
CHRISTIANS AT LAST

AUGUST 1882 – KAMAISHI

Following the required lessons from Fr. Lispard, both families 'did the baptism' at St. Mary's church. With so many new members adding to his flock all at the same time, even the normally low-keyed Fr. Lispard was excited. The event took place at the beginning of mass on August fifteenth, the Feast Day of the Assumption of Mary, for which the little church was named.

Toshi and Ayami, together with their two boys, were seated in the front row bench, while Haruki and Minako, together with their three girls, and Hisa's husband, filled the second row. Each family rose when called, and processed to a large wooden bowl placed next to the altar. One by one, they tilted their heads over the bowl, while Fr. Lispard poured water across their foreheads and recited the sacred words… "I baptize you in the name of the Father…" Then he handed them a clean white towel to dry themselves.

The ceremony was formal and short. For that many baptisms, he didn't want to keep the rest of the congregation waiting any longer than necessary. But the smile on his face as he welcomed ten new Christians into the fold was unmistakable.

Following mass, when they were gathered outside under the shade of a large maple tree, Toshi moved in close to Fr. Lispard.

"Father," he began, "I've been thinking about mass, and I'm worried about making it to mass on Sundays." He spoke in a soft voice and glanced furtively around to see who was listening. "I know when you taught us about the ten commandments, and we even talked about them—I think it was the Fourth Commandment, that said we need to keep holy on the Sabbath day, we were to worship God on that day.

"Now that we have the rice contract at the silk factory, we have to be gone for at least five days every other week. And now, since we've taken on two additional shifts of the fishing boats to cover for our friends who went back to the foundry, that makes four nights a week at sea. Neither Kazuo nor Emiko can go to the silk factory, so that leaves just Haruki and myself. Even if we take turns going to Osaki, I don't know how we'll be able to always be here for mass on Sundays.

"Reading about the Commandments seemed easy at the time. But now, when I try to follow them in real life, it's not so easy."

Fr. Lispard looked up to the sky, as if searching for guidance from the Lord himself. Then he looked back at Toshi. "I understand your dilemma," he said. "And I'm pretty sure our Lord does too. However, at the heart of it, everything we have comes from the Lord, so it is important to honor Him as he instructed in His Commandments."

He looked to the sky a second time, then at his little church. Then he shifted his focus from one side of the village to the other. Toshi thought he must be looking for something in particular, until he spoke again.

"What time does your boat leave on Saturdays?" he asked.

"It depends on the season," Toshi replied. "We usually leave an hour or two before sunset so we can get past the breakers during daylight. I suppose we could leave earlier, before the rest of the fleet, in order to get back earlier in the morning."

"Actually, I was thinking more along the lines of saying mass before you leave on Saturday. I celebrate mass every day anyway, and it might even be convenient for more of our parishioners to offer mass on the 'eve' of Sunday, so to speak. That way, you could come to mass on your way to work. If I did that, would you promise to come? I'd hate to think I changed the schedule just for you, and not have you show up." He smiled his familiar grin.

"Yes, I'll come. It would be a shame for you to share your sermon with an empty house." This time it was Toshi who grinned.

Then Fr. Lispard turned to Haruki, who was standing a few feet away.

"What do you think, Haruki?" If we had a mass on Saturday evening, would that make things easier for you?"

"Yes, it would definitely work out better for us, whether we were going out on the boat Saturday, or leaving for Osaki early on Sunday morning." Then he looked over toward the front of the church, and saw Hideji standing there. "Let's ask Hideji what he thinks," he said.

The three of them walked over to where Hideji was standing, and Fr. Lispard raised the question a third time. "We've been talking about changing the Saturday mass time to late in the afternoon, letting it become the 'Eve of Sunday' mass so you could ease your conscience on the days you can't attend on Sunday."

"For me, since I don't go out every night, I can usually schedule to be off on Sundays anyway, but I know it would be a relief for some of the other boats. Can you really do that? If you can, I know it would be welcome news."

"I believe God knows what is in your heart, and also that he understands your need to earn a living for your family. So I don't consider this a breaking of the rule, more like a 'practical bending,' so to speak."

The following Saturday, Mass was celebrated at four o'clock. Toshi was there with his family, as were Haruki and all his family. There were a dozen other fishermen, most of whom had not been able to attend Sunday mass on a regular basis, because of the requirements of their livelihood.

Fr. Lispard began the mass with an announcement there had been no new cases of cholera reported for the last fourteen days. "Let us give thanks to our God," he exclaimed. He then proceeded with the opening prayers.

PART TWO

Eight Years Later

CHAPTER 11
NIGHTTIME DREAM

JUNE 15, 1896 – KAMAISHI TEAHOUSE

Toshi took ten steps back from his work. He dangled a short length of string between his thumb and index finger. *It makes a good vertical plumb line,* he thought to himself. He carefully studied the freshly painted letters, then paced five steps to the right and studied them again. Satisfied, he moved ten paces to the left and took a long last look. The bright blue color stood out perfectly from the near-white background that covered most of the storefront.

He yelled for Kiyoshi to come and have a look. The year was 1896, and Kiyoshi was a strong and healthy eighteen-year-old. He stood some distance behind his father and read the letters: "1500 NORTH FRONT STREET," he recited. "Everyone should be able to find our store now."

The fish house was fifteen streets away from the wharf. Front Street ran parallel to the Kasshigawa River, on either side. On the north, the street was called North Front, while on the opposite bank, the street was named South Front. Two streets to the east of the fish house, was the location of the physician, while three streets farther inland, to the west, was the church of Fr. Lispard. The junction in the trail leading up to the northern ridge was located a half-kilometer west of the church at twenty-eighth street.

The Kasshigawa River drained rainwater and snowmelt from the mountains on its way to Kamaishi Bay. Narrow in the mountains, it widened as it neared the bay, like a funnel in reverse. The peninsulas on either side of the bay protruded up steep and rocky cliffs to a height of twenty meters. Toshi liked to gaze up to the north from time to time while working outside at the fish house. Not a week went by that he did not reminisce about his first visits up there, flying a kite with Ayami and her cousins.

It had been six years since Toshi and Haruki bought the nearly abandoned storage shed and converted it to a smokehouse and warehouse for their fish and rice enterprise. The small front room Ayami and Minako commandeered for a dining hall was taken over as their display and sales room for an expanding variety of food items. They began selling rice, vegetables, and produce in 1890, bringing stock back from Hanamaki and even Osaki, in an otherwise near-empty wagon.

In 1894, they built a new wing on the west side of the building to house a dining hall. Between the fishing boats, smokehouse, dining hall, food market, and shipping business, virtually every family member from both families contributed to their livelihood. Even Kazuo and Emiko, their two children, and a half-dozen former foundry workers were included in the effort.

When the iron foundry reopened a third time, using coal and ore from the north, it finally found a sustainable formula. Two additional foundry fishermen opted to return to the iron works. Toshi and Haruki purchased their shares of the fishing boats, and when another owner decided to retire, they purchased his boat as well. They now owned enough shares to fish five nights of every week.

Satisfied the new sign met his approval, Toshi returned the paint can to its shelf in the storage room and called to Kiyoshi, "Are you thirsty? How about a cup of tea before we leave?"

Ayami was busy working at the adjacent teahouse. Toshi walked over and asked if he could have two cups of tea for Kiyoshi and himself before they left for the boat. "You're not having tea without us," she teased. "Go sit down, and we'll bring it out."

Toshi and Kiyoshi sat at a bench under the solitary beech tree behind the smokehouse. Presently, Ayami, Minako, Hisa, and Saya came to join them. Kanae stayed inside to serve the teahouse customers.

Saya brought a pot of fresh tea, and Ayami brought six cups. She handed one to each of them and began to fill them one by one. She poured for Toshi first, followed by Kiyoshi. She had just begun to pour into her mother's cup when her feet shifted without warning. She jerked the pot upwards with one hand while trying to maintain her balance with the other.

It was impossible to say who squealed first. Most likely, all six of them shouted in some form or another. "What was that?" Ayami cried.

"Are you okay?" Toshi exclaimed to Saya.

And then it was over.

"It must have been another earthquake," Toshi said.

Saya began to chuckle. "*Uwa*," she said. "I was not expecting that. Did I spill anything on you?" she said to no one in particular.

"No, we're all okay," replied Ayami. "That was unexpected. I'm surprised you kept your feet."

"I thought the bench was going to tip over," Kiyoshi said.

"I'd better go look in the fish house," Toshi said. "I don't think it was strong enough to damage anything, but I'd better check."

"Check on the teahouse, too," implored Minako. "In fact, I think I'll go. There were several patrons in there. I better check to make sure they're okay."

After a quick inspection, none of them found damage from the quake. They convened around the bench for the second time. The tea Saya had previously poured was cool by now. "Who wants a warmup?" Saya asked as she looked around the group.

"Mine's fine," Toshi declared.

"Mine too," said Kiyoshi.

Saya either filled or topped off the cups of the others.

"For some reason, that quake didn't feel quite like the ones we usually get," Toshi offered. He wished Haruki were there for a second opinion. Haruki seemed to have the best advice, no matter what the subject.

The five of them sat quietly for the next five minutes. They waited for the ground to shift again.

Finally, Kiyoshi spoke up. Something that seemed irrelevant earlier, now stuck in his mind. "Do you think there could be any connection between our catches the last two days and these tremors?" he said, looking at his father.

Toshi thought about it. He'd come to appreciate the curious mind of his firstborn. It reminded him of himself when he was young. "Hmmm," he said. "I don't know, but I suppose it's possible. We thought we were just being lucky on Saturday and Sunday, with the number of tuna, especially. It was at least twice as many as usual. I suppose a shift of the ocean floor, if that's what caused the tremors, could drive the fish closer to the surface. Let's see what happens tonight. We'll see if it happens three days in a row."

He turned to Ayami. "I'm sorry I offered to cover for Dai tonight. He wanted the night off to attend the festival, but I'd feel better if I were here, in case something happened."

"I'm sure we'll be fine," she replied. "It wouldn't be the first earthquake we've been through." She looked at Minako and Saya for confirmation.

"We'll be fine," they both agreed.

"Maybe you should close up the teahouse before dark, just in case," Toshi said. "I'd feel better if you were already home. It's hard enough to see the trail in daylight. If any trees were to fall, you might have trouble finding your way, even with a lantern."

"We would hate to lose out on any late patrons, especially with the festival going on. It will probably last until nine or ten o'clock," replied Ayami.

Before Toshi could press his argument, Fr. Lispard called to them from several meters away. "Greetings, my friends. It's by the grace of God that I find all of you here in a moment of rest. Usually, when I find you, you're hard at work." He looked at Kiyoshi with a smile. "Don't let your parents work you too hard," he said. "You need to take time to enjoy the beauty of God's creation—but that's a different story. Do you mind if I join you?" He looked at the group, hoping to find a reply of welcome.

Ayami was first to assure him. "Of course, Father. Would you like a cup of tea? We've just poured one for ourselves." Not waiting for an answer, she stood from her place at the bench and headed to the kitchen for an extra cup.

Hisa's son, Eito, now four years old, ran to the priest with outstretched arms. Hisa could not decide if it was because of his unusual black garment or the priest's easy laugh that attracted her son. But whenever he saw the man, he rushed forward to meet him and grab him around the legs.

"Did you feel the tremor?" Kiyoshi asked. "What do you think it means?"

"Yes, I definitely felt the tremor," Fr. Lispard replied. "But I don't know what it means. I felt one yesterday and the day before as well, but I don't think they were quite as strong."

Ayami returned with a cup for the priest and motioned for him to sit. Eito was firmly anchored to Fr. Lispard's legs, but loosened his grip long enough for him to sit and join the others. Then he held up his arms in a pleading motion, until the priest picked him up and sat him squarely on his lap.

"Were you on your way to the boats?" Fr. Lispard asked as he tried to balance Eito with one hand and his cup of tea in the other. "Do you have time to hear about my dream? Maybe you can help me figure out what it means."

"Yes, of course we have time," Toshi replied. "But I don't know if we can help with a dream. I would be more inclined to think it should be the other way around. What was it about?"

The priest's face lit up even more than usual as he began his story. "I hardly ever dream," he said. "That's what makes this so unusual. Last night I went to bed at my normal time, following nightly devotions. I was more tired than usual because I'd spent much of the day visiting sick parishioners and had done a lot of walking. Maybe fifteen kilometers. Although I'm used to walking, so maybe that had no effect. Anyway, I went right to sleep for several hours."

He paused to organize his thoughts before he continued. "Then I heard someone call my name. It must have been two or three times, until it finally woke me up. Or at least it felt like I was awake. It was a man's voice, a low voice. Lower than mine, I believe. It was a comforting voice. I was startled by it, but not once did I feel afraid. Once he awakened me, he said he brought good news. He knew our church was too small to hold all the parishioners, and thanked me for bringing new souls to his kingdom."

Fr. Lispard stopped again. His face contorted slightly, as if he expected his audience to break out in laughter. He could feel his face flush. It was against all his convictions to point praise in his own direction. Looking then, at the group gathered around him, he continued.

"Actually, you are the ones who've grown our parish," he said, looking at the friends around him. "You, and the others like you who wish only to learn of the great things God has promised His children.

"The voice then said it was time to build a new church, one big enough to last well into the future. It would serve future generations, the voice went on to say. Then He described how it should look. It was like the shape of the cross on which Jesus died. The altar would be at the top, with a wing on either side, to represent where his arms were stretched and nailed to the cross, and finally, the rest of the church would be the longest section, and represent his feet. This, he said, would remind those who came to pray that the Holy Eucharist takes place at the head of Jesus, while those in attendance at mass will sit where the nails pierced our Lord, at His hands and at His feet. He said when the new church is built, it should be big enough to hold many more worshippers than the current one. The voice then told me that details would be up to the villagers who reunite to build it."

He paused. "I'm pretty sure that was the word he used: *reunite*. That's the part I don't understand. I can't imagine why the parish would have to reunite. Do you suppose we're going to have a rebellion within our parish? I can't believe there is a rift among our members. Have you heard any dissention?" He looked primarily at Toshi but scanned the group quickly, looking for clues.

"I've heard nothing." Toshi replied. "Is it possible you misunderstood the word?"

"I've replayed the dream over in my mind a dozen times since last night. I'm sure that was the word—*reunite*. The voice then told me one more thing. He said it should have a window above the main door and that the door should be facing west, and be aligned with the orbit of the earth such that on the Feast of the Assumption each year, when the sun sets in the west, it would shine through the window and project a ray of light slowly from the entrance of the church, progressing up the aisle toward the altar at the opposite end. This would be in commemoration of his mother, the Blessed Virgin Mary, on the day of her Assumption into Heaven."

Finally, with a look of quizzical expectation, Fr. Lispard looked at his band of friends. "What do you think it means?" he asked. "It felt like someone was right there in the room with me, it was so real. I was fully awake by the end, and I remained so for the rest of the night, even though I tried to go back to sleep. I still can't believe our parishioners are divided about something. Why would we need to be reunited?"

"You've taught us that God speaks to us all the time, but most of the time we don't listen," Kiyoshi spoke up. "I think most likely, God was telling you he wants a new and bigger church. When you think about it, we could use a new church. The current one is not only too small, but it's cold in the winter and hot in the summer."

Minako, whose usual demeanor was to remain silent, confirmed Kiyoshi's opinion. "Since you rarely dream, as you've told us, and since the dream felt so real to you, I will speak for Haruki as well as our family. I believe the dream was a request by God to have us build a new church. Why he chose to reveal some details of its design to you, and why he sent you here to share them with us is the bigger mystery to me. Perhaps he wants our family to help with the work. Rest assured, I will speak with Haruki when he returns from Osaki."

Fr. Henri Lispard stood then, a noticeable look of relief spreading across his face. "Thank you, and may God bless you. I have been blessed to count you among my friends here in Japan." Then he turned and headed back toward his church. "I'm going to start right now on a sketch of the new church," he called back to them.

Then Toshi stood and said to Kiyoshi: "It's time for us to go, too. It's time to get to work. If the sea is calm tonight, maybe we'll have time to think about a new church." He walked into the teahouse and quickly placed several cakes and a few smoked fish into sacks for Kiyoshi and himself.

Returning to the group, his eyes were inexplicably pulled to Hisa. He smiled at her as he walked to the door. Kiyoshi briefly touched her on the arm as he followed his father past his cousin, and the two men waved good-bye as they headed down North Front Street, toward the wharf.

Toshi and Kiyoshi were in different boats this night. Kiyoshi had his usual first mate while Toshi was filling in as captain on Dai's boat. The boats stayed close together as they left the bay and headed out to sea. It was just after five o'clock when they hoisted sail. *Two more hours of daylight,* Toshi thought to himself. Then he began to draw a church, in the shadows of his mind.

***

With the men now gone, Minako, Ayami, Hisa, Kanae, Saya, and the children quickly returned to the business at hand. Several new customers had entered the teahouse, talking excitedly about the colorful kites and the musicians roaming the village.

Saya overheard two elderly women talking about the 'heroes' being honored for their victory in the war against neighboring China. "I can still see those medals shining on their handsome uniforms," one of them was saying. "They must have been very brave," replied the other. "I heard one of them talking about getting ambushed while they slept."

But the teahouse workers had little time for eavesdropping. Every seat was occupied. Ayami could barely keep up, taking their orders for food, and Minako was too busy in the kitchen to stop for even a drink of water. This was, without any doubt, the largest crowd since the teahouse opened.

By seven-thirty, most of the customers were gone. Ayami heard several of them talking about heading to the beach for a bonfire and music. "Does anyone want to go and listen to the music?" Minako asked.

"Not me," Ayami replied. "I'm too worn out to want music."

"Same here," Hisa replied. "Do you want to spend the night at our house?" she then asked the other two. "It will be dark soon. You're welcome to stay the night and go home in the morning."

Minako considered the offer.

"Thank you, Hisa," Ayami replied, "but I think the kids would sleep better in their own beds. And besides, that would be a lot of guests for you."

Then Minako said, "Ayami's right. You've already had a busy day. You don't need extra houseguests tonight. I'll walk home with Ayami. If we leave now, we'll be home before dark." The words were barely out of her mouth when the tables around them began to wobble. Everyone looked around to see if anything was falling from the walls. Then it was over. Nothing fell. Nothing broke.

"We should be used to this by now," Saya said, forcing a smile.

"I know," replied Ayami. "I don't know why we can't get used to it. Luckily, nothing seems to come of it." Then she looked around for Isamu and Meisa. "Come," she said. "It's time for us to go."

"We'll come with you," Minako said, motioning to Saya. "We'll see you tomorrow, Hisa. Don't worry about cleaning up. We'll do it in the morning." Then she reached down, lifted her grandson Eita in a long hug, and kissed him on the top of his head. "Good bye, precious one," she said as she put him down again.

On the way up the ridge, Minako looked at Ayami and said, "Why don't you and the children stay with me tonight? Haruki's gone to Osaki, and there's no reason for you to go home to an empty house. I have plenty of room."

The idea appealed to Ayami. Not only was she tired from the busy day, but something gnawed at her about being alone. Normally, when Toshi and Kiyoshi were both away, she secretly enjoyed her time alone.

CHAPTER 12
DISASTER

JUNE 15, 1896 – KAMAISHI

Five kilometers to the southwest, Emiko was busy with her family. After fourteen years of marriage to Kazuo, she was almost as good as Kazuo at taking care of his beloved animals. It was largely due to the fact they had become her beloved animals, too.

Today, when taking fresh water to them, something was amiss. She tried to put her finger on what it was exactly, but could not. They were restless, she recognized immediately, but more than that. They were not interested in fresh water, or even the hay or oats. On any other day, they would run to her the minute they heard footsteps from thirty meters away. Today, they kept a distance, with a look that seemed distrustful. Kazuo had taken his favorite, the beautiful blood bay the Empress was so enamored by. And of course, the mules.

Emiko filled their troughs with water from the stream. It was cold and clear and always brought the horses running. She tried calling them with her familiar voice, but without so much as an acknowledgement in return. *Maybe they miss the other animals*, she thought. *But some of the animals are gone every other week, so why today? Surely, the six remaining horses are enough to keep themselves company.*

In addition to ignoring her, the horses took turns calling out low, guttural sounds. Emiko had witnessed this occasionally by one or another in the twelve years, but this was the first time ever, she'd seen all of them participate. *If only Kazuo were here, he would know what to do,* she thought. *But he won't be home for several days.*

***

By seven-thirty, darkness had fallen across the ocean. On the outbound sail to the fishing grounds the sea was calm, and the offshore wind pushed the fishing boats easily toward their mark. Toshi could already picture a new church, larger than the current one. *How much larger?* He made a mental note to ask Fr. Lispard how big it was supposed to be. He had told them the shape, but no instructions about its size. He dwelt for some time on the concept of the sunlight window, tracking from the entrance of the church to the altar in the afternoon setting sun.

Toshi periodically looked forward, across the bow, relieved the periodic tremors he felt at the teahouse had not followed them out to sea. It was as calm as he had ever seen.

Meanwhile, one hundred and sixty kilometers from Kamaishi, in the depths of a colossal depression in the ocean floor known as the Japan Trench, the pressured movement of two ancient plates shifted, causing a momentary heave deep within the earth. The explosion of ruptured fire and gas unleashed an underwater wave that traveled with such velocity and force that had Toshi been close enough to see, it would have been his final view of this world.

Ayami was glad they had decided to stay the night with Minako. After a long day at the teahouse and the climb up the ridge, she was ready for bed. Meisa's eyelids were drooping, and her arms were getting heavier the longer they delayed. Even Isamu looked forward to laying down his head for sleep. Kanae and Saya felt the same.

Minako finished counting the money they'd taken in for the day and placed it carefully in a canister. "I'm going to bed, too," she said. "I'll see you in the morning."

"Good night," the others replied. All of them were asleep almost as soon as their heads touched the mat.

An hour later, Isamu woke with a start. He sat up and looked around, only to find everyone else sound asleep. *Have I been asleep long?* He wondered. It didn't seem so. The room was dark, and no light came through his window. He laid his head down again and listened. *Did something wake me?* He heard what sounded like wind in the trees, but wasn't sure. *Maybe it always sounds like this at Haruki's house,* he decided. He wished they had traveled the remaining distance to their own house, but it was too late now. After several minutes, he went back to sleep.

***

Fr. Lispard walked along North Front Street from his church toward the wharf. The sliver of a new moon wafted in the sky above. Fr. Lispard knew the village by heart. Even on nights of near total darkness, he could find his way. Tonight, though, lanterns were glowing from every direction. Most every house and shop on both sides of the narrow streets displayed a lantern from the building or a nearby tree. Groups of people milled in the street, many of whom also carried a lantern. Fr. Lispard accepted a small cup of saké from a neighbor across from the church, but politely declined more offers than he could easily count, as he made his way toward the wharf.

Hardly could he move from one group of revelers to the next without a corresponding change in music from one type to another. Some groups, it was obvious, were spontaneous and unrehearsed. Others brought instruments and, stationed at a strategic tree or bench, provided a most pleasant melody or verse. He occasionally stopped to listen, wishing this person or that might consider joining his church. The choir could benefit from their talent.

By nine-thirty, he found himself at Fifth Street. As he continued east, he could see a legion of lanterns at some distance, on the beach to the south. They reminded him of fireflies, as they seemed to flit and jump from place to place. Several larger lights shone from bonfires strewn in a drunken arc along the sand. As he drew close, he heard the cacophony of a dozen different songs, all being sung at once.

He had hoped to engage a few of the soldiers back from the war. They were, after all, the honored guests of the festival. Having reached First Street without finding any, he decided it best not to entangle himself with the beachgoers. They seemed a little too engrossed in revelry for his liking. He looked to the sky and prayed that even the most impertinent among them remain safe and sinless in the eyes of God. Then, aloud, he quietly proclaimed a favorite verse from the prayer of humility. *"Jesus, grant that others may be holier than I, provided that I may become as holy as I should. Amen."*

When he looked toward the beach, he blinked and looked again. He thought he'd become disoriented by looking at the sky and back. There were no lights of any kind, anywhere on the beach. He turned to look in the opposite direction, relieved to find Front Street just as it should have been, with First Street just up the way, followed by Second Street. He could clearly see people, with lanterns aglow. He could even hear the strains of a chorus or two. But the sound was fleeting. Then the sound of music disappeared. Or, to be more precise, the sound of music was overcome by a mysterious and growing sound, much like that of a heavy wind.

He turned toward the ocean once again, expecting to see a thousand lanterns twinkling in the distance. Not a light was seen. Just then, the sliver of moon poked through a passing cloud, and as he strained to look for lights, he caught ephemeral images of people, several meters above the surface of the beach. *They're flying*, he thought. *How can that be? They're even flying upside down.*

At that very moment, the noise reached First Street. It was more than a noise. It was a crashing sound—the sound of a giant wave, smashing against a rocky shore. *It must have been the saké*, was his first thought.

There was not time for a second.

Like all the revelers on the beach, Fr. Lispard was thrashed like a blade of grass in a hurricane. His slender body struggled to stay above water for the mere blink of an eye. Whether he felt the force that hit him would never be known. The giant wave cared not whether it destroyed rich or poor, heathen or Christian. It cared not whether it destroyed the works of man or the works of God.

People, buildings, plants, animals, trees. Nothing mattered. Nothing survived.

The wave was indiscriminate. Up First Street it went. Up Second Street. Up as far as Eighteenth Street. It was not content to take the priest; it wanted his church as well. And on it went. As the valley became progressively narrower, the wave became progressively higher. The tsunami gushed in from the depths of the sea, and with nowhere else to go, it forced its way up the river valley, more and more ferocious the further it went.

Having reached the end of the valley, it then had no recourse but to turn on itself and rush back to the Pacific. It was an action too cruel to fathom. There were still a handful of survivors, virtually all of them from the upper end of the valley, who found a tree or a rooftop to cling to, when the giant wave shifted its momentum.

The sudden shift in direction of the raging current caught them off-guard. By now, not a lamp was lit, and barely a slip of moonlight found its way to illuminate the calamity unfolding below. Too confused and frightened to yell for help, one-by-one, they succumbed to the hungry wave.

As if to assure itself of complete destruction, a second wave followed minutes later. Up the valley it went until it could go no further. Then it cascaded downward to the sea, picking up as much debris and as many bodies as it could along the way. It seemed to be apologizing for the carnage it had created, and tried to remove as much of it as possible.

As quickly as it had come, it was gone.

***

Minako tossed and turned the whole night through. To say she slept fitfully would be an understatement of the fact. At six o'clock, she gave up. Being as quiet as she could, she went to the kitchen and stoked the stove. She added two small lengths of wood to the embers, enough to re-ignite the coals, and heat a pot of water for early morning tea. Then she stood at the window and blankly stared at the adjacent forest.

How many mornings had she done this? she wondered. It was something she looked forward to at the beginning of her day. Most mornings, she would catch the glimpse of a fox or deer, and almost always the sound of bush warblers, as if to welcome her to the coming day.

This day felt different. Maybe it was the lack of sleep. She had probably worked too hard at the teahouse, and now found herself in the kitchen with an anxious heart.

Having gone to bed earlier than usual, Ayami awoke to the sound of quiet footfalls in the kitchen. She hurriedly dressed in yesterday's clothes and tiptoed out to join her aunt. "Good morning, Minako. You're up early."

"Oh, good morning, Ayami. I hope I didn't wake you. I was trying to stay quiet. I started the stove, so we can have tea shortly."

"Tea sounds good. I can't believe how tired I was. I'm glad we didn't go the rest of the way home. Thank you for keeping us. Did you sleep well?"

"Not very," she replied. "For some reason, I just could not settle. I hope I didn't make too much noise. I tossed and turned the whole night through."

"You poor dear," Ayami replied. "You must have worked too hard at the teahouse. I still can't believe how many customers we had. Have you counted the money yet? Surely it was the best day ever, since we opened."

"I did count it last night before going to bed, and yes, it was the best day we've ever had. We took in sixty-seven yen."

"I can't believe it," Ayami exclaimed. "That's better than fishing or shipping rice. Wait until Haruki and Toshi hear that. They'll be jealous of us," she said. Then she noticed that Minako seemed preoccupied by something, so she sat quietly and poured them both a cup of tea.

Before long, Kanae and Meisa joined the two women and poured themselves a tea. Conversation began again, now between the four of them. Mostly, they talked about yesterday's customers and how busy it had been. Meisa blushed at the mention of a particular group of customers, among whom was a handsome young boy about Isamu's age. Naturally, her great-aunt capitalized on the opportunity, and teased her about the boy until blushing turned her cheeks from pink to bright rose. Then Ayami wrapped an arm around her shoulders and gave her an unexpected hug. "He was handsome, wasn't he?" she admitted.

Hearing banter from the kitchen, Isamu rose from his mat and joined the group. He'd slept in his clothing from yesterday, so did not have to spend time getting dressed. His clothes, however, betrayed him.

"Isamu!" his mother exclaimed. "Your clothing! You can't go back to work looking like that! What will our customers think?"

"But, Mother," he pleaded, "they won't care. Besides, they'll be too tired from the festival to notice how I look. And there probably won't be many customers today, anyway."

Ayami considered his reply. He was right, there wouldn't be many customers today. "Let me at least iron out the worst of the wrinkles," she replied. "I can do that while we fix breakfast. Then we'd better get back to the village. There is probably a lot of cleaning up we need to do before we open today. I hope Hisa didn't stay late and clean it herself."

The five of them left Haruki's house shortly after eight o'clock. Minako seemed to release much of her anxiety as they walked the half-kilometer to the junction leading down to the village. She and Ayami were discussing where to start once they arrived at the teahouse, while Isamu, Kanae, and Meisa followed a few steps behind. Meisa was wondering to herself if the handsome boy would come back again today, and Isamu was hoping business would be slow so he could go home early.

Ayami was talking to Minako when they reached the junction. "Isamu can get the stove started when we get there, and I'll..."

Minako was watching her footing when she heard a loud gasp. It sounded more like a snort. She looked up at Ayami, whose face was frozen in horror. She was looking down at the village. Minako turned to look in that direction as well.

Ayami turned to face her just in time to watch her head sink slowly toward the dirt.

"Isamu!" she shouted. "Grab Minako!"

Isamu, by then, had seen Minako slump toward the ground. He rushed the two steps up to her and made a desperate grab for the arm nearest him. Ayami grabbed the other.

"What happened?" asked Isamu as he stared down at her. Then he followed Ayami's gaze toward the village.

"Meisa!" he shouted. "Look!" He pointed to the valley below. But it could no longer be called a village. There was nothing left.

"Where's the teahouse?" Meisa cried. "Where's the church? Where is Hisa's house?" Then the three of them realized why Minako had fainted. Hisa's house was no longer standing. In fact, the three of them had trouble placing where it used to be. No landmarks remained. What once had been stately trees were nothing but broken, twisted limbs. There were pockets of water standing here and there, mixed with broken lumber, broken glass, remnants of once-fine clothing, and a hundred other things.

"Is that the bell from the church?" Isamu asked, pointing down to what he thought might have been Tenth Street. How could it get all the way down there?"

"And isn't that part of the teahouse just beyond?" Meisa continued.

Standing there in a semi-stupor, they continued to stare. Finally, as their wits slowly returned, they saw a few solitary figures walking among the rubble. *Are they survivors?* They wondered. *Or are they rescuers?*

As they stood in horrid grief, they heard the faint sound of moans, practically at their feet. They had forgotten about Minako. Hearing her come back to life, they reached down to help.

"Can you sit up?" asked Ayami. "Don't try to stand. Sit for a minute and catch your breath."

The three of them stood motionless above her as they tried to think of something reassuring to say. No one could. Finally, Minako began to pull herself up from the ground, all the while her eyes reaching to the valley below.

"Hisa," was all that escaped her lips. "Eito…" Tears began to stream from both her eyes. "Haruki," she sobbed. "Poor Haruki. He loved them so much. How can I tell him they're…"

Hearing this, Ayami's brain began to re-engage. Until now, her brain as well as her body were numb. She tried to think what Toshi would do if he were here. Then it occurred to her. *What about Toshi and Kiyoshi? Were they alright? What about the other fishermen? Did the tsunami take them as well?* She dared not bring it up in the presence of their children. She had to push forward on her own.

"Isamu," she said, "run to Kazuo's house and tell Emiko what has happened. Go as fast as you can. Tell her someone needs to ride after Kazuo and Haruki and bring them back." She took several deep breaths, in and out. *What else?* she wondered, then continued. "Meisa, go with Isamu. This is not for you to see. If Hisa or her family survived, you will see them soon enough. If not, then there is nothing here for you. Both of you, stay at Emiko's house with your cousins until we come for you."

CHAPTER 13
THE FISHING FLEET

JUNE 16, 1896 – SOMEWHERE OFFSHORE

Sunrise in the Pacific that morning found most of the boats in the fleet already overflowing with catch and hoisting sails for home. Toshi, at one point in the early morning darkness, called over to Kiyoshi in his nearby boat that it seemed like the fish couldn't wait to get in their nets. Kiyoshi called back that this was the third night in a row they'd had such easy fishing. "Maybe those earthquakes are good for something after all," he joked. He could hear several men in surrounding boats chuckle across the water in reply.

Prevailing winds at this time of year were primarily from the south. The sail home, then, was normally a beam reach with the wind coming over the port beam. This was Toshi's favorite point of sail because it kept the boat moving through the waves with enough force to skim through them rather than bob up and down through the peaks and valleys, as when running downwind.

These were fishing boats outfitted with a mast and small sail, as opposed to a truly designed sailing vessel. Although they did have a keel affixed to the hull for ballast and stability, they were small and not as efficient at maintaining course. On a beam reach, such as today, a wind blowing directly across the beam also had the unwanted effect of pushing a boat sideways as well as forward. From twenty kilometers off-shore, even a light-to-moderate sidewind could push them as much as five kilometers north of Kamaishi.

The remedy was simple, however. At periodic intervals, the captain would simply change course by tightening the sail and heading closer into the wind. By doing this maneuver for approximately one-fourth as long as the beam reach, it kept the boat on course for Kamaishi.

For an hour at a time, then, Toshi had little to do but think. He guided the rudder with one hand, mostly so he could feel the water. It sometimes reminded him of riding one of Kazuo's horses. After years of riding, he could sense the temperament of the horse just by the feel of its barrel chest between his thighs. In a boat, the rudder was always first to signal a change in the wind, or wave, or current. Other than during storm conditions, the rudder maintained a rhythm. A change in rhythm was the signal to stay alert.

Having settled on the first beam reach toward home, Toshi let his mind begin to wander. It was not idle wandering. His thoughts were divided throughout the hour. First, he considered the abundant catch. *Could it really have something to do with the recent earth tremors, as Kiyoshi had speculated?*

His mind walked back to the preceding days when first they felt the quakes. They did, indeed, correlate to the days when they caught so many fish. And, on those same days, it seemed the fish were in schools closer to the surface than they'd been in the past. It almost did seem they were afraid of something and trying to escape. He eventually came to the realization that he needed more evidence before drawing any conclusion. Three days did not seem enough to confirm a cause-and-effect relationship. He wondered if it would continue a fourth day.

Then he turned his thoughts to the new church Fr. Lispard had described the previous afternoon. He was particularly struck by the idea of a traveling sunray, inching its way up the aisle, from the entrance to the altar. Fr. Lispard specified it had to be an exact path on the Feast of the Assumption every year, which was the fifteenth of August. *How would they determine the exact path?* he wondered. It would be a failure, if off even by a day or two. After all, the ray would be plainly visible to everyone who came to celebrate mass, or came only to see the ray, as many likely would. An idea came to him just as the first mate called back to him.

"Time to change course," he shouted.

Toshi pulled on the rope that controlled the sail, causing the boat to list, but also causing it to draw tighter into the wind for a change of course. The boat steered several degrees south of their destination, to make up for the northerly drift of the previous hour. Toshi forgot the church for the next fifteen minutes as he concentrated on navigating the boat. With daylight well underway, he could see as much as half the fleet, scattered at different locations around him. Some were heading southwest while others were heading west; some still on their first segment of beam sailing, others now early into their second.

When he concluded they had corrected far enough south for this segment, he loosened the rope holding the sail and let the boat return to its westerly course. After several minutes, when he felt the rhythm return, he began to crystallize the seed of his idea.

He would start with a pole—the trunk of a small tree, and position it upright on August fifteenth. Then, as the afternoon sun wore on, he would record the shadow as it grew on the east side of the pole. That would show him exactly where the ray of sun would travel and, therefore, the correct alignment for the main aisle of the church. *That wasn't so hard,* he decided.

Then he thought about it further. *How tall does the pole need to be?* And it didn't take long after that to wonder, *How high up should the window be? And how far up the aisle does the ray need to travel?* Followed shortly by, *how big should the window be? How big should the ray of light be, as it travels up the aisle?*

Thinking through each of these details one by one, he found answers that satisfied him. He would experiment with different lengths and build a frame at the top of the pole to simulate the window. He could watch the pattern of light travel along the ground, where the aisle would eventually be.

Finally, it dawned on him. *How can I do my experiments when the current church is already there? Will the new church be in exactly the same place as the old, and if so, what happens while the new one is being built?* He needed to talk to Fr. Lispard right away, to see if he had answers. *He would stop and see him on his way home this morning.*

But his mind would not rest quite yet. There was plenty of time to think, during this segment of the beam reach. *We can't wait until August fifteenth to run our experiments. What if we're wrong or run out of daylight before we get it all worked out? We'd better try it the day before to make sure the idea works. Then we'll do it again for real on the fifteenth.*

He pondered the idea. *We can't afford to have it wrong. I think we'd better start running the experiment two or three days before the fifteenth.* He was proud of himself for being so cautious. *Actually,* he decided, *we better start at least two weeks before the fifteenth. If we have it worked out ahead of time, we can always stop the experiment.*

This time, he was satisfied he had thought through at least the basics of the design. And this, he felt, was the key ingredient of the entire concept. At least from what little Fr. Lispard had told them. He tried to organize his questions for the priest in his head. It was always helpful to have his thoughts in order beforehand. And he wanted to make sure he didn't forget any of them.

Then something distracted him. Something was not right with the rudder. There were no signals from the wind or waves, but something almost imperceptible had changed at the rudder. The rhythm had changed. He bent over slightly from his place at the rear of the craft. He gazed at his hand on the tiller, as if watching it might enhance the ability to feel.

There it was again. Something was dragging against the rudder as they traveled through the water. It felt like something small, nothing that would damage the wooden fin. But it was definitely something out of the ordinary. He watched, listened, and mostly strained to feel even the slightest signal from his hand, as to what was happening below the surface.

As he waited, he felt the disturbance become more pronounced. Whatever it was, it was gradually increasing. He called to his mate, "I'm feeling something below. Do you see anything unusual?"

Toshi gazed at the sole of the boat, half expecting to hear a thump or some other affirmation of intrusion. The rudder was sending regular signals and they were getting louder. As he continued to monitor the rudder, the mate called out, "Driftwood ahead!"

Toshi looked up. The mate was pointing off the starboard bow. He followed the man's arm, and up ahead, some twenty meters, spotted a length of what appeared to be lumber, riding the crest of one wave and slinking quietly down the next. As luck would have it, just when the lumber slithered out of sight below an oncoming wave, a loud noise came from the bottom of the boat on the starboard side. Both men jumped at the sound. They stared behind the boat for the next several minutes, watching for something heavy or large to emerge. When nothing did, they turned their attention back to the bow.

Shortly the mate called out a second time. "Flotsam ahead!" he cautioned. This time he was pointing to the port side of the boat, almost straight across the beam. More lumber. This time it appeared to be several boards nailed together. "Where did that come from?" the mate asked rhetorically. "It looks like part of a building."

The rudder continued to speak to Toshi. The turbulence, whatever it was, was now more frequent. But instead of intermittent brushing with whatever was below, the disturbances were getting longer and larger.

Toshi stood up for a better view and panned the surrounding expanse of ocean. The sea was actually quite peaceful. The swells only a meter or less, which was about as calm as it ever got. But when he looked across the bow and beyond, to the kilometer or so in his field of view, he sucked in a breath. The sea was littered with flotsam from port to starboard for as far as he could see. Now, with a better view from standing, he could also see a change in the color of the water. Instead of the deep blue green he was accustomed to, it was changing to an ugly mix of brown and grey.

A sickening feeling enveloped him. This had all the earmarks of either an earthquake or a tsunami. But surely, they would have felt or heard either one. He looked around at the other boats, hoping to see Kiyoshi or Hajime. He spotted Kiyoshi off the starboard quarter, about three hundred meters behind. He called to his mate and pointed back toward Kiyoshi. "I'm going to sail closer to them!" he shouted.

He loosened the sail until it began to flutter, and the boat began to slow. Then he pulled the tiller toward himself, steering the boat to starboard. As the two boats drew closer, Toshi ran through in his mind how he wanted to report his fears. Finally, when they were within thirty meters, he shouted across, "Have you seen the flotsam ahead? Stay close to us the rest of the way. Have your first mate keep a steady eye so you can avoid it. Some of it looks big enough to cause damage if we hit it."

Kiyoshi waved his reply. Toshi heard him give instructions to his mate.

"Have you seen Hajime?" he then called. "If you do, make sure he sees it too." Then Toshi looked around at other boats in the fleet to see if they had seen the danger ahead. Several boats were already taking evasive action to avoid the larger objects. He could see first mates standing upright at the bow of most of the boats, helping to navigate through the sea of debris.

In the commotion, Toshi lost track of time on their beam reach. He knew instinctively they needed to sail south again to stay on course. He called to Kiyoshi to follow, and proceeded to tighten the sail and veer to the south. *Maybe we'll sail out of it,* he hoped.

Kiyoshi followed, and when Toshi looked around at the fleet, a number of the other boats were doing the same. He hadn't been the only one caught off-guard by the sudden change of events. Toshi maintained this new course for what he estimated a full twenty minutes, owing that he was late in making the correction.

Now on their third beam-reach segment, they still had two remaining. They were halfway home. If this continued, it would be a long trip, when considering maneuvers along the way, to avoid collisions.

Settled, if he could call it that, into the beam-reach, he had time to study the seascape with some semblance of analysis. The flotsam had gotten steadily worse. In addition to scraps of lumber, he saw not only the limbs of trees, but entire trees, floating and bobbing in the swells. Smaller things that looked like clothing and children's toys floated by. He was tempted several times to reach out and pull them into the boat.

Then he heard Kiyoshi call out to him with an obvious note of alarm. When he looked over, he was pointing to an approaching piece of wood. It was about a meter long and a half-meter wide. It was not large enough to cause damage to the boat, and he had to stare at it for a time to see why it captured Kiyoshi's attention.

It looked like a normal weathered piece of brown lumber until it flipped over at the top of a swell. That was when he saw the familiar white with blue colors he had painted on the teahouse only yesterday. It was close enough that he quickly jerked on the tiller to throw the boat in the direction of the floating wood. As he approached, he let loose the rope holding the sail and let it flap in the wind. The boat slowed to a stop just as Toshi reached out as far as he dared, and snared the end of the board between his thumb and two of his fingers. Carefully sliding it closer to the boat with his left hand, he grabbed it with both hands, lifted the wooden piece up and over the gunnel, and let it drop to the sole of the boat. Almost in disbelief, he read the letters:

1500 NORTH FRONT STREET.

With knees of rubber, he collapsed on the seat. Kiyoshi by now had sailed past and was looking back at his father, trying to decide if he was going to set sail again or merely lie adrift in the swells. He loosened the sheet on his own vessel, letting the sail relax and flutter in the wind. Finally, he saw Toshi tighten his sail and the boat slowly resume its forward motion.

Now it was Kiyoshi in the lead, ahead of his father's boat by thirty meters. He stood at the stern and waved in a circular motion as a signal he wanted him to follow. Finally, he watched as Toshi trimmed the sail further, and maintained the speed and heading of his son.

Toshi mimicked his moves for the next twenty minutes, not really conscious of his actions. If his sign was adrift amid the unending sea of broken debris, it could mean only one thing. The teahouse was gone, and with it, probably every building in the village. He wondered about Ayami and their other two children. Then he wondered about Minako and her family. Haruki had gone to Osaki, he knew. What about Fr. Lispard and all the others? Surely, they had somehow survived.

He was trying to convince himself of that when his first mate called to him in a subdued voice. "Toshi, look there!"

Toshi turned to the mate to see where he was looking, and followed his gaze. At first, it looked like a once-colorful piece of clothing. But instead of riding on top of the water like a flat rag might do, it appeared to be rounded, like it had created for itself an air pocket, and bobbed along like a dead fish. He continued to stare, and as he sailed closer to it, he gasped.

There was an arm inside the clothing. Instinctively, he knew the person was dead, but he reached out with an oar to jostle the arm just in case. When it did not respond, he tried to slip the oar under the arm and lift it up and toward him. On the first try, the arm slid from the oar without success. Toshi tried a second time, this time with a better angle.

He managed to lift the arm thirty centimeters before it slid off again. But this time, Toshi saw clearly. There was no body attached. The arm was floating by itself. He pulled back the oar and laid it in the bottom of the boat. Then he plunged his head over the port-side gunnel and emptied his stomach.

Seeing his father's boat begin to flounder behind him, Kiyoshi again loosened the sail and let his boat slow to a halt. Then he trimmed the sail in such a way to force his boat to stall, in spite of the wind, and wait for Toshi to catch up. "What's wrong?" he shouted the short distance across the two boats. He watched as his father collected himself, then stole quick glances at his sail and rudder.

When they closed to within ten meters, Toshi finally replied. "It looks like we've had a tsunami," he started. "I don't know how it could have happened without us feeling it, but it must have. I'm afraid it's caused a lot of damage in the village." He paused before going on. "I'm afraid there will be injuries when we get there. When we get to the harbor, stay close to me. We should stay together as soon as we tie up at the dock." Then his voice trailed off, and Kiyoshi couldn't tell if he said anything more or not.

They performed their course corrections two more times, with beam-reach segments in between. Surprisingly, as they got closer to shore, the amount of flotsam thinned. Toshi began to get his hopes up. Maybe it was not as bad as he had thought. Or maybe, if it was a tsunami, it hit farther down the coast.

From two kilometers offshore, they could see the familiar peninsulas on either side of Kamaishi Bay. The first place Toshi looked was to the top of the one on the north, looking for his house. It was still too far away to see the house, but Toshi thought he could make out a roof, and the trees that surrounded their home.

Then he turned his focus to the village below. *It was odd,* he thought; *he should be able to make out houses from this distance. Or at least rooftops. Or trees.* Nothing matched the image in his head of how it ought to look. He guessed he had never really looked at the village from here. It was a sight he merely took for granted. Perhaps it always looked like this.

He was reminded briefly of his final trip through Tokyo. The one when he noticed many landmarks for the very first time. The one where he vowed to pay more attention to the things he looked at every day but did not see.

The scattered fleet of boats continued to make their way, ever closer to Kamaishi Bay. Soon, Toshi heard the sounds of distant shouts as the first of the boats reached the wharf. From their shouts, he knew with certainty they signaled both alarm and desperation. From this distance, he could make out figures of fishermen leaving their boats. Some were running. Others were stopped in their tracks. Some were shouting—wailing even, while others merely stood and stared.

For some reason, he looked up at the sun. *It must be about nine o'clock,* he thought to himself. Then he looked again at the village. He was now a kilometer from the harbor. He should be seeing a busy village. *Think!* He told himself. *I was here just twenty-four hours ago. What did it look like yesterday?*

He closed his eyes momentarily and tried to remember.

He could see it now. The harbor was busy with vendors buying fish from the incoming fleet. There were people walking on Front Street, going about their business, buying vegetables from a dozen different shops, children and dogs running in the street, smoke from homes and vendors preparing a noontime meal. He looked for the physician's house, the largest house in the village and beyond it, St. Mary's church. It wasn't large, but it had a steeple and a bell. It should be visible, too. But most of all, the trees. The village was thick with trees. Oak, beech, cherry, cypress, pine, and shrubs of all sizes and colors.

Today, nothing.

The only thing he saw, was where the village used to be.

CHAPTER 14
HAJIME

JUNE 16, 1896 – KAMAISHI HARBOR

As the remaining boats pressed closer at the harbor, there became progressively fewer places to dock. Remnants of the pier remained, but none seemed solid enough to secure a boat. The mooring buoys they normally used were not to be found. The only option remaining was the sea wall, now fully occupied by the early returnees.

Toshi pointed the bow of their boat as far as it would go between the sterns of two boats already there. They would have to walk across the other boats to reach what used to be the dock. He lashed his boat to those adjacent, then checked to make sure they were tied to something on land. One of them had a line looped several times around a rock. Whether it would hold them in place seemed questionable, and any other time he would have stopped to correct it. But today, it hardly triggered a second thought.

Once safely ashore, Toshi looked around to see if Kiyoshi was able to secure his boat. He had followed Toshi's lead and was tied just three boats over. He scanned the incoming boats for a glimpse of Hajime, but without success. He turned back to the collection of boats tied randomly in a group, hoping to find Hajime picking his way across the boats, like stepping stones across a stream, but still no sign of him.

Kiyoshi was walking in the direction of the teahouse when he called out Toshi's name. "There he is!" he yelled excitedly.

He pointed to a spot up ahead. Standing alone, staring west, Hajime seemed to be fixated on a location where North Front Street and Tenth Street used to meet. It was where his house should be.

Toshi and Kiyoshi hurried toward him and each put a hand on his shoulder. When they were finally able to see his face, they recoiled in alarm. His face was so pale, they thought at first it was someone else. His eyes were swollen and dark, and tears ran down the sides of his face. His mouth was open, like it was trying to make a sound, but nothing was coming out.

He did not react to the two caring hands placed on either shoulder. Toshi spoke his name softly several times with no response. Kiyoshi looked at his father with pleading eyes that seemed to say, *What can we do?*

Just then, Hajime's knees gave way, and he buckled to the ground. Toshi and Kiyoshi quickly switched their hands from above his shoulders to under his arms, with just time enough to soften the fall.

The two men watched helplessly as Hajime lay limp on the muddy ground. They had nothing to help revive him, much less restore him, once he came to. Then Toshi thought of the boat. They always carried water in the boat. "I'll run to the boat and get some water," he told Kiyoshi. "Stay with him and keep him seated if he wakes up." Then off he went.

He had to look carefully to find the right boat, with all of them crowded together like a flock of sheep. It was not his usual boat, and most of them looked alike. He finally located Dai's boat and hurriedly stepped from one to another in order to reach it. He grabbed the sack containing their nightly ration of food and water and turned to retrace his route.

A man was sitting in a boat nearby, seemingly unaware of the pandemonium that surrounded him. The peculiar behavior caused Toshi to look again. Then he watched as the man lifted a flask to his mouth and took a long drink from its contents. It gave him an idea.

"Hello," he shouted. "Do you by chance have another store of that refreshment? I can put it to good use if you do."

"Whaaat…" he replied. "You asking meee?"

"Yes, I wondered if you had another flask you could spare. A friend of mine needs something to ease the pain." He reached in his pocket and pulled out a yen. "I can pay you for it."

"A yen?" Suddenly, he seemed more alert. "I'll have to look," he said. He fumbled through a bin attached to the bottom of his boat. It seemed like forever. Finally, he held up a flask. "You can have this for a yen," he managed to say. "It's excellent saké. I wouldn't have it otherwise."

Toshi quickly stepped across the two boats separating the men and handed him the yen. The man handed him the flask in return.

"Try it," he said. "Shee if I'm right. It's the besht that money can buy."

Toshi quivered at the remark. Right now, it probably was. Whether it was actually good or not was yet to be determined.

Having acquired it, he hurried back to where he'd left Kiyoshi and Hajime on the shore. Hajime was awake and sitting up, as Toshi had instructed. "Here, take a drink. It will help you."

Hajime lifted the flask to his lips and took a swallow. His eyes momentarily bulged as the potent medicine found its way down his throat. Then he managed a "thank you," and shifted his weight to stand. Both men reached out to steady him as he rose, then stood close, in case he suffered a relapse. This time he kept his stance and looking forlornly at Toshi, pointed to where his house stood yesterday, when he pushed out to sea with the rest of the fleet.

Toshi nodded his head slightly to indicate he understood. "Let's get a closer look," he said, and the three men headed west along what they still considered North Front Street. Making their way past houses washed from their foundations, fallen trees, and every other thing imaginable, Toshi led Hisa's husband up the street.

He tried not to let Kiyoshi see him stealing looks farther west toward the teahouse and the church. It took every ounce of his self-control not to point them out to Kiyoshi. Even from here, he could see they were gone.

When they reached the site of Hajime's house, the three of them carefully approached, almost as if afraid of what they would find. The roof was mostly torn from the rest of the house, and it lay on soggy ground several meters away from the flattened walls. Toshi and Kiyoshi lifted sections of walls as high as they could, while Hajime peered underneath, looking for his parents, wife, and child. Under one section of the roof, he found his parents.

Hajime first pulled his mother from under the debris, and then went back for his father. From the state of their fragile bodies, it was clear the tsunami had hit with vengeance. Both bodies had broken bones. His mother, an arm; his father a leg. The rips and tears in their clothing confirmed the force of the wave.

Toshi and Kiyoshi left Hajime with his parents while they continued up the street to the teahouse. They passed by the physician's house on the way. It fared no better than Hajime's. Toshi gave up hope the teahouse would be any better.

Reaching the location, its remains reflected the same violent treatment as the others. The initial wave had softened up the structure just in time for the receding water to finish it off, as it forcefully returned back into the sea. The rocks, where only yesterday they had shared tea as a family, were still in place as a solemn reminder. Little else was still the same.

Not waiting for Hajime, Toshi lifted broken walls where he could, while Kiyoshi peered beneath, looking for bodies. The first body they found was little Eito. At least he had no broken bones. Not far away was Hisa. One arm lay outstretched as if reaching for her son.

Hajime came just as they were pulling her out to a bare spot on the ground, next to Eita.

He'd lost everyone.

CHAPTER 15
EMIKO

JUNE 16, 1896 – CATCHING HARUKI

Emiko was taking water to the horses when she heard a distant voice calling her name. She finished emptying her bucket into the trough and hung it on the railing. As she came around to the front of the barn, she recognized the voice of Isamu. He was running toward her house, followed closely behind by his sister, Meisa. From the looks on their faces, she braced herself for bad news. Between long-winded breaths, Isamu told her what they had witnessed from the ridge above Kamaishi.

"The village is totally ruined. We don't know if anyone survived. Mother said we should stay here with our cousins and that you should ride after Haruki and send him back," he managed to say.

Trying to catch her own breath, Meisa stood beside him with a look of panic in her eyes and nodded to reaffirm Isamu's short description of the disaster.

Emiko called out to her three children. "Kaneto, saddle up Autumn and Brandi. Suki, fix a sack with rice and cake, and a few carrots. Kensei, fill a water pouch. Hurry, all of you! I need to catch father before he gets to Kitakami." Then she ran to the barn, rolled up a blanket, and pulled a tunic from its hook on the wall. She placed a halter on a third horse, Pepper, just in case.

If she rode all through the night and switched horses periodically, she might catch them in Kitakami, before they left again for Osaki. It should take at least two or three hours to load and unload the wagons in Kitakami. And they would not have been in any hurry, since they were unaware of the earthquake when they left on Monday morning. If she hurried, she might actually make it in time.

Less than fifteen minutes after Isamu and Meisa arrived with the news, Emiko was on her way. She waved goodbye to her children and their cousins and was gone from sight. She stopped along the way long enough to eat a few bites of cake and drink a few swallows of water; then, alternating mounts, she pressed onward.

She caught sight of the wagon just before noon the following day. It lumbered along behind the four mules, contented because they were not being asked to hurry. Low layers of dust flaked behind the wooden wheels. At any other time, the scene would have made a perfect painting, but not today. As soon as she thought they might be able to hear, she shouted their names as loudly as she could. "Kazuo… Haruki…"

Thinking he had heard an unexpected noise, and still concerned about highway robbers, Haruki turned from his seat in the wagon. He didn't recognize Emiko at first, probably because it was beyond his wildest imagination to see her at that location. He held his gaze on the rider until, suddenly, it registered. It was Emiko, leading two empty horses. He called out to the mules and reached for the brake. Pulling the wagon to a stop, he jumped down and hurried toward the approaching rider.

"Emiko!" he shouted. "What's wrong? Did something happen?"

Kazuo was now off his horse and running to Emiko. He had heard Haruki's question and wanted to hear her reply.

"Tsunami!" she yelled. "A tsunami hit Kamaishi. Isamu came to tell me. He said it destroyed the village."

"What?" Kazuo shouted, louder than he'd intended. "It did what?"

"Minako and Ayami were heading to work yesterday morning, and when they got as far as the junction, they could see it all. They sent Isamu to get me and come after you." She was looking at Haruki. I brought extra horses for you to ride back. I'll take your place in the wagon so we can deliver the fish to Osaki. Isamu and Meisa are to stay at our house with the children until they hear from us. Isamu didn't know anything about the fishing boats. He came directly from the ridge."

She climbed down off Brandi, her current mount, and handed Haruki her sack of food. "You might need this on the way back," she said. "Autumn is the freshest horse. You may want to start back on him. I'll help change saddles if you want."

The conversation, from start to finish, lasted less than ten minutes. Kazuo embraced Emiko for almost as long, then climbed on the wagon and called to the lead mule.

She and Kazuo talked from wagon to horseback for the rest of the trip. Kazuo was filled with questions. Emiko had few answers. She'd left in such a hurry to catch them, she explained, that the only news she had, came from her short meeting with Isamu. And he'd not actually been in the village, only on the ridge looking down. He'd told her he had not seen any houses or buildings still standing. He thought there were a few figures moving among the rubble, which he assumed were rescuers. That was all he knew.

When they arrived at Kitakami, both were so busy telling the story to the Empress she finally had to put her hand up in front of them. "I can't listen to both of you at once," she said. She could see they were in panic and wanted to give them time to unload their grief. "I'll have Enji unload the fish while I make us something to drink. Come upstairs with me, and we'll figure out a plan." She led them up the stairs to her living quarters and with a wave of her arm, invited them to sit while she fixed tea.

***

Haruki rode through the night and stopped along the way only long enough to change horses and give them a short rest. Wherever the road passed close by a stream he let the horses drink. He doused himself with the cold river water to stay awake and gulped several bites of the rice cake Emiko had given him. The only thing he could think about during the entire ride was the teahouse and its occupants. Surely, it must have survived. It was a kilometer or more from the bay. He hadn't felt the earth move since the afternoon they left. How could a small earthquake cause a tsunami large enough to reach that far up the valley?

Just when he had convinced himself it couldn't be as bad as Emiko made it out to be, the village came into view. At first, he didn't recognize where he was, because all the landmarks were gone. From two kilometers away, for the first time ever, he could see the ocean. He looked for the familiar cross atop Fr. Lispard's church, but it was gone. He looked for the teahouse, three streets further down, but it was also gone. From where he sat—atop Brandi, from the bay to the ocean, not one roof could be seen; not where it belonged, atop a building. Roofs, or parts of roofs, were strewn in pieces here and there for the entire distance. Broken walls and random boards filled what had been busy streets on the day he left.

Off in the distance, slow movement caught his eye. As he drew closer, figures appeared. He studied the figures long enough to realize they were survivors. Or rescuers. They were lifting leftover walls and other large panels of debris, apparently searching for anyone still alive. He nudged Brandi forward. He was suddenly wide awake and his aching body sprang to life. He sensed the same in his weary horse.

He gently nudged Brandi in the flanks and guided him forward through the tangle of debris. He entered Kamaishi on the main road, which became North Front Street in the village. But it was no longer a street. What should have been the street was a tangle of broken houses and twisted trees. What once was a kitchen sink now rested on its side in the middle of what once was the widest street in Kamaishi. Haruki slowed his horse to a walk. Slowly he maneuvered toward the center of the village.

"Haruki!" called a voice from among the searchers. "Haruki, over here!" it called again.

Haruki guided the horse to what he thought was Tenth Street. Four sullen figures sighed and exhaled loudly as they laid a large section of wall back down on the ground.

"Toshi," he called back when he recognized one of the men. "Toshi, what happened?" He climbed off Brandi and stepped to the earth. His legs nearly betrayed him after so many hours on the horse. He started to sink to the ground but grabbed hold of the saddle with one hand in time to stay on his feet.

"A tsunami," he replied. "A freak tsunami," he added. "It came on Monday night after you left. It happened after dark, so no one saw it coming. The fleet was at sea and didn't feel a thing. It was a monster, Haruki. This is what we found when we returned the next morning."

Haruki looked Toshi in the eyes without speaking. Toshi understood. "Minako and Ayami left for home before it hit," Toshi said. "They are safe."

Haruki stood slightly straighter at the news.

Then Toshi added, in a wavering voice, "I'm sorry, but Hisa and Eito were still at the teahouse. And Hajime's parents were at home. All of them are gone.

Toshi watched tears form on Haruki's haggard face. They started with a glisten, first one eye, then the other. As Toshi watched, they grew. In a moment, they formed two streams, sliding down his cheeks. Haruki stood his ground and held his gaze. Toshi felt his eyes doing the same. He blinked two, then three more times, trying to hold them back. But the tears won out. The two men, lives intertwined by a thousand griefs and joys, simply stood and stared.

CHAPTER 16
HELP FROM THE FOUNDRY

JUNE 17, 1896 – KAMAISHI VILLAGE

The sun was barely above the Pacific horizon on Thursday, the third day following the tsunami, when the three men led their horses back down to the village. Each horse carried as many provisions as the three households could assemble: food, water, blankets, shovels, and basic carpentry tools. Minako, Ayami, and Teruko walked beside their husbands. When the six of them reached the makeshift command center, they found the watchmen seated around a dying fire. The watchmen barely noticed their arrival; they simply sat and stared at the fire as if in a trance, their thoughts lost in the flames.

Haruki shouted as they drew near, but, receiving no reply, shouted a second time. Finally, the third greeting roused them from their reverie. A slender smile crossed their faces when they gazed at the cargo tied across the horse's backs.

The women went to the horses and began unloading food. Teruko pulled tea and rice cakes from several pouches while Ayami filled a large kettle with water they'd brought along. Minako recruited Toshi to help build a framework to hold the kettle above the fire, while Haruki and Hideji rounded up the rest of the men. Most were sleeping on the ground, wrapped in whatever they could find, not far from the growing row of corpses.

Teruko walked among the waking men. "Come and have some breakfast, we brought food with us. You'll feel better after something to eat."

As the tea readied, Ayami and Minako passed around rice cakes, watching to make sure every rescuer ate what was given. Ayami knew they had a long and weary road ahead, with no place in it for starving workers. Even as she handed out the meager rations, her mind was working on a future plan. For starters, she would enlist the children to canvass the ridge, spread the news, and ask for donations of food, especially, but also sleeping mats, raincoats—anything to provide temporary relief.

When every man had eaten a few simple bites and shared sips of tea from a dozen cups, Haruki called the men around, much like he used to do at the foundry years ago. "You have done your families proud," he began. "They would be proud of you for the way you searched every house in the village. There is nothing any of you could have done to prevent what happened. All of us share a burden we will carry for the rest of our lives. Outside help will come eventually, but for today, we must rely on ourselves."

He paused, choosing his words carefully. "Many of you noticed, as I did, that we found none of our loved ones in the streets or open spaces. The only bodies we found were those trapped inside buildings. So far, we've found less than half the residents of our village. The only conclusion I can draw is that the others were washed out to sea.

"I think we owe it to them to try and find them. Do you agree?"

Several men responded. Many were in such a state of disbelief they merely stared back.

He tried again. "Most of us have boats. I'm asking if some of you would be willing to search the bay, and bring back any bodies you find. It will not be easy, especially if you find a member of your family. But wouldn't you want to have them brought back for closure? Especially, if it's family."

This time, the response was stronger, as they thought about the truth of his words. Several men offered to go.

"Good," Haruki said. "Each boat should take two or three men. Even a fourth, if you want, there will be strength in numbers." He didn't need to elaborate. "If you're willing to captain a boat, raise your hand."

Four or five hands raised slowly in the morning light.

Haruki asked the three of them nearest him to come forward. "Thank you," he began. "As soon as you've selected your crew, you can start the search. Bring back any bodies you find, and we'll place them with the others."

One of the three then asked, "What should we do with all the fish in our boats? We still have fish from Tuesday morning."

"Oh!" Haruki said. "I forgot about our catch. It's probably spoiled by now. We better not dump them in the bay. Pile them as best you can at the dock, and we'll look for volunteers to bury them."

Then another of the three said, "We need to do something about the boats. Without moorings, we don't have room for all the boats. There's not enough room at the dock."

"You're right," Haruki responded. "We need to work on that as well. But right now, finding our missing is the most important thing. The longer we wait, the less chance we'll have of finding them."

Then, from the rear of the group, in a loud voice, came an unexpected question.

"Who put you in charge?"

Haruki was caught off guard. So were Toshi and several others standing between them. "What do you mean?" Haruki finally asked.

The man stepped to the front of the group. He was shorter than Haruki, with a stocky, solid build. His black hair was long and matted, even compared to the other men standing around him. With eyes that bore up to Haruki, as if ignited by a mystery fuel, he repeated, even louder.

"Who put you in charge, Mr. 'high-and-mighty'? Mr. 'better-than-us, foundry man.' You aren't even a real fisherman, here only because you couldn't make a go of it at the foundry... Me? My family has fished here for six generations. We've lived in the village even longer than that. So what makes you in charge of finding the dead?"

Now that he was a bit closer, Haruki could see who it was. Bunji Tanaka was, indeed, a longtime fisherman, just as his father, and generations before had been. But Bunji was also a longtime troublemaker. Now, of all times, was not a time for confrontation. What Kamaishi needed now, was unity.

He looked directly back at the man, into his piercing eyes, and wondered what lay behind such behavior. Hunger? Lack of sleep? Fear? *Maybe it was simply the result of what he'd been through. What they'd all been through. Maybe his senses overloaded and he'd simply snapped.* On the other hand, maybe he had a point.

"That is a fair question, Tanaka-san," he began. "To be honest, no one put me in charge. I stepped up to offer suggestions, only because no one else had. I'm sorry if you find it offensive, but correct me if I'm wrong. When I returned from Kitakami yesterday, several groups of people were searching for survivors in a random fashion. When I saw what was taking place, I suggested they split up into teams and search the village in a more organized manner. Were you here yesterday?"

"Of course I was here," Bunji spat back. "I was here all along. I live here, remember? Down here in the village, with the other fishermen. Not high up there, on the ridge. And I was here looking for survivors when you were a hundred kilometers away. So who put you in charge?" Then the man stood down from high on his toes and relaxed slightly as he looked around for affirmation from his fellow fishermen.

Two or three men standing next to him smiled when he finished.

"I commend you for being here to help from the very beginning," Haruki said. "And for all that you and your families before you have done to help build Kamaishi into a successful fishing village." Then he remembered the food he and Toshi had gathered from their pantries for distribution.

"Were you able to find anything to eat until this morning?" he asked.

"That's a dumb question," Bunji snarled. "Everything was gone when we got here. There was nothing to eat."

"Were you able to get a few bites of breakfast this morning, or maybe some hot tea, provided by my wife Minako and her niece, Ayami?"

"Of course," he replied. "We all did."

Haruki waited to see if Bunji would realize on his own that no one had stepped forward to take charge until his return yesterday.

"Do you have a better plan for searching for survivors?" Haruki then asked.

"Well, not right now, I don't. I haven't had time to work on a plan. I've been too busy helping the others," Bunji replied.

"I understand," Haruki said in a softer voice. "While you're thinking about a plan, would you be willing to head up a team to repair the moorings? I admit you certainly have more experience with the moorings than me. It would be a great help if we could move the boats away from the dock."

With a different task to worry about, Haruki was hoping Bunji would not bother further about a search plan.

Bunji looked around at his small group of friends for a reaction. When they seemed agreeable, he replied in a voice that still sounded argumentative, "Yes, we can repair the moorings."

"Thank you, Tanaka-san," Haruki said. Then he turned his attention back to the search teams. "Until we come up with a better plan for searching the bay, let's get started. You can work out the method among yourselves. And come back in for a break whenever you need to."

The three volunteers stepped back into the group to recruit additional help. This would not be a task for the meek.

Then Haruki spoke up again.

"We still need someone to organize the fish disposal, and we're all going to need something to eat. Since we're fishermen, that should be the easy part. Can one or two of you volunteer to go out tonight and bring back some fish? The rest of us will start to work on the houses."

One man offered to be the fisherman.

"Are there any questions?" Haruki asked.

No one responded.

"Okay," he said. "Toshi and I will work with any team that wants our help. Minako, Teruko, and Ayami will be in charge of what food we have. That will be their 'kitchen'," he said, as he pointed in the direction of the fire. "They will keep the fire going and make sure there is tea available, along with whatever food we collect."

Encouraged slightly, simply by the feeling of having a plan and a way forward, the men disbursed to begin their assignments. Toshi joined one of the building teams. Haruki handed out the few shovels, saws, and hammers they had scavenged from home, then headed to the seawall to help dispose of the decaying fish.

The three search boats were first to be emptied of their three-day-old catch. It was turning soft, and it smelled. Without even a sack to collect them in, all they could do was throw them out on the wharf. It was sickening work. Even Haruki was slow to volunteer. Then he thought about the men who were about to use the boats, and decided this was nothing by comparison. He stepped into the nearest one and, taking a deep breath, stooped down and began throwing the mushy fish over the gunnel, into a pile on the wharf.

What a waste, he thought to himself, as he threw fish after fish out of the boat. *Better we had not caught any at all, then to have a record catch and throw them all away.*

"Remember how excited we were that morning, when we said it was like the fish wanted to jump in the boat?" he said to the man helping him. "As if our losses aren't bad enough, the fish have to suffer, too. Not to mention, we could certainly have used them for food about now."

"*Susanowo* must be angry," the man replied. "My grandfather used to tell me stories about the sea god, and what a terrible temper he had, but I thought they were just stories. Now, I'm not so sure. Only an angry god could be this destructive."

Haruki wondered what Fr. Lispard would say about *Susanowo*. He had contended there was only one god, one that taught love and mercy. If only he could talk to Fr. Lispard now. Now is when he needed him. Even as he threw rotten fish from the boat to the wharf, he kept seeing images of Hisa, images of Eito…innocent Eito. So young he had barely a taste of life.

And Hisa…loving Hisa, filled with love and always a smile. How would Fr. Lispard explain such losses?

And then he recalled his words, the day he had helped the physician with the dead man on the road to Kitakami. "Since earth is only a temporary place for man, and eternity is the true goal, then it really doesn't matter how long we're here…"

Haruki stumbled at the words as they came back to him now. That was back in 1882, when cholera visited the village. His family was spared back then. *Was it a gift to celebrate? Or only a few extra years for their love to grow, making it an even greater loss today?* And what about Eito? Eito was not yet born in 1882. Eito would not have been the added loss that he was today. *Fr. Lispard was a priest*, Haruki thought, *he would have to think that way. I'm just a man. I don't have that strength. I can't bear to have them gone. Maybe if I'd had one more day with them… just one more day to tell them how much I loved them…*

Haruki barely noticed the smell or the oily slime that coated the bottom of the boat, so engrossed he was, in the grief of his daughter and grandson. When all the fish were emptied, the other man sluiced several buckets of sea water into the sole of the boat to rinse away the worst of the pungent remains. It was far from perfect, but given the task ahead, it would be good enough.

The captain of this boat then climbed aboard and motioned for his crew to follow. Three men stepped in and solemnly found a seat. Haruki and his helper gave the craft a hearty shove and watched as it drifted from the wharf. When it slowed to a stop, two of the men began to row. The third man took a spot at the bow, watching for bodies, while the captain mapped their course. It would be a matrix, moving back and forth across the bay, and always outward from the shore.

Within an hour, they collected their first corpse. It was a boy, not more than ten years old. He was floating on his back atop the waves, his eyes open, staring blankly at the sky above. Two of the men reached over the gunnel to lift him in the boat. When they laid him down carefully on the sole, the captain remarked, "It's a good thing they rinsed the bottom before we left." Then, as he looked at the boy's face, he exclaimed, "Oh, no! It's Kubo's boy. Kubo is on one of the other boats. I'm glad we found him—Kubo would be devastated."

"Poor Kubo," another man said. "We'll have to stay by him when we get to the dock. He'll need some help when he sees his son."

"We should have room for three or four before we go back," the captain said. He stood from the tiller and looked around for the other two boats. Neither had recovered a body. He sat down again and maneuvered in line behind them. Twenty minutes later, the lead boat altered course. It had spotted someone. Twenty minutes later, it was the middle boat's turn.

An hour later, they saw a body floating face-down. The man at the bow snagged the kimono with a boathook and guided it toward the boat. When it was within a meter from the side, he reached out and grabbed the garment. He could tell it was a woman by the shape of her hair. The man at midship, on her side of the boat, reached out to grab her arm, but after several tries, he could not find it. Then he gasped. "Her arm is gone!" he shouted. "She's missing an arm!"

The man on the other side crossed over to help. He stared down at her empty shoulder and, after catching his breath at the sight, struggled to say, "Can you turn her over? Try turning her over so we can grab the other arm."

The first man stretched out across the gunnel as far as he dared and managed to grip a piece of sleeve from her other arm. He lifted as he pulled, trying to roll the drifting body over on its other side. Having done so, he said to the others, "It will probably take all of us to lift her over the gunnel."

The man in the bow and the captain came to midship, ready to grab her remaining arm or a leg, or whatever they could manage, in order to lift her from the water and into the boat. When the man from the bow reached down to help, he caught a first look at her face.

"Oh no!" he wailed. "Not Ahmya! Ahmya. My sweet Ahmya."

It was the man's wife.

"I'll take her," the captain quickly shouted. He moved forward to take the place of the man holding her arm. "You take the tiller," he said. "I'll help get her in."

The man stumbled to the rear of the boat and collapsed in the captain's place at the helm.

As soon as the body was laid securely next to the others, the captain said, "Quick, look around for her arm. It must be somewhere around here." Then he moved back to the helm, opposite the woman's husband, and grabbed the tiller. "Grab the oars,' he said, "we'll circle the area and look for her arm."

The husband moved closer to her body and wept, holding her remaining hand tightly in his own.

An hour later, the captain looked at the two men rowing and said, "It's no use. There is nothing more we can do." Then he stepped forward toward the woman's husband and gently placed a hand on his shoulder. "I'm sorry," he said quietly. "We'll take them in now. I'm sorry it was us who found her."

"No," the man replied softly. "I'm glad it was us. I'm glad it was me."

When the other two boats saw them heading for shore, they turned and followed. One of the boats had recovered three bodies: the other, two. Seven bodies accounted for, and it was not yet noon.

A small crowd gathered when they saw the boats approaching. Nearly every survivor lost at least one family member; most lost all of them. Kamaishi was a small village. Everyone lost someone.

When the bodies were lifted from the sole of the boat, no one spoke. A single wail filled the air each time a body was recognized. Whether a wife, a son, or a daughter. Sakichi Kubo wailed first for his ten-year old son, and minutes later, at a different boat, for his thirty-year-old wife, Hibiki. But, in a way, Sakichi was lucky. He had recovered both members of his small family. Few others would.

The corpses were placed on a makeshift canvas gurney and carried to the growing row of victims.

Teruko brought tea in a dented metal pail to each of the crewmen. "You should drink something before you go out again. It will keep your strength up."

Few accepted her offer until Hideji stepped in beside his wife. He looked them in the eyes and gave a slight nod of his head. "I brought this down this morning, thinking it might come in handy," he said. Then he held up a jar of his own, filled with a clear liquid. Some of the crewmen watched as he poured it into the pail filled with tea. "I think it might help," he said.

Twelve men got in line for a cup of the newly seasoned tea. Then, with renewed energy, returned to their boats for a second search.

When the boats returned the second time, one of them seemed different. The crew was somber as they approached the dock with their precious cargo, but something in their demeanor was different. A tiny spark of hope appeared on their faces. Workers who saw them tie up walked over for a closer look. The men in the last boat were scrambling beneath one of the seats, searching for something.

Then two or three of them converged together and bent down at the sole of the boat. "I got him," one of them yelled, as he slipped a small bundle under his tunic.

The men from the other two boats came over to witness their strange behavior.

The men from the first boat then stepped up on the dock, surrounding the man with the strange lump protruding from under his tunic. They took turns peering in at the object while the first man held it safely next to his chest.

Filled with curiosity, they headed to the dock for a closer look. As they drew close, they heard the sound of a mournful wail, long and loud, not from a child, but from a cat. A cat that had drifted at sea for three days, with no food and no water. It was an ordinary cat except for his coloring, which was a dark shade of yellow, with a few dark stripes. With a little imagination, it might resemble a miniature tiger.

Not knowing what to do with it, they took it to the kitchen area, hoping to find something for it to eat. Not until Haruki and Toshi arrived at the kitchen did they recognize the poor, bedraggled little creature. It was Fr. Lispard's friendly companion, Tiger. The church cat.

Encouraged slightly, now knowing it was possible to survive, the search teams went out again. If a cat could cling to the branch of a tree, then surely a wife could, too. Or a child. Now, instead of looking only for bodies floating on a passing wave, they would spend more energy looking for something they might have clung to.

But each time brought disappointment. Each time, they returned only with bodies. At every return to shore, the others came to watch, hoping to see their loved one, one last time. Some of the crew asked to be relieved. Others stepped in to take their place. Those who wanted, grabbed a few bites of rice cake or a few sips of tea before climbing back in the boat. But now, the tea was only tea. The saké was gone.

Near the end of the day, the teams agreed to make one last sweep. The recoveries had slowed on the last two trips. Only two corpses were found over the last two hours. But there was daylight remaining, and they were not quite ready to concede to the sea.

The three vessels rowed out of the harbor and past the breakers, then raised sail, just like for a night of fishing. This time, they sailed to the edge of the bay and turned to the south. It was farther out than they had gone before, but not yet in the Pacific. Looking for a body in the vastness of the ocean would be time wasted. But there was still a chance they could find someone in the confines of the bay.

Everyone but the captain had opted to stand at their position by now. It allowed just enough more of an angle to spot objects afloat in the waves. One stood at the bow, the two others at midship, one on port, and one on starboard. Even so, at this time of day, the sun reflecting from the water made viewing to the west impossible. They could only look to the east, north, or south.

The trio sailed south to the edge of the bay and reversed course back to the north, this time fifty meters closer to the shore. Every eye on board scanned near and far with as much intensity as they had remaining within them, hoping to spot a floating object.

When they reached the north edge of the bay, they reversed again and traveled south, another fifty meters closer to the shore. Three times they sailed the pattern. Three times the same result. Not one crewman called out. No sign of a body, anywhere.

"I'm afraid we've found everyone we're going to find," a crewman said, to no one in particular.

"I think we already covered this area once before," another added.

"Look," the first man said, "the other two boats are headed for shore. They must be giving up."

Chikao Sugiyama, the captain of the boat, spoke up. "Let's make one more pass," he said. "I'm not ready to give up on anyone's family just yet. If we don't find anything after one more pass, we'll go in." They had just reached the northern edge of the bay. Reversing course, they sailed south.

Halfway across, the man at the bow shouted out, "Look! Is that a body?" The others looked up at him and followed the direction of his outstretched arm. It led to a point twenty meters ahead and slightly off to port.

The crewman standing on the port side stared intensely at the dark-colored object as it crested a wave. "It could be," he shouted back. "It's so dark against the water that I can't tell for sure."

The captain adjusted the tiller to push them a few meters further east, closer to the object. By now, all eyes were focused on the wave. Then the object appeared again. It was about the length of a person, but maybe too narrow.

"It might just be a blob of seaweed," the man at the bow said.

"No, I think it's a body," replied the man standing at midship. "It definitely looks like a body."

The captain pulled at the tiller again and prepared to drop the sail. If they passed him by, they might never find him again. They were fishermen; they knew how easy it was to lose a person in the waves.

The boat edged closer. All four men stared at the object. It was now close enough to see clearly. It was the body of a man, dressed in a black robe, and he was not Japanese.

Chikao Sugiyama brought the boat to a stop just as it reached the floating corpse. He held it steady as the three crewmen hoisted the Frenchman into the boat and laid him carefully on its sole.

From there, the captain tightened sail and headed straight to the wharf. The other two boats had already moored when they arrived. Since the first two boats came back empty, no crowd gathered for the last one.

Chikao looked at one of his crewmen. "Go and find Hideji, tell him we found the priest."

Hideji was helping one of the building crews not far away. When he heard his name being called, he handed his hammer to another worker and started toward the man.

"We found the priest," he called out. "We thought you should know."

"You found him?" Hideji answered. "Is he at the wharf?"

"Yes," the man replied. "Chikao asked me to find you."

"Tell him I'll be right there," Hideji called back. "I'm going to get Haruki and Toshi."

Then Hideji headed to the kitchen area, hoping to find them there. "They found Fr. Lispard," he yelled out to Minako as soon as he saw her at the open fire. Ayami was close by and moved closer to hear what he had to say.

Teruko saw the commotion, dropped the pan she was washing, and hurried over.

"They found his body," Hideji repeated. "Do you know where Haruki and Toshi are? They'll want to see him, too."

The four of them then started across the broken village, stepping over remnants of furniture, walls, and random boards. Ayami was first to spot them, clearing a path from what used to be the teahouse to what used to be the church.

"Come quick!" she yelled to them. "They found Fr. Lispard." Now, six people rushed toward the wharf.

When the other survivors saw the disturbance, they dropped what they were doing and followed. Most didn't know what was happening at the wharf, but if it was important enough to draw a crowd, they wanted to know what it was.

Reaching the boat, the six of them gazed at the once tall, slender, jovial human being, now lying motionless at the bottom of the vessel. His black garment was unmistakable. The once white collar had faded to a drab sea-green, after three days floating in the sea. His normally tanned and lively face now stared blankly at the sky above, pale and gaunt.

Hideji, Haruki, and Toshi carefully lifted the body from the boat and placed it on a makeshift gurney. They asked Chikao, since he had been the captain, if he would kindly take the fourth position, and from each corner they carried the body from the wharf, past what had been the physician's house, the teahouse, and finally, to St. Mary's church.

Hideji pointed to a small open space, just beyond where the house had stood. "I think this would be a good place to bury him. He deserves to be near his church."

Hideji, Haruki, and Toshi took turns digging. Teruko, Minako, and Ayami stood silently in prayer as they watched. When the grave was ready, several mourners gathered around, and the corpse was wrapped in a blanket and carefully lowered in the ground.

Hideji thanked God for the gift of His servant, and led the others in reciting the Lord's Prayer. Then he gently covered the body with soil.

This time it was Toshi who recalled words from Fr. Lispard, at the grave of the dead man with cholera. "I could drown in the sea a few years from now," he had said.

"Do you think he knew?" Toshi asked Hideji. "Do you think he knew he would be...taken by the sea?"

"I don't know," Hideji replied. "But I'm not sure he would have cared. He would have said he was ready."

CHAPTER 17
HELP FROM THE EMPRESS

JUNE 19, 1896 - RETURN FROM KITAKAMI

It was afternoon the next day when Kazuo and Emiko passed by the final resting place of the unidentified dead man some fourteen years earlier. Kamaishi was only a few kilometers further. The trip home took longer than normal because this time, their wagon was filled with supplies. Not just filled, but overflowing. Twelve former samurai on horseback accompanied the wagon. The Empress had organized their return while Kazuo, Emiko, and two samurai bodyguards delivered fish and rice to Osaki. Kazuo and Emiko waited at camp while the samurai went alone to the silk factory. They came alone, they explained, because of the tragedy in Kamaishi.

Samurai were trained to fight, not to build, but the Empress had many friends and many contacts. She hand-picked a small number who seemed good at anything they tried. In addition to the overflowing wagon, five additional horses were loaded with saws, hammers, nails, sleeping mats, cooking utensils, ropes, shovels, and canvas tents. Whatever she could think of, to help the survivors rebuild their village.

The mules were not happy with the load. They'd already been to Osaki and looked forward to a mostly empty wagon on the return trip home. Osaki to Kitakami was fine, with only Kazuo in the wagon, Emiko riding Autumn, and two mounted escorts alongside. Then came Kitakami. They were herded back to the warehouse, where the wagon was loaded with bag after bag of heavy rice. Then, when they thought the wagon was already full, still more. Potatoes, carrots, and large jugs filled with water. Those were the worst. They remembered how heavy water could be. They would show their disgust by setting their own sweet pace.

When the small band reached the far western edge of the village, it was like entering a different world. Until now, trees had looked normal; the ground, the grass, the rocks—all looked normal. But suddenly, almost like in a land of make-believe, everything changed.

Tree limbs were down, rocks were washed together, and greenery was washed away. Here and there were small pockets of mud, with the remains of decayed fish giving off a pungent smell, and faded gray eyes staring upward at the sun.

As they traveled onward, the damage grew worse. First, trees uprooted, some gone entirely. Then a house; what was left of it—the roof gone entirely, the walls, one atop another. Who's house was it? Difficult to say. Few landmarks remained.

The group moved slower now. The wagon needed more time to navigate the littered street. It was easier for the horses; they could step over rocks or limbs. But not the wagon. Two samurai moved to the front, helping clear a path for the others.

Emiko positioned herself between the samurai and the wagon. She knew the village; she would help guide them. Her eyes scanned the ravaged street, side to side, searching for a landmark, anything to help them navigate the cluttered maze.

Suddenly, she halted her horse and shouted, "Kazuo! Stop the wagon!"

Kazuo took his eyes off the rugged trail just long enough to look over at Emiko, not far ahead. He followed her eyes to a small bundle, some twenty meters beyond. Unsure what it was, he responded to Emiko's request by pulling back lightly on the reins, and then on the long handle of the brake, bringing the wagon to a stop.

He remained seated, waiting, as Emiko rode ahead a few more meters and jumped from her horse.

"What is it?" Kazuo shouted, puzzled by her unexpected movement.

Then Emiko shouted back. "Kazuo! Come quick!" And she bent down for a closer look.

She was down on her knees when Kazuo rushed up beside her. He gasped when he saw what it was.

The two of them stared down at the bundle. The faded cotton cloth was covered by patches of dirt, mud, and broken twigs. It was a blanket, ragged and worn. Barely visible was a face. The face of a baby. A tiny baby. Not more than a few weeks old.

Emiko looked quickly around in search of a mother. There was no one in sight but their samurai escort. She looked back at the baby, this time searching for signs of life. Emiko bent close and gazed at its mouth, hoping for movement, something to indicate it was still alive. When she saw an ever-so-slight movement from its lips, she spontaneously extended her arms, slid her hands gently under the body, and lifted it from the ground.

Holding it close to her face, she instinctively began to talk to it, in a soft and reassuring voice. She was so surprised when it opened its eyes to look up at her that she responded with a gasp, loud enough to scare the baby, which wrinkled up its face and began to cry. It was so weak the cries were little more than muffled whimpers, but the baby was alive. She turned to Kazuo. "Quick! We have to get it to Kamaishi! Someone there will know what to do."

Emiko handed the reins of Autumn to one of the samurai and climbed in the wagon, holding the baby as close as possible, being careful not to put pressure on the little body, in case it had a broken bone.

Kazuo was one step ahead of her, grabbing the reins of the mule team and releasing the brake, almost before Emiko was settled beside him. He swatted the rumps of the mules several times, each time with more urgency, until they began to move. Once they did, he kept at it until the wagon was bouncing along the rocky trail as fast as Kazuo dared to go.

The two leading samurai now moved further ahead, looking for the safest route, while the others rode close behind, jumping down to clear the way of rocks, limbs, and even the occasional fallen wall.

With the baby now in her arms, Emiko stopped staring at what remained of the village and looked up only occasionally, hoping to see the physician's house come finally into view. When the wagon reached Twenty-Eighth Street, nothing there but scattered walls, twisted roofs, and broken lumber. The same at Twenty-Third Street. At Eighteenth Street, four workers were busy trying to hoist a wall.

"Where is everyone?" Emiko finally asked Kazuo in desperation. "Where is the physician's house? Shouldn't we be seeing it by now?" She held firm to the baby in her arms, looking down at it every chance she had.

Kazuo kept looking for the church. The fish house was three blocks past the church and should come up just ahead.

At Thirteenth Street, where the physician once lived, only flattened walls remained.

"Nothing looks the same," Kazuo complained loudly. "I don't know where we are. Do you?" he asked Emiko.

"No, but we have to find the physician's house. Who else can help the baby?"

Surely, we must be getting close to the fish house by now, then just two blocks more to the physician, Kazuo thought. When they reached Tenth Street, Kazuo realized his mistake. They had driven too far. They must have passed by the fish house without realizing it. Emiko had not recognized it, either. Nothing was where it should have been. And the samurai could not have known.

Nearly impossible to back the wagon up from here with a four-mule team, the only recourse was to turn around. Fortunately, most of the trash and debris had been picked up from this area, for use in yesterday's funeral pyre, but the streets were narrow, even without the litter and the rubble. Approaching the next upcoming cross street, Kazuo veered first as far to the right as possible, avoiding a section of wall close to the open street, then guided the mules to the left, making the arc as wide as he could, to maneuver up the cross street. The left rear wheel of the wagon moaned while it scraped a fallen roof, as it made the turn. Kazuo held his breath until it passed.

Unknown to Kazuo, they were on Eighth Street and now headed north toward the makeshift kitchen. His plan was to turn left at the next intersection, and back to where the fish house ought to be. Approaching that street, however, he could tell it was too narrow to make the turn. They'd have to continue to the next. As he guided the team and wagon to the far-right side, to set up for another wide turn, Emiko grabbed his arm and pointed farther north. There, a cluster of people were gathered around a fire. She could clearly see smoke lifting from the center of the group.

Kazuo pulled up on the reins and studied the scene. It was not so much the smoke that caught his attention, as the open space that surrounded it. From here, it looked like it offered plenty of room to turn the wagon around. He was just about to flap the reins for the mules to go when he noticed someone near the smoke look in their direction and wave. Presently, another arm went up, and then a third. They seemed to be beckoning them to bring the wagon. He looked at Emiko, who gave a reassuring nod, and he signaled for the mules to go.

The wagon and its samurai escort came to a halt twenty meters short of the fire.

Ayami was first to reach the wagon, and extended an arm to help Emiko down when she noticed the faded, muddy blanket wrapped in her arms.

"We need the physician!" Emiko said, almost shouting. "We found a baby along the road about two kilometers back. It's barely breathing. I don't know what to do for it. We need the physician!"

"We don't know where he is!" Ayami shouted back. "We haven't seen him. His house is ruined, and he may have washed out to sea. Hand me the baby while you step down."

Emiko looked down at the baby in her arms and kissed it gently on the cheek before handing it to Ayami. Then she quickly looked around at what remained of the village and stepped from the wagon. "It's worse than I expected," she said. "Where is everything?" Then answered her own question. "Everything is gone."

"Yes," Ayami replied, "just about everything." Then, looking down at the baby, it became her only worry. We have to find it something to eat. Is it a girl or a boy?" she asked, almost rhetorically.

"It's a girl. I checked while we were bringing her in the wagon. She must be two or three months old, so has probably only ever had her mother's milk. Do you think we can find a wet nurse? Or a recent mother?"

"No women from the village survived," Ayami replied, now in a near-normal voice. "Only the men who were out fishing survived, because they were at sea when it hit. We set up a makeshift kitchen over there. We can at least give her a little water to drink. I don't know where we'll find any milk."

Turning to Minako, who was standing alongside and also staring down at the baby, Ayami said, "Minako, you have more experience than me. What can we do? She has to eat something. Who knows when she last saw her mother? Probably the night of the tsunami. She can't survive much longer without milk."

Minako stared blankly at Ayami and didn't answer.

Ayami and Emiko looked at Minako's face and waited. Finally, Ayami started to say again... "What can we..."

But before she could finish, Minako cut her off.

"I can't keep up!" She sobbed. "A minute ago, we were trying to figure out how to feed seventy workers, and now, all of a sudden, it's a new crisis. How do we feed an infant? We don't have any magic. We can't do it all." Then, as tears started down her cheeks, she inhaled deeply and sighed. She held her face in her hands and cried.

Haruki stepped up beside her and placed an arm around her shoulder.

"I'm sorry," she sobbed. "I should be happy just to be alive. But this is too much. It is simply too much."

"Yes," he agreed. "It is too much."

A minute later, he added, "But we have no choice. We have to keep going."

Then Haruki looked up at Kazuo, still sitting in the wagon, waiting for a decision on where to unload its overflowing contents.

"Kazuo, could you take one of your horses and look for a new mother? Or a cow? Up on the ridges, there must be someone with fresh milk. Or maybe one of your neighbors? Anywhere. We need to find some milk. If you take a horse, you might be able to find someone, or some milk. I'm pretty sure Hideji doesn't have any animals. I don't know who else might. But surely..." he trailed off.

"I can take the horse Emiko was riding. It's ready to go," Kazuo said, and he jumped from the wagon directly to Autumn's back and headed west, in the direction he had just come.

"Tell everyone you see that we need help down here," Haruki called out. But Kazuo was already too far gone to hear.

Ayami handed the infant back to Emiko. She was the one who found it. "Bring her over to the kitchen," she said. "We can try to get some water down her, at least. She can't live without water."

The three women headed quickly to the kitchen area. "There's water in a jug beside the stove," Ayami said. "Pour some in a cup. We don't have a spoon, but we can wet her lips and see if she responds."

When Emiko looked down at the listless body cradled in her arms, its eyes were closed. They fluttered occasionally but didn't open. But there was movement—she was still alive.

"Sit on this log," Ayami said to Emiko. She held a cup filled with water in her hand, and held it out to Emiko. "Dip your finger in the water and wet her lips."

When Emiko touched the infant's lips with her wet finger, the mouth began to quiver. Emiko wet her finger a second time and softly massaged the baby's lips. They quivered again, but nothing more.

"Keep trying," Ayami said, as she and Minako watched.

A third time, Emiko coated the baby's lips with water from the cup. Then, as the three of them stared down at her, the smallest tip of tongue appeared between her lips. The tongue then extended just enough to test the liquid.

Emiko's heart raced as she watched. She quickly doused her finger in the cup and carefully touched it to the little tip of tongue, covering its lips in the process.

The baby responded by extending its tongue a small bit further, this time licking the liquid from its lips.

"If only we had a spoon," Ayami said. She spoke in a quiet voice, trying not to frighten the baby with her voice.

Minako jumped up and headed for Haruki, who was with the group of men staring at them from a short distance away. Work had come to a halt. The entire camp, it seemed, was holding their collective breath over the fate of this tiny baby girl.

"We need some kind of spoon," she said. "The baby is responding to water on her lips, but we need to get some in her mouth. Can you find something? Or make something? It doesn't have to be fancy, just something to get water into her mouth. If we use a cup, I'm afraid she'll choke on it, with so much at one time."

The workers standing nearby heard everything, even with Minako using a soft voice. They looked at Haruki and, almost as one, dispersed from the group in search of something, anything, that resembled a small spoon.

Ten minutes later, one of the men presented Minako with a handful of sea shells. "I think one of these might work," he said. "I found several different sizes. Surely one of them will fit her mouth. You use it just like a spoon. If I had some tools, I could even make a handle for it."

While Minako was sorting through two of the smaller ones, another man approached. "I carved this little spoon out of wood," he explained as he held it out. "It's kind of crude, but if it works, I can make a better one. I could make one any size you want."

Now Minako had two choices to consider. She was about to take both of them over to Emiko when a third man rushed up excitedly. "I found an old piece of tin that I was able to make into a baby-sized cup," he said. "It is not very pretty, but it's small enough; I think it might fit her mouth. If she likes it, I can make a better one, I was in a hurry on this one, so you could see if it works."

For a short time that late afternoon, it seemed the entire remaining villagers forgot their own calamitous plight, in favor of a two-month-old baby girl they did not know.

Minako handed Emiko a small seashell, no bigger than the baby's mouth. Emiko dipped it into the cup of water and held it level, containing just a sip of water in the curve of its shallow shape. Then she teased the baby's lips with the wet of her finger, gently pressed the makeshift spoon to her mouth, and let the water dribble in.

The three women watched intently for a reaction. The men, still at a reserved distance, did the same. Hardly a sound was heard as they waited anxiously for the baby to take its first drink since being found.

Emiko saw a tiny bobble in her throat. She had swallowed the water. Then her tongue extended, and she touched it to her lips, moving around them, for something more to drink. Emiko quickly refilled the shell and poured another swallow into her mouth. This time, there was no delay. She swallowed the second sip.

"Hand me a bigger shell," she said to Minako. Then she filled the larger shell with water and gently trickled it down her throat. This time, not only did Emiko see a telltale bobble in the baby's throat, she watched as its eyes fluttered open and gazed up to meet her own. They were beautiful eyes, brown eyes, but not yet clear enough to focus. Whether the baby could see her face, Emiko did not know. But its eyes were open.

Emiko filled the shell once more and eased its contents into the mouth of the foundling. This time her eyes stayed open, still gazing up at Emiko, and she swallowed once more.

The men, several meters distant, could not see clearly what was taking place, but realized the baby was taking water. A collective sigh of relief swept through the group.

Emiko repeated the process several more times, until a tiny frown covered the baby's face and its arms began to move. Then it uttered several muted cries.

"The poor thing is too hungry to cry," Emiko said. "We have to find something for her to eat, before it's too late." She looked at Ayami, and then at Minako for an answer.

"Maybe Kazuo will find us some milk," Ayami offered hopefully. "He should be coming back before too much longer. Until then, all we can do is keep giving her water. That will help. She won't live without something to drink."

"Maybe we can find something to mix with the water," Minako added. "What if we boiled some vegetables and drained off the water? It might provide a little nourishment."

"It's worth a try," Ayami agreed. "Emiko, bring her over to the kitchen area, and let's try it."

When Haruki saw them walking away, he took it as a signal there was nothing more for them to see, and it was time for them to return to work. They would start by unloading the wagon.

***

For hours, Kazuo had listened as the imaginary sounds of a baby's cries reached his ears from every small, dark image along the way. He sometimes stopped, going in for a closer look. When they turned out to be nothing more than a rock, a bucket, or a tangled, washed-up kimono, he returned to his horse and continued on. Nothing was the same since the night of the tsunami.

It was after midnight when he returned to Kamaishi, his pace constrained by the animal following reluctantly behind. Kazuo's pants were stained from sweat, and his loose cotton shirt was soaked with dust. He struggled to keep his eyes open, and his shoulders sagged from the weight of the day and the overwhelming disaster. Adding to his worries, the village was in total darkness. With hardly a moon to guide him, and landmarks no longer where they ought to be, he could barely find his way. In the distance, light from a single lantern sputtered from the makeshift kitchen area, his destination.

Afraid he might accidentally lead Autumn into a remnant wall or a broken piece of roof, Kazuo pulled the horse to a stop and climbed off, leading his horse the rest of the way. Better to stub his own foot or shin, than to injure his horse. Keeping the distant light in view, he carefully threaded his way through the dark, street by street, until he reached the lantern that had guided his way.

Just beyond the light were three tents, sent by the Empress. Assuming they were for the three women, he approached quietly and stopped at the first. He listened for voices or other sounds, but heard nothing. Then he cautiously pulled back the flap and peered inside. There was just enough light from the lantern behind him to make out a silhouette. Someone was sleeping, and seemed to be holding something in her arm.

Kazuo treaded carefully over to the mat and bent down close. Emiko started when she opened one eye and saw him standing there.

"Kazuo?" she whispered. "Is that you?"

"Yes, it's me," he whispered back.

Now awake, she opened both eyes and smiled up at him.

"Did you find a wet nurse?" she asked, relieved by his return.

"No, I couldn't find anyone."

"Did you find a new mother?" she then asked, hopefully.

"No, I couldn't find a new mother, either," he said.

"A cow? Did you find some cow's milk?"

"Not exactly," he replied. "I couldn't find any cows, either. But one of our neighbors loaned us their goat." Then he waited for her reaction. "They thought it might work," he explained, "and it's all I could find in a hurry. If it doesn't work, I'll go back tomorrow and look some more."

Emiko then carefully shifted the baby to the mat and began to rise.

Kazuo froze. A dark shadow rose from the mat and moved slowly toward his feet. He was so surprised he had no time to shout, which surely would have awakened everyone around them, including the baby. Then, from the light of the lamp, he recognized the furry figure. It was a housecat, colored like a jungle tiger.

Fr. Lispard's cat had adopted Emiko. Or the baby. Or maybe both.

Emiko struggled not to laugh at Kazuo's reaction to the friendly feline. She looked at him tenderly for a long moment. Kazuo had saved her from the factory and had become her loving protector. He meant everything to her. Tonight, for the first time, he looked older. She saw the wrinkles, now lining his kindly face, and the strain in his eyes. *Has this happened since the tsunami?* she wondered.

"The baby has been cranky ever since you left," Emiko said. "She finally went to sleep about an hour ago. It was not until Tiger came over and snuggled in beside her. I think the sound of his purring helped her settle. I don't want to wake her, even for milk. We can try it when she wakes up."

Kazuo looked down at his wife. "Where are Toshi and Haruki?"

"They couldn't take her whimpering any longer. They went to find somewhere more peaceful."

"Should I go find them?"

She reached up and took his arm. "Lay here with me until she wakes up. There's room beside me on the mat."

Kazuo quietly slipped down beside her, careful not to jostle the baby, still wrapped in Emiko's other arm. He placed his hand lightly on top of hers with a tender squeeze. After a few minutes, he said, in barely more than a whisper, "I can't believe this is happening to us."

Emiko squeezed his hand in return. "I know," she whispered. "Neither can I."

Just then, the oil lamp, hanging a short distance across the way, sputtered noisily, and the night went black.

CHAPTER 18
MILK FOR THE FOUNDLING

JUNE 20, 1896 – KAMAISHI VILLAGE

A ray from the early morning sun found its way through a seam in the tent, hitting Kazuo squarely in the face. He opened his eyes and looked around, then moved his arm slightly to see if Emiko was still at his side.

Barely asleep from worry about the infant lying beside her, she stirred at the touch of Kazuo's hand on her arm. She opened her eyes and looked over at the baby. Then she raised up on one elbow and peered closely at its face. When she saw the two tiny lips working as if searching for something to eat, Emiko sighed in relief.

"Quick," she said to Kazuo, "take that cup and get a little milk." She pointed with her free hand to a battered cup just beyond her reach, near the wall of the tent.

He rose from the mat as quietly as he could, picked up the cup, and headed for the opening. The goat, apparently tired from his unexpected travel, was sleeping in the dirt not far away. Kazuo patted him on the head and then behind the ears. He was not familiar with the Bovidae family, but if it worked for mules, it might also work for goats.

The goat looked up at him and bleated her obvious displeasure. But it did raise the goat to its feet, where she stared back at him with a look of defiance. Kazuo looked around for something to bargain with and noted a small bucket of water not far away. He brought it to the goat and held it slowly closer to its face. When the goat stretched her neck to get a drink, Kazuo set the bucket on the ground and looked around for something to feed the animal. He didn't know what they liked, but had been told they would eat almost anything. He went to his horse and retrieved a handful of oats from the leather pouch he always carried. Then he spread them on the dirt next to the bucket of water. The goat lost interest in the water when he saw the oats and began to lick them from the ground.

It gave Kazuo just the opportunity he needed to kneel down beside the goat and cautiously squeeze two of its udders, just as its owner had shown him only hours before, squirting two small streams of milk into the cup. When it was barely half full, he stopped and ran back to the tent, holding the cup carefully in his hand.

Emiko was sitting up with the baby when he entered, the infant cradled carefully in her left arm. "Hold the cup where I can spoon some in her mouth," she said, and taking one of the seashells in her right hand, carefully filled it with milk, and dribbled it into the baby's mouth.

At first, the baby wrinkled its nose and turned away from the makeshift spoon. Emiko and Kazuo watched as it seemed to be judging whether the taste was good or bad. Then its lips began to move. It turned its little head first in one direction and then the other, looking for the source of the strange new liquid. Then her eyes, still faded from hunger, but now with a sign of hope, stared up at the face of the woman holding her close.

Emiko quickly scooped another dribble into the spoon and poured it slowly into the baby's mouth. This time, it swallowed the substance and reopened its mouth. Emiko scooped several more times, raising her hopes with each successive swallow.

Ayami and Minako heard what was happening and came over to watch.

At first, Ayami subconsciously held her breath, watching for the infant to swallow. When she did, and saw it turn its head for more, she turned over to Minako and touched her arm. Ayami watched as Minako mimicked the baby's movements, trying her best to help it drink and swallow each small sip of the newly found substance.

Once Emiko and the baby found a rhythm, Ayami found herself counting the sips. "Seven, eight, nine," she counted. "Thirteen, fourteen, fifteen." At twenty, she finally stopped counting and then began to worry.

"Maybe she needs a break," she said to Emiko. "She is probably so hungry, she won't know when to stop."

The words were barely from Ayami's mouth when a small geyser erupted from the baby's mouth and fresh, warm goat's milk covered the baby's face, arms, and chest. With some still left in her mouth, the infant began to choke.

"Quick!" Minako shouted. "Turn her over!"

Emiko had raised three children of her own, and did not have to wait for instructions. She turned the infant to its stomach in her left hand while gently thumping its back with her right. After three good thumps, the baby stopped coughing. Emiko instinctively brought it to her shoulder and held her tight.

"You poor thing," she cooed in her ear. "I'm sorry. I gave you too much at once. I forgot you hadn't eaten for so long. I won't do that again. I know you're hungry, but we're going to have to take it a little slower from now on."

Ayami found an old piece of towel and held it out for Emiko. "It looks like we're going to need some fresh clothes for her. I guess you could use some, too."

"I wonder if the milk is too rich for her," Minako offered. "Maybe we need to mix it with water until she gets used to it."

"That's a good idea," Ayami said. "I didn't think of that."

Emiko wiped the baby as best she could with the towel and said, "Shall we try it again? I don't think she has any of it left in her stomach."

Just then, the baby began to cry.

"Add some water to what's left in the cup," Emiko said, "and I'll see if she can keep it down."

Half an hour later, Emiko put the spoon on the floor and lifted the infant with both hands to her shoulder, patting her on the back. By the fifth pat, it burped so loudly that it made the rest of them jolt with surprise, and then laugh in relief.

"Kazuo, I think you should go get a little more milk." Emiko's voice was quivering. "I think she's going to make it."

Kazuo, who was still holding the cup for Emiko, set it on the ground. "I'm going to need a bigger container," he said, looking around. Minako was standing near a makeshift serving table and handed him a porcelain jar someone had found in the rubble.

Kazuo turned back to Emiko as he headed for the goat, just in time to see Tiger drinking eagerly from the leftover cup of milk. He turned and rushed for the cat, an instinctive reaction, but Emiko stopped him.

"Tiger was the only one who could get her settled last night. I think he deserves a little reward. Besides, the goat will give a lot more milk than this little girl can drink." Then she smiled at Kazuo with a look he could not resist.

"Yes," he muttered, "I'll be happy to milk a goat so the cat can have milk to drink."

***

After two days of steady milk, the foundling was a different baby. She cried when she was wet or hungry; she moved her arms and legs; she occasionally found her mouth with her thumb; and her eyes tracked Emiko whenever she was close.

"What are we going to do now?" Emiko asked on the third morning. "I can't stay here with her forever. We need to be getting back to our homes at night, to at least make sure they're okay. If I take her home with me, I don't feel I can stay there with her. I should be helping the rest of you. And the trip would be hard on her if I took her back and forth every day. Even more important, who will take care of her from now on?"

She secretly wondered if Minako would consider taking her in, now that she had lost her daughter Hisa, and her grandson Eito. Emiko looked at her with pleading eyes. "Is there any chance you and Haruki could raise her?"

"I'm too old, Emiko," she said, without hesitation. "She needs someone younger. Like you. You should ask Kazuo about keeping her."

CHAPTER 19
AFTERMATH

JUNE 22, 1896 – KAMAISHI VILLAGE

"We're too old," Kazuo said for the third time. "We're too old to raise another child."

"We're not *that* old," she replied for the third time. And besides, who else is there? Someone has to raise her, and the children will help. There are no families left in the village."

Kazuo stared at the infant in her arms and then at Emiko's face. He tried to avoid her eyes, but they were like magnets when he looked at her. He might possibly have maintained his resistance had she not held out the baby to him. He could hardly shun her implied request to hold the baby. It would be downright rude.

Reluctantly, he extended his arms as Emiko placed the baby into one of them and pressed her close to his chest. It was pure instinct when he looked down at the tiny thing in his arm, with big, round eyes looking back. He stood silent as he gazed at her.

"We'll help, Papa," Suki pleaded. "Won't we, Kensei?"

"Yes, we'll help," Kensei replied. He turned to his big brother. "Right Kaneto?"

"We'll all help," Kaneto affirmed. "Mama's right, someone has to take her in."

Kazuo was still looking at the big brown eyes he held in his arm. Without wanting to, he bent down close to her face and talked to her in a voice he hadn't used since Kensei was a baby.

"What do you think, little one? Do you want to live with us?" Then he tickled her cheek with his other hand and watched as her eyes brightened.

"I guess that's a 'yes'," he grinned. "You win. But not without a name. If you're going to live with us, you have to have a name."

Emiko moved over and kissed him on the cheek. "You are the best thing in my life," she beamed. "You won't be sorry."

"What about 'Tiger'?" Suki asked. "Can we keep Tiger, too? He's the one that helps her sleep."

"She's right," Emiko added. "I think the baby likes him. And Tiger seems to like her, too."

"This isn't fair," he said. "You are all taking advantage of me. Okay—but only until Fr. Lispard's replacement gets here. Tiger belonged to the priest. When the new priest comes, he can take Tiger back, if he wants.

"Now, what about her name? I suppose you have that figured out, too. It would have been easier if you'd just told me what we were going to do. It seems like you have it all figured out."

"Actually, I do," Emiko said. She smiled at Kazuo and then looked down at the baby. "There is only one name that fits her...Mamiko. It means 'daughter of the sea.' What do you think? It fits her perfectly. It was the sea that brought her to us. That should be her name."

It was settled. Her name would be Mamiko.

***

By the end of the second week, rebuilding houses of the few survivors had settled in. The four-man teams were actually becoming good carpenters. Fishing skills had little in common with woodworking skills, but they had one of the most important requirements. They knew how to work together. Every man on a fishing boat was dependent on the others. The captain was in charge, but every man had to pull his weight. It was the same for building a house.

At the end of the week, the volunteers from the foundry went back to work. It was, after all, their means of livelihood, and the furnaces were not affected by the tsunami. Only the railway had been damaged. It was one reason it was so hard for others to comprehend the disaster. The village was decimated, but beyond the village, it was almost as if nothing had happened.

The foundry volunteers did manage to build a usable smokehouse before they left, and to clear the remaining streets throughout the village. Carts, horses, and even wagons could now maneuver wherever they needed to go. It proved particularly helpful for moving the lumber in rebuilding, but also for transporting fish from the harbor to the smokehouse.

At communal supper one evening, Haruki asked if he could use the samurai volunteers to help rebuild the teahouse. Since neither he nor Toshi needed help with their houses, it seemed a reasonable request. But he had forgotten about his previous encounter with Bunji Tanaka.

"What makes you so special?" Bunji asked loudly. "I thought we had this settled once before, but I guess you have a short memory."

"Tanaka-san, It's not that I consider myself special, it is simply a matter of foresight—what month is it?"

"What month? That's a dumb question. It's June. See, everybody? No wonder I have to keep an eye on him."

Turning back to Haruki, he continued. "You pretend to be our leader, and you don't even know what month it is. Are you sure the tsunami didn't thump you on the head with something?"

"That is correct, Tanaka-san. It is June. Right now, it is June. Where will you be eating in December? Are you going to fix your own meals when your house is done? What about the rest of you? Will you be able to fix your own meals without a wife? Or would you rather come to a teahouse and meet with your friends? Will all of you have new stoves before the snow flies? Where will you get them without any income? Are you going to take turns using this one? Maybe you think it would be fun to cook on an open fire in the yard, but probably not every day. If we rebuild the teahouse, it will be a place everyone can come for meals until we're all back on our feet again. So it benefits everyone, not just me.

"Does that seem like a reasonable solution?" he then asked.

Bunji was silent as he looked around at the group. Then he looked over at the solitary stove, sitting in an open area just beyond. He watched as a column of gray smoke rose from its modest chimney.

"Well, if that's the reason, you should have explained it first," he managed to say.

Not a person to celebrate winning a confrontation, Haruki replied, "Yes, I probably should have. Thank you for raising the question."

"With that question now answered, does anyone else object to having the samurai work on the teahouse?"

The group remained silent until finally, came a voice from the rear, "We need the teahouse. I'll help, too, if you need me."

"I'll help too," another voice said.

Several other voices agreed.

"Toshi and I can finish the inside later," Haruki said. "We should have plenty of time before winter to make it better. But at least we'll have a place to cook, and to store the food."

Two weeks later, the teahouse was usable, though far from finished. The cooking stove was moved from its open area in the dirt to a kitchen area in the teahouse. The chimney was extended, venting smoke through a roof.

Haruki and Toshi could make the benches later.

CHAPTER 20
DESIGNING THE CHURCH

JULY 28, 1896 – KAMAISHI TEAHOUSE

One night during supper at the new teahouse, Haruki, Toshi, Kazuo, and their families were seated together, talking. Toshi got quiet, and his look seemed kilometers away. "Do you remember our last time together with Fr. Lispard?" he asked.

The others nodded.

"Remember how he told us of his dream, and how he went on to describe a new church?"

Again, they nodded.

"At the time, we couldn't figure out why God described to him how to build a new church. Granted, the other one was small, but didn't seem to be in bad condition."

No one spoke. Each person seemed to retreat into a memory of that warm afternoon with the priest from France. He'd been almost timid at the time, wondering if he'd really had the dream and what it meant. Now it was obvious. It was a premonition, a signal from God that the church would *need* to be rebuilt. It did not reveal that Fr. Lispard would not be there to see it. But in retrospect, that must be why the priest came to reveal his dream to them. And to describe the major features of its replacement.

"That same night, out on the boat," Toshi continued, "I found myself designing segments of the church to pass the time. I remember clearly, how I thought we could position the church exactly as Fr. Lispard had relayed it to us, so the setting sun would shine a beam of light directly up the aisle, to land on the altar each year on the Feast of the Assumption of the Blessed Virgin Mary."

He went on, "I remember thinking to myself, Where is the new church supposed to be? Are we to tear down the original and rebuild on the same site? Are we to build it adjacent to the old one? Should it be somewhere else entirely? If we rebuilt on the same site, could we build the new one around the old one first, then tear down the old?

"Now it's clear. The old one was destroyed. It seems to me we are meant to rebuild right where it was, only bigger. And I think we're supposed to start on it right away, even without a priest. Surely, if we build it, a new priest will come."

The others considered his proposal. Finally, Haruki responded. "With most of our houses now habitable, it would give us something new to focus on, and also provide a worthy project for those who wanted to help. Especially, since there is no longer a big demand for fish… We don't need to fish every day.

"There aren't many parishioners left, but others might want to help, just for something to do. There is still some lumber we could use. And we should be able to salvage at least some of the altar. It would be a chance for fishermen to learn the fine art of a skilled craftsman," he chuckled.

Together, they began to draw out variations of a plan on scraps of paper. Toshi explained his ideas on how to get the orientation exactly right for August fifteenth. If they hurried, they had time to begin trial observations in time for the final test, just over two weeks away.

Toshi was already working on a plan. "Tomorrow, we'll clear away debris from the site. Then we'll select a tall tree to use as the marking pole. And we'll build a wooden frame to attach to the pole, to simulate the window."

For the next seven days, sketches, plans, measurements, trial-and-error, sawing, digging, and a dozen other tasks kept at least half the remaining residents too busy to dwell on everything they'd lost in a single night. Fr. Lispard had left them a parting gift. The gift of community.

Excitement continued to build as, day by day, they determined and laid out the exact measurements of the church-to-be. The first shadow test was ready on August seventh. Time was running out.

"I don't know why I didn't think about this sooner," Toshi lamented. "I don't see how we can possibly be ready by the fifteenth. That's only one week away."

"We have to do it," Ayami said. "We have to do it for Fr. Lispard. We'll just have to work a little longer every day. I'm sure we can figure it out by the fifteenth."

Using the longest boards they could find, they laid out a cross-shaped footprint, representing the perimeter of the church. The boards were placed along the ground at its intended size, which meant wherever the ray of sun tracked at sundown, is where it would shine along the floor of the church. The marking pole was cut from a ten-meter, fresh-cut pine, stripped of its branches for a clean shadow when the sun crossed the afternoon sky. Atop the pole, just as Toshi had envisioned, their most skillful craftsman attached a rectangular frame, with a starting dimension of one meter by one and a half meters. They might have to change the size as they progressed, but this was a place to start.

The pole was planted in a hole where the front doors to the church would eventually be located. It represented the only fixed location of the design. All other measurements would be determined using that point as their basis. The objective was to line up the rest of the church with that point such that on the fifteenth, the sun bore directly down a line from the window above the front door to the altar at the opposite end of the church. If necessary, they could shift the footprint boards left or right.

On the first day, Toshi attached a length of rope to the base of the pole and stretched it loosely to a point fifteen meters distant, where he planned for the altar to be located. As the sun lowered in the sky, he planted a stake in the ground at the end of the rope, in a line parallel with the shadow of the pole.

Everyone in the village gathered around as the sun continued to set. Some of them understood his logic and were pleasantly surprised to find, as the last of the day's rays reached the earth, they could watch its progress along the ground toward the stake. Others were not convinced. "Maybe he should stick to fishing or shipping rice," one of them mumbled under his breath.

The next day, Toshi had a better idea of what to expect, and with a few adjustments, had high hopes for improvement. For one thing, the pole was too high, which prevented the sunray from traveling the full distance. But it also dawned on him that Fr. Lispard had not specified at what time of day the phenomenon was supposed to occur. The height of the window made a difference. At any rate, he would try again. He had five days remaining.

The crowd gathered again as the sun began to set. This time, they had a better understanding of what to watch for. Some even offered ideas or suggestions. It had become a source of pride for most of the village. The height was better this time. Toshi could see the sunray streaming through the window frame well enough to watch it track along the ground on its imaginary line, toward the imaginary altar. Although he didn't think to time it, at the end he thought it took between thirty and forty-five minutes. It seemed like a good figure. *Did Fr. Lispard envision the travel to take place while he said an afternoon mass?* he wondered. If so, then forty-five minutes to an hour would be perfect.

One of the suggestions was to make the window more realistic. A simple framework was not really enough to truly trace the path of the ray. "We need to see the shadow that surrounds the window," they said. "That way, the outer areas will be dark, and we'll only see the ray of the sun."

Toshi conferred with the chief craftsman. The request went out for remnants of heavy fabric or sail cloth that could be used to simulate a wall surrounding the window. It needn't be large; even a half-meter covering on each of the four sides of the window frame would be enough to demonstrate the effect. The craftsman quickly added a second frame around the first. It was simply a frame within a frame when he finished. Then he nailed the bits of fabric between the two frames, leaving the window opening free.

On the third day, just as the crowd assembled to view his progress, clouds gathered in the sky. In his many hours of planning, cloudy skies had not once come to mind. The only thing they would learn this day was whether their shadow pole and its make-believe window could withstand a light wind and a shower of rain.

Undeterred, Toshi spent the evening drawing pictures with lines and angles. He had three more days to get it right. All he needed was for the sun to shine.

The fourth day was more productive. Even the crowd was surprised at how much better they could track the path of the rays, now with the imaginary wall providing more shade. It was almost mesmerizing to watch the rectangle of sunlight move slowly along the line of rope until it reached the stake at its end. Toshi moved the stake several centimeters to the north as a result of today's test. He knew it would have to move a little each day now, until the fifteenth. That was the whole purpose of starting early. It gave him time to first confirm the process, then to fine-tune the measurements. And since the trajectory of the sun changed daily, so too would the location of the imaginary altar.

Convinced he was close to the mark, he decided it was time to devise a better altar. He sadly wished Fr. Lispard were there to guide him. *How big would the altar be? Should it be centered exactly at the intersection of the vertical and two horizontal wings? Or should it be at the upper tip of the cross-shaped building?*

Following a restless night of tossing and turning, he awoke with a plan. Without Fr. Lispard, he realized, it was up to him. While his mind worked on the question overnight, it occurred to him that as long as the alignment was correct, the placement of the altar could be moved closer or farther from the front door by Fr. Lispard's successor. For now, he would carry the damaged altar from the old church and place it at the intersection of the two planes of the cross.

He shared his plan during breakfast at the teahouse. It was a daily ritual now. All the survivors gathered at the teahouse for meals. A half dozen of them volunteered to retrieve the altar and somehow nail or tie it back together at the end of Toshi's shadow rope.

By the time the sun reached the western sky that afternoon, the altar crew had resurrected the altar at a spot Toshi pointed out to them. Anticipation grew among the regulars to see how close it was going to meet what they now understood to be the goal. At three o'clock, the rays from the sun shone through the simulated window and rested approximately three meters from the entrance to the church. The crowd watched as the minutes ticked by. At four o'clock, the heart of the ray was half-way up the imaginary aisle. By five o'clock, the ray was directed exactly at the makeshift altar. It continued to move along its intended path until, by six o'clock, it disappeared somewhere up the eventual eastern wall of the church.

Somehow, Toshi had not considered that the rays would travel much faster than expected. After seeing it in practice, it seemed obvious. The distance between the sun and the earth compared to the distance from the front door to the altar created a distortion in its movement. Nevertheless, the concept worked. Not knowing the exact requirements of Fr. Lispard's dream, Toshi felt he had come as close as God would expect of him.

Of course, being Toshi, it still nagged at him. Overnight, another idea came to him. While technically, it might be considered cheating, he envisioned a floating window. One that could be adjusted up or down, and left or right, to allow for minor corrections, if the need arose. For one thing, he wasn't sure if the trajectory of the earth and sun would remain constant over time. It seemed possible that one or the other might move a degree over the course of several years. An adjustable window would help control the path of light as it made its way up the aisle.

August fifteenth was a Saturday. Toshi thought it would be more appropriate had it been a Sunday, but that was beyond his control. To his amazement, a crowd began to gather at the church shortly after noon. Families from the ridge, families of foundry workers, and others from as far away as twenty kilometers, trickled in to watch the free event. Word had spread day-by-day about the priest's dream and Toshi's ingenious concept of controlling sunlight so as to travel up the aisle of the church.

The teahouse was open for business, but it was not prepared for the crowd that came. Ayami pressed every available family member into service, preparing tea and even coffee for the more adventurous. It would be good publicity for the emporium, and also for the teahouse. The more people who tried it, the more who were bound to want more of it. They had plenty of smoked fish on hand, but Ayami stirred the embers in the cook stove, and hurried to boil a small amount of rice, just in case.

When the spectators realized the teahouse was open, a few walked the three streets down, simply to pass the time while waiting. Little by little, the few became more, and by the time the first rays of sun landed inside the make-believe door of the make-believe church, the teahouse had produced its biggest day since the tsunami. And the best part was most of them had cash money from the foundry. A few still had to barter, and a smaller few reluctantly accepted charity, 'in honor of Fr. Lispard,' they were told.

Ayami might as well have closed the door after three o'clock, however. Every resident and every visitor sat or stood as close as possible to the future church, grasping for a view of the magical *March of the Sun*, as it came to be called. They watched as it shined through the fake window atop a pine pole, and during the next two hours, marched up an imaginary aisle to rest briefly on the makeshift altar. Due to the angle at that hour, and the height of the altar, the sun actually seemed to dwell on it for a longer period of time. The effect was that it seemed to pause momentarily at the altar of the Christian God. Without an actual wall behind the altar, it was difficult to determine when the march was complete. At some point, however, it would march its way beyond the altar and up the wall behind, until the sun was gone.

But while it rested briefly on the broken wooden table, with its hand-carved features and built-in storage, two hundred or more spectators broke into shouts and applause at this unique and marvelous trick of human engineering.

Satisfied the layout was as close to perfect as he could make it, Toshi made his way around each and every length of lumber, hammering stakes firmly into the rocky soil.

Having come this far, the last thing he needed was for a storm, the wayward step of a horse, or even one of his faithful workers, to kick one of the precious marking boards out of position before a permanent floor could be completed. There was just enough time to drive the last wooden stake before dark set in.

Tomorrow, he and a crew of others, could finally begin for real.

CHAPTER 21
REVELATION

AUGUST 16, 1896 – KAMAISHI TEAHOUSE

The first task would be a solid foundation. Using hand carts, they carefully collected nearby stones from an ever-increasing arc surrounding the church. There were lots more prior to the tsunami, but many had washed away. On the bright side, several new ones appeared as well, coming from the foundations of houses that used to be.

Next, the team did the same for flooring materials. They adhered to Haruki's mandate that any material located on an owner's property belonged to that owner, unless it could be shown to belong to a neighboring property. It didn't matter whether the original owner had survived or not. Until relatives were notified and given a reasonable period of time to claim the remnants, they were not to be confiscated. This still allowed for the scavenging of materials found in vacant lots or on public property between the houses.

One evening at the teahouse, Toshi alternated between staring at his bowl of rice and the window facing east toward the heart of the village. Ayami had to ask him twice what was troubling him.

"I'm afraid we won't have enough wood for the floor," he finally said. "I want all of it to match. It will look bad if we have to piecemeal different sizes and varieties of wood. I've searched everywhere I can think of, but so far the only wood that matches is from the physician's old house. And we can't wait for his relatives to decide if they want any of it. I'm not even sure if he had any, or if he did, where they live. It could take months to find them."

At the sound of his name, Ayami's face tightened. She tried to hide the tension that gripped at her. When she turned away from the others, Minako knew something wasn't right. "Are you okay, Ayami?" she asked quietly.

Ayami continued to stare out the window so intently that Minako followed her line of sight to see what she found so captivating. There was still plenty of daylight to take in whatever activity might be going on beyond the window. For a fleeting moment, the others half expected to see a giant wave come crashing in on them. Ayami was trembling.

"What is it?" Toshi asked. "What's wrong, Ayami? Are you okay?"

Slowly, she turned back to face Toshi. "It would be wrong to use anything from the physician's house for the church," she said, hardly louder than a whisper. "It just wouldn't be right."

Toshi smiled, almost to the point of a chuckle. "Oh, Ayami, I wouldn't take the flooring without approval. Surely you didn't think I was planning to steal his flooring to put in the church. I agree it wouldn't be right."

Her face did not change expression. "That's not what I was worried about," she said.

The others waited to see if she was planning to explain.

"I mean, he was not a nice person," she finally continued, still barely more than a whisper.

"Oh, now I understand," Toshi tried to console her. "He was pretty rude in how he hounded us to move down to the village, where he said we'd be safer. I agree he could be disagreeable, but he finally stopped pestering me. Now that I think about it, consider the irony. He repeatedly told us to move down here so we'd be safer, and it turns out the village was most dangerous of all."

"Yes, that's true," continued Ayami. "But that's not what I mean, either. The physician was not a nice person. After Kiyoshi and Isamu were born…" she turned to look out the window again. "After Kiyoshi and Isamu were born, he made several trips up to see me while you were working at the foundry. He said he just wanted to make sure I was recovering.

I had no idea what to expect after having a baby, especially with Kiyoshi. He said it was just routine that he should examine me. At first, I believed him. But after several visits, I began to suspect he just wanted to see and touch me, in ways that didn't seem logical. I was afraid to tell you at first, because I didn't expect you to know either, but then later, because I was so ashamed of myself, for falling for his tricks.

"Eventually, I convinced him to stop coming. But when Isamu came along, it started all over again. This time I was better prepared, but he was persistent. Finally, I tied the door shut and would not let him in. Then I threatened to tell his wife. That seemed to convince him. By the time Meisa came along, I guess I was too old for him to bother with. Or maybe he had a new infatuation by that time. At any rate, he stopped harassing me. I think the real reason he wanted us to move to the village was so it would be easier for him to slip away and see me, and you would be further away, at the foundry."

Minako reached across and placed the palm of her hand on top of Ayami's as she stood, and bent to be closer to her. Toshi and Haruki sat with faces as rigid as stone.

A small group sitting next to them sensed a sudden change in the tone of the conversation. There was little doubt among them regarding what they had unintentionally heard. Soon every table and every discussion within the room went quiet. Even those who had not heard, felt the weight of the event. Something bad had happened to Ayami. Word would get around. Eventually, they would know.

Toshi's eyes began to mist. He moved to Ayami and placed a gentle arm around her shoulder. He placed his head close to hers and whispered something she alone could hear. She shook her head almost imperceptibly, but could not fight off the tears.

Eventually, one of the workers helping with the church floor approached their table. "I've been thinking about the floor," he began. "There were several members of Father's church who will never come back. Their entire family was taken. I think they might consider it an honor if something from their house could be used for the new church. Maybe it's okay to change our rules in this case. We could put up a sign in the church giving their families credit for donating materials. We don't have the money to buy anything new."

The worker was fully aware he was trying to distract Toshi and Haruki and their wives from their sudden grief, but hoped he could be forgiven. Besides, he spoke the truth.

Still clinging to his beloved Ayami, Toshi looked briefly at Haruki, then back to the man. "Yes," he replied, "I think it might be time."

The workers in the teahouse, instead of lingering as usual to share new stories and retell old ones, soon dispersed. "See you tomorrow," some said. "Good night," others replied, and the teahouse emptied out.

Both couples walked home with hands clasped tightly together.

Toshi condemned himself for not noticing the agony his wife must have been going through, and not searching for a cause.

Minako retraced her memory for the signs she must have missed.

For his part, Haruki tried hard not to be happy about the physician's unfortunate demise.

Toshi did not thank God that night, as he often did before falling asleep. In fact, he did not pray at all. Only one thing filled his mind, and he could not push it out. The physician. A man of trust. A man looked up to by nearly everyone in the village.

He thought of Ayami. His beloved Ayami. He replayed her explanation over and over. *I had no idea what to expect…it was just routine…I was ashamed of myself for falling for his tricks.*

Then he thought about himself. *How could I have been so blind? Why didn't I see what was happening? I should have asked Haruki how often the physician came to visit when their children were born.*

Nothing helped ease the pain. He turned on their mat and gazed at Ayami. She was breathing steadily, but was she sleeping? He gently placed a hand on hers. At first, it did not respond. Then, after a minute, she wrapped her open fingers around his and held them tight.

"I'm sorry," she whispered. "I should have told you long ago. At first, I was too afraid, and then I was too ashamed. Can you forgive me?"

Toshi released her hand and rolled over enough to place an arm across her chest. He could feel the trembling as she began to sob.

"Of course, I forgive you, but it's me who needs the forgiving, not you," he whispered back. "I should have noticed something wrong. I must have been so excited about the babies that I didn't pay enough attention to you. I am so sorry."

Toshi then released his embrace and took hold of her hand. Together, they stared at the ceiling in silence.

Ayami was almost asleep when she finally heard Toshi speak. "How much more?" he murmured.

"What?" Ayami asked.

"How much more?" Toshi said, this time a little louder.

"How much more what?" she asked.

"How much more can we take?" he replied. "What's next? Another plague? Another flood? How many more loved ones are going to die?"

Now it was Ayami who turned on her side and placed an arm across her husband.

"Oh, Toshi," she said, as her voice began to tremble. "We'll make it, no matter what else happens. I love you. Don't ever forget that. I've loved you since that first time I saw you walking home on the path from work. Think about all the good things we've had in our lives—when we met at Saya's birthday party, when we first flew kites up on the ridge, our wedding, our children. They are all safe and strong. God has saved us for a reason. Whatever is still to come, we can handle. And if we can't, we've already had a better life than most."

"What about Hisa? And Eito? Poor Minako and Haruki. I don't know how they keep going. And Hajime. He lost everyone. Even his parents—he lost everyone."

"I know. I don't understand why, but no matter what, we have to keep trying. We have to keep going. We'll have to help take care of Hajime. Maybe that's why God spared us. Spared you. Maybe he wants you here to watch over Hajime."

They were both quiet for some time. Then Ayami thought of one more thing. Actually, it might be the most important of all.

"No one else understands how the new church is supposed to work. Maybe God wants you here to finish the church."

CHAPTER 22
PLEA FOR A PRIEST

AUGUST 1896 – KAMAISHI

Toshi wrote three letters to the Jesuits following the tsunami.

25 AUGUST 1896

Dear Fr. Bishop,
*   I am deeply saddened to report to you the recent death of our beloved Fr. Henri Lispard. You may have received reports of our terrible earthquake suffered on June fifteenth of this year. The ensuing tsunami devastated our village of Kamaishi, and carried your servant out to sea, where his body was later recovered.*
*   Several of his surviving parishioners buried his remains at the site of St. Mary's church, which was ruined by the disaster.*
*   I am writing to ask that you send a replacement for Fr. Lispard as soon as possible.*
Awaiting your reply,
Toshi Ozawa
Surviving parishioner.

***

21 OCTOBER 1896

Dear Fr. Bishop,
   I am writing once more to send additional condolences on the death of your servant, Fr. Henri Lispard, on June fifteenth of this year.
   Having received no response from you, a handful of surviving parishioners (myself included) have taken it upon themselves to rebuild St. Mary's church using whatever materials we could salvage from the original structure, along with usable material from surrounding homes or buildings that were abandoned.
   For that reason, we are eager to receive your replacement servant, in order that we may continue to celebrate mass and other sacraments and prayers when the structure becomes operational once again.

Awaiting your reply,
Toshi Ozawa
Surviving parishioner.

***

23 MAY 1897

Dear Fr. Bishop,
   I am writing to you once more, seeking a reply with instructions for a replacement priest at St. Mary's of the Assumption Church.
   We are continuing to rebuild the church with a planned completion date prior to August fifteenth, 1897, at which time we had hoped to celebrate the Feast of the Assumption of the Blessed Virgin Mary. That is a special occasion for us because on the eve before he died, Fr. Lispard shared with us a vision he received during a dream, regarding basic features of a new structure. We have tried our best to honor his vision. However, it would be of comfort to give his successor time to make final adjustments prior to the Holy Day.

Eagerly awaiting your reply,
Toshi Ozawa
Kamaishi Village, Japan

The Difficult Years of Toshi Ozawa

By the end of June, Hideji, Toshi, Haruki, their families, and the few other surviving parishioners were frustrated and losing heart. Not a single letter had arrived from the bishop. Toshi was convinced he must have sent them to the wrong place. Fr. Lispard was the only one who knew who and where his superior was. And he was long since unavailable. Toshi posted the letters to Paris, since he knew Fr. Lispard was French. He remembered Fr. Lispard occasionally referring to the Provincial, and understood that to be the 'management office' of the Jesuits, but he was unsure where their office would be located.

Together, they decided that if they had not heard from the bishop by the first of August, they would have to settle for a holy day without a priest. Toshi or Haruki would have to make do by leading a few prayers on their own. Ayami volunteered to search for as many Bibles and prayer books as she could find. And Minako offered to search for a songbook and organize a choir.

Late in July, Toshi received a letter from the bishop.

23 JUNE 1897

Dear Mr. Ozawa,
  In future, may I request that you adhere to commonly accepted practice of addressing a bishop of the church as 'Your Excellency.' Had our departed servant and brother been there to assist you, I'm sure you would not have committed this error.
  Regarding the assignment of a replacement for Father Henri Lispard, S.J., our missionaries serve countries throughout the world as evangelists of our Lord. Only those called by the Lord to serve his mission make themselves available to His service. There are far more needs than available servants. It is particularly challenging to procure a replacement who speaks your language, on account of the Island of Japan isolating itself from the rest of the world for over two centuries.
  However, because of the outstanding legacy left behind by Father Lispard, and in honor of his memory, I have requested the service of an American order to continue the work begun by him.

He has been authorized to sail from San Francisco, California, his current assignment, at his first opportunity.

Please welcome Father Katz, and provide for him whatever necessities he requires. He should arrive in time for the Feast of the Assumption.

As regarding your re-construction of the church, it is common practice for the pastor in residence to make all decisions regarding form and function within his church. Whatever 'vision' was relayed to you by Father Lispard will be considered only as a 'suggestion,' subject to actual requirements you will be provided by Father Katz upon his forthcoming arrival.

Yours in Christ,
Felix-Auguste Beguinot, S.J.
Bishop, Diocese of Nimes, France

Toshi studied the date on the bishop's letter and considered the date of its eventual arrival. He should not have been surprised, then, at the slow response by 'His Excellency,' determined in large part by the slowness of mail delivery to and from a foreign country. It being almost the end of July, Toshi then considered the tasks still to be completed prior to the church's grand re-opening. There were three benches still to be constructed and placed at the rear of the church. The altar and other related functional structures were loosely assembled and arranged as closely as Toshi could remember from the original structure. He purposely refrained from securing the altar to the raised flooring because he was not sure where Fr. Lispard would have wanted the sun to concentrate during its march up the aisle. Once the new priest gave his approval, it would not take long to secure it properly in place.

Toshi was convinced the result of their combined efforts would make the new Fr. Katz proud. He had consulted Hideji, Ayami, Haruki, Minako, and any other parishioner who took an interest, whenever there was a choice between two, or even more possible alternatives. Whenever there was indecision, they consulted their collective memories and tried to mimic the way it had been before. Several times, after reaching a decision, they felt as though Fr. Lispard had actually participated in the discussion. At least in spirit.

The Difficult Years of Toshi Ozawa

By afternoon on Friday, August sixth, 1897, when Fr. Katz had not yet arrived in Kamaishi, Toshi was losing faith. He, Haruki, and a host of others had been working on the church for over a year. The last of the benches were completed and placed. Toshi estimated the new church would easily seat two hundred people, almost twice what the original church could hold.

Granted, there were not two hundred Catholics living in Kamaishi, but the whole idea presented by Fr. Lispard was to build for future growth. He was already beginning to feel the despair of having to wait another year to see if his measurements and planning were accurate. Even without a mass, he concluded, he could still stand at various locations within the structure and confirm the movement of the sun's stream of light. But he could not shake the disappointment Fr. Lispard would have felt, his final dream not yet fulfilled.

If only the bishop had told him how the priest would arrive, it would have been easier to anticipate his arrival. Toshi assumed it would be on the packet ship from Tokyo. But what if he came overland, possibly using the same road from Kitakami they traveled routinely with the mule team? They might well have been able to meet the priest and expedite his arrival, if given some clue as to where and when. As it was, there was nothing to do but wait and hope. Toshi's patience was growing thin.

***

Toshi and Haruki still maintained their Friday night shifts on the fishing boats. Accordingly, on Saturday morning, they guided their respective boats behind several others lined up at the wharf to unload their nightly catch. The sun was already causing a steady stream of sweat to drip from their temples. It had been a good night's work; the take was better than most nights. Both men were considering to themselves how much fish they should buy from the other boats. The Kamaishi Trading Company found itself to be influential in the fish market, following the tsunami. Not so much by design as by accident. The silk factory gave them the luxury of a small but steady demand for fish, with payments always made in currency.

As Toshi tied his boat to an available post on the dock, excited conversations from nearby caught his attention. He secured the boat and waited for Haruki to do the same, then they headed toward the animated discussion between the dockmaster and several other fishermen.

"...he came last night. I saw him myself," the dockmaster was saying. "I know it was him by the way he was dressed. He was a priest, all right; there was no question about that. He was dressed in a black robe and wore a little black hat, just like Fr. Lispard. He also had a sash around his waist, with a big string of wooden beads hanging from it.

"No," he continued. "I didn't get a chance to talk to him myself, but I was able to overhear his conversation with some others who were waiting here for the boat to arrive. I would have to say he was a little hard to understand, but maybe it was only because I wasn't close enough. I couldn't say where he was from. He was speaking in Japanese, but he definitely had an accent of some kind."

Toshi's heart quickened. The new priest must finally have arrived. He smiled at Haruki, then said, "We'd better unload our fish in a hurry and find him. Do you think he'll be ready to celebrate mass tomorrow? It would give him a chance to try out our new church before the Assumption, just like we'd hoped."

Haruki was already moving toward his boat with a cart to offload the nightly catch. Toshi followed close behind. They worked together and quickly unloaded both boats. Then they tossed their belongings on the cart and hurried to secure the boats at their moorings. The ferryman gathered them in his dingy and shuttled them back to the wharf.

Together, they pulled and pushed the cart from the dock, up North Front Street to the trading company building on Fifteenth Street. All the while, they searched in vain for signs of the new priest. "He's probably at the church," Haruki offered, "although I don't know if he would have spent the night there. It really wasn't intended as a residence."

"We can look there first. If he's not there, we'll have to start checking with neighbors to see if anyone has seen him. Maybe he took lodging at someone's house."

They left the cart at the smokehouse and headed toward the church on Eighteenth Street. Opening the front door with an excited jerk, Toshi peered in. Light soaked through the windows, but it took a minute for his eyes to adjust. He scanned the benches for some sign of a priest. Not finding any, the two men walked slowly forward, approaching the altar. Out of reverence, they refrained from speaking. Reaching the intersection of the main aisle and the two side aisles, which simulated a cross, they looked in both directions.

Suddenly, from behind the altar, a crash. They both stiffened where they stood. Then, a loud expletive outburst from behind the altar, followed by muttering and words obviously spoken in anger or frustration, in a language that was not Japanese.

"Hello, Father," Toshi uttered. "Are you alright?"

Silence replied.

"Hello?" Toshi repeated. Louder this time.

The sound of footsteps replied. They watched as the sounds made their way from behind the altar and stopped only meters away.

"Hello," came a voice in broken Japanese.

The three men gazed at one another for a long minute, until Toshi spoke again. "You must be our new priest, Fr. Katz. Welcome to Kamaishi. I am Toshi, and this is my uncle, Haruki. We helped rebuild the church. We hope you like it."

Fr. Katz looked around with obvious ceremony. He neither smiled nor frowned. He merely looked. Finally, he offered, "Yes, I am Fr. Katz. I was sent by my bishop. He told me you rebuilt the church on your own volition, without guidance from the church. That was unfortunate, but under the circumstances, I suppose it was understandable. It will have to do, at least for the present time."

Fr. Katz was not as tall as his predecessor, but held a slightly larger frame. His once-blonde hair had turned mostly white. He wore a tuft of facial hair around his chin, but was clean-shaven otherwise. His eyes were a faded blue, most likely from age. In his younger years he would, no doubt, have been described as handsome. In fact, even now, he could be considered so. And the way he carried himself presented a certain air of dignity.

Toshi and Haruki stood together in silence, wondering how to proceed. This did not feel like a hopeful beginning. Fr. Katz was not Fr. Lispard.

"Will you be celebrating mass tomorrow?" ventured Toshi, in a hopeful tone.

"Is tomorrow Sunday?" The priest replied rhetorically. "If tomorrow is Sunday, then yes, I'll be celebrating mass. I'm used to having mass at nine o'clock. I assume that is acceptable."

Toshi looked quickly at Haruki, then back to the priest. "Yes, nine o'clock will be fine," he replied. "We will tell as many parishioners as possible. They have been anxious for your arrival."

The priest continued to gaze at the men but did not speak. Presently, they concluded their audience was over, turned and headed for the door from which they had entered only minutes before.

"Well, that was interesting," Haruki began. "I hope he's just annoyed by his travels and not about his assignment here."

"It will be a sorry shame if he lets all of Fr. Lispard's hard work fall by the wayside. With that attitude, I wouldn't be surprised if people stopped coming to church. Maybe he's just exhausted from the travel. He is not exactly straight from the seminary, by the look of him." They both laughed.

Toshi and Haruki split up to spread the word. They each grabbed a clump of charcoal from the smokehouse and used it to write makeshift signs along Front Street wherever they could find a suitable space. They ducked quickly in and out of every shop that was open, to announce the upcoming mass in the new church. When they had searched every location they could think of, they met back at the smokehouse and unloaded their nightly catch. Minako, Kazuo, Emiko, and a few others were already at work cleaning the fish and preparing the charcoal for smoking.

Saturday, being another of their assigned nights on the water, they agreed to leave an hour earlier than usual in order to be back before nine in the morning. They would come directly from the boats, but both knew Minako and Ayami would insist they bathe and change their clothes prior to showing up for the very first mass at the new St. Mary's of the Assumption Church.

CHAPTER 23
FIRST MASS AT ST. MARY'S

AUGUST 08, 1897 – KAMAISHI

Both fishermen tied up at the dock before eight o'clock on Sunday morning. They hurriedly offloaded their catch into the cart and shuttled their boats to their respective moorings. Together, they pulled the cart to the trading company, left it, and washed themselves in a tub of water, fresh from the adjacent river.

Meanwhile, Minako, Ayami, and their families were settling in at the church, taking special care to welcome the several other people filtering in. Ayami tried not to let anyone notice her frequent glances out the window in search of Toshi and Haruki. Several minutes before nine, the two women made their way quietly to the sacristy, where Fr. Katz was donning his vestments, and knocked respectfully at the open door.

"May I help you?" the priest inquired.

"Good morning, Father. I am Ayami, and this is my aunt, Minako. We'd like to ask a question." She paused to analyze his response. His countenance remained the same.

Finally, he replied. "What is the question? I'm preparing for mass."

"Yes, of course. We are sorry for the intrusion, but have not had a chance to discuss it with you until now. We just wanted to know if it is acceptable for our choir sing, and do you have any favorite hymns we should sing, and at what points during the mass would you prefer?"

If his initial countenance was one of disregard, Ayami felt sure it had changed to disgust by the end of her question. She had to wait once more for a reply.

"You have a choir, you say? I didn't see any evidence of an organ or a piano. Or any instrument, for that matter. How can you have a choir without accompaniment?"

Ayami tried to smile along with her response. "No, I'm afraid we have no musical instruments. There was a piano, but unfortunately, it was destroyed by the tsunami. And without a priest to offer regular masses, we haven't been able to collect money to replace it. We sing *a cappella*."

Fr. Katz made little effort to hide his dismay when he raised his chin slightly and rolled his eyes toward heaven. "You have a choir with no organ. Tell me, how long have you been rehearsing this choir, *a cappella*?"

"We've been practicing ever since we learned you were coming. Several weeks now, at least."

His expression hardly relaxed at the news. "How many are in your…choir?" he asked.

"Everyone in our two families, plus several from other families. About fifteen people if they all show up today," she replied. "Two of the children have especially good voices."

At this, the priest seemed to relax slightly. The mention of children invoked memories of children's choirs he had heard over the course of his career. Of course, the Vienna Boys' Choir was his favorite, but none came even close to them. Still, a children's choir could almost always be counted on to bring a few smiles to the congregation.

"Very well," he finally agreed. "We'll try it today and see how it goes. You may sing one song following communion. As for a favorite, since we are at St. Mary's, does the choir know *Ave Maria*?"

"Oh yes, Father. It's one of our favorites. Thank you. We'll sing *Ave Maria* right after communion. Thank you." They turned and left quickly, hoping to be gone before he could change his mind.

By nine o'clock, about twenty-five people had taken their place on the benches. Toshi and Haruki were among them. Those who had rehearsed in the choir grouped together in the section to the right of the altar, which more or less filled the area, while several people were scattered here and there throughout the remainder of the church. On short notice, there were a number of people who had not gotten word of the priest's arrival, but would have attended, had they known.

Father Katz was slightly bewildered and noticeably humbled, as, when he exited the sacristy and ascended the altar, he saw face after face in solemn reverence gazing back at him. Most, he could hardly help but notice, were looking back at him with misty eyes. A few had droplets of tears partway down their cheeks.

Much of the mass, in 1897, was celebrated with the priest facing away from his congregation, toward the altar and the tabernacle where the sacred hosts were stored, with a large cross behind. But at selected points during the liturgy, notably the sacred readings and the sermon, he turned to face them. At those times, he was visibly reminded why he'd chosen the priesthood as a vocation. He tried not to stare at the many among them who were still dabbing at their eyes with a cloth, or the sleeve of their clothing. He recognized them as tears of joy at being able to honor their Lord after all this time, and all they had suffered.

The sermon he'd spent hours preparing during his weeks of travel to get there, now seemed irrelevant. The words he'd spent so much time putting on paper, he realized, were words based on a reluctant acceptance of his assignment. With only a few years remaining until he could officially retire, coming to a foreign land to piece together remnants of a tiny parish in a mostly Confucian country, was not what he wanted to do. His prepared sermon had reflected that feeling.

Catching himself in time, he decided at the last minute to simply offer a short introduction of himself and welcome them back. It may have been the shortest sermon ever heard at St. Mary's, but the twenty-five people present that day felt its sincerity. He was not Fr. Lispard. But he might be a good Father Katz.

The mass continued, and, since there had been no opportunity to hear confessions since the previous July, Fr. Katz offered a general absolution to all those present, followed by a prayer of contrition to allow everyone who wanted, the chance to receive communion. He felt obliged to announce they should all make a formal confession at their first opportunity, however.

Thus, nearly every person in attendance that morning approached the altar to receive the Eucharistic host. Fr. Katz then proceeded to wash and dry the chalice, and organize the altar for the upcoming dismissal prayers. Lost in reverence and amazed at the warming of his heart during the last forty minutes, he jolted slightly at a sound he could not identify.

It resembled a whistle, but it wasn't. And the sound it made was a single note. A musical note, he decided, and was trying to determine which note it would correspond to on the piano when it fell silent, just as quickly as it began.

Then voices emerged. Singing voices. It was a hymn he knew by heart. *Ave Maria*. At first, there were two voices, young, clear, in perfect harmony. "AHH-veeeyyy ma-RHEEEE-eeee-yaaahhh." He stood motionless at the altar and let the sound fill his ears and his senses. He found himself waiting for the next phrase to follow. "GRAT-zhee-aaah PLA-aay-naaah."

At the repeat of Gratia Plena, the rest of the choir softly added a dozen voices to the two young girls, in a blend of perfect harmony. The fourteen singers were too busy staying in time and in tune with one another to critique their own performance, but to the rest of the congregation, it was by far the best they had ever sounded. Not a sneeze, a sniffle, or any other sound emitted from within the church as they sang the soothing hymn. It was magical. Perhaps a miracle. *Did the Blessed Mother herself intervene at this humble celebration?*

Fr. Katz not only lost his place in the service, he lost his voice as well. When, at the final dismissal prayer, he turned to the congregation and waved the sign of the cross to all those present, he found only a lump in his throat where the words should have been.

A few did not notice his lack of words. The others noticed, but understood.

Following the dismissal prayer, Fr. Katz processed down the aisle to the front entrance. A few steps past the door, he turned and waited to greet his newly inherited parishioners. When Minako and Ayami approached, flanked by Haruki and Toshi, he greeted them, then looked down, as if he'd just noticed one of the sandals was missing from his feet. "Would you have time to stay for a few minutes before you go?" he asked timidly. "I'd like to talk with you about the mass for next weekend."

"Of course," they replied with a combination of voice and gestures. "We'll wait for you inside the church."

With only twenty-five congregants at the mass, Fr. Katz's farewell greeting did not take long, at the entrance to the church. He made his way back inside to find Kazuo, Emiko, and their three children, alongside Toshi, Haruki, and their families. Together, they comprised nearly half the worshippers.

"The bishop told me about some kind of special window that was requested by my predecessor. I'm curious how that came about. Do any of you know the story behind it?"

Since most of them were there on that fateful afternoon of the tsunami, they weren't sure who was best qualified to respond. Then, because Toshi had been the one most instrumental in figuring out how to build the moving ray of sunlight, he relayed the story to Fr. Katz.

When he finished, he looked around at the others to see if they had something to add or correct, in his description of the event.

Fr. Katz simply listened as Toshi relayed how the new church should take on the shape of a cross, and that it should be positioned such that on the Feast of the Assumption of Mary into Heaven, the sunlight rays should travel exactly down the main aisle to the altar and eventually up the rear wall until the sun dipped below the western horizon. He explained that Fr. Lispard didn't realize the old church would be destroyed and mostly washed out to sea. His vision only revealed that a new church should be built, with those few specific requirements.

"It is highly unusual the bishop—any bishop—would consider such an unreliable event worthy of designing a church... as alluring and fascinating as the dream may have been. I can't think of another example that comes even close, during my nearly forty years of priesthood." He saw the looks of disappointment cross their faces as he spoke. Then he continued, "However, what's done is done. On behalf of the bishop, I want to personally thank you for taking the initiative to rebuild, using only salvaged lumber and volunteer labor. You have done an exceptional job, given the means available."

He raised his eyes upward, scanning the interior of the church above the entrance. "If I'm following what you said, that must be the window meant to light up the aisle when the sun begins to set in the afternoon sky." He pointed to the rectangular window directly above the doorway. "And, next Sunday being August fifteenth, the day of the Assumption, I presume you are interested in making the most of it."

Toshi could not refrain from smiling back at the priest. "Yes, we were hoping to make the most of it," he said.

"Well, if we're going to watch the sun march up the aisle to the altar, I guess mass will have to be celebrated later that day. August being what it is, sundown will be well toward evening. I didn't pay particular attention last night, but it seems to me that dusk arrived around seven o'clock. Is that right?"

"Yes, that would be very close. We can test our premise later today, or even the next couple of days, but I would think a five o'clock mass next Sunday would be perfect for the celebration."

Father Katz looked at Toshi. "Are you an engineer by any chance?" he asked.

"I was educated as an engineer, but I've been a fisherman for several years... Why do you ask?"

Fr. Katz fought back a chuckle. "No reason," he replied. "You just seem to have an interest in details." Then, changing the subject back, he continued, "So we'll plan on mass next Sunday at five o'clock, subject to confirming your premise this afternoon. I'll be here to watch the sunlight through its travels, and let you know if we need to change the time."

Turning to Ayami, he said, "I'm not sure I've ever heard a more pleasing hymn than the one your choir sang today. Do they know any other hymns? Next week, I'd like them to add several others as part of the service. I'm not sure our Blessed Mother herself could have done it better."

"I think she just did," Ayami quipped.

"Do you think we'll have a bigger turnout next week since we have more time to alert everybody?" the priest asked, to no one in particular.

Haruki responded, "I think we'll have to get here early if we want a seat. Everyone in the area knows the story of Mary's sunlight. They will come to see it for themselves, whether Catholic or not. I hope that's okay."

"Nothing would make me happier," he replied with a smile. "Come by the church tomorrow, and I'll give you a list of hymns."

Toshi and Haruki tried to find someone to trade for next Sunday night on the schedule, but no one wanted to miss the event. In the end, they decided to take that night off.

***

By noon on Sunday, people began to gather in the village.

In anticipation of a repeat of the initial sunlight test from a year earlier, the teahouse was open for business. Everyone was pressed into service. Emiko's three children were there, plus their new daughter of the sea, Mamiko. Ayami's three children were there. The kitchen was a flurry of moving figures. Kiyoshi and Isamu seated customers and placed their orders. Meisa and Emiko's Kaneto brought drinks and cleared away dishes to make room for the next group. Emiko's Suki and Kensei, now aged eleven and nine, were assigned to dishwashing duty under the close supervision of their mother.

Every visitor at the teahouse knew Mamiko, or at least knew of Mamiko. She had been the talk of the region ever since the tsunami. Stories of her recovery still brought an uplifting smile as neighbors or friends recounted the miracle. How many of the stories were true and how many were imagined was hard to say. It seemed that nearly everyone for kilometers around recalled being there, watching Mamiko take her first sip of water, and seeing firsthand the fluttering of her tiny eyes as she 'came back to life' that day. Few thought to remember there were but forty survivors and thirty volunteers actually there. But it didn't matter. What did matter was that the entire village took her in. Not just Emiko and her family, but everyone. And every one of them seemed to want their turn at watching and holding the toddler, now almost a year and a half old.

By one o'clock, business was brisk, and it grew from there. Toshi and Haruki barely had time to wipe perspiration from their heated faces throughout the afternoon. By three o'clock, they began to worry about finding space to sit at the five o'clock service. Finally, Toshi sent Kiyoshi to the church to see if he could save enough seats for their families.

He grabbed a spool of twine on his way out, thinking he might be able to close off two or three benches. When he arrived at the church, Fr. Katz was standing at the doorway in an apparent state of bewilderment. He now understood what Haruki meant last week about an overflow crowd.

They had not previously met, but when Kiyoshi introduced himself as Toshi's son, a noticeable sigh of relief crossed his face. At least he now had help. How it was going to solve their problem was not yet clear.

"What about the choir?" Fr. Katz asked. "We need to save room for the choir."

Kiyoshi lifted his small spool of twine to show the priest. "I brought this in case we needed to rope off a section," he said. "I was thinking about our families, but you're right, the choir is more important."

Kiyoshi followed as they hurried to the section of benches to the right of the altar, where the choir had sat the week before. Luckily, the early arrivals preferred seating along the main aisle in order to have a firsthand view of the light stream as it traveled toward the altar. Fr. Katz hovered around the open benches to keep anyone from claiming them, long enough for Kiyoshi to unwind and wrap a strand of twine around all four of the benches as a signal the seats were reserved. Then the priest scurried to the sacristy in search of something to write on. He returned with a quickly scribbled sign that read simply: CHOIR. He pinned it to the strand of twine in what he hoped would be plainly visible to anyone attempting to claim the seats.

As for their own families, Kiyoshi reluctantly concluded that whoever was not in the choir would have to take their chances with whatever space they could find. Fr. Katz seemed to have the same thoughts, though not a word was spoken in that regard. He looked around the church as it continued to fill. The section to the left of the altar was still mostly vacant, again because people were drawn to the center aisle. He nudged Kiyoshi on the arm with a motion to follow, and together they proceeded to the left side of the church. He signaled for more twine and, in a low voice, told Kiyoshi to rope off two of the benches. Then he returned to the sacristy to make another sign.

He quickly pinned it to the twine before Kiyoshi could read the words. When he finished, he smiled at Kiyoshi and looked around the church once more. It was filling fast, with an hour and a half still to go. He began to perspire. It was then that he wished he had spent more time on the sermon for today.

"I have to get back to the teahouse," Kiyoshi told him. "Is there anything you need from us? We should be back in an hour."

"I'm glad you came when you did," Fr. Katz replied. "No, there's not much more any of us can do but wait, and then get through it. Thank you." He turned and made his way down the main aisle, making sure to welcome those already seated with his best smile.

When the priest moved away from the benches, Kiyoshi caught a glimpse of the makeshift sign pinned to the twine. It caught him off-guard. It read: TOSHI FAMILY

By five o'clock, St. Mary's church was standing room only, with a number of people gathered outside. The church, built with seating for 200 people, today held half-again that number. The rays of the sun were shining distinctly in a rectangular shape on the aisle, several meters from the altar. Those who came early had already watched it march slowly forward with the movement of the sun. Some were intrigued simply by the idea, while others felt a special presence of God himself. Barely a sound was emitted by the congregation, in spite of their cramped quarters. Even Toshi, seated on his bench to the left of the altar, was taken by the solemnity of the occasion. *If only Fr. Lispard could be here*, he mused.

Then Fr. Katz gave the signal, and a sound came from the right side of the altar, where the choir was seated. It was a single note, one still not determined by the priest, but which allowed a dozen members of the choir to begin their hymn on exactly the right note. The choir sang an entrance procession for the priest as the congregation stood. Following communion, when they sang his cherished *Ave Maria*, he was grateful to have his back to the congregation, so they could not see him blink away the mist.

At the end of mass, now facing the worshippers and visitors, he made a sweeping motion with his face as he slowly raised his arms out wide. The intended effect was to gather in all those present on this warm summer afternoon. A smile filled his aged, still handsome face as he began, "Thank you, all of you, for joining us for a grand celebration of new life. I know many of you are not Catholic in your belief...that you came to see the fruits of some of your own, and to see for yourselves whether the light would actually find its way up the aisle to the altar and out the other side toward the heavens. I have to admit, I was as anxious as you to see it happen. You are welcome here at any time.

"Are the birds and animals Catholic? No, I believe not, yet St. Matthew assured us not one would fall to the ground without the Father knowing of it. You are welcome here, always.

"Because many of you were blocked from the view, on account of our crowd, I'm going to celebrate the mass here every day, at five o'clock in the afternoon, until the end of the month. I know the light will be moving slightly off course day-by-day, but it should still be a very close trajectory for the next two weeks. I ask only that if you had a close-up view today, please select a different view on your next visit, so someone else gets a better view next time."

He turned then, to his left, to acknowledge the choir, mostly women and children. "I don't expect them to be here for every service, and I know you will be disappointed when they are not. Their voices bring a new joy to the service." He turned then to his right, to acknowledge Toshi and his other family members not seated in the choir. "I want to thank Toshi especially, but all of you," he said, extending his arms toward the congregation, "every one of you who helped bring this church back to life after complete disaster. I simply cannot imagine how you managed it."

Then he made a sweeping sign of the cross with his right arm toward the congregants, turned to the altar, bowed his head, offered a short silent prayer, then turned and processed slowly down the aisle toward the door.

He was surprised when no one followed him out. In all his previous parishes, there were always a few who felt the need to race him to the door. He waited patiently just outside, ready to greet the exiting crowd. He began to wonder if he had forgotten some final part of the ritual. *Did the Japanese have a tradition following mass he hadn't been told about?* He was about to re-enter the church when the first few families began to emerge. Judging by the smiles on their faces, they seemed not to be alarmed or confused by his actions. As the crowd trickled out, he realized they were merely taking their time, some still gazing at the rectangle of light as it traveled up the far wall, behind the altar.

Finally, he recognized the face of Toshi, still one of the few he could identify after one week in the village. He was joined by Ayami and their family, followed closely by Haruki, Minako, and their family. He thought he could detect a look of relief on all their faces. It had not occurred to the priest it was their reputations being judged that day, not his.

Toshi spoke first. "Well done, Father. I'm glad you welcomed the visitors. We're going to have a lot of empty space when only the Catholics come," he joked. "We've been thinking about you, not having adequate quarters and no place to take your meals. Haruki and I will organize a group to build a place for you to live. We already have several volunteers ready to help, and there's still some usable wood from the deserted properties we can use to get started. In the meantime, we'd like you to come to the teahouse for your meals. We're there every day, starting at eight o'clock."

"Thank you," he said. "I would like that."

PART THREE

The American Dream

CHAPTER 24
ISAMU GROWS UP

OCTOBER 1897 – KAMAISHI

Isamu looked forward to the Kitakami trips. He loved the beauty of the pine-covered mountains, much like his father, but most of all, he craved time with his father's almost mythical friend, the Empress. At seventeen, he was already serious about how to spend his life. He listened intently as Toshi told stories of his university days, the foundry, being a fisherman, and finally, being a merchant. He seldom talked about the short tenure at his father's furniture factory.

Isamu loved, in particular, stories of far-off places. Something about the very word "importer' caused his mind to paint a thousand pictures of exotic goods. Coffee, spices, and other things he could not even imagine, must be out there somewhere, just waiting to be 'imported' to a different country, a different continent. From countries like Brazil. Like Africa. Like Germany or England. The excitement of such a life kept him awake at night.

He could study maps for hours. He had traced the route from Kamaishi to Osaki at least a dozen times before Toshi took him on his first trip. His most prized possession was the hand-drawn map his father had given him from his first trips to Kitakami and Hanamaki. That was back in the days when there were no roads, only crude trails running through the mountains.

Ayami loved her family dearly. Even after twenty years, Toshi still sent tingles through her body when he touched her tenderly on the arm or on the shoulder. It was a different love than the one when they were young, but it was stronger now. Deeper. Like iron at the foundry, it had been strengthened by the fires, both tragedy and joy.

And Kiyoshi, her firstborn, how she remembered the difficult delivery and her own near-death. He'd grown into a man to be proud of. At nineteen, he'd already been the captain of his own boat for two years. He was good at fishing, and he liked it.

Toshi, Kiyoshi, and even Haruki, all spread their time working the boats, buying, selling, and shipping grain, rice, and lately, vegetables.

Meisa, now fourteen, helped Ayami and Minako at the teahouse every day. When she was younger, she helped wash vegetables and dishes, clean tables, and a variety of other duties. By now, she had become an expert at cooking meals and even dreaming up new menu items. Her aunt and mother both agreed, she had an eye for business as well as for cooking.

But Isamu...Isamu was special. Even though Ayami tried desperately to fight it, deep inside, she realized he was her favorite. Then again, Isamu was pretty much everyone's favorite. He was four or five centimeters taller than his peers, which caused him to stand out, without trying to, in any way. He parted his thick brown hair down the middle of his head, which gave him the look of an intellectual on one hand, and a whimsical one on the other. It suited him exactly.

Girls as young as twelve and grandmothers as old as seventy, went out of their way to smile at Isamu when they passed him by. And oddly enough, their men didn't seem to object. In spite of his handsome good looks, they displayed no animosity or envy toward him. There was something about his presence that attracted men and women alike. Probably because he put others first. He always asked how they were feeling, or what they thought of whatever was being discussed. And he always listened intently at what they had to say.

He was curious, like his father, and diligently recorded his thoughts and ideas in a journal, just as Toshi had done in his early days at the foundry. Reading was one of his favorite pastimes, and he made a habit of freely trading books with anyone, for a book he had not yet read.

Even his brother and sister held Isamu in high esteem. Ayami watched children in other families sometimes argue and bicker about this childish thing or that, but not once that she could remember, did Isamu cause disagreement with his siblings. On the contrary, she could recount any number of times overhearing Isamu shed praise on one or the other for something good they had accomplished.

But of all the things Ayami cherished about her second son, it was his heart that topped the list. He smiled at everyone he met, with a look that said he was happy to see them. It never occurred to him, that she could tell, that his smile was bigger, or better, for the pretty, the handsome, or the powerful. In fact, she was pretty sure it was just the opposite. His greeting was based more on how much the other person needed it, than on how much Isamu did.

She could not help but eavesdrop occasionally on his conversations with friends or strangers, and soon learned one of his secrets. Somehow it must have come from birth, as it was not a secret she or Toshi would have consciously known themselves.

Conversations were never about Isamu. They were always about the other person. If he knew them, he asked about their family, their friends, their work, their favorite things to do, or even for their advice. Not once, ever, did she hear him embarrass, shame, or belittle another person, whether present or not.

So, proud as she was of all her family, Isamu found a special place in the heart of his mother. And that is why, whenever her favorite son mentioned a far-away place called America, her eyes misted, and she found it hard to speak.

***

In August 1896, it was decided that Kiyoshi would join Kazuo to make deliveries to Hanamaki and Osaki, leaving Toshi and Haruki free to work on construction in the village, the teahouse, and especially the church. That way, they could more easily check on the smoke house, keep the charcoal trimmed, change the vents, whatever needed done, and quickly return to their other duties.

Kazuo would always be the partner in charge of the animals and wagons. However, because of his initial meeting with Cho at the silk factory, under the false guise of a Ministry of Labor agent, they all agreed he must stay away from the factory. It was an inconvenient arrangement none of them anticipated when they first went in search of Emiko. The Empress had considered Haruki and Toshi, but not Kazuo. Back then, she had no way of knowing Kazuo and Emiko would fall in love.

Toshi accompanied Kiyoshi on the first of his trips, to introduce him to Cho and his cousin at the Osaki Emporium. After a few trips, Kiyoshi, in turn, took his brother Isamu. The two of them soon became the face of the *Kamaishi Trading Company* to their customers. That was where Isamu honed his skills as a future entrepreneur.

The Empress, who met him when he was just a toddler, watched him grow from a distance, over several years. When he followed his brother into the emporium for the first time as a merchant, she was instantly smitten. He smiled the only smile he seemed to know, which made her think it was hers alone, then bowed politely. The Empress was taken aback by his formality, but managed to return the bow before pulling him into a short but embarrassing embrace, and then laughed to relieve his consternation. "Your father reacted the very same way," she exclaimed. "He was a shy one at first. But he got over it." She turned to the back of the emporium. "Enji," she called, "come out here and meet Toshi's other son. You're going to like him, too."

On every trip thereafter, the Empress requested, in a manner the brothers felt they could hardly refuse even had they wanted, to spend the night in her elegant housing on the second floor. Of course, the evening started with a dinner of more food than either could eat. She always offered, and they always declined, a cup of her very best saké.

The first thing the Empress asked as they reclined to eat was a full report on her 'adopted' daughter, Emiko. She wanted to know about Kaneto and Kensei, her boys, and what they were doing each week, but most of all, about her daughter, Suki. She still struggled when she spoke that name. It brought back the memory of her namesake from years before. And she always asked about Mamiko, the newest member of their family.

Following a full and complete report from Kazuo regarding his family, she next wanted to know everything new that had happened with Toshi, Haruki, and their families. Her guests learned early on that her interest was more than polite conversation. These people were more like family to her than her own.

Eventually, when all the questions from the Empress were duly answered, Isamu felt comfortable asking a few of his own. He always made sure to start with questions about her family or friends, but he had a way of guiding the conversation to questions that truly interested him. He did so without deceit or duplicity. It was simply his natural instinct, and it was based on a genuine desire to learn. Of course, when he smiled and made eye contact, it was hard for anyone to ignore his requests.

"How do you know what to stock on your shelves?" he would ask.

"Look around at your customers," she would reply. "Find something they need and supply it. Everybody needs food. Everybody needs clothing. Not everybody *needs* something sweet, but almost everybody *wants* something sweet. They consider it a treat. Maybe they've accomplished something difficult and want to give themselves a reward. Or maybe their 'Suki' has, or their 'Ayami.' Whoever. They see something fun and want to forget about the hardships in their lives."

"Where do you go to get the best prices?" he would ask.

"Sometimes the best prices are not the lowest prices," she would reply. "You must be careful to make sure the price is fair for what you get. If the food is not good, if the sweets are not sweet enough, they not only won't buy it again, they might not even come back again." Looking at the brothers, she continued, "Ask your father about the very first time I bought smoked fish from him. I tasted it first, but I also told him if it didn't sell, I would not buy more of it."

What surprised Isamu most was the difference in answers to his questions.

Cho's cousin, owner of the emporium in Osaki, to the same question answered, "The best price is the lowest price. So what if they don't like the quality? By the time they come back, they'll have gotten over it. And it means they'll have to come back to my store that much sooner. I can always blame it on whoever made it, if they complain too much."

At the silk factory, Cho explained it like this: "I'm not buying anything to resell. The only things that interest me are to keep workers healthy enough to work hard, and happy enough to do a good job. The cheaper I can do that, the happier I am."

Isamu remembered the stories his father told them when working at the foundry, how in that first year of production, in 1880, the director offered a bonus to whichever furnace could out-produce the other. He remembered how they set new records every day in those last few days, trying to earn the bonus.

"Have you ever thought of giving workers a bonus if they reach a production goal?" he asked Cho during one of their deliveries.

"Yes, we used to pit one group against another, hoping the competition would motivate them to work harder. It worked for a time. But not enough to continue."

"What if you offered a special meal for each week they reached a certain standard? Since they get rice three times a day and fish once or twice a week, maybe you could entice them with a little something extra if they met a certain goal."

Cho seemed to consider the idea.

Isamu continued, "But instead of dividing the workers into groups, do you think it might work to have everyone on the same team, with an overall production goal to meet?"

Cho thought about it. "Yes, I can see where that might be a possibility. That way, they would all be pulling together for the factory, instead of causing resentment between the groups."

"Do you think the workers would put pressure on their peers, for any worker not doing their share of the work?" Isamu asked.

"I'm sure of it," Cho replied. I know how I'd feel if someone caused me not to earn a special meal."

"Those are great ideas," exclaimed Isamu, trying to drive home that Cho could take the credit for them. And we have just the thing to make it worth their while. Since the tsunami, until we get back on our feet, we have a temporary excess of fish. We could double the shipment of fish and only charge half the normal price for the extra allotment. This is only a temporary offer until the village gets back to normal again. Do your workers still like our fish?"

Trying to hide his enthusiasm, Cho held a straight face as he replied, "Yes, they seem to like it. We haven't received many complaints, at least." He looked eagerly toward his assistant, hoping she would not betray him with the number of compliments she'd heard from the reelers.

"Excellent," Isamu quickly asserted as he bowed politely. "On our next trip, we'll bring an extra order of fish."

"But you'll only charge for half an order. Right?"

"Yes, we will only charge for an extra half-order." His relaxed smile was so natural that Cho responded with one of his own. What caused stress and anguish for many, came so easily for Isamu that he didn't realize he had a gift.

Using the same easy manner at all their stops, Isamu created agreements to ship excess produce from farmers in Hanamaki to Osaki, Kitakami, and Kamaishi.

To fill the void in Kamaishi, Toshi and Haruki located an available plot on Twelfth Street and rebuilt an empty shop there to become an emporium of their own. They recruited two former fishermen to run the shop and little by little, its shelves began to fill, mostly from shipments of the Kamaishi Trading Company.

Isamu played an important role in its development. He was receiving a better education, he decided, than what he might have received at university. He had a front-row seat in watching an economy transform from virtually nothing, into a growing and thriving community. It was almost like his private laboratory. He watched the farmers growing crops, the warehouses in Kitakami and Kamaishi, direct consumers like the silk factory, retailers like the three emporiums, as well as shippers like the Kamaishi Trading Company. He could personally relate to the special problems associated with every aspect of an economic society.

He was preparing himself for America.

CHAPTER 25
A LOOK THROUGH THE MIRROR

MAY 1898 – OSAKI DELIVERY

It was early on a Monday morning in May when the mule team departed Kamaishi on its biweekly route to Kitakami and Osaki. Kiyoshi sat in the driver's seat, and his younger brother Isamu sat behind him in the rear-facing seat that Toshi fabricated soon after the hold-up years ago. It allowed the passenger to scan the horizon behind the wagon and at least provide time to prepare for an attack.

It was an easy project for Toshi. The hardest part was finding an abandoned wagon with a usable seat. Then it was simply a matter of mounting it behind the original seat, facing the opposite direction. It had the added advantage, they all agreed, of granting the driver more room to maneuver his team. Kiyoshi was able to stay seated in the center of the wagon, which made it easier to see around his mules.

Kazuo, meanwhile, was free to roam ahead or lag behind, always on the lookout for suspicious activity. Today he was riding Autumn, the beautiful five-year-old chestnut. Spring flowers bloomed in clumps and clusters along the way. Songbirds darted among the trees as he rode along. The warmth of the sun was welcome on his back. When he realized he was outpacing the wagon farther than he'd meant, he tugged the reins slightly to the left. The river was just a few meters from the road; a more peaceful place could not be found, to wait for the wagon to catch back up.

As he sat in the morning shade, immersed in the sounds of surrounding beech leaves rustling in the breeze, the ripple of the water as it ghosted toward Kamaishi Bay, and the cacophony of bird songs among the trees, it occurred to him this was the spot where they'd found the cholera stranger some fifteen years before. It seemed longer. He nudged Autumn through the trees to a small mound of earth and rock. The eternal resting place of the mysterious man. The makeshift cross Fr. Lispard had placed atop the mound was no longer visible. Two rotting branches lying in the grass might once have been the marker. So much had changed since then. His three children were born. Fr. Lispard was gone. The village, mostly gone. Even now, Kazuo wondered who the man could have been. Did he have a wife and children? Was he a good man? Was he on the run? He had a good horse; that is all Kazuo knew for sure. And the horse was also gone.

As he reminisced, he heard occasional snorts from one or another of the mules, mixed with snippets of a conversation between the two brothers as they traveled along. The mules brayed when they saw him approach the roadway from the trees. They seemed to wonder why the horse could stop to rest, but not them.

The trio traveled west in silence.

Kazuo still wondered about the man in the grave.

In the driver's seat, Kiyoshi let his mind travel to the fishing boats. He wondered if they were bringing home a good catch from the night. They should be approaching the harbor soon. It was a favorite time for him, knowing the night was over and a fresh new day lay ahead. The sense of an honest night's work never got old, as the village came back in view. On a good night, the emotional high of a successful catch. On a bad night, relief that he was safely home, with hope for better luck tomorrow.

In the seat behind, Isamu was reliving a conversation he once had with the Empress. She had been very clear…the most important thing about a successful business was to 'find a need and fill it.' He thought through several examples she had used to reinforce the simple concept.

It was past mid-morning by now, and for Isamu, facing the rear, the sun warmed his face, not his back. The sound of the wheels in constant motion along the hard-packed ground, combined with the warmth of the sun, finally succeeded in forcing his eyes to close, in spite of it being early in the day. Isamu dozed as the wagon traveled west.

The wooden front wheel on the right bounced up and over the branch of a recently downed limb just as the rear wheel on the left dipped into a rut. The combination jarred Isamu alert enough that, in a half-awake state, her advice still lingered in his mind. *Find a need and fill it.*

Maybe it was because his mind was mulling it over during the short nap, or maybe it was because he was facing the wrong way in the wagon. Everything he viewed was moving away from him. It was the opposite of 'normal.' *It was like looking at everything in reverse,* he thought to himself. The idea intrigued him. *What if he looked at other things in reverse? What would he learn?*

He started with the advice from the Empress. Every time he considered her words, he was looking at them from the perspective of the buyer. It was an easy concept. *What do buyers want?* Then provide it.

By looking from a different point of view, he managed to formulate a new thought. From the fishermen's point of view, *we have an abundance of fish. How can we create a demand?* It seemed such a simple concept, once it entered his head. He could not understand why it had not occurred to him before. *We have excess fish; how can we create demand for it?* He rode in silence for several kilometers, not once feeling the bumps in the road.

The trio stopped for lunch at their usual spot, a rocky meadow surrounded by evergreens. The river splashed noisily nearby. Overhead, a crow cawed.

"Have you ever been to Tōno?" Isamu asked Kazuo.

"No, I haven't been there, but I've often wanted to. Why do you ask?"

"I've been thinking," he replied. "What if we added Tōno to our route? Surely, they must have an emporium of some kind. We might be able to provide them with something they need and don't even know about." He chuckled. "They are too far from the coast to have easy access to ocean fish. And actually, they might be too far from Hanamaki to have good rice. We might just be able to solve both their problems."

Kazuo looked at Kiyoshi for a signal. Kiyoshi looked back at Kazuo for a signal. Then, in unison, they both looked at Isamu with a grin. "I think you're on to something," they said.

A few minutes later, Isamu spoke again. "Have you ever stopped in Oshu? It's just off the main road on our way to Osaki."

"No, we've never taken the time to stop there," Kazuo replied. "It seems like we're always in a hurry, either to deliver supplies to Osaki, or to get back home to Kamaishi."

"What about Ichinoseki? Or Kurihara? They're both on the way to Osaki." Isamu continued. "Would you be willing to call on them if Toshi and Haruki agree? We would need to work out a new schedule, and it might add an extra day to our route. But if we could help out the fishermen, it would be worth the effort."

"I couldn't agree more," chimed in Kiyoshi. "I'm sure the fleet would be in favor. Most are barely making it, since the tsunami. Why didn't we think of this before?"

"You're usually better at avoiding the ruts," laughed Isamu. "But thanks for shaking me from my meditation this time. Maybe we should try it more often."

CHAPTER 26
ISAMU'S DREAM

AUGUST 1898 – KAMAISHI TEAHOUSE

Isamu was a hard worker in a hard-working family. Although his primary responsibility was to make the biweekly deliveries, he had many other days available, to fill in or help out in other parts of the family enterprise. Sometimes he even filled in for a friend on one of the fishing boats. Like his father and uncle, he was a good fisherman, but it was not his favorite assignment. He helped smoke the fish on many occasions, but neither was it a favorite. It was too confining and lonely, just tending the charcoal and keeping the temperature steady. It was, in a word, boring.

His favorite 'other' assignment was working at the teahouse. He loved the bustle of people coming and going with friendly conversations, and interesting discussions with patrons. He was not surprised, though not totally expecting, to see Fr. Katz enter the front door of the teahouse at what must have been two minutes after eight on a Monday morning. Whether for food or for companionship, he did not yet know.

Fr. Katz asked for tea when Isamu seated him in the early morning shade of a canvas awning. The awning replaced what once had been a tree where they spent many happy hours with Fr. Lispard. That tree, along with most of the others, was taken by the tsunami. But the shade was welcome, even if not provided by nature.

When Isamu brought his tea, the priest cordially asked if Isamu had time to sit with him for a few minutes. Since he was the only patron at the moment, Isamu could hardly deny the invitation. Three refills of tea and one hour later, a friendship had taken root. From that day forward, Isamu volunteered for as much time at the teahouse as he could. Most days, Fr. Katz would appear for one or another of his daily meals.

Early in those visits, Isamu, for whom it was simply a part of his nature, asked the priest about his previous travels. How was it that an American had found his way to Japan?

In reply, Fr. Katz said simply that he'd traveled to many countries in service to God. His vows as a priest required him to go wherever he was needed. And where he was needed was determined by his bishop.

"Do you have a favorite?" Isamu asked.

Without hesitation, he replied, "Yes, I do have a favorite. My favorite assignment was the one in San Francisco. I spent the last ten years there as an associate pastor at St. Mary's Cathedral. I fell in love with the city, and I miss it very much. I've thought about it many times since coming here. The weather is quite similar. Although San Francisco, I believe, is a few degrees warmer than Kamaishi. Of course, San Francisco is much larger, but the topography is quite similar. It is located on rugged terrain, overlooking a large bay, which is part of the Pacific." He was quiet for a time, then continued, "You might say the two cities are like mirrors, one on either side of the ocean. I hadn't considered that until this very moment," he mused.

Isamu was enraptured. Something inside himself, which he could never quite capture, surfaced with clarity. It was adventure he cherished. Learning new things. Meeting new people. Hearing their stories. It explained why he was bored on the fishing boats and in the smokehouse, and why he preferred the teahouse and the delivery route. San Francisco offered the answer. From that day forward, it was an effort not to overwhelm Fr. Katz with questions about his life prior to Kamaishi. And especially about his life in San Francisco.

***

With his dream now clarified, Isamu began to plan. Gaining approval from Toshi and Ayami to emigrate to America hardly compared to making a sale at the emporium in Tōno or Kurihara. This would require a more thoughtful and serious effort. He took solace when he considered how his father, with help from others, rebuilt St. Mary's church in Kamaishi from the ground up, with nothing but an image in his head and scavenged materials. And look how it turned out. It took a year to complete, but it had worked. People flocked to see the result.

Isamu's dream could take a year as well. That would be his goal.

From that day on, no matter what Isamu was doing, planning for a trip to America was also churning somewhere in the back of his mind. He created a checklist of arguments in his head, listing every reason he could think of, as to why his parents would object. The first would be simply, *you're too young*. Followed by, *you won't know anyone. You won't be able to find work. We won't be able to see you again. What if you get sick?* And these were just the obvious, easy questions. There were many others he couldn't think of. That is why he kept the thoughts to himself. Secrecy was an overriding element of his plan.

He consciously downplayed his many questions to the Empress, and other emporium owners for answers about inventory, prices, and what were wholesalers, and when did they require contracts, and how did you employ them. He made sure to ask only one or two of his questions at each delivery, and to not ask the same questions of each customer on the same trip. Otherwise, Kiyoshi, who was not particularly interested in that aspect of the business, would begin to wonder why his younger brother was asking all those questions. Isamu tried to make them seem more a matter of polite conversation than actual learning, which of course, it also was.

At the silk factory, he used a different series of questions, all of which Isamu thought might be useful in America. For example, who buys your silk? Does it all go to a single buyer? Do you offer a discount for any reason? Is it shipped to other countries and are there taxes to be paid? Again, Isamu spaced his questions far enough apart not to cause suspicion, by either Cho or Kiyoshi. He had allowed himself a year to gather the answers.

On the days he fished with the fleet, he made sure to absorb everything he could about their methods, the weather, how to read the waves, and the sky for on-coming storms. Though he'd always been observant on the boats, he worked hard not to appear overly enthusiastic, for fear of divulging his secret plan.

Hardest of all, was to control his excitement when having tea with Fr. Katz. Every day Isamu thought of something new he wanted to ask about San Francisco. He made sure to casually ask about his assignment in Germany and his parish life in England, in Ireland, and other places where he'd previously lived. But at carefully planned intervals, he made sure to ask if the priest still had any friends or contacts living in San Francisco. And if he did, quickly excused himself long enough to head for the kitchen and write down their names.

One morning in November, the weekly packet ship from Tokyo was still docked at the harbor when he returned from overnight with the fishing fleet. Isamu saw a man dressed in what surely must be the captain's uniform, standing near the gangplank, waiting for someone to either arrive or depart. Seizing the opportunity, he hurried over to the ship, named simply *City of Tokyo,* and approached the man. "Excuse me," he began. "Are you the captain of this ship?"

"Yes," he replied. "What can I do for you?"

"I was wondering if you have any ships that sail to America."

"America, you say? What part of America? Do you mean North America or South America?"

Isamu stammered, realizing it was not a very precise question. "North America," he replied. "Actually, San Francisco. In California, North America."

"Are you in a hurry to go?" came the next question.

"Well, not exactly," Isamu replied. "Sometime next year."

"I've seen postings near our dock, but since I have no plans to go there, have not paid attention to the dates. I suppose I could bring one of the postings on my next trip, if you're sure you want to make the crossing. It's a long way, you know. I see you're a fisherman, but crossing the ocean is not like fishing a few kilometers off the coast. You prone to seasickness?"

"So far I haven't been sick from it," Isamu replied. "But then, I've only been out a few kilometers, as you said."

"Well, that's a good start," the captain replied. "So then, is that what you want? It will cost you a *yen*. Not so much for the posting, but of course I'll have to go out of my way to find one and then remember to bring it, and so on. Is it worth a yen to you?"

It seemed an exorbitant amount, but he could not think of an alternative. Isamu reached in his pocket. Most days he did not carry money on the boat, but today he had exactly one yen. *Maybe this is an omen of good luck*, he thought as he handed it to the captain. "My name is Isamu. If I'm not here when you bring it, hide it under that rock over there." He pointed to a medium-sized rock a few meters away. "Thank you, captain. I'm very grateful. If I can return the favor one day, rest assured that I will." Then he hurried back to off-load his nightly catch into a cart and headed for the smokehouse. He could hardly contain his excitement. *How much longer could he keep the dream to himself?* he wondered.

Each week, Isamu checked under the flat rock for a posting from the captain. The packet ship normally came only once each week. It had been a Monday when he'd talked with him. Nothing was there the following Monday. Surely it would be there on the second Monday. Still nothing. *Maybe he wasn't even the captain*, thought Isamu. He merely tricked me for an easy yen. *Maybe instead of a promising omen, this was meant to teach me a lesson*: to be *very careful who you trust*. He wished he had the yen back. They were not that easy to come by.

On the third Monday, in spite of knowing the result, he hurried from his fishing boat to the shipping dock, tried to look inconspicuous when he walked over to the rock, and lifted it. Tucked there, where it would not be seen unless specifically looking for it, was a posting, with the image of a large sailing ship, and a series of dates printed below. It was the schedule.

His heart raced as he held it up and scanned the words. *Occidental and Oriental Steamship Company* displayed in large letters across the top. Below was a rendering of the largest ship Isamu had ever seen. It must have been more than a hundred meters long, with four masts in addition to a large stack in the middle, which billowed black with smoke. Even in the rendering, the ship appeared to be streaking through the waves. He read down the page for information about sailing dates. There, printed in black and white, a date etched in his memory.

08 June 1899. Departing Yokohama for Honolulu.
18 June 1899. Departing Honolulu for San Francisco.

Isamu could not believe his eyes. His dream might actually come true. Then he noticed another section of the poster that announced the fares.

Yokohama to Honolulu – fifty yen.
Honolulu to San Francisco – thirty yen.

His heart sank almost as quickly as it had soared moments before. Where could he come up with eighty yen in seven months? Not once had he considered how much it would cost to cross the Pacific. After all, he knew not a single person who had made the trip. How could he have known?

Shaken back to the reality of the moment, he nearly forgot to return to his boat and collect the nightly catch. It was not the behavior of one who aspired to travel halfway across the world by himself. Frustrated by his new knowledge, he walked slowly back to the boat, loaded his catch in a cart, and headed to the smokehouse. Maybe it would seem better after a good night's sleep.

The sharp dose of reality hit Isamu directly in the face. After sleeping on it, things had, in fact, become more clear. He had to decide if this was a real dream or a 'pipe' dream, the name used for one induced by opium. By morning, he knew this was his dream, and it was real, and if he wanted to achieve it, he could not give it up simply because it was going to be difficult.

Keeping the dream to himself while secretly working to gather ammunition to argue his cause, was now beginning to feel somehow untruthful. Whether it was or not, he wasn't sure, but he knew only that it was starting to feel like a plan of deceit to those around him. Even if he had not worked out all the details, financial chief among them, he vowed to share his dream by Christmas, barely a month away.

The next four weeks found Isamu constantly running ideas through his mind about how to save the required eighty yen for an ocean crossing. He would worry about additional money to get settled in America later. He studied his work schedule day-by-day. Maybe he could fish one extra shift by adjusting his hours at the teahouse. He was already helping to open at eight o'clock, but maybe he could work a few extra hours in the evenings.

As for the boats, there was limited demand for fish, so would it even help to add to the supply? Their own Kamaishi Trading Company was already the largest customer for fish, between the smokehouse and the teahouse. He would need to find more customers along their delivery route to actually increase demand. If he shared the dream with his family, maybe they would have ideas on getting new customers. Surely, the Empress could help. Maybe even Cho. Isamu felt sure Cho trusted and respected him. Each of his ideas, however, seemed more fragile the longer he considered them.

Finally, with no revelations forthcoming, Christmas was upon them. The weeks of Advent found Isamu becoming steadily more inward and withdrawn. No one could put a finger on it, but he did not seem himself. Ayami hoped it was part of his natural maturity. She hoped he was taking the Advent season to heart, and preparing himself spiritually for the upcoming birth of the Lord.

**

At midnight mass on Christmas Eve, Fr. Katz, and indeed, all the parishioners, felt a buoyancy from the season. Especially when the now-legendary *Ave Maria* hymn filled the church with song.

Candles at every window, on the altar, and scattered throughout the church, helped to create a joyous environment. For one brief moment, not a single burden rested on the shoulder of almost eighty souls, tucked into St. Mary's Church, Kamaishi, Japan.

By previous agreement, Fr. Katz had accepted the Ozawa family's invitation to dine with them on Christmas Day.

Haruki's family, Kazuo's family, and Hajime, Hisa's only surviving family member, also joined in. As a matter of practicality, they convened at the teahouse. It was the only place where they could all sit together, and it had the additional advantage of an extra-large kitchen, complete with all the necessary supplies.

Fr. Katz, not surprising to anyone, arrived early. His residence was still under construction, and the teahouse served as his daily dining room, anyway. But he was given to feel like one of the family, and no one was surprised when he stepped in to help with whatever task he could find to help. His major task on this day, however, was simply to offer a prayer of thanksgiving and grace before the meal was served.

Toshi surveyed those seated around him and offered his own silent prayer of thanks. There was nothing he could think of that he wanted or needed, that was not within five meters of him at that moment. Namely, his family and his friend, Fr. Katz. Between sips of tea and leisurely bites of fish, rice, sweet potatoes, carrots, and beans, conversation bounced freely from person to person—sometimes speculating on what the Blessed Mother must have been thinking and feeling on this day twenty centuries ago, sometimes speculating on whether snow was in the air, sometimes predicting an increase or decrease in the number of fish at their offshore fishing grounds.

During an easy lull in the conversation, Fr. Katz decided to change the direction with an innocent question to everyone in general. "Now, with the new year almost in sight, what are each of you hoping for in 1899? It will be the last year of this century, a milestone by any measure. Do any of you have milestone hopes or dreams for the coming year?"

Isamu blushed, as if the question had been directed to him alone. *Had the priest read his mind all along? Had he given himself away with his endless line of questioning, when he thought he was being so subtle?* He lowered his chin just a little, hoping the others wouldn't notice, as he shifted his eyes quickly around the room. No one was staring at him. Not even Fr. Katz. *Maybe it was only a coincidental question, after all.* He continued to look down, hoping someone else would respond. After what felt an eternity to Isamu, Toshi took the lead.

"My dream for this year is to finish your residence," he said. "We would have built it along with the church, but we didn't know what wishes or rules you might have, and we decided to wait until you arrived so you could tell us yourself. The church, on the other hand, we felt we had enough guidance based on the previous structure and what was told to us by Fr. Lispard. We're glad you approve of the church. And we'll be glad when you finally have a place to call your own."

"Most likely, so I'll stop coming to the teahouse for every meal," the priest retorted with a laugh. The others laughed along, but assured him he would still be expected for meals.

When no one else took up the discussion, Fr. Katz decided to press forward himself. "And Minako, what is your dream for 1899? Do you have any special plans you hope to accomplish in the coming year?"

Minako was not an extrovert by nature, and preferred to remain away from the spotlight. But she was now on the spot as a result of his direct question, and felt it would be impolite to sidestep it. He seemed genuinely interested in her future hopes. She had to think about an answer before she could respond. Finally, she found it. "I would like to renew my relationship with my sister," she said. "We have not been close since I married Haruki. I can't say we didn't get along, but it's just that we were never close. She liked Haruki from the beginning, so that was not the issue. Now, since we make deliveries to Kitakami and Hanamaki twice a month, I'd like to ride along and spend some time with her."

Everyone fell silent. Color was draining from the usually rosy cheeks of Fr. Katz. He chided himself internally for opening up what must have been a long-festering wound for Minako. Whether Haruki was even aware of it, he could not tell. But he sat for a time, wishing he had not called on Minako.

Haruki was first to speak. "I think that's a good idea, Minako, and I don't know why none of us thought of it before. You can ride with the deliveries as often as you like. And stay for as long as you want. We have plenty of family to cover for you at the teahouse." He looked around at the others, hoping to see agreement on their faces. Every head was nodding.

Now, afraid he might open another wound, Fr. Katz kept his silence for a time. Then it occurred to him this was not the best of discussions to end with. He would try once more, this time choosing someone he felt would be a safe target. As he looked around the room, he saw his frequent tea companion, Isamu. *Aha,* he thought. *We talk several times a week, and I know almost as much about Isamu as his parents do. He will be a safe way to end this discussion.*

Looking across at him, he smiled with what he hoped was a comfortable countenance, and quietly asked, "How about you, Isamu? You've become quite a man, even since I arrived here. If I'm not mistaken, you'll soon be nineteen? From all I can tell, you've already proven yourself as a promoter and a salesman. I've heard how you added four new accounts to the trading company this year. Do you have a special dream for next year?"

It was just the opportunity Isamu had hoped for, yet he tensed at the thought of it. He was fully aware that everyone was looking at him, awaiting his reply. "Yes, I do have a dream," he croaked. "My dream is to travel to America and set up a new outpost for the Kamaishi Trading Company."

The words blurted out of his mouth like they had been locked there for months, which, as a point of fact, they had. He tried to gauge the reactions of his mother and father without looking directly at them. He saw enough to know he was walking on thin ice.

Ayami's face was tense. Her eyes were open wide, and staring directly at her son. The easy smile from just one minute earlier had completely disappeared. *Not again, she thought. Not America again. I thought we got past that in 1880, when Toshi wanted to use his bonus money to travel to America.* Mist came to her eyes as she relived that night. *It would have been better to go then, when the children were little. We would have all been together, at least.*

Toshi was staring at him with a blank and unreadable look. There was no hint of a smile or a frown. Then he turned his face to a nearby window and moved his gaze to something unseeable in the distance. He thought back to that December day when the foundry director awarded his hundred yen bonus. The most money he'd had at one time, since. But in the end, he could not leave his friends. *What would our lives be like now?* He wondered, *if we had gone when we had the chance.* Only when Isamu began to speak did he turn back to look.

Regaining control of his breath, Isamu launched forward. Looking directly at his father, he said, "You've taught me a dream without a plan will always remain a dream. I've been working on a plan, and I think I have it worked out, except for one thing. I know you probably think I'm too young to go to America, but I'll be nineteen in May. You weren't much older than that when you left home to come to Kamaishi." He shifted his gaze to Ayami. "And you weren't that old when you came here from Hanamaki."

Ayami blinked at the reminder. She felt so much older at the time. And besides, it was different. Times were safer then. And she was forced to come.

"As for being mature enough, or experienced enough," Isamu continued, "I've been making deliveries for almost two years. I've been going out with the fleet off and on since I was little, and I've been working in the teahouse and the smokehouse almost since they began. And, like Fr. Katz said, I've been able to add four new customers to our accounts." He looked briefly at the priest sitting across from him, to acknowledge his affirmation.

The priest, still reeling from his innocent attempts at holiday conversation, forced a meek smile and quietly massaged the porcelain cup in front of him with both hands.

"Kaneto is getting old enough that I'm sure he could take my place on the deliveries, and that way he could spend time with his father along the way, which I think they would both appreciate.

"I've been learning everything I can from our customers about how their business works, which I expect would be helpful in America. They've helped me learn about suppliers and distributors, financing and shipping, and even tariffs. When I get to San Francisco, if Fr. Katz agrees, I hope to contact some of the people he knows there, to help make introductions. In the meantime, I know I can get a job. With my experience, I could work on a fishing boat, a teahouse, a smokehouse, a delivery company, or even take care of livery animals. I don't require much to live on, and I'm sure I could make a living until I get the trading company up and running."

Isamu paused for a moment to catch his breath, but almost by instinct, to create a pause; to change the direction of his argument.

"Our entire family has been working almost every waking hour, at four different jobs, just to make a living. We catch fish, we smoke fish, we run a teahouse, and we buy, sell, and deliver fish, rice, and vegetables. Yet we're just getting by. It seems obvious the government is interested only in exports. They favor iron foundries and silk factories, while they punish the farmers with high taxes. Silk workers make barely enough to stay alive. And too many of them can't even do that." He looked at his aunt Emiko for affirmation. "The only reason more girls haven't starved to death or been worked to death at the silk factory is because we basically subsidize their kitchen. If we hadn't tricked them, they would still be serving barley water for three meals a day. How many girls throughout Japan are starving in other factories, do you suppose?"

Luckily, he was not able to see Emiko's face, which reflected her painful time at the Osaki factory. She hoped he didn't know the worst part, the part about the supervisors, who could punish and intimidate with impunity. And especially, about Orochi.

He paused again, to let them consider his argument, and then continued, "Did the government step in to help our fishermen when the tsunami came? They hardly bothered to see if we needed help. And what will become of our trading company if the country encounters a drought? We wouldn't be able to provide rice to Osaki. Could they afford to serve only fish to their workers? Could we survive selling only fish? How would our family survive without at least two major products to sell? Could we survive on just the teahouse? Or the smokehouse? If it weren't for us, there wouldn't be much demand for fish, so how would the fleet survive? America is ahead of us in many ways, and if we're smart, we'll expand our horizons. We need to reduce our dependence on a few small markets by adding new ones. Not just outside our region, but outside Japan."

The Difficult Years of Toshi Ozawa 215

Even Kiyoshi and Kazuo were watching him with eyes open wide. Neither had an inkling that Isamu had gathered all this information during their routine deliveries. Having finally unburdened himself of his secret dream, he felt the tension slowly drain away. Even if he received a resounding 'no' from his father, it was good to feel normal again.

At this point, even a 'no' seemed acceptable. Maybe he was chasing a rainbow after all. Why would he even consider himself ready to travel five thousand miles alone, to a country whose language he could not speak?

He was busy critiquing and second-guessing himself, when he was interrupted by the sound of his father's voice.

"It seems that you have, indeed, been thinking about this for some time. You have considered several things which I certainly would have questioned.

"But I noticed you didn't mention the piece of your plan you haven't worked out yet. What piece is that?"

Isamu dropped his shoulders slightly, a telltale sign he was not comfortable, or maybe just not confident, with the major roadblock to his plan. It was, after all, the primary requisite for all the other parts. Without it, everything else was moot.

"I've checked into the cost of travel," he began. "There is a steamer, the *S.S. Coptic*, which sails in June to Honolulu and then on to San Francisco. It would take three weeks, or a little longer. The timing is good, but the fare is eighty yen for both excursions. I don't know where to come up with eighty yen. I've considered additional shifts with the fleet, or additional hours at the teahouse or smokehouse, but since all of those are essentially 'family' income, I don't see how it would help. And since there aren't many places to work in Kamaishi that pay in currency, and if I went to Kitakami or somewhere else, then I'd have to pay for food and lodging...even if I did find work. I'm out of ideas."

"That's a lot of money, true enough," Toshi said. He looked at Ayami, to see if she wanted to speak. The color was mostly gone from her cheeks, and he could see she was blinking back misty tears.

Then he looked over at Fr. Katz. "I guess you've given us a Christmas dinner to remember this year," he said. "How about we save any more dreams for another day?" He tried to smile, but Isamu could tell it did not come easily. Nor did it provide an answer one way or the other. "We'll talk about this later," he finally said, looking at Isamu.

Isamu stood, and offered to collect everyone's dinnerware and take it to the kitchen.

***

Since most residents of Japan were not Christian, most did not celebrate Christmas. The teahouse was closed on Christmas Day, to give themselves a family day of rest and celebration. The day after Christmas this year was a Sunday. The teahouse was open for business because, fundamentally, they needed the income. Toshi and Haruki still held the weekend schedule for fishing, but opted to spend the time with their families instead. This did not prevent them from helping out at the teahouse, however, along with Emiko and most of the children, Isamu included.

On Monday, Toshi announced he would be late arriving at the teahouse, due to other pressing business. He did not offer what the pressing business was, and if Ayami knew, she kept it to herself. Kiyoshi and Isamu thought better of asking. They assumed Meisa was also in the dark.

Toshi arrived at the teahouse before noon but went directly to the smokehouse and busied himself with the fish and the smoke. Together at supper that evening, Toshi remained quiet and slightly aloof. Isamu thought he saw a few fleeting glances between Toshi and Ayami, but for the life of him, could not decipher any messages contained therein.

When Fr. Katz visited the teahouse for his regular meals, the other patrons were puzzled as to why he'd taken a sudden interest in the weather. The weather was all he ever asked about, since midnight mass. They wondered if he was worried about another tsunami coming.

Every other Tuesday and Wednesday were Isamu's normal shifts on the boats he shared with three other men. On the opposite weeks, he made deliveries with Kazuo and Kiyoshi. This time of year, it was a struggle to endure long nights on the water, far from shore, but it was long understood that complaining would gain him nothing. It was part of the life of a fisherman.

As he packed a lunch at the teahouse and prepared to walk to the harbor, Toshi motioned for Isamu to sit. Isamu's breath tightened, and he felt his pulse quicken in spite of efforts to calm it. Sitting down beside his parents, he tried to capture their faces without staring.

Toshi began before Isamu was completely settled. "We have been thinking about your dream, Isamu. I guess we always knew you had an adventuresome spirit, but never did we think you would consider leaving Japan."

Isamu tried to speak, but his father held up his hand as a signal to wait.

"I can see my seed fell close to the tree," he said. "When I heard your arguments, I could almost see myself pointing out piece by piece each of the points you made to us. I could tell you spent a lot of time thinking through the arguments before you presented them. I can remember many times in which I did the same. And it's a good thing for you that you did. Without your arguments, I would be inclined to dismiss the idea as nothing more than a child's fantasy. But when you reminded me that you have several valuable skills you can put to use until you get established, I realized you were thinking more like a man than like a child."

Isamu was starting to hope this might actually lead to an approval.

"Then, when you reminded all of us how hard we work as a family, with little hope of a better life, it forced me to consider your future and not merely our own. Sadly, I have to agree with you. Our government seems to care more about its reputation around the world than it does about its people. Your grandparents hardly scratch out a living in Hanamaki, even with us paying cash for as much of their rice as we can afford. I don't know if you knew this, but we've been helping them with their taxes since we were married. Otherwise, Kunio would not have been able to spare Ayami. He was about to contract her to a silk factory to raise the money for his taxes."

Isamu was not sure if he heard correctly. His mother, sent to a silk factory, like Emiko? What a horrible life! All of a sudden, going out on the boat at night, in December, did not seem so bad.

"You have our approval if you still want to go," Toshi continued. "Of course, there is still the major obstacle you mentioned: money for steamship fare. I went to the foundry yesterday to make inquiries. There are still a few people there who I worked with years ago, and they were able to help. They introduced me to the director, and I told him about my years there, and also about my son, who is more promising than his father was, when he started working there."

Isamu began to blush at what he considered the ultimate compliment.

"I explained that you might be interested in working there until June, if there was any work available. He said there was a low-level opening in the coal yard, if you are interested. It would be hard work and dirty. But it pays one yen per day. That would give you over one hundred yen by the time you have to leave. It should be enough for passage and a little extra to get settled in San Francisco."

Isamu was smiling so wide he could barely contain himself. He was so taken by surprise that it was the only time he could remember actually being lost for words. He just sat there and looked at his parents. First at Toshi, to make sure it was not a joke, then at his mother, to see if she agreed. When he saw the mist in her eyes, he knew it was real, and it made his eyes mist in return.

"I explained to the director that you have to work your shift with the fishing fleet tonight and tomorrow," Toshi said. "He said if you are interested in the foundry job, you should come to see him on Thursday. But for now, we'd better let you get on down to the dock and off to work. You are never late for your shift. They'll worry about you if you're not there on time."

Isamu stood, hurried to the kitchen and grabbed his overnight meal sack and a jar of tea. He waved with a smile as he headed the several blocks to the harbor. When he arrived, he could not remember a single step.

Climbing aboard the boat, he finally collected himself. It took all the discipline he could gather to think about fishing, but he knew instinctively how quickly things could go wrong if he was not paying attention. For the next two days, he had to dedicate himself to being the best fisherman he could be.

***

The return sail early on Thursday morning, his last shift on the boat, seemed to take twice the normal time. Was it the wind? Or was he just so eager to meet the foundry director that it only felt that way? But eventually, he found himself back at the dock, unloading his catch. He stopped at the teahouse only long enough to say good morning, and was on his way up the ridge toward home. He hated to take the additional time, but felt he should bathe and change from his fishing clothes before going to the foundry. The fish smell might put the director off.

He could afford to take no chances, even with the favorable connections of his father.

CHAPTER 27
LIFE AT THE FOUNDRY

JANUARY 1899 – KAMAISHI FOUNDRY

By ten-thirty, he was approaching the two furnaces, which seemed much larger and more intimidating than they ever had on his previous trips. Isamu visited a few times when he was younger, with his father. But this would be the first time ever, as a prospective employee. The heat and the noise had already caused his pulse to quicken, and he was still fifty meters away.

Finding his way to the familiar but now-aging director's office, he straightened his shoulders, forced his chin up, stretched his shoulders as wide as he could, and climbed the two steps to the door. At the center of the room, sitting at a rather small table, was a young man not much older than himself.

"Good morning," Isamu said. "I'm here to see the director about a job as a coal tender. My name is Isamu Ozawa. I think he is expecting me."

The young man looked down at one of several papers strewn on top of his table and, after finding the one he was looking for, looked back at Isamu with a faint smile. "Yes, I see your name is listed. Wait here, and I'll see if he can see you now." He stood and retreated through a doorway located along the wall behind his table.

Presently, he returned and said, "The director will see you. Please follow me." He turned and motioned for Isamu to follow him through the door and into the adjacent room.

Isamu bowed politely when the director saw him enter. The director was seated at a table of his own, though it was much larger than the one in the first room, and very ornate. Isamu made a note in his head to ask about the history of the table, if an opportunity arose.

"Thank you for seeing me this morning," Isamu began. "I know you are very busy. My father, whom I believe you spoke with on Monday, told me there might be an opening as a coal tender for which I could apply."

"Yes, of course," he replied. He seemed to make the connection only now, after Isamu's account of the introduction. "It is not easy to be a coal tender," he began. "A lot of men start at that job, but most don't last very long. It's a hot job. It is also very dirty, because, of course, the coal itself is dirty and rubs off on your clothing as well as your skin. But it is a very important job, because it is imperative we keep the furnace at a specific temperature. Otherwise, it affects the quality of the iron, and of course, that is the whole point of our existence."

He looked Isamu up and down slowly. "You seem to be a strong and healthy young man. Do you think you would be up to the challenge? The days are long; you would be working twelve hours every day, except Sunday. A lot of young men your age prefer to spend time with their friends, and don't have the discipline to report for work on time, day after day. Do you have the discipline for that?"

"I do," he replied. "I am currently working several jobs and have never been late for any of them." Then he added, "It is the way my father brought me up."

"Very well. If you want the job, we'll give you a chance. The last person we hired only lasted two days. See if you can do better. Be here at six o'clock tomorrow, and the foreman in charge of the coal facility will be waiting for you in front of his building. Do you have any questions?"

"No questions," he replied. "Thank you for this opportunity. I will work hard for you." Then Isamu bowed politely once more, turned, and exited through the same outer office as his father had done those many years before. He regretted not having the opportunity to learn about the beautiful table, but perhaps there would be another time.

Isamu hardly slept at all, he was so anxious about starting his first day. Lying on his mat, he laid first on one side, then on the other. It had not occurred to him until tonight that he had never worked for anyone other than his family. Nor had he received an explicit wage for doing so. Working as family was contributing to the livelihood of them all. No one in the family got paid, but they all received the benefit. It was just part of family life.

Tomorrow would be different, he realized in the darkness of his room. *Will I be able to do the work? What if the supervisor doesn't like me? Will I be strong enough to do the job? What if I make a mistake and set the coal on fire?*

Here I am, almost nineteen years old, and never really with a 'real' job, he thought. *What makes me think I could travel to America and be successful in a foreign country when I've never really had a job? Maybe this whole dream is just that—nothing more than a childish dream.*

That was the last thing Isamu remembered until he jolted awake hours later. His first instinct was to look at the window, searching for daylight, hoping for darkness. He exhaled when he saw only the faintest hint of a morning sun—hardly a tint of pink in the eastern sky. Even so, he bolted from the mat and dressed quickly. A light reflected underneath his bedroom door. *Mother must be up*, he thought with a smile.

When he entered the kitchen, she was indeed, up, and heating the stove for a pot of tea. She smiled through tired eyes, and Isamu knew instinctively she had spent a restless night as well. She would not wake him unless it was clear he was oversleeping, but she was there and prepared, just in case. This was the mother he'd always known. This was the mother he would truly miss.

She made him lunch in spite of his objection that he could do it himself, as he nervously gulped down a breakfast of rice, eggs, and hot tea. She set a lantern by the door next to his lunch, gave him a smile that, without speaking, told him how much she loved him, and headed back to her mat next to Toshi, as Isamu pulled on a coat and walked out the door.

Daybreak was still a half-hour distant, and the lantern helped light his way. A few of the early-rising birds were calling from treetop to treetop, much as they might have done twenty years earlier when his father walked this very route on a similar dark morning.

Thirty minutes later, the lights from the foundry poked through the trees as he neared the factory. He'd been told to report to the coal hut, a short distance to the south of the main office. As he drew closer, he could see the movement of a man inside, his shadow moving in front of a small window at the front of the hut.

Isamu knocked lightly on the door and entered without waiting for a response. The man inside was looking down at what appeared to be a ledger of some sort and looked up with surprise at the sound of Isamu's voice.

"Good morning," he said. "My name is Isamu Ozawa, and I was told to report to you as a coal tender. I hope I didn't disturb you," he added, almost as an apology.

"Good morning, Isamu; my name is Jin. No, you didn't disturb me. I was expecting you. Just not quite so early," he smiled. "I can see that you are your father's son," he continued. "I had the privilege of working for your father many years ago. He was the best supervisor I ever had. He and his uncle, Haruki. They were two of the best who ever worked here. I wish they still worked here, as do most of the other men who knew them. Your father and Haruki were always the first ones to arrive for work. I think they must have had a competition to see who could get here first. That's why I see your father in you. You must have that same habit. I'm sure you will be as good a worker as he was." Jin smiled at Isamu.

"I see you brought something for lunch. Come with me, and I'll show you where your storage bin is located. Then you'll need to pick a pair of boots and protective clothes. Most of your time will not be near the furnace, but when you are, you need to wear protective gear. Otherwise, your skin will melt. It is very painful."

Isamu was not sure if it was said in jest or as a warning, but decided for the moment to consider it a warning.

Jin led him to a large wooden bin filled loosely with heavy leather boots. "Find two that match your feet and bring them along," he instructed. He pointed to a stump of pine that was apparently used as a place to sit while trying on the various sizes of boots. "It's easier to get the right size if you're sitting down," he said.

Isamu found two boots of matching size and tucked them under his arm along with his lunch and the lantern he still carried. Jin led him to a room off the side of the foundry, which he indicated was a place for him to change and store his regular clothes until the end of the day.

Then he led Isamu to a shed near the supervisor's hut. "Most of the shovels are the same," he said, "but find one that feels good in your hands. It will be your most important possession. It is best if you can find one with a cushioned handle," he joked. "By the end of the shift, your arms will be so tired you won't feel them, but by the time you get home again, they should start coming back to life." Jin watched as Isamu's shoulders tightened up again.

From there, he led Isamu to the rail station just beyond his hut. He pointed to the cars resting there, mostly in darkness. Isamu could see the silhouette of dark mounds heaped within their walls.

"The coal is shipped to Kamaishi from Hokkaido and then by rail to our foundry. Your job is to make sure there is always plenty of coal at the furnace to keep it going." He pointed to a nearby barn with several horse and wagon teams resting out front. The other drivers should be arriving soon...they are not as prompt as you. When they arrive, I'll introduce you to one of them, and you can ride with him today. Once you learn the routine, I'll assign you to a wagon of your own. There will be extra hands at the rail car and the furnace to help load and unload."

Isamu spent all that day making short trips from the rail car to the furnace and back again. By mid-morning, his back and shoulders were beginning to burn. Loading and unloading coal was a lot more work than sitting in a boat or riding a delivery wagon. By lunchtime, he felt blisters starting to form on both his hands. He finally got the joke Jin had told him: to pick a shovel with cushions. He couldn't help but chuckle in spite of the growing pain.

By lunchtime, he wondered if he could survive the afternoon. Every muscle in his body was in active rebellion. Finally, when the sun was well down the western horizon, Isamu heard the welcome shrill of the foundry whistle, the end of his shift.

When the horses had been cared for, Isamu returned to the changing room and dressed in his regular clothes. Without the heavy boots, he might actually have enough energy to make it home. Darkness was setting in, and he lit his lantern for the journey.

Arriving home to an empty house, he had to decide if he was more tired than hungry. He wanted to go directly to his mat and sleep, but was afraid he would be too weak to work another day if he didn't eat. Instead, he stirred a fire in the stove and put water on to boil. It would be another meal of rice, eggs, and tea.

When Toshi, Ayami, and Meisa came home from the teahouse later that night, Isamu was sound asleep and snoring loudly. He didn't stir in spite of their veiled attempts to accidentally awaken him.

Ayami listened intently the next morning, in case Isamu was too tired to wake on his own. When she saw beads of light through her bedroom door, she pulled a night coat over her shoulders and joined him in the kitchen. She could barely wait to hear about his first day at the foundry. But when she saw his sagging eyes and disheveled hair, she decided not to press him for details. Instead, she smiled and asked if she could help.

Isamu shook his head and poured them both a cup of tea. Ayami watched as he ate, then handed him the lantern and his lunch as he headed for the door. "Tomorrow you can sleep in," she said. He smiled at her, but was too tired to reply.

Jin greeted Isamu with a smile when he arrived. "You are your father's son," he said again. It was a greeting he would express every morning of Isamu's short tenure.

Isamu smiled in return. "I was already in bed when he came home last night, but I will tell him that we met," he replied.

"He will be pleased to know I'm in your care." Then he headed for the changing room and prepared himself for the day ahead.

When his teammate arrived, Isamu climbed aboard the wagon for the short trip to the rail yard. Each wagon took one half hour to load. The trip from the railyard to the foundry was ten minutes. The ten-minute breaks during each trip were the only things that kept him going. Finally, it was lunchtime; only a half-day remaining until he could lie on his mat and forget the rest of the world. Tomorrow he would sleep until at least noon, he decided. The thought sustained him until the final whistle sounded.

It was Isamu's first payday, albeit a short one. Jin handed each worker their earnings as they marched past his table in single file. When Isamu's turn came, he was handed two yen. It was the first time Isamu had money that belonged to him alone, money he had earned by his own accord.

Isamu was almost giddy with excitement at the feel of two yen in his pocket. It was entirely his, and he could spend it however he wished. It crossed his mind to go to the village and buy something special. He envisioned how Kiyoshi or Meisa would envy his new silver ring or bracelet, or maybe even an inexpensive new watch.

It was his intention to head to the shops on his way home, then later to the teahouse for something to eat, and show off his purchase. But the closer he got to the trailhead, the more he remembered the purpose of his labor. With two yen already in his pocket after two days of work, he needed only seventy-eight more to pay his fare. Next week, after six days, he would have another six yen, for a total of eight in all. Once he'd saved eighty yen, then, only then, could he spend part of what he earned on other things.

He decided to go to the teahouse instead of home. Buoyed by the thought of a day off tomorrow, he was anxious to tell his family about the rigors of his new job. And of course, to tell his father about his foreman, Jin.

Isamu was so excited by the two yen that it had not occurred to him to wash his face along with his hands, in the changing room. Consequently, he did not understand why everyone in the teahouse, his mother in particular, stared at him when he entered. He hurried over to her with a hand outstretched, tightly holding his earnings. "Look, Mother!" he exclaimed. "Look at what I earned already!"

Ayami broke into a huge grin, betraying her underlying embarrassment at his blackened face, readily apparent to all the diners. "That's wonderful," she said. "I'm very proud of you. I can only imagine how hard the work is. Your father told me it was not a job for the weak." Then, almost as if an afterthought, she added. "You have a smudge of black on your face; why don't you slip into the kitchen and wash it off before you eat? You must be starving by now."

Meisa brought him supper from the kitchen and then sat down next to him, eager to hear all about his work. Toshi and Ayami were close behind. Kiyoshi was fishing and not at the teahouse, or he would have been right there as well.

Isamu started by telling about his supervisor Jin, and the kind things he'd said about Toshi and Haruki. Then he told them about the rail cars and the shovels and how hot it was near the furnaces. Toshi laughed when Isamu told him how Jin advised him to select a shovel with a cushioned handle.

They walked home from the teahouse together. Isamu was still wide awake from the thrill of his earnings, but as soon as he lay down on the mat, his eyes went closed. Ayami heard his lingering snores until she fell asleep herself, later that night.

Isamu's plan to sleep until noon was interrupted when he heard movement in the kitchen. He opened his eyes just enough to see a stream of sunlight climbing slowly up the bedroom wall. That was the moment he remembered it was Sunday. Not only a day of rest, but more importantly, a day of worship. He was not working. There was no reason he could not attend Sunday mass with his family. He slowly rose, dressed, and made his way to join his mother in the kitchen.

The four of them headed off together for St. Mary's of the Assumption, just after eight-thirty. It was a twenty-minute walk from home to the church. Arriving late to mass was not an option at the Ozawa household. They were seated and settled, with time for a private prayer before the priest stepped to the altar.

Isamu prayed for a safe and successful passage to America.

Next to him, Toshi prayed that Isamu would find a career that was suited for him and make him happy.

Ayami and Meisa prayed that Isamu would change his mind and stay in Kamaishi.

CHAPTER 28
FR. KATZ'S CONFESSION

FEBRUARY 1899 – KAMAISHI TEAHOUSE

Following Sunday mass, as had become the custom, Fr. Katz made his way to the teahouse for lunch. Kiyoshi was back from his overnight shift on the fishing boat and joined the group as well. The teahouse was closed on Sundays, except for these family dinners. It was a quiet and peaceful place to congregate. Haruki and his family, along with Kazuo and his family, were always included. It was an ideal way to start the week. With so many members having different schedules, this was often the only time they could all be together, to visit and enjoy being a family.

At the end of the meal, Fr. Katz made a point of asking Isamu to join him for a walk. "I've been eating too much, thanks to the teahouse," he said. "I feel better when I go for a walk after eating. Especially during the winter months when I don't get out as much."

The two of them slipped out while others finished a serving of sweet cake and berries or yet another cup of tea. "Let's walk down to the wharf," suggested Fr. Katz. "I always enjoy watching boats in the bay, or even at their moorings."

Neither man spoke for the first block as they headed east from the teahouse. Then Fr. Katz spoke of the chilly weather, and the two of them pondered as to whether it would be a long winter or not. Eventually, Fr. Katz said, "Have you ever regretted something that you said, even though it was the truth, and not spoken with ill intent? But all the same, something you wish you hadn't said?"

Isamu's first instinct was to laugh. It sounded an awful lot like Fr. Katz was about to make a confession. The thought of a priest confessing to a nineteen-year-old struck him as more than ironic. But something in the voice of the priest caused Isamu to turn away, so that even the possibility of giving away his amusement would be avoided. Finally, he replied. "I'm not sure I know what you mean," he said.

"I want to apologize for sharing my stories of San Francisco with you. Looking back on them now, I realize they could easily have sounded like wonderful stories of travel and adventure. I'm quite sure those stories helped convince you to go there yourself. Those stories were a display of my vanity, and I see that now. I took a vow of humility, and the first thing I did when your family took me in was to talk about myself." He waved his arm in a sweeping motion across the empty village plots of ground where houses used to be.

"Look around us. The entire village was swept away, countless lives with it. Many families are gone forever. Others, like yours, have struggled every day since, and will never be the same. Instead of telling you stories about San Francisco, I should have been asking how I could help restore Kamaishi. I was sent here to serve, not to plant dreams of faraway places in your head."

Isamu didn't know how to respond. Fortunately, his familiar instincts took hold, and he chose to simply listen instead.

"San Francisco is as different from Kamaishi, as night is to day," he continued. "You are safe here, and your soul is safe here. San Francisco is a dangerous and sinful place."

Fr. Katz spoke slowly and quietly, making it clear to Isamu he was choosing his words thoughtfully. "It was named after a famous saint," he continued. "St. Francis of Assisi. That's an irony in itself. St. Francis was known for his vows of poverty, humility, and chastity. Those virtues are pretty much the direct opposite of what the city actually stands for today. Most of the city leaders are known for their greed, and the city, for its loose morals and arrogant personality.

"When gold was discovered, it created an influx of people from all over America, even from other countries, convinced they would find instant wealth. Some were well-meaning, hard-working families simply seeking a better life. But many were ruffians, scoundrels, thieves, and criminals who would do almost anything to get rich quick. Very few ever did, by the way. But now, fifty years later, the city is still reeling from them or their descendants. The explosion of a ne'er-do-well migration takes a long time to normalize, even with well-meaning people and overflowing churches.

"There is an area there called the Barbary Coast, which houses opium dens and female…companionship. It is not uncommon, even today, for young men to enter the Barbary Coast and never be seen again. Some are shanghaied and sold to ship captains, as crew to who-knows-where destinations around the world. Others are simply killed and dumped in the bay, for something as bold as smiling at the wrong woman.

"There are many…even people of the cloth…some are friends of mine, who plead for God's help to destroy the city. They liken it to the cities of Sodom and Gomorrah in the Bible. They wish God would strike it down entirely."

At this, Isamu finally mustered the courage to speak. He was sincerely curious, but he also wanted to make sure the priest knew he was listening. "What about you?" he asked. "Do you think it should be struck down?"

Fr. Katz smiled at Isamu. This was the young man he thought he knew. Isamu was mature enough, even at nineteen, to question and gather as much information as possible before making a decision. "No," he finally replied. "No, I don't think it should be struck down. I know from experience there are many good and God-fearing people who live there. God told Abraham that even if ten righteous people were found living in Sodom, he would spare the city. I can personally attest there are more than ten righteous people living in San Francisco. So, I don't think God is going to destroy the city and all its people."

They had reached the wharf by now, and stood to peer across the bay and as far as they could see across the Pacific, toward California. Finally, the priest turned back the way they'd come. Isamu followed, and they headed toward the teahouse.

"I suppose it is possible," Fr. Katz said, "that God could send the city a warning. But I don't think he would destroy it completely. If you go to San Francisco, please promise me you'll never visit the Barbary Coast. Or if you do, go only with one or two trusted friends, in daylight. And stay away from the opium dens and the saké houses. Who knows what kind of drops they might put in your drink? If something happened to you, I could never face your family."

"I promise," Isamu replied.

"There is another matter," the priest continued. "We've talked about your soul. Let's talk about your happiness. 'Prejudice' is not a word you've probably ever used or needed in Kamaishi. It means that someone forms an opinion about a person or a group of people, without knowing anything about them. In America, there are many forms of prejudice, and California is no exception.

"The gold rush created a demand for safer travel to California from the eastern half of the country. That prompted them to build a railway all the way from Omaha, in the middle of the country, to Sacramento, in California. It was a distance of over twenty-eight hundred kilometers.

"The track beside us here, leading to the foundry," and he paused to wave an arm off to the northwest, where the coal train was located, "is something like fifteen kilometers. Can you imagine the effort it took to build twenty-eight hundred kilometers of railway? The manpower to build it? It was dangerous, hot, cold, dirty, and demanding work. To make matters worse, there were still hostile Indians in parts of the area.

"The only way they could get workers to do the job was to bring them in from China. More than fifteen thousand Chinese immigrants were brought in. Just imagine how many shiploads of people it must have been.

"They were spread out along the route between Salt Lake City and Sacramento while the line was under construction. But when it was completed, there was no other work available for all those Chinese workers. Most of them returned to San Francisco because that's where they originally landed, when they came there."

By now, they had arrived back at the teahouse. It seemed obvious that Fr. Katz was not finished with what was on his mind, so they kept walking.

"Back in San Francisco, no one would hire them either. Only the most menial or dirtiest of jobs were available to them. Most could not speak English, so it was difficult for them even to apply for work. They had to settle for jobs as housekeepers and nannies. Mostly, they had to congregate together and run their own businesses. Laundries were among the most common, and profitable. Caucasians were not above having their laundry done at cheap prices. It was a simple drop-off and pick-up procedure where they did not have to spend much time with the shopkeepers.

"This is where prejudice comes into play. Japanese are victims of prejudicial treatment just as the Chinese are. Especially those who don't speak English. If you go there, it will be extremely difficult for you to find work for which you are qualified. You will most likely have to take a menial job, such as washing dishes or laundry, just to survive.

"The Chinese have banded together in an area called 'Chinatown.' Almost every Chinese person lives and works in Chinatown. Those who work as domestic help have to walk, often long distances, to reach their place of employment. A select few are shuttled to work by their wealthy employers, but it's not an easy existence. There is also a 'Japantown.' It is not as large, but exists for the same reason. Caucasians don't want to mingle with 'foreigners.' Especially foreigners from Asia.

"My point is simply this. I don't know how happy you would be in a place like that, where you are often judged by how you look. You will have trouble finding work. Especially work befitting a person of your intellect and ability. And there are very few women of marriage age in California. You might even have trouble finding friends. I just want you to be happy."

Isamu was quiet as they walked. They were already beyond the church. He waited to see if Fr. Katz had finally spoken his mind. It was most assuredly a lot to share. Isamu knew it must have been weighing heavily on his mind. He slowed to a stop to see if the priest would follow suit. When he did, Isamu looked briefly at him and turned. As if by unspoken signal, they headed back to the teahouse.

Walking back, Isamu said, "Thank you, for telling me this. I can see you are thinking of my well-being. I value your opinion and your advice." They walked a bit further, and Isamu continued, "Do you think it necessary to tell my parents about our talk?"

"I think you are mature enough to tell them what you think they should know. I will leave that to you," he replied.

They walked another block before Isamu asked, "Could you teach me some basic English words? Maybe enough to get me started, at least?"

Fr. Katz smiled. "I guess that means I haven't talked you out of it? In that case, yes, I can help you learn some basic English."

They agreed to spend two hours every Sunday. They would start next week.

CHAPTER 29
ENGLISH LESSONS

FEBRUARY 1899 – KAMAISHI TEAHOUSE

Fr. Katz wrote down numbers from one through twenty. Alongside, he wrote the English graphic for each number, followed by the phonetic sound of the number. Then he had Isamu say each number in English, from one through twenty.

Every day after that, Isamu would count his shovels full of coal using English. One, two, three, four…up to twenty scoops. After twenty scoops, he would start over again at one and repeat the process.

On subsequent Sundays, Fr. Katz introduced common phrases such as 'Good morning,' 'Good afternoon,' 'Good evening,' 'Hello,' 'Excuse me,' and so on. Following each new exercise, Isamu spent the following week at work practicing the phrases. After that, he memorized the days of the week and the months of the year.

For the next three months, Isamu practiced his English vocabulary to help get him through the physical labor of his days. He counted every time he scooped a shovel of coal. He recited the days of the week. He carried on conversations with himself at times throughout the day.

"Good morning, sir."
"Good afternoon, ma'am."
"Good evening, gentlemen."
"Which way to St. Mary's church?"
"Thank you."

Jin learned to simply smile to himself and shake his head when he encountered his young charge talking in nonsensical sounds. He was getting the work done. In fact, he was the best worker Jin could remember at that job. He tried not to think about the day when Isamu would give it up, and leave for America.

But the day did come. It was Saturday, May twentieth, 1899. Isamu was scheduled to depart from Yokohama on the eighth day of June. Before leaving, he wanted to make one more trip on the fishing boat, and one more delivery to Kitakami and Osaki. There were a lot of goodbyes he needed to say before leaving.

Arriving home from work on the twentieth, Isamu hurried to his room and added this week's six yen to his hidden jar. He counted it every week, and today was no exception. He counted one hundred and ten yen. After paying his remaining steamship fare, he would have forty yen when he arrived in America. It should be enough, unless he had trouble finding work.

Meisa showed him a special money belt she made for him. He was to wear it under his kimono, where no one could see it. Fr. Katz had warned them about the dangers of traveling to big cities, and he explained what a pickpocket was. Toshi, having grown up in Tokyo, was already aware of them but chose not to cause further alarm to Ayami by bringing it up in her presence.

Isamu enjoyed his last fishing trip, but it was not an emotional experience. It was a different matter, however, for the trip to Kitakami and Osaki. He enjoyed the stops at Tōno, Oshu, Ichinoseki, and Kurihara. Largely because he had formed those contracts himself.

But when they reached Kitakami and found the Empress waiting on the veranda, he knew it would not be an easy parting. He stepped down from the wagon and toward the legendary woman. While still some distance away, he could see her fighting back tears. The samurai warrior, veteran of multiple combat battles, and intimidating simply by her presence, was fighting back tears. Isamu had not prepared for that. He slowed his step and tried to glance left and right, pretending it was simply a routine encounter, forcing the best smile he could muster, but knowing it was fake.

When he reached her, still unprepared, the Empress wrapped him in her large and muscular arms and held him motionless for what seemed forever. He had to force his breathing to compensate for the tightness in his chest and abdomen. Eventually, she released him and stood back a step to simply look at him.

"You've grown into a man," she said. "A handsome one at that," she continued, as a smile appeared on her face. "Toshi must be very proud of you. And Ayami, too. They have raised a good son. You will make them proud from America, too. I'm sure of it. Just don't forget who you are or where you came from. When you get lonely, think of us and remember that we're thinking of you in return."

Then she acknowledged Kazuo and his oldest son, Kaneto, who was taking over Isamu's place in the wagon. "So, what have you got for me today, my friends? Did you bring any special surprises to commemorate Isamu's last trip?"

Her voice had returned to normal, along with her business woman's disposition. They unloaded the shipment of fish, shared a lunch of tea, rice, and smoked fish with the Empress, then loaded rice from the warehouse and headed south to Osaki. "We'll see you again the day after tomorrow," Kazuo said as the wagon pulled away.

Isamu could not help but repeat it: "I'll see you soon." But he said it in English, so no one else understood. Finally, a half-kilometer down the road, Kazuo began to laugh for no apparent reason. He had figured it out.

The final reunion with Cho was unexpected. This was a man Isamu had never quite figured out, much as Toshi and Haruki had never figured him out. At times, he seemed only interested in profit, without regard to friendships or relationships. At other times, he could show a different side. He was always pleasant enough in his dealings with Isamu, but Isamu was never sure how much trust to place in him. It was true; he did seem to be treating the workers better. He was buying more food, at any rate. Isamu could only assume it was finding its way to the workers. And they appeared to be better fed on the occasions he was actually able to see them. But when he tallied it up, Isamu felt justified in thinking the relationship was based purely on profit.

That is why, when they entered the factory and were led up the stairs to Cho's office, they were surprised when Cho greeted them with the biggest smile any of them had ever seen. And even more so when he picked up a small wooden trunk with both hands and presented it to Isamu.

"Here is a little gift for you," he said. "In appreciation for what your company has done for our factory. We want to wish the best of luck to you on your travels to America. It must be a very exciting proposition for you. If I were a younger man, I would be eager to join you," he added.

Feeling it would be impolite not to open the trunk, Isamu felt obliged to do so. He took more time than necessary to unhook the two latches that sealed the lid, giving him time to consider his response. When he slowly lifted the lid, he was even more surprised to find what must have been a hundred spools of fine silk thread, separated in rows by what seemed to be every color of the rainbow.

"I thought you might enjoy having a few examples of what we actually make here in the factory," he explained. "You have called on us many times over the years, but I don't think you ever really had a chance to see the results of our work. These are samples of what I consider the finest silk thread made in Japan.

As you can see, there are dyes to make every color you can dream of. And every one of them a perfect example of our work. Our standards are unmatched anywhere," he said, "not only in Japan, but even in China or England. Some people think China produces the best silk, but that isn't true. It might have been at one time, but no longer. Japan makes the best silk in all the world. And we make the best silk in all of Japan."

Following the silk factory, they made a stop at the emporium of Cho's cousin in Osaki, and then returned to Kitakami. The Empress beamed as she presented Isamu with two durable, if noticeably not lavish, travel cases. "You should not look too prosperous," she explained, "otherwise, you will be an obvious target for the unscrupulous. These may not look expensive, but they are excellent quality, and they will last for many years.

The trip back to Kamaishi seemed the shortest he'd ever made.

PART FOUR

The Voyage

CHAPTER 30
TIME TO SAY GOODBYE

JUNE 05, 1899 – KAMAISHI

Not one cloud filled the early morning sky on Monday, June fifth, 1899. Isamu gazed eastward from beneath a towering pine just beyond the garden, where he'd spent countless hours helping his mother while growing up.

He tried to remember the rules of a game he'd played with Kiyoshi and Meisa when they were little. The one where they watched for the flaming round crest of the sun, as it broke free of the watery horizon at dawn. They each made a wish at that very moment. But he could not remember how it ended. *Did they have to see if their wish came true in order to win the game?* He wasn't sure. For today, he wanted merely to collect the image of the sunrise forever in his mind, in case he never saw it again.

Lost in reverie, he jumped lightly at the sound of his father's gentle voice behind him.

"Do you remember when you were little?" he asked, "and I told you the sun was a giant ball of fire? When it began to rise into the sky, you asked me why the water didn't put out the fire."

Isamu laughed at the memory. "I guess it was a childish question," he said. "To me, it looked like the sun came up out of the water in the morning, since there was no other horizon except the water."

"Actually, it was a very good question, which is why I never forgot it. For a five-year-old, it told me you had a very curious mind. If the sun actually lifted from out of the water, then why indeed, would the water not douse the fire?"

Both men watched as the sun rose in the eastern sky. They silently absorbed the colors, changing across the horizon for as far as they could see.

Then Toshi said, "You have always displayed a level of maturity above your years. If not for that, I could never have consented to let you leave. Fr. Katz told me there are many dangers in California. I have faith you will choose wisely in your decisions, just as you have always done while in our care. He also told me it will be a difficult life for you, and that, in spite of the possibilities for success, it could also end in disappointment. Promise me that, if at the end of one year, it is not turning out as you planned, you will come back to us. I will gladly pay your fare, if necessary. We'll do our best to find you work that makes you happy."

Then he turned his gaze down to the harbor, hoping Isamu couldn't see his face. He stopped talking only because he felt his voice begin to crack.

Isamu dared not turn to face him either, for fear of losing his own, as well as his resolve. "Thank you, Papa. I will."

The entire family met at the teahouse for the final trek to the harbor. Haruki and his family, along with Kazuo, and his family were there, too. Fr. Katz went so far as to reschedule daily mass in order to join them. The packet ship was scheduled to leave at 10:00 sharp. At 8:30, the group left the teahouse, with Isamu surrounded by his parents and siblings. Kiyoshi carried one travel case, while Kaneto carried the other. Meisa asked him multiple times if he was wearing his special money belt, just to make sure.

Kamaishi was the end point of the packet ship's coastal route. It made the trip from Yokohama weekly, arriving on Sunday night and returning on Monday morning, with stops along the way. The *S.S. Coptic* was scheduled to depart on Wednesday afternoon for Honolulu. If everything went according to plan, the packet would arrive in Yokohama early Wednesday morning. Isamu said a prayer, asking for an uneventful trip. If anything went wrong, he might miss the *Coptic*. His only choice would have been to leave Kamaishi one week earlier. It was tempting, but then he considered the cost of staying in Yokohama for a week. He decided to take the chance and save the money.

Not many passengers boarded the packet at Kamaishi. Not many people had the money or a reason to travel. He finally took a travel case in each hand and walked up the gangplank to find his place. Nearing the top, he turned back and broke out in a giddy smile, in spite of the fears gnawing at his stomach. He rested one of the cases on deck long enough to wave good-bye to his parents, his family, his friends, and the village of Kamaishi, which had watched him grow since infancy. He found himself blinking more frequently the longer he viewed the familiar scene. At one point, he glanced across the harbor to see the early-returning fishing boats, home from a night at work. He waved to them as well.

One by one, as they realized who it was, they stood and waved back with arms high in the air.

Then he heard a command from the captain, followed by deckhands unlashing the thick, heavy ropes tied to the dock. He smelled the fresh burst of smoke emitting from the stack and felt the thrust of steam making its way to the powerful propeller. A blast from the horn filled the air, and the boat began to move. This was something altogether different than his time under the sailing power of a fishing boat, and it brought a smile to his face. He shifted to the rear deck as the vessel picked up speed. There he set down both cases, spread his feet apart to brace against the motion of the boat in the waves, and waved until he could no longer make out the figures waving back.

The packet pushed offshore just far enough to keep the coastline in distant view. Once away from the harbor, it set a course south-southwest to the first stop at Ofunato. Beyond that, they would stop at a dozen or more ports, the names of which Isamu had never heard. Names like Haragama, Choshi, and Okitsu. By Chikura, Isamu could only wonder if they were still on schedule.

He searched throughout the decks and companionways of the small ship, looking for a map of the intended route. Finding none, his only option was to continually inquire of one of the deckhands. Their reply was always the same: "We're exactly where we're supposed to be," which did not serve as comfort to Isamu. It had not exactly answered the question.

Unable to sleep, Isamu roamed the deck for much of the night, and noted with excitement when, sometime just before midnight on Tuesday, a lighthouse off the starboard bow beamed a stream of light far into the night at regular intervals. He remembered hearing one of the crew telling another that when they reached the lighthouse, they would meet for a 'seaman's salute' in gratitude for a safe return. From the sound of their voices, he gathered the salute was something more in the form of raising a cup than raising a hand. He decided to walk the deck to see if he could find the two sailors performing their salute.

As he expected, the decks were empty. At this time of night, the only activity of any kind was that of a few dark shadows, reflected in the window of the captain's bridge, high above the deck. But he felt the motion of the ship as it turned in the direction of the light, the shift to a northerly course. If that were true, they would soon be entering Tokyo Bay. His muscles relaxed at the thought of reaching Yokohama. He wondered how crossing the Pacific would compare to a sail down the coast, where land was always just within reach.

Approaching the dock at Yokohama brought back the words of Fr. Katz regarding Kamaishi and San Francisco. The harbor at Yokohama was also as different from the harbor at Kamaishi as night was from day. Isamu counted at least twenty large ships, either tied at the pier or anchored just beyond. The dock was filled with people walking, waiting, and milling, dressed in every color imaginable. Even from a distance, the noise of the crowd carried to the deck of the *City of Tokyo*. His tension rose in unison with his excitement. Never had he seen such a throng of people going in so many directions, seemingly all at once.

CHAPTER 31
YOKOHAMA

JUNE 08, 1899 – YOKOHAMA

Passengers on board the *City of Tokyo* began to form a line as soon as the packet approached the pier. Having been told nothing about the process, Isamu simply gathered up his belongings and followed along. He waited in a line behind thirty others, each with a travel case or bag close at hand. They watched as the dockhands grabbed the ropes and tied the vessel with no more effort than taking a stroll through the park.

Then, at the command of the ship's captain, the railing was removed and the gangplank lowered in place. The captain stood at the rail, smiling politely at each departing passenger. To his right stood the first mate, followed in line by the second mate. Unlike the captain, they each held one hand extended, on the hopeful chance that a departing passenger might feel obliged to hand over a coin or two in appreciation of their safe voyage.

Isamu was unprepared for the encounter, never having traveled before. By the time he realized what was happening, it was too late to set down his luggage and search for a coin without disclosing the secret money belt beneath his clothing. Grateful for the safe passage as well as a natural desire to do what was right, he regretted not having something to give. He could only bow to the mates and offer a sincere smile without holding up the remaining passengers.

Once off the vessel, his first priority was to find the *S.S. Coptic* and secure his passage. He thought he'd spotted it as the packet was making its way to the wharf. Now, however, with so many people milling along the pier, he could barely see above them to find his way. He held his two cases tightly, one in each hand, and slowly jostled his way toward the far end of the pier. Even though it was still early morning, he began to worry about the time. How soon prior to departure he needed to be on board, he didn't know.

The day was beginning to warm, and Isamu was beginning to worry. He felt beads of sweat form beneath his clothing. Carrying two travel cases only made matters worse. He was hungry and especially thirsty, but dared not stop at one of the many available vendors until after he obtained his passage.

Adding to his anxiety was the seemingly endless stream of intoxicated patrons traveling the walkway. Every fourth one seemed intent on bumping into Isamu. At first, he was polite and smiled at their apology for being so clumsy. But he found himself becoming jaded the longer he walked. Bumping him was one thing, but occasionally he felt a hand against his side or back. Surely the bumping was bad enough, without needing his body to regain their balance. And why would so many people be drunk this early in the day? It was disgusting. Then he remembered what Fr. Katz had told him about San Francisco, about opium dens and saké houses, and the general state of decay of so many of its residents.

Still making his way toward the *Coptic*, another of Fr. Katz's cautions finally came to mind, and when it did, Isamu froze in alarm. Pickpockets! These are not drunks; he finally realized, they are pickpockets! He quickly turned away from the row of ships, toward the less crowded section of the walkway. There he found a small space empty of people, set down both his cases, and tried as inconspicuously as possible to feel the special belt Meisa had made for him.

At first, he could not feel anything underneath his clothing, and panic set in. He looked quickly around to see if he was being watched. Satisfied that he was not, he felt the area just to the left of his belly button, hoping to feel the presence of a small pad that was not part of his clothing. He almost shouted in relief when his fingers confirmed its presence. Meisa had saved the day. He would write to her the minute he was settled on the *Coptic*.

He still had his money, but time was running out. He grabbed both cases and hurried back to the boardwalk, this time staying farther away from the crowded throng. Making his way along the wharf, searching the bow of each successive ship for the name *Coptic*, he glanced to his left, and whether by accident or divine intervention he couldn't know, just in time to see the words *Occidental and Oriental Steamship Company, Ticket Office*, painted prominently on the front of a small building adjacent to the pier.

He changed his course and headed directly for the sign, which was located above the door of a sturdy but austere wooden structure. He held both bags tightly, one under his arm and the other by its handle, while he pulled open the oversized entrance door. Once inside, he saw a line of six or seven people waiting their turns at the counter labeled *ticket agent*. He stepped to the end of the line and, with little time to spare, inquired of the last person ahead of him. "Is this the line to purchase tickets for the *Coptic*?"

The elderly man smiled back at Isamu. "Yes, young man, this is the line. Are you sailing to Honolulu?"

Isamu nodded his head in reply. "Yes, thank you for the information." The line moved slowly. Isamu began to perspire as his anxiety increased. He relaxed slightly as first one, then another traveler filed in line behind him. Apparently, there was still time for them to board.

When Isamu's turn came at the head of the line, he gave the man his name, "Isamu Ozawa, from the village of Kamaishi. I have a reservation on the *S.S. Coptic* bound for Honolulu, and from there, on to San Francisco," he said.

The man opened a ledger and fanned through several pages. Isamu watched as the man scoured each page, looking for the name. "Ozawa?" he asked.

"Yes," replied Isamu. "Isamu Ozawa."

The beads of sweat began to form again. First on his forehead, spreading to his brow, then down the back of his neck.

The man turned to another page in his ledger. As Isamu watched his finger slide methodically down the page, line by line, it faltered, and then halted. "Isamu Ozawa," the man repeated. "Transport on steamship *Coptic*, from Yokohama to Honolulu, then to San Francisco, California," he continued as confirmation.

Isamu exhaled the breath he had not realized he was holding. "Yes, that's me," he gushed. "How much is the remaining fare?"

"You made a deposit of ten yen, dated February twenty-six," he replied. "Your balance before boarding is seventy yen. You can pay it now." In his hurry to find the ticket office, Isamu had neglected to remove the fare from his money belt. To retrieve it now would let every person in the ticket office know of his secret belt. He would be an easy target once alone on the ship.

He tried to think of a solution, but nothing came to mind. He then tried to stall for time while he continued to think. He reached into each of his visible pockets, padding them profusely, in an effort to demonstrate his intent. Finally, he admitted to the agent behind the grated window. "I seem to have misplaced my money packet. I must have put it in one of my travel cases. It would be rude to open them here for other passengers to see. Do you by chance have a storage room or closet I might retire to, long enough to search my luggage?"

The agent looked over Isamu's shoulder at the line. It was still growing at the end as fast as it was shrinking at the front. "I don't have all day for this. In future, you must remember to have your payment ready when you reach the window. Since you're obviously a newcomer, I'm willing to allow it just this once. See that doorway at the back of the lobby? Knock and tell the person who opens it I have granted permission for you to enter. But you have only five minutes. If you're not back by the time I finish the next customer, you will have to go to the end of the line and start over. Perhaps your parents were wise to send you away if you're unable to make simple decisions."

Isamu blushed as he grabbed his two cases and hurried to the door at the back of the room. He knocked, then waited for it to open. When nothing happened, he knocked a second time, this time with more urgency. Again, he waited. Finally, he saw the handle turn, followed by a crack in the opening. As the door opened further, a man in uniform peered back at Isamu with a quizzical look on his face. Isamu tilted his head toward the grated window, behind which, the agent glanced back at the two of them and nodded. At that, the man behind the door opened it enough for Isamu to quickly squeeze through and allow the door to close behind him.

Isamu first looked around the room, which appeared to be a rather plush parlor or library. The walls were dark paneled wood with intricate trim. There was an electric lamp glowing at a small table in the center of the room and another in each of the corners. Two large windows opened in the direction of the wharf. Looking out, Isamu could clearly see the Steamship *S.S. Coptic*, tied at the pier, just across the way.

Isamu saw no other people in the room, much to his relief. Surely this man, dressed in a distinguished uniform, would pose no threat to the exposure of his secret money belt. Isamu looked at the man, bowed, and said, "My apology for disturbing you. In my rush to find the ticket office, I neglected to retrieve my payment. And I was reluctant to retrieve it in front of others in the lobby, whom I do not personally know. With your liberty, may I please retrieve it now, so I can pay the remaining fare and secure passage on the *Coptic*?"

The man looked at Isamu with soft, almost sparkling eyes, and nodded. Without saying a word, the man then walked to the window and, with deliberate movement, gazed intently out, as if something nearby was the sole focus of his concentration. When the man finally cleared his throat gently, Isamu grasped his meaning.

He quickly untied the *obi* from around his waist, pulled the right-hand side of his *Nagigi* robe out from under the left, and slipped a hand next to his stomach until he felt the secret belt. Then he opened the special flap Meisa had sewn, and pulled out several paper bills. He counted them, then reached in to retrieve several more. He counted them a second time, then placed one of the bills back in his belt, closed the flap, tucked one side of his robe under the other, and re-tied his *obi*. Then he signaled to the man with a gentle clearing of his own throat.

Isamu could not wait for further expressions of gratitude; his five minutes were almost up. "Thank you, kind sir," Isamu said as he turned to leave. "You have been very helpful." With that, he bolted for the door with a case in each hand and made his way back to the head of the ticket line, waiting for the current traveler to finish. He then handed the agent his seventy yen, fresh from the money belt. The man, in return, handed Isamu two paper documents.

"These are your permission slips to board, both here and in Honolulu. Whatever you do, do not lose them...like you did with your payment," he added. "Your passage is for steerage-level deck. You may claim any unoccupied berth. All luggage must be stored in one of the lockers provided. You are not to place anything on the floor beneath your berth. You will understand why on your way across the Pacific. Keep all belongings in your storage locker. Steerage passengers...that includes you, will begin boarding in one hour. Do not be late, or you will miss the boat," he chuckled. It must have been his favorite joke, as Isamu heard him repeat it to every passenger.

Isamu gripped both his cases protectively as he exited the ticket office and proceeded back to the pier. He considered buying chicken on a stick from one of the vendors working the crowds among the travelers, but decided instead to get a closer look at the *S.S. Coptic*.

Fighting the crowds, he made his way close to the ship. The mooring lines tied to the dock were the biggest he had ever seen. He stifled the urge to grab hold of one with his hand to see if he could reach all the way around it with this thumb and fingers, mostly because he didn't want to let loose of either travel case with so many strangers close at hand. Or, just as ominous, what if one should accidentally get knocked into the water? It would be as good as lost. Measuring the mooring line is something he could do while bored at sea.

He slowly walked the length of the ship, unable to fully concentrate on how large it really was because of his lingering fear of pickpockets. Each time he felt someone brush against his arm or back, he reacted with a jerk and a stare. Even so, the size of the ship was not lost on him. It was the largest he had ever seen. He tried to count the number of steps between the bow and stern, but with so many people in the way, he lost count.

There were already a number of first-class passengers strolling about on the upper deck, able to board before everyone else. He tried to guess how many first-class cabins lined the perimeter, and then he wondered what the steerage deck was like. There were no portholes along the entire side of the ship. *They must be on the other side,* he decided.

As he gazed at the magnificent vessel, he saw movement on the dock. Passengers were starting to take their place in line. He remembered the agent's instruction to take any berth available, and he wanted to be among the first to board. He made his way to the sign that read, *Steerage Boarding*.

The crowd had thinned by now. First-class passengers were already on board, and those remaining at the pier were in steerage class like himself. The line continued to grow, but not yet move. A large Japanese man stepped into the line behind Isamu.

Even though Isamu concentrated on the line ahead of him, as well as his two cases and always his money belt, he sensed someone standing behind and turned just enough to catch a glimpse from the corner of his eye.

He winced at the size of the man. He was more than a head taller than Isamu and nearly twice as wide. He appeared to be in his mid-twenties, maybe even thirty, though he might have looked older because of his size. Trying not to be discourteous, Isamu turned back and forced his attention to the forward portion of the line.

As time went by and the line failed to move, he joined the others in becoming restless. More than an hour had passed since the agent told him they would begin boarding. He turned to view the line behind him, curious at how much it had grown since he had joined. This time, he had little option but to acknowledge the man directly behind. Trying to strike up a friendly conversation, he first bowed politely to the man, then addressed him, "I thought the line would start moving by now."

The man bowed respectfully in return and smiled briefly, but said nothing.

Isamu felt awkward. Should he try again to show his openness toward the man, or simply ignore him and turn back around? His instinct was to turn around, but something nudged him to try again. It occurred to him to ask a question rather than simply make a statement. That way, the man would be forced to respond. And if he didn't, then Isamu would turn and respect his privacy.

"Are you staying in Hawaii or going on from there?"

The man gazed back at Isamu, and his face began to flush. His eyes held Isamu, and his face contorted ever so slightly. Then his cheeks and lips began to quiver before a short series of "C...Ca...Ca..." emerged from his mouth, followed by the word "Cali...f...for...fornia!" Then his face relaxed in a sigh of relief, and a small smile returned.

The otherwise formidable man was burdened with a speaking disorder. He stuttered.

Isamu had only known one person who stuttered. It was one of the patrons at the teahouse. He recalled how difficult it was for the man to order his food.

Isamu felt sorry for the man behind him as he thought back to the patron at the teahouse. He responded, "I'm also going to California. This is my first trip away from home, and I'm a little nervous about it. Would you mind if I stayed close to you along the way? Maybe we could even find two berths close together."

The man smiled back at Isamu. "Y...Y...Yes," he replied simply.

Just then, the line began to move.

CHAPTER 32
NOT CHO AT THE DOCK

JUNE 08, 1899 – YOKOHAMA WHARF

Facing toward the ship as the line progressed, Isamu noticed three men, not in the line, but close enough to see their faces and hear their voices. He stopped short when one of the men briefly looked in his direction during what appeared to be an argument between them. The man looked so much like Cho from the silk factory that Isamu was just about to wave to him. Then he realized it wasn't Cho, but the resemblance was unmistakable. Isamu then took note of the two companions. One was decidedly younger than 'Cho' but could possibly have been his son.

The other, about the same age as 'Cho,' wore a uniform of the military police. At least that's what he assumed. Isamu had never seen a real *Kempeitai* before. He'd only heard about them from the Empress.

He watched the trio as the boarding line inched slowly closer toward them. The young one seemed to favor his left leg as he stood. He had not walked much while Isamu watched, but he definitely limped when he did. When the line passed by where they stood, Isamu was able to hear a short exchange between two of them.

"It's your choice, Orochi," the man in uniform said, speaking to the young one. "You either board this ship or return to prison. If you board the ship, you may disembark in Honolulu, or stay on board to San Francisco, or even transfer to a different ship bound for Australia. But today, you have only two choices. Get on the ship or go back to prison. If you board this ship, you are forbidden ever to return."

The young one glared at the third man, the one Isamu thought might have been Cho. The man glared back. "I warned you. You're lucky to have a choice at all." Then he turned away from the younger man.

The boarding line moved steadily, if slowly, taking Isamu and the large man past the trio standing alongside the line. Isamu, of course, was only a boy when the holdup occurred on the road from Osaki. He might have heard Kazuo and his father recount the frightening experience over the years, but it was not a memory close at hand. The name 'Orochi' did not connect.

Of greater concern for the moment was finding a berth, and safely stowing his few belongings. Neither Isamu nor the large man behind him gave the trio another thought. Neither had a feeling, though perhaps they should, that having a criminal on board could surely lead to trouble.

As his turn to show boarding documents drew near, Isamu paid close attention to the man ahead of him. His habit of trying to always be prepared was hard to break. The ship's mate assigned to clear them for boarding held a list of names, dutifully checking to make sure anyone who attempted to board was registered and paid in full. The mate then asked a few questions to confirm it was the person noted on his list. Name, destination, occupation. They were easy enough questions, as long as the person was actually who they purported to be.

When Isamu's turn came, he was ready with his answers almost before the ship's mate was able to ask. Isamu Ozawa. San Francisco. Fisherman. He could have answered multiple ways to the last question and still been truthful. The mate followed Isamu's answers as he looked at his list of names. Satisfied by Isamu's answers, he was about to read him a list of boarding instructions.

That's when Isamu thought of the large man behind him. Would the man's stutter be cause to deny him passage to America? Before the mate could begin reciting his list, Isamu set his two precious travel bags on the deck, turned to the man behind, and motioned with one hand for him to step forward. Then he looked quickly into his face as he reached for the man's left hand, the one holding his boarding document.

"We're together," Isamu told the mate. "My friend is timid, so I sometimes speak for him."

The mate eyed Isamu carefully. He shifted his gaze to the large man standing next to him. Then he addressed the large man, "Is that true? Do you wish for him to do your speaking?"

The large man, noticeably tense, managed a smile that appeared sincere to both Isamu and the mate. He nodded his head and mouthed a nearly silent, but definitely vocal, "Y…Yes."

The mate continued to gaze at the man as he asked the same three questions: "Name? Destination? Occupation?"

Isamu stole a quick look at the name on his ticket and replied, "Matsu Konishi. San Francisco. Fisherman."

The mate then looked sternly at them both as he read from his list.

"It says here you're a carpenter," he said to the large man.

"Yes, that's true," Isamu quipped. "He is both a carpenter and a fisherman. Like myself, he has several occupations. We are hoping it will make finding a job easier in America if we have qualifications for more than one type of work."

The sailor considered his response briefly and then motioned for them to step on board. Whether he believed Isamu or was merely pressed to get passengers boarded on time, Isamu could not determine. But he let them pass.

"Follow the line ahead of you down the stairs to steerage deck, also known as 'S' deck. At the bottom of the steps, turn right. Look for an empty berth and claim it by placing an item on the bunk. That is where you will spend most of your voyage. You may visit the upper deck daily between the hours of 6:00 a.m. and 7:00 a.m., and again between the hours of 4:00 p.m. and 5:00 p.m. Those are the only two hours you are allowed on the main deck.

"Keep your boarding pass with you at all times. Notice that it contains a large letter 'S' in the upper corner. That identifies you as a passenger in steerage. If you are caught on the upper deck at any time other than the aforementioned hours, your document will be confiscated. Without your document, you will no longer be allowed on the main deck.

"Meals on the steerage deck will be served at 7:00 a.m., 12:00 p.m., and 5:00 p.m. The serving lines will remain open for one hour. After that time, food will not be served. If you miss a meal, it is your fault only.

"Any luggage you do not want to keep in your bunk must be placed in a storage locker along either outside wall of the ship. The lockers do not have locks. If you want to purchase a lock, see the ship's purser. The Purser's Office for 'S' deck is located at midship. The galley on 'S' deck is located at the bow, forward of the Purser's Office. No luggage is to be stored under your berth. If you store anything under your berth, it is guaranteed to get wet. Unless you want to wear soggy clothing, do not place it under your berth. If there are no questions, proceed to your berth."

Isamu moved forward to the stairwell, one suitcase in each hand. His fellow passenger followed close behind. The doorway was propped open, but when they descended downward to the steerage deck, sunlight slipped farther away with every step. At the bottom, an oil lantern hung from a wooden beam, which gave out just enough light to find their footing. They both stopped to let their eyes adjust before entering the large, open chamber. One side of the aisle was lined with a row of double bunks, as far as he could see. On the other side, the outer wall of the ship contained a row of lockers, one above the other, also as far as he could see.

Isamu instinctively began walking toward the rear of the ship, looking for a pair of empty bunks. He had taken only a few steps in that direction when Matsu tugged on his arm.

"M...M...Mid...dle s...sh...ship," Matsu said amidst his stutters. "M...M...More s...st...stab...stable." He continued.

Isamu looked first at Matsu and then around the ship. Passengers were filing in behind them, and one by one, claiming their berths.

"We need to hurry and find a place," he said to Matsu. "They're filling up fast." He started again toward the rear of the ship.

Matsu tugged at his sleeve a second time. "N...No," he said. "F...Fol...Follow m...me."

Then Matsu picked up his luggage and headed for the middle of the ship. The aisles were getting more and more congested as passengers continued to file down the stairs. With the big man leading the way in front, Isamu grabbed one case in each hand, so tight that his fingers were turning white, and followed along behind.

Matsu peered through the shadowy light, searching for two empty bunks as close to midship as possible. On the far side of the ship, he spotted two, on the starboard side, one aisle away from the storage lockers. "At least we'll be close to our luggage," Isamu said.

They each laid claim to a bunk by placing their luggage on it. Isamu motioned for Matsu to take the lower bunk while he claimed the upper. Having completed their mission, they looked around at their surroundings. There were oil lamps scattered at intervals throughout the area, but without windows, it was hardly enough even to be considered moonlight.

Then a stench caught their senses. It was not a common odor, though parts of it seemed familiar. The smell of workers at the foundry came to mind. That smell when Isamu was so hot and tired he could hardly move—the smell of sweaty coal workers at the end of the day. But there were other smells mixed in as well. The one most foul, reminded Isamu of the last time Meisa was sick and threw up her supper of fish and beans. But there was yet another odor as well. One that reminded him of little Mamiko, when she ate too much applesauce and filled her underwear with a smell that made him hold his nose until she left the room.

Sitting on the edge of his bunk and gazing to his left, toward the stern of the ship, he could see only a glimpse of the vast sleeping area surrounding them. The movement of heads, arms, luggage, and items he could not identify obscured his view. The noise of conversations, too numerous to count, added to the hectic scene. Across the aisle from where he sat came the sounds of multiple conversations at once. "Where are you from?... Where are you going?... My name is... What's your name?... They didn't give us much room in here... Have you ever sailed before?... I hope we don't get seasick..."

Isamu, trying to force the scene into a semblance of logic in his mind, began by cataloging the layout of the ship. He knew they had entered the ship on its port side, which, from his fishing experience, he knew to be the left side of a vessel when standing at the stern and looking toward the bow.

Once they boarded and descended the stairs, they crossed over to the other side, the starboard side. They had selected bunks as close to midship as they could find. They were in the next-to-last row. By climbing up and sitting on his bunk, he counted sixteen rows between the two exterior walls of the ship. They were in the fifteenth row. Matsu claimed the lower berth, and Isamu took the upper.

Next to each of them, in row sixteen, were identical bunks. Only a small slat of wood separated a bunk from the one adjacent. Just as he was evaluating the layout, a rumpled, unkept man who appeared several years older than Isamu threw his luggage on the berth opposite him. "This bunk available?" he asked with what seemed more like a statement than a question.

"Yes." Isamu replied, with a disappointment he tried not to show.

A second man, seemingly traveling alone, followed close behind and claimed the lower berth, next to Matsu.

It was understood from the beginning, that every berth would be taken for the crossing, yet Isamu held out a whisper of hope that for some reason, whoever had spoken for it might somehow have a last-minute change in plans and not be able to board the ship.

Curious about how many passengers there were, he tried counting bunks, but with so much congestion, he settled for a rough estimate. Counting as many as he could see, he arrived at two hundred and fifty. Since he could only see a fourth of the area, he multiplied his count by four and came up with one thousand passengers. No wonder it was so noisy and crowded. It crossed his mind to calculate the *Coptic's* revenue from just this single crossing, but it could wait until later.

As he continued to scan the dim quarters, a hand touched his right foot, which only then did he realize was dangling off to the side of Matsu's berth, directly below. Isamu bent down to peer at his new companion, prepared to apologize for leaving his smelly foot so close to Matsu's head. But Matsu merely smiled and pointed to the row of storage lockers along the starboard wall just beyond row fifteen.

"C…C…Cho…Choos…Choose?" he was finally able to say.

When Isamu looked over at the wall of lockers, he saw a small number of passengers beginning to stow their belongings in one of the many available compartments. But it didn't take long to realize that once passengers had selected their berth, they would soon be making their way to the lockers.

This was the second time since boarding that Matsu had offered good advice. It was a good suggestion to find theirs early, while the selection was good. If they hurried, they should be able to find empty lockers close to their bunks.

Realizing a conversation with Matsu would be even more difficult with the noise and chaos surrounding them, Isamu formulated his question to allow a minimal reply. "Can you stay here and guard our bunks while I stow our luggage?"

Matsu nodded.

Isamu quickly scaled the short ladder down from his upper berth, grabbed one of his cases and the one belonging to Matsu, and made his way forward up the aisle to the end of their row, then back down the next aisle, which contained the lockers. He found two that were adjacent, directly across from their berths, and just as with their berths, one locker was up and the other below. He placed his in the upper and Matsu's in the lower. They would be easy to remember, and they were also within easy viewing distance from their berths.

He closed the locker doors, noticing there was provision for a lock, as they had been told at boarding. He wondered if he should purchase one.

He made his way back to their berths for his second bag. It was already more congested than when he began. The movement was made worse because of everyone scrambling with their luggage. *If we ever have to evacuate this space...* But he would not let himself finish the thought.

Reaching their bunks, he lifted the second bag from its place on his bunk, smiled at Matsu, and headed back up and around the aisle for his second trip. Already, he noticed passengers opening locker doors and peering in to determine if they were available. Nothing nefarious, he felt, just looking for an empty locker. But the fact that it was so easy for anyone to open a locker made him uneasy.

He stowed his second bag. This was the one with the silk thread samples from Cho, his notebook of names, and his year-long accumulation of ideas for setting up a trading company in America. It also contained the address of St. Mary's Church in San Francisco, in case Fr. Ramm was not there to meet him at the wharf. He took the first bag out of the locker and placed this one in first, then put the first bag on top, hoping to use it as a buffer to protect the second, smaller bag. The larger bag contained all of his clothes, but he could replace clothes. He casually placed his hands just above his waist and felt for the familiar pouch beneath. His money was safe.

The aisle back to his berth was, by now, not really an aisle at all, but simply a constant stream of humanity, all seemingly headed in opposite directions. He was relieved not to be encumbered by his luggage on the trip back.

With the aisle so busy, he was surprised to see Matsu standing, in front of his berth when at last he reached it. He turned to Isamu with a somber look. "Th...Th...that man with Kem...Kem...Kempei...Kempeitai," he started.

"The man we saw when we were boarding?"

"Y...Yes. He w...was h...here. He tr...tried t...to cl...claim y...your b...b...bunk."

"Are you sure it was him?"

Matsu nodded.

"What did you do?"

"I g...got... up from my b...b...bunk and th...then I l...looked d...d...down at h...him...and said N...No. It's t...taken." Then Matsu grinned.

"But I d...don't t...tr...trust h...him. His e...eyes are f...fil...filled w...with e...ev...evil."

"I'm afraid you're right, Matsu. It seems like I should know him from somewhere, but I can't figure out where. I think we should get locks for our lockers. It would be too easy for someone to pilfer from them while everyone is in the mess hall or sleeping. I can get one for you if you want me to. Until then, we should probably make sure one of us is always here to keep an eye on things."

Matsu nodded in agreement.

"I'll go right now, and maybe it won't be too crowded."

Matsu nodded again.

This time, Isamu had to find his way out of the sleeping quarters and forward of midship, if he remembered what they were told at boarding. Once clear of the bunks, there was hardly any congestion. He easily found his way forward until he encountered a huge space, almost as large as the sleeping quarters.

In place of rows and rows of berths, however, it was filled with rows and rows of tables. Closest to him, near midship, were two rows of tables, running perpendicular to the others. *Those must be the serving tables,* he decided. Matsu had been smart to realize the smoothest part of the ship would be close to the middle. He tried to envision feeding a thousand people with some semblance of order.

But he did not see the ship store. He was sure the crewman at boarding said it was between the sleeping quarters and the dining quarters, near the middle of the ship. There were fewer lanterns lit on this end of the ship, presumably because it was not yet mealtime.

The thought occurred to him about having to abandon ship in a hurry. Looking to both port and starboard, he spotted two forward stairwells leading up to the main deck. *It would be good to remember those,* he noted. He would bring Matsu on an exploratory tour as soon as they felt secure about the lockers and their bunks.

Turning inboard again, he scanned the deck for some sign of a store or even an office where he could inquire about the store. On his second look, he noticed a doorway with a small sign above. The letters were not in Japanese, so he was not sure what they said. But he did recognize the letters as English, based on his tutoring from Fr. Katz.

Approaching the door, he first knocked gingerly several times. He was sure he heard noises from within, but no one replied. Finally, he tried the latch to see if it was locked. The door squeaked loudly as it opened, putting Isamu on guard as to the consequences, if he were not allowed to be there.

Once open, he saw that it was indeed, a store. The lighting was significantly better than everywhere else on deck. There was a man behind the counter and another man standing in front of it. They seemed to be engrossed in a transaction of some sort, and Isamu, not wanting to intrude, stood back from them, waiting his turn.

At last, the man in front of the counter turned and walked out of the store. Isamu took his place at the counter and waited for the clerk to acknowledge him. "What do you want?" he finally asked.

"I would like to purchase two locks for the storage lockers," he replied. "Have I come to the right place?"

The man reached under the counter and pulled two padlocks from what must have been a large supply. He handed them to Isamu with no sign of emotion and simply said, "Two yen."

Isamu tried not to show his shock. Two yen for two locks, which should not have cost more than fifty *sen*. It was next to robbery. But what choice did he have? He knew instinctively the inflated cost would prevent many from locking their belongings, which made it even more prudent to put locks on their own.

"Do we get to keep the locks, or do we have to return them at the end of the voyage?" he asked.

"It's up to you," he replied. "We'll buy them back for twenty-five sen each, or you can take them with you."

At least they had sixteen days to decide, he thought. And then it occurred to him they might have good use for locks once they reached San Francisco. From the stories of Fr. Katz, thievery was not exactly an unknown sin there either. He grudgingly pulled two yen from the side pocket of his kimono and handed them across the counter.

He tried the key in each lock to make sure it worked to both lock and unlock each device. Then, on a whim, he traded keys to make sure they did not work in the other lock. He pretended to ignore the sarcastic look from the clerk, but the keys were not interchangeable.

Isamu bowed politely to the clerk, turned, and exited the store.

With the two locks now in hand, he headed directly for the storage lockers. The aisle was already more congested than when he'd left minutes before, but without luggage to slow him down, he was able to make his way to the two lockers. He quickly peeked inside each one to make sure their bags were still secure, then latched and locked them both.

He looked across the aisle, catching glimpses between the moving heads and jostling bodies. Matsu was looking back at him from his bunk. They exchanged short smiles of relief that both their luggage and their bunks were safely secured. His mission completed, Isamu turned to exit the busy locker aisle and return to their bunks.

Suddenly, and without warning, the air was filled with a loud wailing sound, almost like the moan of a giant animal. It was alarming, yet almost soothing. Isamu stopped where he stood, and when he'd gained enough composure to look around, he saw that everyone else was doing the same.

Nearly the entire 'S' deck stood frozen in place. Only a few continued with whatever they were doing. Of those, a few smiled, knowing the familiar sound of a ship's horn. They knew a single, long blast of the mighty horn was the signal they were about to depart.

Complete silence then turned to quiet murmurs as word spread of the impending movement. Isamu could feel the excitement beginning to grow. Tightly held faces up and down the aisle began to loosen. Eyes opened just a little wider. The adventure, in which every passenger was complicit, was about to begin. There was no turning back.

They were leaving their homeland—some of them forever.

CHAPTER 33
LEAVING JAPAN

JUNE 8, 1899 – YOKOHAMA WHARF

The sound of the ship's horn added to an already high sense of urgency, and passengers throughout the deck all seemed to want to be somewhere else from where they were. Those stowing their luggage carefully into lockers now tossed their bags with abandon and closed the door, heading for their bunks.

Those at their bunks felt the need to catch a last glimpse of the wharf and headed for the stairwell. That they were not allowed on main deck was lost in the moment, as they climbed as far as they could up the stairs. The first few only, were able to see the tops of a few nearby buildings, forced to shield their eyes from the bright summer sun.

Isamu continued toward his bunk, to find Matsu and give him the key to the locker. With passengers moving in all directions, he was able to fall in behind several others heading in that direction. Handing Matsu the key, he asked, "Do you want one last look? I know a place we can try."

Matsu nodded.

"Follow me," he said, and he led Matsu out of the sleeping quarters and toward the ship store. As soon as they left the sleeping area of the ship, the crowd diminished to almost nothing. The two of them hurried to the forward stairwell on their starboard side. The stairs were empty. It had not yet been discovered by other passengers.

They climbed to the top, where they were at least on equal footing with the main-deck passengers. By standing on tiptoe, they watched a small crowd of well-wishers waving back to friends or family members on board the *S.S. Coptic*.

As they scanned the dock, trying hard to etch the scene in their memory for as long as possible, the figures began to move slowly away from the ship. More accurately, the ship moved slowly away from the figures. As they strained to watch the heavy timber posts along the wharf, any doubt about their movement drifted away, like the dock.

From the stairwell leading below, the sound of a hundred cheering passengers wafted upward toward them. Passengers on the upper deck joined in the excitement, waving and cheering to those on land below. But the adventure for those three hundred on the main deck was in stark contrast to the thousand or more below. Theirs, an adventure of exciting new marvels of the world: below, a life of hope, hard work, and for most, disappointment.

The two men continued to gaze at the Yokohama skyline as it edged further from their view. Finally, they looked at one another and, without the need for words, returned to their bunks, relieved that no one else had claimed them during their absence.

Passengers still milled through the aisles, however, searching for an available berth. Isamu and Matsu sat next to each other on Matsu's bunk, as a signal they were taken. It crossed Isamu's mind briefly to offer his bunk to someone else, but he quickly concluded it would have no real impact. What they needed were more bunks.

As if reading his mind, a crew member came through the aisle with a message. "Those of you without a bunk, follow me..." he said. It began with a trickle. By the time he reached the stern and back up the adjacent aisle, it was growing. The man continued to weave down one aisle and up the next until they were mostly out of sight from aisle fifteen. After walking all the aisles, the group exited from aisle one, along the port-side lockers, and headed forward, toward the area of the ship's store.

Behind the store, in a darkened area Isamu had not seen earlier, was a rack of foldable cots, stacked from floor to ceiling. Pointing to the stack, the man instructed the line following behind. "Take a cot from the rack and find an available space to set it up. It will be your bunk for the duration of the trip. You can use the open space where we're standing now, between the ship's store and the portside gunnel. You can set up next to a friend, but you cannot block any aisles. Every man should also take a bucket. What are the buckets for? The buckets are for keeping your vomit off the floor. You can empty them in a trough at the back of the ship." Then he added, "Pleasant dreams," and walked away.

By now, Isamu could feel the motion of the ship while it picked up speed, as it navigated its way through Tokyo Bay and toward the Pacific. He felt the rhythm. It reminded Isamu of his nights on the fishing boats. This was going to be a pleasant journey, he decided, in spite of the darkness of their quarters. He climbed into his bunk and stretched out fully, enjoying the gentle motion of the waves below.

Gradually, the conversations and other noise subsided. Most of the passengers, just like him, realized they were tired. After days, even months, of planning for the trip, boarding, and finding their bunks, they were exhausted. Finally, they could relish the voyage and dream of what awaited them in Hawaii or California.

Isamu considered the words of the crew member. "Pleasant dreams," he told them. His tone suggested one of sarcasm, but at this moment, pleasant dreams were precisely what they were having.

In the lower bunk, Matsu dreamt of a small carpenter shop in a quiet section of town. He could see a wall of the shop filled with pegs and shelves, each peg holding a special saw. This one with large teeth for cutting rough wood, that one with small teeth for detail work. On another wall were carefully stored lengths of lumber, some of pine, some of oak, others of cherry or apple. In the middle of the shop was a large, sturdy table. That's where the real work was done. He would clamp together pieces of a table or chair, even cabinet doors or dressing table drawers. Windows across the front provided ample light on all but the cloudiest of days.

In the upper bunk, Isamu had a similar dream, though somewhat more grandiose. In his dream, he saw a modest shop in a busy part of town. A prominent sign out front clearly identified *Kamaishi Trading Company* as the occupant, behind large glass windows, along a crowded street. Inside, two, maybe even three other workers were busy taking orders from well-dressed customers. Behind the shop, just out back, was a large warehouse, larger even, than Kazuo's barn. It was filled to capacity with a dozen different items, just arrived from Japan. Rice, mostly, and silk. People in San Francisco had money for silk.

The ship's bell awoke Isamu just when, in his dream, an exceptionally wealthy-looking man entered the shop with a beautiful young woman at his side. It took a moment to reconcile the charmed life of a successful California business owner with the smokey, smelly, sleeping quarters of the steerage deck that surrounded him. He sat up in his bunk, looked around, then down to the lower bunk to see if Matsu was awake. His new friend was grinning up at him with a look that said, "How can you sleep at a time like this?"

"W…w… want t…to g…go up?" he asked, pointing to the main deck above. The bell was their signal that below-deckers could visit the main deck for an hour before the evening meal. Passengers from every aisle were heading to the stairs leading up.

Without bothering to answer, Isamu jumped down from his bunk, while Matsu rose from his. He looked at Isamu and tilted his head in the direction of the forward stairs, where they caught their final titillating views of Yokohama just hours before.

They hurried as much as they could while trying to not be noticeable to the other passengers, still unaware of the second set of forward stairs. They would find them soon enough, but for the moment, it was a tactical advantage. Once at the stairwell, they ascended two at a time, reaching the main deck and a clear view. Driven by an age-old human instinct, they proceeded directly toward the bow, where they'd have a panoramic and unobstructed view of whatever there was to see.

Their timing could not have been better. Off the port bow, the Sunosaki lighthouse marked the western tip of the peninsula. The finger protruded ten kilometers west into the tailings of Tokyo Bay. *Or maybe it was actually Sagami Bay at this point.* Either way, Isamu knew they were getting close to the Pacific. A few more kilometers, and the *Coptic* should bear to port, rounding the southern tip of the Boso Peninsula and clearing the Nojimasaki Lighthouse.

The landmarks were still familiar from his arrival yesterday on the packet ship. But they were easier to see from the higher deck of the *S.S. Coptic*. By now, the main deck was mostly filled, with passengers from below. They seemed to realize this would be their last chance at fresh air until tomorrow morning. To some, the fresh air was as important as their very last view of the country they were leaving behind.

Hardly had they adjusted to the sunshine and fresh air when the clanging of a bell captured their attention. It rang louder as the crewman approached from the stern. Their time for today was up. "Please return to the lower deck," came the instruction. "This deck will be available again tomorrow at six o'clock. Please return to the lower deck," he repeated as he circled the main deck, until it was finally emptied of its inferior guests.

Below deck, new lines had already begun to form. The mess hall was about to start serving. It seemed obvious to Isamu there were not as many benches as there were bunks. Those near the end of the line would have to wait for the early ones to finish eating in order to have a place to sit.

As they slowly approached the serving table, both men peered eagerly ahead to see what was about to be served. Next to two large tubs of rice were several baskets containing small portions of bread. There were also a number of smaller bowls, filled with olives, lemon slices, and one with something that looked like ginger roots.

At the first table, a worker handed them each a tin bowl and cup. "Keep these for the remainder of the voyage," he said. "You will use these for every meal. If you lose them, you will have to pay for a replacement at the ship store." Never having traveled on a ship before, Isamu could only assume this was the way of travel. He thought to himself how this would never happen at the teahouse. Every bowl and cup were thoroughly washed after every use. But this was not the teahouse, and he could adapt.

One deck above, first-class passengers would soon be served with spotless glassware, porcelain, and hand-carved wooden bowls or cups. Most did not have to adapt, however. They were accustomed to the luxury.

Isamu made sure to follow Matsu in the line, and he watched with disappointment at what he considered the skimpy portion of rice slapped into Matsu's bowl when he held it out for the server. When his turn came, Isamu received the same frugal portion as Matsu. He tried extending his hand a little longer, hoping the server would get the message. But in return, he received only a glare and the same tilted head motion Matsu had received, meaning to move along.

Maybe we'll get enough other items to round out our meal, he thought.

When Matsu held out his bowl to the second server, his reward was two small portions of bread. Next, he received a spoonful each of olives, lemon slices, and the things that looked like ginger root. Isamu received the same.

"Good for your seasickness," the server said.

Matsu spotted space for the two of them at the end of one of the far benches and motioned for Isamu to follow. "S... Sea...s...sick...? Matsu managed to say before he took his first bite. He suddenly realized how hungry he was. It took only a few bites to finish off the small serving of rice.

Trying to speak for him, Isamu said, "That was odd. No one seems to be seasick." Then he added, "But we haven't reached the ocean yet; we've been protected by the bay. Once we round the peninsula, we'll be in open water for five thousand miles. That might be a different story."

Matsu picked up the olives and the lemon slices. Holding them up to Isamu, he simply gazed at him with a look of confusion.

"I'm going to save mine," Isamu said. "They might help, in case we start feeling nauseous. I've heard ginger can be helpful to prevent it, but I've never tried it. I guess we're just supposed to chew on it." He looked around at other passengers who seemed to have the same confusion. Getting up from the bench, he reminded Matsu, "Don't forget your cup and bowl. I wish we had somewhere to rinse them out."

When they returned to their bunk, the area was quiet. Most of the passengers were still in the mess hall, finishing their meals. "Let's walk to the stern," he invited Matsu. "Maybe we'll find a place to rinse our bowls." As they walked aft down their aisle, Isamu found himself counting bunks. When they arrived at the very end, he announced, "Thirty—more than I thought."

At the end of the aisle was a bulkhead running from beam to beam, with openings that aligned with the two outermost aisles of bunks. On the other side of the bulkhead was a dead space with a long trough, also running from beam to beam. There were wooden seats mounted on hinges above the trough in such a way they could be folded up against the stern or down, atop the trough. Each seat had a hole in the center, approximately twenty centimeters in diameter. It was obvious now. This was the toilet for a thousand people.

Looking toward the starboard beam, he saw a pump handle, with a spigot that emptied into the trough. Walking over to it, he decided to pump the handle to see how it worked. After two pumps, water splashed into the trough. The trough sloped from each end toward the middle. In the dim light, made worse by the presence of the bulkhead, he was barely able to make out the silhouette of a similar pump on the port side. He stuck a finger into the trickle from his spigot and raised it to his mouth. It tasted salty. It was not drinkable, but certainly usable to rinse their bowls. He pumped the handle again with his right hand while holding the bowl under the spigot with his left. Then he pumped the handle while Matsu rinsed his bowl.

Back at their bunks, other passengers were beginning to trickle back from their meal. It was noisy, but not chaotic like before. Isamu sat next to Matsu on the lower bunk as they watched men alone or in pairs make their way to their respective bunks.

Isamu turned to Matsu. "My parents run a teahouse in Kamaishi," he said. "One of their regular patrons had trouble getting his words out when I first met him. But over time, I didn't notice it anymore. I thought maybe I'd just gotten used to it, but then I made sure to listen when he spoke, and I realized he had nearly gotten over it. So much so, that I asked him about it." Isamu looked away from Matsu to avoid putting pressure on him to respond. He waited long enough to see if Matsu was going to speak, and when he did not, Isamu continued.

"He told me that he'd learned an exercise that helped him. I don't know if it would be of interest to you, but he said every time before he tried to speak, he would take two or three deep breaths. Inhale, exhale. Two or three times. It seemed to loosen his speaking muscles and calm his nerves. I wish I'd paid more attention to what else he told me, but that was the gist of it. He tried to calm himself before saying anything. He said it also gave him time to clarify in his head what, exactly, he wanted to say."

Then he paused to see if Matsu might be turning red with anger, or if not, whether he seemed at all interested in his story.

Matsu seemed quiet and thoughtful, at least on the surface, so Isamu continued. "If that is something you might be interested in, we could practice it together every morning and evening when we get our time on deck. It would be quieter up there, and we'd have a little more privacy than down here with people all around."

The response was immediate and positive. Matsu smiled what might have been the biggest Isamu had yet seen from him. He nodded, and then, as if to solidify his answer, inhaled deeply once, twice, a third time, then replied, "Y… Yes!"

***

Matsu was sitting in his bunk when the crew member walked up and down the aisles. This time, only every other aisle. "Upper deck is open for those who want it," he repeated periodically as he rang his bell. He stood to see if Isamu had heard the announcement.

Isamu's eyes were barely open as he peered over the side of his bunk. He startled slightly when he saw Matsu grinning back at him. "I guess you're ready to go topside," he said.

Matsu took three deep breaths, then relaxed his shoulders and replied, "Ye...Yes."

Isamu hurried down from his bunk, and the two men walked the few steps to the end of aisle fifteen, then to the forward stairwell on the starboard side. Climbing the stairs two at a time, hoping to get on deck before it became overly crowded, they exited at the top and stepped out into the rising sun.

They had just begun to walk toward the bow when Isamu spoke. "Matsu, I don't really know if this will help or not. I'm sorry I can't remember more details about what our friend at the teahouse did to improve his speech. Do you still want to try it?"

Matsu nodded.

"Then let's practice your greetings. Good morning."

"G...g...g...good m...m...morning." Matsu repeated.

"Good afternoon."

"G...g...g...good a...after...n...noon."

"Good evening."

"G...g...good evening."

"My name is Matsu Konishi."

Matsu smiled at this one. "My n...n...name is Matsu K...Konishi"

By now, they had reached the forwardmost part of the deck. The sun was low in the sky and directly in front of them. There was nothing to see from the bow but miles of ocean. They looked in every direction. Nothing but water, as far as they could see. Neither man had been so far from land in his life. Without speaking, they simply stood in silence.

Trying to hide their concerns from one another, in a meager attempt to scan the horizon, they both made a mental note of where the lifeboats were stored. How to get to them from below, in case of an emergency, was a question neither cared to ponder.

As they stood transfixed at the bow of the ship, all other thoughts emptied from their minds. There was nothing there but them and the sea. They did not think of what was left behind or what was yet to come. It was a moment almost spiritual. They simply stood and gazed at the vastness of the Pacific. How little they were—hardly more than a grain of sand, or a pebble in the sea.

What does a life matter to the world? Isamu wondered. *Can God see me? A small speck of life, from far above.*

Their reveries collided with reality when the crest of the wave below no longer supported the bow of the *Coptic*, sending it down through a trough with a mighty plunge. Salt water splayed the front of the ship from its bow to its midsection. The sudden shift of the ship caused both men to stagger as the deck momentarily dropped away below their feet. When the bow settled again at the base of the trough, their knees bent to absorb the strain of landing on the heavy liquid surface.

There they stood, hardly able to breathe, waiting for the next wave to come. They grabbed hold of the railing, which helped to protect the deck from the waves and spray of an open sea. With both feet firmly planted and hands gripping the rail, they waited. They felt the bow slowly rise and watched as it overtook the oncoming wave. They sucked in a breath and tightened their grip, riding the bow as it slowly lifted upward. When the weight became too much to bear, down it crashed again. Over and over, it repeated. Up on the crest, down in the trough. Spray flooded the bow in a torrent, then drained away in rivulets.

Isamu had experienced this on his fishing boat. But this was something different. His stomach grew queasy as they rode the waves. Then he remembered what the server told them as he scooped those small portions into his bowl. Especially the olives and ginger. If they served them this morning, he would ask for more.

After several more cycles of waves and spray, Isamu looked at Matsu. "Let's move to midship. It will be smoother, and we'll be protected from the spray back there."

Matsu nodded and followed Isamu as he tried to synchronize his movements with those of the ship. The closer they got to the middle, the more settled it became. He turned to Matsu with a smile as he thought back to their bunks near the middle of the ship. "You were right about our bunks," he said. "Thank you for selecting them."

Matsu smiled.

When they reached a spot protected from wind and spray, between the first-class cabins and a long row of lifeboats, Isamu found an empty spot along the rail where they both could steady themselves while they continued Matsu's exercises.

"Are you ready?" Isamu asked. When Matsu nodded, he said, "Be sure to take several deep breaths each time first. Good morning…"

They continued the exercise until a crew member made his way carefully, if not begrudgingly, around the perimeter of the ship, ringing his bell as a signal their time on deck was over. They made their way down the forward stairs, where a serving line had already started to form.

Having attuned themselves to the rocking motion of the ship while on the main deck, they were now fully aware of its motion on 'S' deck. Without fresh air or a view of the horizon to assist them, Isamu could only imagine what lay in store for the hundreds of passengers confined there. When his turn at the serving station came, he opted only for the ginger, olives, and lemons.

By afternoon, seasickness had struck most of the passengers on steerage deck. Isamu could not tell if the upper deck fared better, since contact between the two decks was restricted. Isamu and Matsu spent most of their waking hours lying in their bunks, trying to nap or distract themselves as best they could. Isamu retrieved a notebook from his locker and, little by little, wrote a letter home. In it, he made sure to ask if Ayami could learn more about the stuttering treatment of their teahouse patron.

Sleeping, whether daytime or nighttime, was difficult to attain with the continual sounds of snoring, heaving, moaning, and the banging of pails as passengers either filled them with vomit or emptied them at the trough. By the second day, the smell from the sickness was as bad as the sickness itself. It affected even those who weren't sick, and the stench was unavoidable.

The only relief came an hour before the morning and evening meals, when they were allowed on the main deck. At least there, the air was fresh. Matsu faithfully continued his speaking exercises during every excursion. Fewer passengers visited the deck for the simple reason they were too sick to go, which made it easier for the teacher and his pupil. Matsu was unencumbered by curious bystanders, which helped to reduce his anxiety.

In spite of Matsu's diligence, Isamu could not see progress in even simple responses. He considered calling off the lessons but could not bring himself to tell Matsu it wasn't working. The more he thought about it, the more he decided that for Matsu, hope, even if not well-founded, was better than giving up. He vowed to keep trying. Which, when he considered it, was not much of a sacrifice, since they had sixteen more days together with absolutely nothing to do.

Confinement to steerage deck brought Isamu a feeling he'd never had before—boredom. He'd been required to help with whatever chores he was old enough to accomplish for as long as he could remember.

Now, twenty-two hours of every day were limited to a deck shared by a thousand other passengers, bored like himself. Making matters worse, was that on 'S' deck, day and night were nearly the same. Without windows, the light was limited to a few oil lamps scattered throughout the area. It did help that some of the lamps were extinguished after the evening meal. It made sleeping slightly easier and moving around slightly more difficult. It tended to keep the men in their bunks.

***

On the second day since departure, following their noon meal, Isamu lay in his bunk, thinking about what he could add to the on-going letter to his family. The letter was on its third page, and Isamu had written about every major happening since leaving Kamaishi. He'd told them about Matsu and his speaking malady. He'd also written about the man he mistook for Cho at the silk factory, the military man, and the other man with a limp, who was now on board and had tried to take his bunk. Other than that, the days seemed destined for boredom until they reached San Francisco.

Lying on his back in the upper bunk, his eyes wandered aimlessly to the ceiling above. Always interested in how things worked and how things were made, he studied the pattern of the beams overhead and the planking that ran from beam to beam. He wondered if there was a chamber between his ceiling and the floor of the deck above. Turning his head slightly to the nearby starboard wall, he noticed for the first time, a large circular grate in the ceiling above aisle sixteen. It appeared to be almost a meter in diameter, made of metal, and apparently designed to allow for the movement of air.

He slipped down from his bunk for a closer look. Because the grate was directly over the aisle, he could stand beneath it, and when he did, could see a small reflection of light at its top. The light seemed to be coming from the direction of the stern, which Isamu quickly deduced would be the sun, since they were heading east and it was well past noon.

He decided to search for the tube on the main deck later that afternoon, when their turn came to go above. To mark the location, he walked down the aisle toward the stern, counting his steps until he came to the stairway leading up. Twenty-three was the magic number. He returned to his bunk, and when Matsu looked up at him with quizzical eyes, he explained what he'd found. "When we go topside later, I want to look for that tube. I'm pretty sure it's a vent to provide fresh air below, but I'm curious about how it works," he said.

When the crew member came by at four o'clock, clanging his bell as a sign they could use the upper deck, Isamu and Matsu were eager to go. This time, they went up the aft stairwell, and once on main, Matsu followed, as Isamu began counting twenty-three steps toward the bow.

He had only reached step number sixteen when he saw the large white tube rising up from the planking just ahead. The diameter was something less than a meter and extended as high as his shoulders. It curved at the top such that the opening was facing the stern of the ship. Standing next to it, he could now see that the upper section, the curved portion, was a separate piece, attached to the straight pipe in such a way that it could swivel three hundred sixty degrees. He counted three retaining bolts that held the curved section in place. The bolts that held the swivel were unusual. In place of a traditional wrench-shaped head, there were short metal wings welded perpendicular to the bolt. The obvious conclusion was that these were designed to be tightened or loosened by hand.

Isamu looked around for a crew member close by. He studied the vent pipe for a moment and recognized immediately that if he could turn the curved pipe to face the front of the ship, it would scoop in the twenty-knot breeze and force it down into the deck below. He tried to look down into the pipe, which was at a convenient height, but was unable because of a grate covering the opening. When he stood close enough to look into the pipe, the stench forced him back.

He put a hand on both sides of the curve to see if by chance it would rotate, but the three retaining bolts were tightened down and it would not budge. He wanted badly to loosen the bolts and try again. But his respect for authority and the property of others precluded his curiosity. He might have to resort to that later, but first he would pursue the proper channels. He looked again for a crew member, but seeing none, motioned for Matsu to continue their walk. With luck, they might find a crewman along the way.

Isamu then began his speaking exercises with Matsu. "Good morning... Good afternoon... Good evening.... My name is Matsu Konishi..."

Matsu practiced his deep breathing, relaxing his body, and responding to each phrase. Isamu began to mix in new phrases periodically to keep it interesting, but also to introduce an added level of stress to his student. Then he remembered something else the patron had told him. He said he loved to sing. And when he sang, he didn't stutter. *I wonder if that could help Matsu*, Isamu thought to himself.

The two had walked the circumference of the ship twice when Isamu spotted a crew member near one of the lifeboats. They approached him respectfully, and Isamu bowed lightly before he spoke. "I am sorry to interrupt your work," he began, even though the crewman seemed mostly to be trying to hide from his superiors. "I have a question regarding the ventilation pipes. I counted twelve pipes as we walked the length of the ship. It appears the pipes have been engineered in such a way that the funnel attached to the vent can be rotated to face in any direction. Do you know if that is correct?"

The crewman, eager to display his expertise in regard to the workings of the ship, replied, "Yes, that is the case; the *Coptic* employs the very latest engineering concepts available anywhere in the world. So, the funnels, as you call them, are designed to rotate in whatever direction the captain calls for. Not only that, they are designed so no special tools are required to make the necessary adjustments. Every crew member is capable of making the precise adjustment as required. I, myself, have adjusted the ventilation tubes many times during my years as a crewman aboard the *Coptic*."

"That is quite remarkable," replied Isamu. "In that case, I have an additional question. Would it be possible to rotate the funnels to face into the wind? That is to say, into the direction we are moving. If I understand correctly, we are traveling at approximately twenty knots, which would therefore provide a steady breeze of twenty knots of ventilation into the funnels. Do you agree it would be so?"

The crewman considered the question at some length, daring not to expose his true lack of expertise, before answering, "Yes, I believe you are correct regarding your calculation. And yes, we do rotate the funnels at various times throughout the voyage. But we are allowed to change their settings only by orders from the captain. As I'm sure you would agree, it is the captain who controls all settings on a ship as modern and sophisticated as the *Coptic*."

"Yes, I understand completely. Given your long years of experience and what I presume to be your strong and much appreciated relationship with the captain, when you see him later this afternoon, would you suggest to him that you believe all the passengers on steerage deck would be more comfortable, and most likely, less prone to seasickness if the ventilator funnels were turned to face the bow. All, except perhaps, the ones most aft. Those might well remain pointing aft to allow air entering the front of the ship to exit at the rear."

Again, the crewman considered the request. The way the stranger had worded his request made it difficult to refuse. After all, he had a certain image he needed to maintain, even cultivate. If he refused, the stranger might wrongly assume he was not as experienced or as highly regarded by the captain as he pretended to be. *But to see the captain this afternoon?* That would be more difficult. *When was the last time he actually talked with the captain?* he wondered. *Certainly not yet on this voyage.* But he was smart. He would find a way.

"Yes, you may be assured I will take up the matter with the captain at my very first opportunity. We are both busy men, as you have rightly indicated, so it might be tomorrow before our schedules allow for such a meeting."

"Excellent. May we meet here tomorrow, at this same time and place? I look forward to hearing about your conversation with the captain. I expect he will be pleased with your observations regarding the well-being of your passengers."

"Ah… yes, a good idea," he stammered. "I will meet you here and report to you about our meeting."

***

Isamu knew the result well before their meeting. He was lying in his bunk the following afternoon when he felt the difference. Not only did he feel the difference, he could smell it. A fresh-smelling sea breeze wafted down aisle sixteen from the bow toward the stern. The bunks he and Matsu selected between aisles fifteen and sixteen placed them within three meters of the ventilator's incoming air. From his upper bunk, he gazed around at his nearby neighbors, watching for their reaction to the unexpected change. Some were dozing and didn't notice. Others either raised their heads or sat up in their bunks to look around. Something had changed, but they were not sure what. Isamu smiled as he watched them one-by-one inhale deeply, then exhale and repeat the process until they were convinced it was real. Several of them smiled and then dropped back on their mats.

By four o'clock, the accumulation of stench had noticeably decreased through the simple circulation of air: fresh coming in through the front, stale purging out through the rear.

When Isamu and Matsu reached the designated meeting location, the crew member was there and waiting. His smile confirmed what the two already knew. Both men bowed to the crewman.

"I spoke to the captain," he began. "He was very pleased with my...with our recommendation, although it was not a request unexpected by him. He told me he had already anticipated the change and was about to give the order to have them adjusted. He explained that until now, the choppy seas sent too much spray on deck, and that had the vents been facing forward, they would have allowed spray to enter the deck below. The seas have calmed enough by now that it's safe to adjust the vents. He added that in the event of rough seas, the vents would have to be repositioned to face the stern."

"You have our sincere gratitude for your intervention," Isamu said. "There is already a vast improvement in the 'fragrance' of the air below." All three men chuckled at his euphemism. "Kindly relay to the captain how much the steerage passengers appreciate his action. And the same to you for resolving the matter so quickly." The two men bowed once more and proceeded with their daily ritual: exercise and speech therapy.

CHAPTER 34
TROUBLE AT SEA

JUNE 11, 1899 – THE PACIFIC OCEAN

By the third day of the voyage, life on steerage deck fell into a dull routine. Three meals, two one-hour stints on the main deck, and the remainder spent sleeping, napping, or exchanging hopes and dreams with adjacent neighbors. If idle minds are dangerous minds, as the Empress had once proclaimed, then steerage deck was fertile ground for mischief. Added to that, there were no females among them, and most of the passengers were between the ages of sixteen and thirty. Ages at the peak of youthful energy. A population not content with lying in a bunk day after day.

It was no surprise then, to either Isamu or Matsu, when small groups began to meet in out-of-the-way corners, discretely at first, for friendly games of chance, mostly as a means to pass the time.

The two men stood nearby to observe, on occasion, although neither felt the desire to participate. It soon became apparent the level of noise was inextricably linked to the number of sen being placed on the table. As far as they knew, there were no rules forbidding the rolling of dice or the playing of cards on board the *Coptic*, but it seemed intuitive to Isamu that risking your much-needed savings before reaching your destination was a bad idea. Eventually, the two observed that stakes had risen from sen to yen. A distressing notion to them both.

This day, as they stood some distance away, Matsu nudged Isamu's arm with his elbow and tilted his head toward a man huddled at the center of a group. "The m…man w…we saw w…with the s…sold…soldier," he managed to say.

Isamu focused on the man for a closer look. "Yes, I think it's him. Something about him worries me," he said. "It doesn't surprise me that he's trying to take other people's money."

They walked a few steps closer for a better view. Several men were huddled in the group, watching the man in the middle, who seemed to be the leader. It was definitely the man they had seen with the military soldier. They watched as he shifted his weight periodically from one leg to the other. He grimaced slightly when shifting to the left leg, the one he favored when walking.

The two watched as he laid three cards face-down on a makeshift table of someone's luggage trunk. Then one of the other players laid a yen down beside one of the cards. The man in the center made a sour face, one designed to reflect a look of defeat, followed by great fanfare of turning over the selected card and holding up a jack of spades. This was followed by an overblown sigh of relief by the man in the center and a chorus of groans by several of the others around the huddle. He ceremoniously turned over the remaining two cards, holding up the queen of hearts for everyone to see. Then the man dealing the cards picked up the yen and discreetly slipped it in his pocket.

"Who's next?" he asked.

One of the other men raised his hand and threw down two yen. The dealer pretended to look alarmed. "Two yen?" he asked. "That's too rich for me," he said.

But the crowd grew more excited. "Two yen!" a few of them shouted. Others echoed their encouragement.

With an anxious face, the dealer wiped sweat from his hands, closed his eyes briefly as he looked upward to the ship's rafters, and, with great fanfare, mixed the cards several times to confirm they were thoroughly shuffled. He showed them to the group, then laid them face down on the trunk, one by one.

The new player studied the three cards carefully for a long minute, then placed his index finger on the middle card.

The dealer slowly lowered his hand to the card and methodically turned it over in a manner that displayed its face to the rest of the group. He drew a sullen face when cheers went up all around. The card he displayed was the queen of hearts. The player won.

The dealer shook his head mournfully but reached in his pocket and extracted two yen. He handed them to the player with what was obviously a forced grin and said, "Congratulations. You have a very perceptive eye."

The dealer then gathered his cards and looked around the group. "See how easy it is to beat the dealer?" he asked. "Who wants to beat me again? I knew I shouldn't have accepted a bet for two yen. It brought me bad luck. I should have stayed with a single yen. Who else wants to try their luck?"

The first man, encouraged by the success of the second player, raised his hand once more and threw two yen on the trunk. The dealer raised his hands in protest at seeing the proposal. But the crowd standing around them broke into cheers of encouragement. One of them shouted "Three yen!" which brought even more remorse from the dealer, who began shaking his head.

Someone shouted, "Five yen!" There were, at first, gasps, then cheers. "Yes, five yen!" Followed by "Coward" and a general clambering for upping the ante. In the excitement, the player reached deep into his pocket and withdrew a small roll of yen, from which he unfolded three more. He laid them on the trunk next to the first two and gave the dealer a daring look in the eyes, bringing the excitement of the group to a frenzied level.

After a perfectly orchestrated delay, the dealer inhaled deeply several times, closed his eyes again, looked up as before, then proceeded to shuffle the three cards. Then he looked carefully around the entire group, finally settling on the player across from him, and winced as if he knew he was about to be defeated two games in succession. Slowly, he laid down the three cards, one by one, while staring at his opponent. The player, on the other hand, was concentrating on the three cards, trying his best to follow where the queen would land.

The entire crowd fell silent as the player carefully made his selection. This time, he placed his finger on the card to his right. That happened to be the correct choice for the previous player.

The dealer once again displayed a sense of profound anxiety and worry before turning up the selected card. He turned it up for the crowd to see first, then flipped it over to see for himself. Of course, the groans from the crowd told him what he already knew: it was not the queen of hearts and he had taken another naive and gullible passenger for five yen. He pretended to be at once, relieved and surprised as he placed the money in his pocket.

Isamu and Matsu had seen enough. It saddened them to see the player lose money he would surely need once he reached Hawaii, or California. They turned and walked back to their bunks.

"I...I've s...seen that g...game before. T...The dealer has p...p...part...partners. They have s...sig...signals t...to make it l...look l...like you c...can win. T...To entice other p...players."

"I wonder if that's why the *Kempeitai* was with him when we boarded," Isamu said. "I think we need to keep our eyes open whenever he's around."

"I a...a...gree," Matsu replied.

***

Fortunately for those who craved quiet surroundings in order to sleep, the pockets of gambling took place only in the afternoons, between the noon and evening meals. Whether from boredom and the hope of impending sleep or some other unknown reason, the end result was a generally quiet atmosphere throughout all of steerage deck.

Isamu routinely spent those waking hours adding to his letters to family or reviewing the list of English phrases given to him by Fr. Katz. He voiced the verses silently in English, concentrating on using the correct phrase to match his meaning. But he could not shake the feeling that when it came time to actually converse in English, all the words and phrases would come to him in a garbled fury, and he would reply with nothing more than a blank stare.

On this night, the pretend conversation in his head was continually interrupted by thoughts of the *Kempeitai* man, as he now referred to him in his mind. *How dangerous was he? How much money did his victims lose to him,* in what was almost certainly a game of cheating? *Could there be a way to stop him—maybe even convince him to return their money?*

With no windows or clocks on the steerage deck, Isamu could only guess the time of day or night, but after lying in his bunk for a lengthy period of time, practicing his English, he finally dozed off. Even so, having had no physical exertion to tire his bones, sleep came lightly. Small noises which would not have awakened him after a day on the delivery wagon, for example, now caused him to roll over or shift position in his bunk. It caused his ears to listen for a secondary sound, which, if heard, would allow his eyes to open slightly, in a half-woken state of mind. If no other sound followed, his body relaxed again, and he returned to sleep.

Something about a sound tonight rang familiar. He awoke enough to listen for a repeat of the sound, trying to place what it was. There was a lull, but eventually the sound again. He lay still with ears tuned on high alert. He was lying on his back, so his eyes could focus only on the rafters above his bunk. When the noise occurred again he recognized the sound. Nothing more than a storage locker being opened and closed. He relaxed momentarily until the sound repeated. Surely whoever needed to retrieve something from his locker, although not an unreasonable action, would not find the need to continually open and close the door. He lay quietly, waiting. Again, he heard the sound. But it seemed to have moved further away. Was it possible that several passengers remembered something in the middle of the night that could not wait until morning?

He rolled over on his side and lifted his head slowly, looking at the row of starboard lockers just one aisle away. The lamps were trimmed to their overnight setting, providing only enough light to identify aisles and faint images of the rows of bunks, barely enough to make out a human figure five meters away, but as Isamu concentrated on the lone figure peering into a locker, he sucked in a quiet breath at what he saw. It was the *Kempeitai* man.

He was holding open the door of a locker and appeared, from where Isamu lay, to be reaching into it in search of something. Presently, he closed the door, holding it all the way so as not to let it slam shut with unnecessary noise.

Then Isamu scolded himself. It would be perfectly normal to need something from your locker. Most likely, he had misplaced something, remembered it during the night, and was anxious to see if he had left it in his locker.

He forced himself to relax and laid his head back down on the bunk.

Then he heard the sound again. Rising on his mat for the second time, he could see it was clearly the same man, but this time, a different locker. As before, the man was reaching into the locker and rummaging through its contents in search of something. This time, he found something he apparently wanted, as Isamu watched him pull a small bundle from the locker and place it in his pocket.

Isamu could not make out what it was or which locker it was taken from. But he was able to isolate the locker within a range of four, or maybe six, possible locations. With that, the man quietly closed the door, turned, and began walking up the aisle toward him. Isamu quickly laid back on the mat so as not to be noticed while the man continued up the aisle, turned, and crossed over to the port side of the ship. There was no doubt whatever that the man was limping, favoring his left leg as he went. It was definitely the *Kempeitai* man.

Isamu laid on his bunk for the remainder of the night. But sleep would not come.

***

A few nearby bunkmates were already making their way to the nearest stairwell the next morning, while Isamu lay sleeping in his bunk, snoring lightly.

Matsu stood up beside his bunk and touched Isamu lightly on the shoulder as he softly called his name.

Isamu jumped at the sound. He was not only awake, but ready for, almost expecting, a confrontation. As soon as he saw that it was Matsu looking back at him with a look of bewilderment, he released an audible sigh and let his body relax. He smiled sheepishly at Matsu.

"Did I oversleep? Sorry, I didn't sleep very well for most of the night."

"I didn't m...mean to startle y...you," Matsu replied. "B...but I th...thought you w...would w...want to g...go for our w...walk."

"Yes, I do want to walk. I have to tell you what I saw!"

Matsu nodded and moved back so Isamu could hop down. When they reached the main deck, Isamu considered where to begin, then relayed to Matsu everything he could remember, with as much detail as possible. He finished by saying he thought they should find the crewman who helped them with the ventilators and ask him to inform the captain as soon as possible, before the *Kempeitai* man caused even more mischief.

Matsu listened intently to everything Isamu told him. At the mention of reporting it to the captain, he held a hand up toward Isamu as a signal to wait. "We n...need m...more evidence," he said. "He c...can't g...go anywhere until at least H...Hawaii. We should g...get m...more evidence fi...first."

Isamu looked at him but did not speak. Matsu was older than he, probably by ten years. Matsu was perceptive. He was the first to recognize the man as the person they had seen when boarding the ship. He was intelligent. It was his suggestion to find a bunk close to mid-ship to minimize seasickness.

In several aspects, at least, Matsu was more capable than he himself. Yet because of his stuttering impediment, Isamu had somehow assumed he was superior enough to make the decisions for both of them. For a brief instant, he wondered how many other times he had ignored, or underappreciated someone, simply because of a first impression. He vowed to add this lesson in his journal.

"What do you think we should do?" He then asked Matsu. "We can't let him take advantage of others like that. Who knows how much damage he'll do before he leaves the ship?"

"We n...need more evidence. M...More p...proof. O...others to help w...watch his movements. We c...can take t...turns w...watching t...the c...card game. See who w...wins. He h... has p...partners at c...cards. M...might be alone with lockers."

The two walked with purpose around the main deck of the *S.S. Coptic*. The deck was crowded with steerage passengers taking advantage of their one-hour morning access to sunshine and fresh air. Since the view from every vantage point was identical—the vast blue ocean—some walked for exercise, others were content to stand at the railing and simply stare at the horizon. Of those who walked, it seemed to Isamu that half were moving in their direction while the other half were coming toward them from the other.

"I have never seen him up here," Isamu said. It was not necessary to identify who the 'him' was.

"M...Me n...neither," replied Matsu.

It struck them both at the same moment. With so many steerage passengers on main deck during their outings, 'he' would have ample opportunity to plunder the lockers down below.

"We definitely need help to watch his movements," Isamu said. But how do we find people we can trust? He has accomplices at cards. For all we know, he has lookouts posted for his locker raids. If we happened to confide in one, they would tell him immediately, and our plan would be over. Not only that, he would probably want revenge. I wouldn't put anything past him, even..." But he didn't finish the sentence. "We'll have to be especially careful."

They walked together in silence along the port side, from the bow to the stern. Then Matsu continued, "W...We s...split up. W...Watch c...card game. W...Whoever w...wins, we stay away f...from. W...We find his b...bunk and see w...who bunks n...next to h...him. We stay away f...from them. We see w...who he eats w...with. Stay away f...from them. W...What y...you think?"

Conversations with Matsu were more work than with other people. Isamu had to continually force himself to listen to the meaning of his words rather than to his natural instincts of guessing the next few words and jumping to a response before Matsu finished speaking. Gradually, he had learned to be patient, let Matsu speak, and then reflect on the entirety of what he'd said.

"Yes," he replied, when they reached midship on the starboard side. "It would be better if we split up. Especially since he has seen you and would surely remember your face, after you confronted him at our bunk. By splitting up, we could spend more time watching the games without being quite so obvious."

Silence again, until they approached the bow on the starboard side. "We could sit far apart in the mess hall. That would make it easier to spot him when he comes for meals. Most likely, he'll return to his bunk after eating. Since he knows you, I'll follow him from the mess hall and see if I can locate his bunk."

They had just begun another trip around the deck, when a crew member came around clanging his bell. Time was up for the morning walk. Steerage passengers needed to return below. Following the crowds to whichever stairwell they were closest to at the time, they headed down to the mess.

Isamu joined the serving line first. Matsu hung back to allow several groups to join the line ahead of him. From now on, they would avoid being seen together except at their bunks. Their eyes were already busy scanning the crowd in search of the 'Kempeitai man.'

It would take practice to search for someone without appearing to.

CHAPTER 35
LOCATING THE TARGET

JUNE 14, 1899 – SIX DAYS AT SEA

Isamu, after receiving his morning portion of rice, bread, and tea, made his way to the second row of benches. It was far enough away that he could be just another face in the crowd, for those coming through the line. It was the perfect location to watch for their man. From there, he could see anyone approaching from the sleeping quarters, all the way through the serving line. His difficulty now would be to pretend to be interested in those seated next to him while focusing on those coming through the line.

He made brief eye contact with Matsu when he started through the line a few minutes later.

Matsu carried his breakfast in one hand and tea in the other, to the forward end of the mess hall. He found an empty seat three rows from the end. Like Isamu, he would be able to observe diners leaving the line and looking for a place to sit. He hoped they would be more focused on empty seats, just as he was, than looking at faces.

Satisfied their plan was now in place, both men began to eat. After a hearty beginning, it occurred to them they would need to pace themselves if they were going to monitor the entire shift. If the 'Kempeitai man' was trying to avoid attention, he would most likely come late for meals, when the benches were less crowded.

Isamu had not considered the difficulty of eating slowly, surrounded by diners who gulped down their food to quench a constant hunger. The servings were bland and sparse, and second servings were officially not allowed. When the food was gone, the line was closed, so the ones who suffered, were those coming late. He tried striking up conversations with his neighbors, but doing so risked losing his focus on the serving line.

An hour passed. Isamu looked at his bowl, now empty. He sipped his remaining tea until there was nothing left in the cup. There were no more passengers joining the line. The kitchen was beginning to close. He had not seen the 'Kempeitai man' anywhere. *Was he here, and I missed him?* Then a more sinister thought. *Was he pillaging the sleeping quarters while everyone was having breakfast?* With no longer any hope of seeing him now, he picked up his bowl and cup and headed back to his bunk. Matsu spotted him from his position at the forward bench and followed him out.

When they met at their bunks, the look of disappointment was clear. "Maybe our plan isn't as good as we thought," Isamu said. "It never occurred to me that he would not come to breakfast."

"H...He has t...to eat s...sometime." Matsu replied. "C...could s...s...somebody be t...taking food t...to him?"

"I never thought of that," Isamu said. "Let's split up and walk every aisle. Maybe we'll see someone eating at their bunk. Or maybe we'll just see him. I'll start down aisle one and check every bunk. You start at aisle sixteen and do the same. If we spot him, we'll make a note of his location and keep going. What do you think?"

Matsu nodded in reply. Then he headed for aisle sixteen to begin the search.

The two met in aisle eight as they made their way in opposite directions. A brief eye contact indicated that neither had seen their man, but they both kept walking.

Back at their bunks, they looked at one another in disappointment. Where was the 'Kempeitai man?' Why hadn't they seen him? Was he not staying on their deck? Surely, he wouldn't have upper deck status. If he did, why would he be spending his time on steerage? The two were pondering possibilities when Matsu slapped his hand on Isamu's mattress and looked at him with a smile on his face.

Isamu watched as he breathed deeply several times, then let his shoulders sag with relaxation. "H…He b…boarded late," he said. "And he t…t…tried to t…take your b…b…bunk. He must be s… s…staying in the o…overflow s…section. One of the c…cots."

Neither man had given thought to the overflow quarters since the first day of boarding. It was located between the ship store and the port beam. Whenever they went above deck or to the mess hall, they always took the starboard side, since that was the side their bunks were on. They'd completely forgotten about the cots.

"I'll go look," Isamu said, "since he doesn't know me. Anyone not sleeping there will probably stand out to them as an outsider. If anyone asks, I'll pretend to be on my way to the store."

"Be c…c…careful," Matsu replied with a nod.

Ten minutes later, Isamu returned. He was smiling. "You were right, Matsu. He was sitting on a corner bunk. The perfect location for him to slip in and out late at night without waking his neighbors. He was talking to three other men. I think I will recognize them if they're with him at the card game."

Matsu grinned.

***

That afternoon, Matsu went first to the dark corner, where they'd seen the card game the day before. 'Kempeitai man' was not among them, but a small group was huddled together, some of them quite excited.

"Have you seen the card man today?" asked one of them. "He was here yesterday, and I made an easy five yen. I hope he comes back today. That was the easiest money I ever made. All you have to do is follow the queen. He shows you three cards, then lays them down. If you're paying attention, it's easy. Just pick out the queen after he lays them all down."

"Yeah, I was here yesterday, too. I only made two yen, but today I think I'll go for more. That poor dealer. He'll be lucky if he has any money left by the time we get to Hawaii. He should know better than to play the game, as laggard as he is."

Matsu noticed they seemed to be talking to a third man in particular. His neck hair began to prickle as he realized they were trying to sucker him in. The 'mark,' he'd been told when he was younger. Retreating a number of paces, he found one of the flooring timbers to stand behind, to watch the game unfold.

Sure enough, it was not long until the 'Kempeitai man' casually approached the group. "How about a quick game of 'Find the Lady'?" the first man called out to him. "Maybe your luck has changed today!"

'Kempeitai man' looked at him with a sigh. "I'm not sure I can afford to keep playing," he confessed. "Yesterday was not a good day for me."

"Just a few quick hands," the other man taunted. "Your luck is bound to change."

"Maybe you'll get your money back today!" one of the other men said.

Just as Matsu anticipated, the dealer finally agreed to play a few rounds. And just as he knew they would, the two taunting men easily won their one-yen bets with the dealer. By then, he had also figured out the scam. Whenever the dealer was betting against one of his fellow scammers, he would lay down the three cards in the same order as when he showed them to the opponent.

But when betting against the 'mark' he would make it as plain as possible which order the cards were in, then deal from the bottom when laying them down. The 'mark,' then, was certain he had watched the queen as it was laid, only to find it was not where it belonged. And the dealer won.

This time, the dealer played a variation where he actually let the 'mark' win his first bet of one yen. He counted on the 'mark' getting confident enough to play a second time, for higher stakes.

The dealer initially feigned reluctance to play a second round, but the equally feigned taunting and encouragement by his two accomplices eventually convinced him to take the gamble. And of course, while the 'mark' was on a roll, why not up the ante to five yen? Caught up in the excitement and fresh from his first win, it was easy enough to convince the 'mark' to raise the bet. With a fanfare and the ultimately reluctant agreement that Matsu had witnessed the day before, the dealer soon showed the three cards for all to see: Jack, Jack, Queen. Then he turned them over and laid them down directly on the wooden planking.

The 'mark' gleefully laid down his five yen next to the third card and picked it up, expecting the queen. His face fell when the card revealed the jack of spades. It seemed so obvious where the queen should be. He was stunned as the dealer picked up the money and gasped a "finally" to the group. "Finally, my luck is turning. Who's next? Who's ready to play?" He turned to the first conspirator and asked, "You ready for another round?"

The first conspirator declined. "Enough for me today; I'm out."

Not finding other takers, the game broke up. Of course, that was part of the scheme as well. Too much talk aboard the ship could work against him. Orochi, the one they called the 'Kempeitai man', had sixteen days at sea to work his trade. He was satisfied with a little each day. If this continued, he could accumulate close to a hundred yen by the time they reached San Francisco. A very nice grubstake indeed. Not to mention the plunder from his 'night job.' Sailing might turn out to be the best job Orochi ever had.

Matsu watched as the losing man turned from the group and slowly walked away. Even from this distance, Matsu could read the man's despair. His shoulders drooped. His head tilted down. His feet barely lifted from the deck as he walked away. Assuming that he was headed back to his bunk, Matsu sidestepped the post he was standing behind and walked at an angle to cut him off. Reaching him, he fell in stride beside him, which was easy because he was moving so slowly.

The man was talking to himself. *"What was I thinking?"* Matsu heard him say. *"It looked so easy,"* he went on. *"What am I going to do for money in San Francisco?"* he wailed softly to himself.

"L...Looks like you had b...b...bad luck t...today," Matsu said quietly.

"It looked so easy..." he repeated.

"Y...You ever p...play before?" Matsu asked.

"No. This was the first time. I wish I'd never, ever tried it."

"Will y...you talk t...to my friend? He might b...be able to h...help."

"I don't see how he can help me now. I've already lost four yen. I don't have any more to lose. It was money I needed when I get to California...to get started."

"C...Come with me. It w...won't t...t...take long."

He led the man back to their starboard bunks, hoping Isamu would be waiting there. He was sitting up in Matsu's bunk when they arrived. Seeing them approach, he stood to greet the two.

"T...T...This is Isamu," Matsu told the man beside him. "He is a g...good man. Tell him w...what h...happened. M...Maybe he c...can help."

"My name is Isamu," he said to the man. "And the man next to you is Matsu. We are interested in your story. If there is a way we can help, it would be our honor to do so," he said with a sincere voice.

"My name is Akio, but I don't know how you can help. I did a foolish thing, and I suppose I deserve the result. I bet money at a card game, and I lost. It was money I had too little of to begin with. It was money I'll need in San Francisco, until I find work. I watched two others play the game and win, and it looked like a sure thing, so I tried it. The first time, I did win. I was so excited that I played a second time, betting more than I should have, and that's when I lost. I must have lost my concentration the second time because of the excitement and the shouting from the other players. I thought sure I knew where the queen was, but she wasn't there. She was a jack."

Isamu looked into Akio's face. Then he said, "Akio, you are not to blame. It is probable that every man on board would have done what you did. The dealer is the one to blame. The game is a trick, and the others who won are in on the trick. The dealer allows them to win in order to entice innocent players. When they see how easy it is for the others, why would they not want to add a cushion to whatever money they have saved for San Francisco? And to give them even more confidence, the dealer will often let them win the first round, as an enticement to raise the stakes.

"It's human nature to respond just as you did. It's unfortunate the game is allowed to take place. In fact, I'm pretty sure the captain would forbid it, if he knew. Matsu and I hope to inform him, but to do that, we need more evidence against not only the dealer but also his partners. Does that make sense to you?"

Akio nodded.

"Would you be willing to help us gather more evidence and identify the others?"

Akio nodded again.

"Did you get a good look at the players who won? Good enough that you could point them out to the captain, if necessary."

"Yes, two of them, for sure. I don't know if there were others. It all happened so fast, and I was trying to watch the cards more than the people."

"That is what they count on," Isamu replied. "They try to blend in and be as inconspicuous as possible. They don't want to be identified. Do you think you could attend the game again tomorrow and act like you're considering whether or not to play?"

Akio thought about it. "I can try," he said. "What's the purpose? Do I have to bet money again?"

"No, you are not going to enter the game; only be an interested bystander watching the excitement. Your real purpose will be to get a good look at the players who walk away with winnings. They will be the ones who are in on the scam. Be very careful not to stare at them or let it be known they are your primary interest. Just look at them carefully as they place their bets. That is a time when everyone's attention will be on the game and not the people. Do you think you could do that without being too conspicuous?"

"Yes, I think so," Akio replied.

"I'm sure you can," Isamu said. "But remember, if at any time you feel something isn't right, or that the dealer is watching you directly, you should take the first opportunity to walk away. He may recognize you from today and try to entice you back into the game. If he does, you can say you're thinking about it, and maybe tomorrow, or whatever comes to mind.

"We think he is the type of person who might seek revenge, so the most important thing is not to give him any cause for suspicion. Do you still think this is something you can do? We'll understand if you don't."

Akio thought about the four yen he no longer had in his small purse. If he had lost it in a true game of chance, it would be one thing, he could blame himself for that. But losing it in a game where there was no chance of winning was another matter. He wondered how many others had already been caught in the snare. And how many more, before reaching San Francisco.

"Yes, I'll do it," he finally answered.

"I know you can do it," Isamu said. "Remember the goals: identify his partners, avoid arousing suspicion, and, if possible, also identify the victim. The more victims we recruit, the better our chance of putting an end to it. Come back here tomorrow after the game and tell us how it went. Matsu will be watching you from a distance, so you won't be totally alone. One more thing. We should not be seen together unless absolutely necessary."

The three men bowed, and Akio moved to the end of aisle fifteen, then turned right, toward the portside beam.

"I w...wonder w...w...where his b...bunk is," Matsu mused aloud.

"Tomorrow, we'll ask him. Maybe he's close enough to the lockers to keep watch on them."

"Do you t...think we n...need to keep our watch in the m...mess hall? We k...know w...who his p...partners are."

"Hmmm..." Isamu pondered. "Yes, I think we should keep watching. There may be other partners we haven't seen yet. And maybe we'll manage to overhear something about items disappearing from lockers. It would be helpful if we found someone who had actually been pilfered. They might be able to help us put a stop to it."

***

The following afternoon, Matsu stationed himself behind the wooden post and leaned against it, facing away from the card game. He could pivot easily, to get a glimpse of the proceedings, yet to anyone watching, seem nothing more than another bored passenger.

Meanwhile, Isamu endeared himself to a group of three men walking around the steerage deck for exercise. With subtle encouragement, he was able to guide the group, now a foursome, past the area of the deck where he knew 'Find the Lady' would be taking place. The group halted their discussion about Honolulu and San Francisco long enough to observe the game.

Isamu focused on the interaction between the dealer and the other participants. Watching the players instead of the cards made it easier to see the pattern. He kept himself from smiling when he saw Akio standing just outside the inner circle of players. Akio seemed so interested that Isamu was afraid he might actually enter the game. But when he looked closer, he saw that Akio was intent on memorizing the faces of the winners.

Isamu also noticed how the dealer kept sneaking glances at Akio as he dealt the cards. He looked behind him at Matsu, who was also watching Akio with a concerned look. They made fleeting eye contact to confirm their alarm.

Isamu was trying to think of a way to signal Akio to abandon the game and move out when he did just that. Akio gave a weak smile to the dealer and whoever else might have been watching him, and walked casually away. Isamu watched the dealer's face, hoping for a telling expression, but saw nothing. He was a hard one to read, which made it even more troubling.

The foursome stayed to watch another round of the game, which was fortuitous because the next player lost what Isamu thought was at least five yen. He turned to make eye contact with Matsu, who nodded. Then Isamu turned to his group and turned the conversation back to dreams of San Francisco. It was a skillful maneuver that caused them to resume their walk, forward toward the bow and away from the game.

Matsu, like the day before, fell into step with the losing player shortly after reaching a safe distance from the leftover card group. This time, however, he followed the man to his bunk. He knew Isamu would still be walking with his three new friends. And Isamu was a much better spokesman than him. "My friend w…will c…come by to s…see you. He may b… be able to h…help." Then he hurried back to his bunk, in order to be there when Akio came by to give his first report.

"They were the same men," Akio told them when Isamu returned. "I would recognize them anywhere. There are three of them. They must take turns playing the game. Only two of them play at a time. Yesterday, it was a different two. I know all three of them now. And now that I know the scam, I see how he does it. But when you're actually in the game, you're not looking at his hands as much as trying to remember where the queen is." He looked at the two of them eagerly. "Did I do what you wanted? Do you think we can stop them? I can't believe they would take advantage of their fellow countrymen. Especially after we've worked so hard to save for the voyage."

"I honestly don't know if we can get your money back, but we're going to try." Isamu paused to look first at Matsu and then back at Akio. "There is more," he said in a voice low enough that no one else could hear. "And it might make all the difference."

He was eye level with Akio and close enough to smell the perspiration on his face. "We are almost certain the dealer is pillaging the lockers that don't have locks. I heard someone going through them two nights ago in the middle of the night. I am certain it was him, but I don't know what he took or who he took it from. What we need are more witnesses who can swear to the captain that he is the man they saw pilfering from lockers. Would you be willing to help keep watch on him? And before you answer, remember, we consider him to be not only evil, but also dangerous. Who knows what he might do if he gets wind of a snitch?"

Akio considered the situation. "What would I have to do?"

"We're hoping to find a few trustworthy men willing to take turns watching the lockers. That's all you have to do. You would stay a safe distance from the lockers and watch for anyone who seems to be snooping in a locker that is not their own. The man I saw was opening every locker, one by one, and reaching in, searching for something of value. I don't know if that's his normal routine or whether he sometimes just checks one or two lockers at a time, acting like they're his own. It probably depends on whether anyone is nearby. I couldn't see what he took from the lockers or what he did with what he took. But my suspicion is that he later deposits it in a locker of his own. Our plan is to find that locker, and when the time is right, ask the captain to open it for evidence.

"It's not really much of a plan, but it's the best we've come up with. If we can convince the captain that the man is a thief, then we think the captain will also agree that he has been scamming innocent victims at his card game as well. And if we're really lucky, the captain will force him to return his winnings. We trust you because we believe you were an innocent victim. But we have to be very careful about who we trust, because if the dealer gets wind of our plan, he will almost certainly want revenge."

Isamu told him more than he had wanted, but knew of no other way to convey the gravity of the request, as well as the risk. He looked at Matsu, wondering if he'd gone too far, or perhaps not far enough. Matsu simply nodded. Isamu pulled back from Akio to give him space to think without intimidation.

Akio smiled as Isamu's plan came into focus. "Count me in," he said. "Just tell me what I need to do."

"You can start this afternoon," Isamu said. Still speaking softly, he continued, "Matsu and I both go for a walk on the upper deck at our assigned hours. We wonder if he is checking lockers while most other passengers are also up there. Would you be willing to stay below and keep watch during those hours? And if you see anything suspicious, stay as inconspicuous as possible. Go to your bunk and lay down if necessary. What we need to know is, if he actually takes something from a locker, what does he do with it? Try to follow him close enough to find out. If you can't determine the exact locker, don't worry about it. Eventually, we'll stake out the area and watch for him when he comes back. For now, we just need to learn his procedure. The dealer has already had an encounter with Matsu, so we don't want him to be involved. I will be taking my turn the same as you. Can you do it? Remember, he already knows who you are, so he'll be suspicious the minute he sees your face."

"I'll be careful," Akio replied.

"Good. Can you also take the early shift tonight? Usually the deck gets quiet by nine or ten o'clock. I doubt he would try anything before that. Could you keep watch between ten o'clock and two o'clock? You can stay in your bunk or somewhere dark and pretend to use the latrine every once in a while. Use whatever technique you find useful. Depending on where your bunk is, you can probably watch a section of lockers directly from there. These are our bunks, so Matsu and I can watch the rear half of the starboard lockers from here. You can concentrate on the port-side lockers. We'll try to find another helper to watch the starboard forward section. Above all, don't raise suspicion. Not to anyone. Even your bunkmates. Remember, we won't know who we can trust until we're done. If anyone confronts you, say you couldn't sleep and just went for a walk, or to the toilet. Pretend to be seasick if you have to. Just get away from the encounter and don't feel like you have let us down. If you feel threatened, come to our bunks. Matsu and I will stand by you."

When Akio left their bunks and headed back to his own, Isamu turned to Matsu. "Were you able to talk to today's victim?" he asked.

Matsu nodded. "I w...w...walked him b...back to his b...b...bunk," he said. "And I t...told him I had a f...f...friend who might b...be able t...to help. Shall w...we g...go see him?"

Isamu hopped down from his bunk as Matsu stood in the aisle to leave. Two steps later, Isamu stopped.

"I'm not sure we should be seen together, even here in the sleeping quarters," he said. "Why don't you go get him, and I'll meet you both at the forward stairwell...on the starboard side," he added.

Matsu nodded, then headed over to aisle five, where he'd followed the man earlier. His bunk was midway through the aisle, on the left-hand side. Only a few passengers lingered in the aisles at this time of day. A few had apparent visitors who were standing near their bunks, having quiet conversations of one sort or another. Matsu concentrated on recognizing the man again, though it had not been long since their meeting. But if he were lying in his bunk, it might be difficult to see his face.

Approaching the midpoint of the aisle, he subconsciously noticed two men standing at the bunks on the right side. They were speaking in low tones, too soft for any conversation to be heard from this distance. He was replaying in his mind the exact location where he'd left the man, scanning with his eyes, that section of the aisle.

It caught his attention when one of the two men standing in the aisle looked directly at him as he approached. Matsu looked back at him and reacted with a start. His face paled in spite of his attempt to ignore the man. It was one of the conspirators. Of that, he was certain. He could not see the second man or the man in the bunk, but one or both were likely the other conspirators.

Matsu was in a panic. Had the man recognized him? Or was he merely looking up the aisle to see who was approaching? They were directly across the aisle from the man he had been going to see. Not only could he not stop at the man's bunk, he could not risk the man seeing him walk by and speaking to him. He tried not to look at the man who'd seen him, and hoped to pass as a random passenger simply walking down the aisle.

Then, in a totally instinctive and spontaneous move, he placed one hand across his stomach and the other across his face and mouth. He bent forward slightly and tried to make himself seasick. He managed to make a muffled gagging sound just as he drew even with the two men and pretended he was about to retch. He picked up his pace as he went past, hoping they would assume he was heading straight to the latrine at the rear of the ship.

He dashed through the portside entrance and bent over the trough with an open mouth, this time hoping no one would realize nothing came out. Then he quickly stroked the seawater pump several times to send a cleansing rinse down the trough and out to sea.

He raised his head to see if the men had followed. When he didn't see anyone, his nerves started to settle. Then he began to reassess his actions. By making a scene, did he only succeed in raising their awareness of him? The better course would have been to merely tilt his head to the floor and walk on by, as a normal random passenger might have done. Isamu would not be pleased with his instinctive reaction. Even more important, though, was that he'd proven himself to not be reliable in an emergency. He dreaded having to tell his story to Isamu.

Once collected again, he exited the latrine via the starboard entrance and tried to walk as naturally as he could toward the forward stairwell where Isamu would be waiting. Resisting the urge to look behind to see if he was being followed, his mind continued to race. With no time to decide the better course, he headed for his bunk instead. He quickly laid down and pretended to be taking an afternoon nap, while raising one eyelid just enough for a glimpse of anyone walking by.

While it seemed like ten, it was more likely only three or four minutes that he maintained his position on the bunk. Just to be sure, he waited another ten…or three or four. Then, seeing no one other than his usual neighbors, he sat up and cautiously looked up and down the aisle. Isamu would be worried by now. He rose and walked as normally as he could toward the stairwell.

Watching as he approached, Isamu knew immediately that Matsu was under stress. The meeting had obviously not gone as planned. "What happened?" he asked. "Are you alright?"

"Two men from the c…card g…game were t…there. R… Right across t…the aisle from him." He went on to tell Isamu how one of them looked at him when he approached and that he was afraid the man might have recognized him. Then he told Isamu how he'd feigned seasickness and dashed to the latrine, and how he'd then gone back to his bunk in case they were following him.

His color had not fully returned, even as he finished recounting his story to Isamu.

Isamu listened patiently and with full attention. Finally, he said, "Matsu, you handled that much better than I would have." Then he was silent for some time, as if lost in thought. Then he looked at Matsu's face and said, "What do you think we should do?"

"W…What? D…Do about w…w…what?"

"Maybe we should forget about the card games—and the lockers. After all, it's none of our business. If men choose to gamble at cards, it's their decision. And if they choose not to padlock their lockers, that's the risk they took when they came on board. Maybe we're just bringing trouble on ourselves. Something about the dealer scares me. I wouldn't put anything past him; if he finds out we're trying to expose him… What do you think?"

Expecting Matsu to ponder before responding, Isamu was surprised that it was immediate.

"I'm s…s…scared t…too," he said. "B…But w…we c…can't let him g…get away with it. If it w…was a fair g…g…game, then m…maybe. But to cheat men who c…can't afford it is w…wrong. We need to s…stop him."

Seeing the determination on his face was enough. He smiled at his friend and said, "You're right, Matsu. We have to stop him."

CHAPTER 36
THE NET TIGHTENS

JUNE 15, 1899 – TWO DAYS FROM HONOLULU

Matsu stepped cautiously into aisle five and looked down it far enough to confirm the two men were gone. He proceeded toward the bunk, trying to appear as just another passenger headed for the latrine. When he got close enough to the designated bunks, he looked first to the left to see if his target was there, then to the right to see if the other man was there. His target claimed the upper bunk, which made him close to eye level, as Matsu walked by. With one swift motion of his left hand, Matsu slipped a small, folded paper just under the man's arm as he lay on his back, looking at the rafters above.

Isamu hung back about twenty paces. Matsu was so smooth with his delivery that it was hardly noticeable, even as he watched. The hand-off completed, Matsu continued down the aisle while Isamu remained where he was, and pretended to search his pockets for something he might have forgotten. He wished he were as clever as Matsu but could think of nothing except to continue padding his clothing, stalling for time.

His assignment was to wait and see if the target read the note and followed its request. *Meet me at the forward stairwell on starboard side. A friend.* Matsu would be there, waiting, in case he came. Isamu would wait in the aisle to watch him leave, but more importantly, to see whether the target would first talk to his neighbor across the aisle and whether that neighbor would also follow the target.

Knowing the note had been delivered, Isamu retreated to the end of the aisle. From there, he could still monitor the movement of both the target and his neighbor. And, importantly, for his own safety, he would be less obvious from that distance away.

This time it was Isamu who felt the minutes tick by in slow motion. He thought he saw movement in the target's bunk. Possibly shifting his arm enough to retrieve the note. Then nothing. Was it five minutes? Ten? He finally started counting to sixty slowly, mostly to pass the time, but in a half-hearted attempt to actually count the minutes.

It surely must be approaching four o'clock, the hour when the bell would sound for their turn on the upper deck. If that happened, the aisles would quickly fill with men heading for their turn at sunshine and fresh air. And of course, the stairwells would become like fish in a net as passengers scrambled for their place in the queue. There would be little hope of their target finding Matsu if that happened. Isamu began to worry. What could be their backup plan? He should have stated a meeting time on the note. Next time, he would know better.

Then, with a hurried motion, the target hopped down from his bunk and began walking toward Isamu. He was not headed in the direction of the latrine; he must be headed for the stairwell. Isamu's first instinct was to move away from his position at the end of the aisle, but it occurred to him he might miss the man across from the target by doing so. Instead, he walked toward the target, trying hard to catch a glimpse of him while at the same time keeping an eye on the bunk across from him for movement. The two men passed in the aisle. The target seemed preoccupied, by the look on his face, and hardly bothered to look at Isamu, let alone acknowledge him. It was a hopeful sign.

There was no movement across from his bunk. Isamu tried his best to see the occupant's face as he walked by, but the man was asleep. Isamu continued to the end of the aisle, then turned up the adjacent aisle and made his way to the starboard stairwell.

The Difficult Years of Toshi Ozawa

From a distance, he could see Matsu and the target standing together just inside. Isamu slowed and scanned first left, then right, looking for anyone suspicious who might also be watching. Taking extra precaution, he walked past them the first time, making his way to the mess hall. Then he continued the circle by returning through the temporary sleeping quarters to portside of the ship's store. Without daring to get close, he scanned the area surrounding the dealer's bunk, looking for any sign of activity. Although not close enough to be certain, it looked like the dealer was lying in his bunk. Isamu, satisfied that Matsu and the target were not subject to scrutiny for the time being, hurried back to the stairwell.

His mind shifted to the new urgency. How to confirm whether the target was somehow affiliated with the dealer without exposing their plan to trap him.

The target looked up at him as he approached. "T...this is the f...fr...friend I t...told you about."

Isamu smiled at the man. He was older than Isamu but still a young man. He had a worried look. His shoulders slumped, and his eyes were clouded.

Without giving his name, Isamu smiled and said, "Thank you for meeting with us. I understand you had a bit of bad luck at cards today. We're sorry to hear that."

The man gave a quick nod but struggled to smile as he replied quietly, "Yes, I should have known better than to play a game I know nothing about."

"So, this is the first time you've played the 'lady' game?"

"Today was the second time. The first time was a few days ago. I won a yen the first game but lost it again in a second game. Today I watched two other men play and win, so I decided to try again. But today I lost five yen. I watched so carefully that I was sure I knew which card was the queen, but somehow I was wrong. I should have known better than to try again. It was money I'll need when I get to San Francisco."

Isamu looked at Matsu, who nodded once.

"How did you happen to enter the game originally?" Isamu asked.

"I heard two men talking to the man who bunks across from me. I don't think they knew I was listening, but they were talking about how easy it was to make money at some card game over in the corner of the deck. They both said it was the easiest money they'd ever made. A 'sure thing,' they said. After they left, I asked my neighbor where the game was held, and he showed me, so the next day I went. That's when I won at first, and then I lost."

"Did your neighbor ever play?"

"I don't know. I didn't see him the day I was there. He might have gone on a different day. If he lost, he probably didn't want to tell anyone. That's the way it was for me; I was too ashamed to tell anyone. If your friend here hadn't found me, I would not have admitted it to anyone."

"Do you know the name of the dealer, by any chance? Did anyone call him by name during the game?"

"Yes, one of the other men called him Orochi. At least I think that's what he said."

"Orochi?" Isamu repeated. Then he looked at Matsu.

"Yes, I think that was it. Orochi."

"What about the other two men? The ones who visited your neighbor. Did you catch their names? Are they the same two men who played the game when you did?"

"Yes, they both played on that first day. Today, one of them played but not the other. I'm sorry I didn't catch their names. I guess I was too busy trying to follow the queen to pay attention to their names."

"Did both of them win on the days that you played?" Isamu asked.

"Yes," he replied. "They made it look so easy. They must have played the game a lot more than me."

Isamu looked at Matsu again. Without having to ask, Matsu knew the look. He nodded to Isamu. They were both convinced this was another innocent victim and not related to the dealer or his gang.

"In truth, it has nothing to do with your experience. Or your luck. The dealer is actually in cahoots with the other players. He lets them win to draw in victims like yourself. Then he might let you win a game to boost your confidence, but he manipulates the cards so you always lose in the end."

The victim looked at him in disbelief.

"Yes, that is the truth. They are very good at it, so you would never suspect the scam. But it is a scam, and their victims never win. The players who walk away with money are part of the scam. They can walk away with as much money as the dealer wants because it all goes back to them. They can use it over and over to draw in new players."

The man had nothing to say. He looked at Isamu and then at Matsu with a look of embarrassment.

"That is why my friend and I are trying to find a way to stop it," Isamu said. "We know gambling is forbidden on the *Coptic*, though it is often overlooked. In this case, since it is outright cheating, we're hoping the captain will take action against the scammers, but we need witnesses who will speak out against them."

He looked at the man with what he hoped was a neutral face.

"Do you think you could speak out against them if we need you to?"

"Does the captain actually care what happens down here?" the man replied. "You see the way they feed us. And our bunks. Not to mention how we're packed in. What makes you think they care about a few lost yen on the steerage deck?"

Isamu looked back at the man. He had a point. In fact, he was probably correct; the captain of the *S.S. Coptic* had more important things to worry about.

"You may be right," he finally said. "The captain might not care about us. Especially when compared to the upper deck. But he did turn the vent pipes for us. Maybe that is just standard procedure once we're underway, but he didn't turn them until we asked.

"The truth is, I don't know. But don't we have to try? Not just for you, but what about the others? He is cheating them, too. All of them. We're sure of it. It's not like he is just lucky. He is cheating."

The man looked down at the planking for a long moment, then lifted his head to search the deck around him. Finally, he looked at Matsu, and then Isamu.

"Yes," he said. "Orochi is a disgrace to our country and all of us who are trying to find a better life. If I can help put a stop to it, you can count on me."

"Thank you," Isamu replied. "But first, you need to be aware; we don't know how dangerous Orochi might be. My friend and I think he could be very vindictive if he found out we were trying to expose him. Are you willing to take the risk that he might come after us?"

"Yes," he said. "He needs to be stopped. I'll take the chance."

"In that case, may I ask your name?" Isamu then asked the man. Then he quickly retracted the request. "No, instead, we'll call you Takeo. That will be our secret name for you. You should call me Tomoki, and this is Takeya," as he tilted his head toward Matsu.

"You told us the dealer's name is Orochi. That is most helpful. Do you think you could learn the names of his partners? We think he has three of them. They take turns on different days so as not to be too obvious. Could you try to learn the names of the two who met with your neighbor? Maybe he could tell you their names. We don't know if he is part of the scam or not, so you will have to be very careful. Or you might be able to overhear Orochi say their names during a game."

Takeo considered his instructions and nodded.

"Good. Let's plan to meet here twice every day. Once at nine in the morning and again at three in the afternoon. In an emergency, you can come to our bunks at this end of aisle fifteen. Just make eye contact or leave a note, and we'll meet you here as soon as possible."

Takeo nodded again. Then Isamu walked away. After some distance, he turned to see Matsu and Takeo leaving in different directions.

Isamu was satisfied they were on the right track. It was time to contact the captain and tell him what they knew. When they met again back at their bunks, he told Matsu it was time to find the crewman.

CHAPTER 37
OROCHI MIZUNO

JUNE 15, 1899 – OVERFLOW QUARTERS ON THE S.S. COPTIC

"After we leave Honolulu, we need to find more players."

Three young men sat across from Orochi's bunk. They leaned forward to catch his every word. "We're running out of time," he continued. "After Honolulu, we only have a few days left. We need to 'up our game,' he said. "Do you think you can find more new players?"

The oldest of the three, barely out of his teens, spoke first. "Yes, I think we can, but I thought you didn't want more. When we left Yokohama, you said we should keep a low profile and not bring attention to ourselves."

"Yeah, but that was Yokohama. Now I'm talking about Honolulu. When we leave Honolulu, we only have five days left to make our money. Every man who boards in Honolulu will be coming from the cane fields, and they'll have money in their pockets...and they'll be more than ready to find something to pass the time to California.

"You know what that means for us? It means we'll have a whole new crop of our own. Get it? New crop? Fresh from the sugar cane fields?" He laughed at his play on words and watched as the three impressionable young men laughed along with him.

"But won't we draw attention to ourselves if we bring more players to the game?" one of the other men asked.

"Nothing to worry about," Orochi said, with a confident tone. "Think about it. Look at the size of this ship." He stretched an arm in both directions to help make the point. "How many times have you seen the captain of the *S.S. Coptic?*—and he made a face as he spat out the last words—join us for supper? How many times have you seen him prance from table to table, asking about our...dining experience, aboard his splendid vessel? Again, he twisted the words as he spoke, to emphasize his distaste for the upper deck.

"As a matter of absolute fact," he continued, "how many times have you actually seen the captain, anywhere? None, I imagine. Because that's how many times he's been on our deck since we left Yokohama. Have you even seen anyone wearing a seaman's uniform since we left? Other than the poor sots who slop our bowls three times a day, with something they call soup. The only other uniform I've seen is the bell ringer, the guy who gives us 'permission' to see daylight for two hours every day.

"No, the captain is not going to show his face on the lowly steerage deck just to look for a few lost yen among the six hundred, or whatever there are, passengers down here in the dark."

"I never thought about it that way, Orochi. You sure are smart. You've thought of everything. How did you learn all this?" the youngest of the three asked.

"I don't like to brag about myself, but my mother always told me how smart I was. But all mothers say that, right? My dad used to tell me that as well, which meant a lot more. But it was not until I went to university that I found out how smart I really was."

"You went to a university?" the young one asked in amazement. "Which one?"

Orochi was caught off guard for a moment. He didn't expect them to ask for details. "Oh...which university? Ah, the big one, of course. The one in...Tokyo. But I only went for a year. At the end of the term, one of my professors—that's what they call the ones that teach—pulled me aside and told me I was already as smart as he was, and there was nothing more they could teach me."

"Uwa!" the young man said. "No wonder you can figure out all this stuff. Who taught you to play the card game? The 'Find the Lady' game?"

Again, Orochi had to think quickly. *I can't tell him I learned it in prison.* "Oh, that," he said. "It's funny you should ask that," he began, "because nobody taught it to me. I thought of the game all by myself. I was bored one night after going home from the factory, so I sat down and started fiddling with some old playing cards. Half the cards were missing, so I pulled out the cards with pictures on them. Then I was just mixing them around, and before I knew it, the game popped right into my head. That's how the game began."

"Uwa!" the young man said again. He rubbed his hands together with excitement. Never had he been befriended by such a fascinating man.

"You worked in a factory?" one of the others asked.

"Yeah, that was after I left university. My uncle had a small silk factory up north. I don't know how he managed to acquire the factory, but he could barely keep it going. When he found out I was leaving the university, he asked if I would go up there and run it for him. I didn't really want to, but my father thought I should. After all, it was his brother, and he needed the help. So I went."

"What was it like, running a factory? Was it hard? Why did you leave?"

Orochi seldom regretted making up stories about his life. The lies were so much more interesting. But this time, it seemed like it might be a mistake. *These guys are asking too many questions.*

"Well, first of all, I would not say it was hard work. Not for me, at least. I guess it must have been very hard for my uncle. Probably for most people. But it was easy for me. Mostly, I just had to make sure everything was in order and the workers were doing their work."

"What did you like best about it?" one of them asked.

Orochi thought for a minute before responding. Part of this would actually be true. "The best thing about it," he began, and then leaned in closer to the three, "the best thing was actually the workers. Almost all of them were girls." His eyes brightened as he thought back to the girls. "And of course, since I was in charge, all of the girls wanted to…wanted to be…special, if you know what I mean."

The three young men now had his full attention. "You mean they wanted…to sleep with you?"

"I hate to put it quite like that, but yes, that's what they wanted. Most of them wanted to marry me. Some of them told me about their dreams. They dreamed of having a good husband, a fancy house, and lots of children. I felt sorry for them most of the time.

"There was one girl in particular. She begged me to marry her. She was beautiful. If I had it to do over again, I probably should have married her. I had a secret name for her. It was a number, actually. Number 8-8-0. That was her employee number. She was the eight hundred and eightieth person to work there. It was our secret code, so the other workers didn't know who I was…attached to. Her real name was Emiko, but of course I couldn't call her that when anyone else was around."

"Why did you leave, if it was such a good place to work?" another one asked.

"Why did I leave? Well, I guess it was what at the university we would call a difference of management style, between me and my uncle."

Orochi actually stopped for a few minutes as he secretly reminisced about that fatal day. If only he'd known there was going to be an inspection by the labor department, he never would have taken advantage of that serving girl in the pantry. And for his uncle to find him there. It was a disaster.

It was only then, as he was packing his few things to leave, that he overheard his uncle's assistant say the name Emiko. She said Emiko and her friend Suki were leaving today, and she needed their employment records. *My life would be totally different if not for that inspection. It was all the fault of the Labor Ministry.*

The three young men sensed a change in the mood of their newly found mentor, as the mentor wisely changed the direction of their conversation.

The oldest one spoke first. "I'm sure we can find a few more 'marks' for the game after Honolulu. But if it's anything like leaving Yokohama, there might be a lot of seasick travelers the first day. Maybe we should wait until the second day to start our game."

Orochi smiled at the man. "You may be right," he said. "We'll wait and see how it goes." Then he laughed at his pun. "See…get it…seasick…we'll wait and see."

His three minions laughed along with him.

Then the oldest one turned serious. "Have you decided…when do you think…you said we would split the winnings. I…we were just wondering when we will…get our share."

"Oh, that," Orochi replied. "Don't you worry about that; you'll all get your share. But I won't know what your share is until we reach San Francisco, will I? When we dock in San Francisco, I'll tally up all the winnings. I keep half, and the rest of you share the other half. Just like we agreed. That's why we need to bring on more players during those last few days. And we need to up the ante besides. It will be our last chance before getting off the ship."

CHAPTER 38
REACHING OUT

JUNE 16, 1899 – SOMEWHERE IN THE PACIFIC

Shortly after four o'clock, when the two emerged on main deck, Isamu went clockwise while Matsu went opposite, and they both made their way around the perimeter of the ship. When they met after one lap, neither had seen the crewman. Matsu gave Isamu a slight shake of the head and kept on walking. On each successive lap, they altered their route slightly, one time staying inboard of the lifeboats, on another lap, taking the outboard side.

First-class cabins took up much of the space on this deck, but there were also lounge chairs arranged neatly in rows for napping in the sun, or reading a book, or whatever other purpose the 'uppers' desired. In addition to the large vent pipes, there were numerous pipes and doghouses for ropes, spars, life vests, and other necessities. Surely a crewman would be somewhere on deck.

Finally, on what must have been the seventh or maybe the eighth lap, Isamu failed to meet Matsu at their usual location. He had no choice but to keep walking. Matsu must be waiting for him along the route. Halfway through his next lap, Isamu spotted him, standing with the crewman between two lifeboats.

Isamu approached the two and tried to anticipate how much Matsu had already been able to explain. The crewman greeted Isamu with a very big grin as he approached. He had apparently ingratiated himself with the captain to some degree, as a result of their previous encounter.

Isamu bowed in a show of his continued respect. The crewman reciprocated. "Did Matsu tell you about the scammers on steerage?" he asked.

"Yes, a little," he replied. "What are you expecting of me? The captain normally doesn't involve himself in matters between steerage passengers. He knows there are bound to be games of cards or dice for money, but he considers it a way for them to pass the time. And if men choose to throw their money away like that, then it's a lesson they must learn for themselves."

"But does he feel the same when the game is actually fraud and there is no way for the victim to win? This game is not really gambling at all. It is stealing. The victims never win; only the dealer and his partners win."

"The captain would not be happy about such an activity," the crewman replied. "If you have proof, he would most likely arrest the men."

"There is more," Isamu added. "We are pretty sure the leader is raiding lockers as well. I have seen him from a distance. We're starting to watch his movements, and we hope to determine where he keeps his plunder. It is most likely in another locker. One of his own."

"If there is theft taking place, then the captain would most certainly want to know about it. But he would need to have some level of proof before he could confront the man. Do you happen to know his name?"

"The dealer's name is Orochi," Isamu replied. "As of yet, we don't know the names of the others. But we are working on that. Also, we don't think the others are involved with the thefts, only Orochi. But we're hoping to confirm that with our surveillance. One other thing you should know is that we both have a very uneasy feeling about Orochi. We think he could be a spiteful man. If he finds out we're watching him, he might retaliate."

He looked at Matsu, then back at the crewman. "What I'm saying," he added, "is that if something happens to either of us, we would like for you to investigate Orochi. It would most likely be because of him."

The crewman suddenly took their discussion more serious. "I understand," he said.

"If you agree," Isamu said, "I can write a letter to the captain about everything we have seen and heard about Orochi and his small gang. That way, if something does happen, you will at least know what we've learned. I can bring you the first letter tomorrow morning at the beginning of our morning walk. We could meet you here, and I could provide an update each morning, of any new evidence. Would that be helpful to the captain?"

The crewman nodded. "Yes, it would be helpful. I will see that he receives your information." Then he bowed to Isamu and then to Matsu, who turned and continued their respective walks.

As soon as Isamu returned to his deck, he went straight to his locker, retrieved a tablet, and carefully recorded everything they had learned about Orochi, and how he had seen him in the middle of the night systematically going from locker to locker. He wrote the dates and names of the known card game victims and the identities of his co-conspirators. It was not yet complete, but would be enough to inform the Captain of Orochi's capers in the event something happened to either Matsu or himself.

On their early morning walk the following day, they found the crewman waiting for them between two lifeboats, just as they had agreed. Isamu scanned the deck surrounding them and handed him the letter. "Please give this to the captain," he said. "I have provided a record of everything we have seen and heard. We don't have names of the co-conspirators yet, but we're working on it. We are hopeful none of them will be disembarking in Honolulu. I don't think we'll have enough proof against them by then."

"We're scheduled to reach Honolulu the day after tomorrow," the crewman said. "The captain will know Orochi's destination from the passenger list. If you learn the other names, we can check on them as well."

"We'll do our best," Isamu replied. The meeting was short, and the three men parted.

Sitting together on Matsu's bunk after breakfast, they made plans for the day. Matsu would watch for a third victim in the card scam. Isamu would confirm the appearance of the three co-conspirators. This time, he would try to follow them when the game was over, in hopes of locating their bunk locations. He guessed they were in the overflow cot area, probably neighbors of Orochi. That was the most likely way he would have recruited them.

They had barely finished their discussion when Akio approached from the rear of the ship. Looking up, they quickly scanned the aisle around them and then greeted him with smiles. They stood and fell alongside when he reached their bunk. The insinuation was for him to keep walking. Isamu took the lead, heading for their now-favorite meeting place in the forward stairwell.

As they walked, Isamu asked, "Have you learned anything new about Orochi? Have you been able to pinpoint his locker?"

"Yes," Akio replied. "He has two lockers. They are well aft on the port side. He stopped at one of them in the late afternoon and retrieved something from it. Possibly a kimono, but I couldn't tell for sure. I think it might be his normal locker. Then, well past midnight, he stopped at the other locker. This time, he placed several small articles in it. Again, I could not tell what. It was dark, and the items were small. I think that's where he keeps his pillage."

"Good work, Akio," Isamu said. "Do you think you can get the two numbers? If the captain needs to look in them, we want to make sure we have the right ones. Is there any kind of marking on the locker or even in the aisle or the ceiling you could use to pinpoint the exact one?"

"The two of them are adjacent, one above the other. I know I can identify them within a close proximity, but not precisely. I'll look for something to mark them from. I'm two aisles away. When I see him coming next time, maybe I can go to the latrine and get a closer look."

"Akio, you are brave, but don't do anything to cause suspicion. Orochi is obviously clever and probably very cautious. At least now we know the general location. When we reach Honolulu, a number of passengers are bound to depart. That will free up a few of the bunks. If we're clever too, we might be able to procure a bunk just across the aisle from them."

Matsu and Akio both smiled at the idea. Isamu was proving to be rather clever himself. Neither of them had considered the possibility. For a youngster, he was more than they'd given him credit.

"If you have anything new to report, walk by our bunks again tomorrow," Isamu said. Then, without further prompting, Akio turned and headed toward the port-side lockers. Isamu and Matsu returned to their bunks.

That afternoon, Isamu realized he might need additional writing paper in order to record their findings. He had only three pages remaining in his current tablet. And he already felt guilty about not writing more to his family in Kamaishi. They would certainly be anxious to hear everything about crossing the Pacific on a steamship. He was living an adventure they would likely never have.

For that reason, he entered the ship's store on his way back to their sleeping quarters, following lunch. He swung open the door and walked in, only to find himself again, second in line at the display counter. The man in front of him was of familiar build, but from behind, meant nothing particular to Isamu. He was having a conversation with the clerk behind the counter, which at first Isamu tried not to listen to. His upbringing did not condone eavesdropping.

But in the small space in which they found themselves, it soon became evident to Isamu that the man was interested in padlocks, and as he listened, the man had apparently lost the key to his, and was asking for a master key in order to get inside his locker. He was in need of medicine, which was locked inside, he told the clerk.

After half-listening for several minutes, something about the conversation triggered an alarm in Isamu's head. He looked squarely at the back of the man in front of him, at his neck, his hair, tied in a knot, and his kimono. Only then did he notice the man shifting his weight from one leg to the other, favoring the left.

Now he listened with complete interest. Why would Orochi, if this was him, want a master key to the storage padlocks? He tried not to panic.

The man pleaded with the clerk. Without his medicine, he would be in great pain. "For his leg," he said. "It was an old war wound while fighting the Sino-Japanese war. He was decorated for his service," he told the clerk.

Again, he pleaded, "Just loan it to me for long enough to go straight to my locker, retrieve my medicine, and I'll come straight back here with the key. I'll buy a new padlock to replace the one with the missing key. I'll leave a security deposit of ten yen for the few short minutes I'll be gone. I need my medicine. Surely you can understand my plight."

And much to Isamu's dismay, he did. The clerk handed the man a new padlock, making sure the key was attached. And then a separate key, which, from his limited view behind the man, Isamu thought looked almost like the one on the new lock. Overjoyed, the man thanked the clerk profusely, handed over the promised ten yen, then turned and headed for the door.

Isamu barely had time to tilt his gaze to the floor as the man turned to leave. Then he shifted his gaze toward the display counter, trying to look as if he were pondering something to purchase. But there was no longer a shadow of doubt. The man was Orochi.

It took a few minutes for Isamu to collect his thoughts while the clerk stared at him. Finally, he stammered, "One writing tablet, please."

The clerk gave Isamu his change but was still making out the carefully written receipt when Orochi returned. Without fanfare or even a pretense of courtesy, he stepped in front of Isamu, slapped the key on the glass countertop, and demanded his deposit back.

The clerk looked at Isamu with a look of apology and stopped working on the receipt. Instead, he opened his money drawer and retrieved nine yen, keeping one as payment for the new lock and returning the rest of his deposit. He picked up the master key, looked at it carefully, and rubbed it with his fingers.

"It feels like there is wax on it. Why does it feel waxy?" he asked Orochi.

"Oh, that," he replied. "It was stiff when I tried to use it, so I put candle wax on it. Just enough to provide a lubricant. Haven't you ever done that? It works great for sticky locks. Don't worry, it doesn't hurt the key. If anything, it will keep it from rusting in the salty air. I won't even charge you for it," he chortled. Then he turned and left, leaving the clerk with a puzzled look on his face. Orochi did not wait for his receipt.

"Some people," he said. "You see all kinds on a voyage like this. Especially down here in steerage. I'm trying to get promoted to the main deck, but it takes seniority. Maybe the guy up there will decide to move on. Then I could get his job."

Isamu glanced down at his unfinished receipt. The clerk, an observant person, recognized the signal and finished the receipt, handing it to Isamu.

When he got to his bunk, Matsu could see that he was pale and trembling. "D.. did you g.. get your t.. tablet?" he asked. "What's wrong? D.. did s.. some... something happen?"

"Orochi was in the store just ahead of me. I didn't see him until it was too late to leave. He said he lost the key to his storage lock and needed a master key to get medicine from his locker."

"D…Did they g…give him one?"

"Yes, he offered to leave a deposit and pleaded about needing medicine for his bad leg. He said he was injured during the war with China. He wasn't gone for long. I was afraid he would just keep it and assume the clerk would not take time to track him down, but he brought it back while I was still there. He said he had to put candle wax on it to get it to work better."

"C…Candle w…wax?"

"Yes, that's what he said. He said it acts as a lubricant to make the lock work easier."

"This w…was for a m…master k…key?"

"Yes. That's why Orochi needed it. So he could open his lock. But he brought it right back. I was still there when he came back."

"The w...wax was for m...making a m...mold. Orochi must have m...made an image of the k...key so he c...could m...make his own."

Isamu's face fell at the thought of it. Matsu was right. That had to be the reason for the wax. "Is it hard to make a key? Do you think Orochi could make one on board, or will he have to have it made in Honolulu?"

"It depends on the k...key. He might be able t...to m...modify the original k...key with a hand f...file. It d...depends on t...the shape. If they're a l...lot different, then he'll have t...to have a n...new one m...made. I d...don't think he c...could do that h...here unless he has a h...helper in t...the ship's repair s...shop."

"We have to let the captain know," Isamu said. "He can alert the repair shop. I'll put that in our report for tomorrow morning. For now, we need to prepare for today's card game. It will be starting soon. I'll meet you in the stairwell if you're able to bring another victim today."

Matsu nodded.

"Do you think we should ask Takeo to help with the locker surveillance? I'm afraid Orochi is preparing to increase his plundering, especially if he gets access to lockers with padlocks."

Matsu nodded again. He liked questions with yes or no answers. He could respond without speaking.

***

The *Coptic* arrived in Honolulu on June sixteenth, with a two-day layover before sailing on to San Francisco. Isamu and Matsu had wanted to spend time on the luscious, mid-Pacific island, admiring its palm trees and unbelievable flowers and birds. But their time was cut short.

They continually circulated the steerage deck, watching for disembarking passengers. When they found someone emptying their locker and taking whatever few possessions from their bunk, they quickly laid claim to the open bunk. Akio, Takeo, and Masaru, all victims of Orochi's crooked card game, were helping. They had mapped out strategic positions along both storage locker aisles, particularly near Orochi's lockers.

If they claimed one bunk within the target area, and later a better one opened up, they were quick to make a move to the better one. By sailing time on Saturday, they were satisfied they had done all they could. Between the five of them, they now had unobstructed views of all the lockers, and from three of them, a clear view of Orochi's.

The crossing from Honolulu to San Francisco would take seven days. Not much time to close the trap for Orochi and his friends.

Orochi, on the other hand, was filled with optimism. He had inherited a whole new manifest of potential victims. For every passenger who disembarked at Honolulu, a replacement boarded for San Francisco. And most of them with more money than those who left. These men came from the cane fields. They had money in their pockets and were newly released from years of sweaty, tedious servitude in snake-infested sugarcane. They'd been dreaming of this day since their first day on the plantations. A yoke had been lifted. They were ready, and long overdue for even a small taste of freedom.

They were perfect candidates for the kind of entertainment Orochi provided his clients. He salivated at the thought. The hardest part of this voyage would be controlling the number of players each day.

His skills had definitely improved since leaving Yokohama, but he still depended on having only one or two 'marks' at every game. Otherwise, it was too hard to control the winners and losers. He still remembered a game where one of the 'marks' actually walked away with his money. Usually, if they walked away a winner, they would come back for more, on another day, but in that particular instance, Orochi never saw him again. He still watched for him at mealtime and when walking around the deck.

But Orochi had other ways of increasing his wealth. Especially with his magic key.

***

Matsu and the victims now took turns watching the games from a distance. He and Isamu agreed they didn't really need additional spies after Honolulu, but they did need to know if Orochi had recruited new partners. Matsu confirmed that Orochi was still sleeping in the overflow area, and his partners were still in their original bunks.

The first night at sea, the five investigators were surprised that not once did Orochi meander through the storage lockers. Had they misjudged him, or were they too late? Had he already pilfered everything he could carry off the ship in San Francisco? It would be a disappointment if they could not detain him on charges of stealing. Stealing was more serious than gambling.

Having slept little in the night, they each took several short naps throughout the day. It would be impossible to stay awake again tonight without getting sleep during the day. They decided to forego watching the card game.

It was well past midnight the second night, when Akio heard the quiet sound of footsteps at the forward end of aisle sixteen. A few of the newcomers were still ailing from seasickness. Most likely, one of them was headed for the latrine to retch their meal. Alert, he lay motionless in his bunk. The sound came closer. *Was it headed to the stern and a visit to the latrine?* The footsteps faltered just when they were next to his bunk.

Akio was not brave. In fact, he was afraid. His heart was beating so loudly in the night that he half expected the man to turn and stare at him. To Akio, it was loud enough to drown out the nearby sounds of heavy breathing and assorted snoring.

There was no sound coming from the man, yet Akio dared not lift his head or even shift his body for a better look. Then he heard a very quiet sound of metal on metal. It was followed by a distinct but quiet click. Then another metallic sound as the padlock opened and was removed from the latch. Finally, the unmistakable sound of a door opening on rusty hinges. Then quiet. Akio lay as still as he possibly could, trying with all his might to control the breath as it rushed in and out of his open mouth. *Breathe deep and slow*, he kept telling himself.

Then, as he listened, he heard rustling sounds. Not sounds he could distinctly articulate, but what he could only interpret as the sound of rummaging through a locker, searching for something. The sounds came and went.

When Akio heard someone in a nearby bunk snore at a new volume, he seized the chance to slither quickly to his side. Then, hearing no new noises from the aisle, he opened one eyelid just enough to peer through the tiny slit. Through the opening, he saw the silhouette of a man standing before him, not more than two meters away. *Long, deep breaths, in and out,* he told himself. He watched as the man placed a small wooden travel case on the deck, next to his feet. Beads of sweat formed on Akio's forehead and trickled downward toward his mat. He inhaled one deep breath and held perfectly still as the man swung the door back to its closed position.

Then came the familiar sound of a padlock snapping shut. And without wasting a moment, the man picked up the case and made his way down the aisle toward the stern. Akio never saw his face, only his profile from behind. But he walked with a limp.

Wishing he could alert Isamu, who was now using a bunk just across the aisle from Orochi's locker, Akio knew he dare not try. All he could hope was that Isamu, or at least one of the three on that side of the ship, were still awake. *We still have a few more nights though, in case they're not,* he told himself.

He could barely wait until morning to rendezvous with the others. Specifically, to learn if they had seen Orochi store his latest pillage. Using the strategy they worked out in Honolulu, Akio would meet with Matsu in the aft starboard stairwell, and Isamu would meet with Takeo and Masaru in the forward one. That way, they would minimize being seen together, in case Orochi became suspicious.

Matsu and Isamu would meet separately after that to relay information between the two groups.

Akio could not contain his excitement when Matsu reported back to him. All three had watched Orochi approach his lockers. Isamu, being the nearest to it, was able to pinpoint the locker number. And he watched as Orochi placed the small travel case into it. But the best was yet to come. Isamu had recognized the wooden case. It was filled with silk threads of every color, given to him by Cho at the silk factory in Osaki. It would be identifiable, and confirm the theft.

Isamu was already writing his daily report for the captain. He and Matsu would deliver it to the crewman later that morning. Matsu was so enthused he could barely get the sentences out of his mouth. He, like Akio, had to keep telling himself to breathe long and deep, in and out.

Watching Matsu labor through his breathing ritual when trying to speak, Isamu thought about the patron back home at the teahouse. "Can you sing?" he asked Matsu.

"W…What?" Matsu replied.

"Do you ever, you know…sing?"

"S…So…Some t…times when I'm a…alone."

"I didn't think of it earlier, but the patron at the teahouse told me that when he sang, he didn't stutter. Maybe you should try that."

"N…No," he said. "I'm n…not g…going t…to sing. I…It w…would n…not be g…g…good."

"What if you just pretended you were going to sing the words, but then spoke them instead? Kind of a mixture. Maybe it would help."

"I w…will have to t…try that w…when I'm a…alone," he said.

That night, long after late-night discussions were replaced with a symphony of snoring sounds, Isamu, Matsu, and their three anxious helpers lay quietly in their bunks, listening for the sound of footfalls, moving across the wooden floor.

This time it was Takeo who first heard the sound. Very faint to begin, but gradually louder as it neared the area of his bunk, along the portside lockers. He often slept on his side, so it was an easy position for him to maintain as he waited patiently for Orochi to make his move.

Like Akio, he kept his eyelids as closed as possible while he peered toward the aisle. The dark silhouette of a man approached from the direction of the overflow quarters. The figure walked past his bunk for several meters before it stopped. Takeo opened his eyes fully now and stretched his neck for a better view.

The Difficult Years of Toshi Ozawa 337

The figure studied the pair of lockers now facing him, then pulled something from his pocket and moved both hands toward the padlock of the bottom locker. Takeo heard a faint clicking sound as the lock unlatched. The figure glanced quickly up and down the aisle to ensure the coast was clear. Then he swung open the locker door and stooped partway into it while submerging one arm completely down into the bottom.

Takeo watched as he pulled something from the locker and held it close to his face in the shadowy light. He moved it to his ear and shook it lightly, as if trying to divine the contents. He set the package on the floor next to his foot and once more thrust his arm deep inside the locker. Finding nothing more of interest, he closed the lid and replaced the lock.

Then, without moving, he repeated the process on the locker directly above the first. Takeo watched as he poked around the contents of the second locker. Even from a distance, it was obvious the locker was filled with an assortment of items. Several times, Orochi pulled something from the bin, looked at it carefully, even held it up to the light of a nearby lamp.

Takeo fought the urge to shout at him, even charge after him in the night. The gall. Pillaging the luggage of innocent passengers, and with the added audacity to select only the items he considered most valuable.

Takeo watched as Orochi placed two items on the floor next to his previous bundle, closed the door, and replaced the lock. He then tucked the first package under his arm, lifted the other two with his left hand, and proceeded with purpose down the aisle.

Isamu was ready. He had also seen and watched, as Orochi raided the two lockers farther up the aisle. The only thing Isamu was really interested in now, was which of Orochi's three lockers would he use to store the plunder. Isamu assumed one of the three was Orochi's personal locker, and therefore he would not put stolen goods in it. The other two were for his bounty. That way, if anyone challenged him, he could open his locker and demonstrate his innocence.

Orochi placed two of the packages he was carrying into one of the lockers. He had to shove and rearrange in order to get them both to fit. The third package, the one under his arm, he placed in the second locker. Isamu noticed with a certain satisfaction that he used only one key. Matsu was right. Orochi had somehow fabricated a master key.

Orochi, with his night's work now complete, turned back up the aisle and headed to the overflow quarters. Even in the darkness, Isamu saw the haughty look across his face.

CHAPTER 39
THE CAPTAIN'S TEAM

JUNE 21, 1899 – THREE DAYS FROM SAN FRANCISCO

Early the next morning, Isamu updated his report for the captain. When he and Matsu rendezvoused with the crewman, he surprised them with a report of his own.

"The captain has asked me to inform you that he will launch a raid on Orochi tomorrow. He has developed a plan of action in which I am to become a victim in the card game. You are to meet me in the forward starboard stairwell at two-thirty. From there, one of your helpers will lead me to the game. I am to enter the game, even if I have to invite myself.

"One of you will lead my companion to your viewing location, where he will watch the game for himself. If he concludes that Orochi is cheating at the game, he will initiate action. Once that begins, and you will know when you see it happen, your men are to remain in the background and stay out of the way. The only assistance he will want from you is confirmation of which of the players are part of the conspiracy. If, as you suspect, Orochi is dangerous, the captain does not want any of you close during the confrontation. I will meet you here in the morning to confirm our plans. And to accept your report if you have any new information. Oh, and the captain wishes to thank you for bringing this to his attention. He takes pride in his vessel and its passengers."

The two men were so excited that even Isamu had trouble speaking. Maybe they actually could put an end to Orochi's antics. They split up to tell the others of the coming plan. Takeo would be the one to watch the game today. His instructions were simply to confirm the daily routine…the same three partners, any new victims.

They watched Orochi through that night, but with the same objective as at cards. Watch for the possibility of an additional locker to store his plunder. Watch for any deviation in his behavior.

The next morning, a Thursday, the sixth day since Honolulu, Isamu and Matsu met the crewman between two lifeboats on the main deck. The day was sunny and warm. It would have been uncomfortable except for the twenty knot breeze created by the speed of the ship. Two days from now, they would be walking down the gangplank in San Francisco.

"Everything is as I reported to you yesterday," the crewman said. "I will meet you at two-thirty in the stairwell. Have your man available to take me to the card game. And you are to take my companion to a place where he can safely observe until he decides to act. Oh, and one more thing. We will not be wearing crewmen's clothing. We will be dressed as passengers."

Both men nodded in response. "We'll see you then," Isamu said. The crewman disappeared while Isamu and Matsu walked away in opposite directions. Hopefully, for the last time.

Following breakfast, they each returned to their bunks. They agreed that Akio should be the one to take the crewman to the game, since he was the first of their helpers to be recruited. It had also been a while since he'd played the game and seemed to them, at least, the one most likely to return to the game before arriving in San Francisco.

Try as they might, neither man could relax. Too many things could go wrong. What if Orochi didn't show up today? What if he played the game honestly? Maybe he would realize he was being watched, or that the crewman was a setup. What if he wouldn't surrender to the authorities? Was it going to be just the crewman and his 'companion' to launch the raid? Surely Orochi and his three partners could overpower just the two of them. Would Matsu and Isamu have to help capture him if he ran? *But the crewman told us to stay at a distance.*

The more they thought, the more apprehensive they became.

When two-thirty finally arrived, Isamu, Matsu, and their three helpers were waiting at the stairwell. At that very moment, the crewman and another man, older and distinguished-looking, descended the steps to the dim and smoky steerage deck below. They would not have recognized the crewman had he not told them he would be dressed as a passenger. The man with him looked familiar to Isamu, but he was too nervous to give it thought. The thought that did prevail was that there were just the two of them.

This is not going to work, he concluded. But it was the captain's plan, and the captain surely knew what he was doing.

Isamu introduced Akio to the crewman, and the two of them headed across the deck to portside, to the empty space between the regular sleeping and overflow quarters.

Isamu led the older man to a viewing location several meters from the game, behind the heavy wooden beams. Matsu and the two other helpers remained behind, at the bottom of the stairwell. They were standing with their backs to the steps, watching where the others had gone, when they were surprised by a group of eight, ten, maybe a dozen men descending from the stairwell behind them. Main deck passengers never came below to steerage. These men were dressed as passengers. Why on earth would they be coming below?

The three men moved politely aside to let them pass. The two men in front headed quickly in the direction that Akio and the crewman had gone. The others dispersed down different aisles between the dining tables, also heading to the portside section of the ship. Then they were gone.

The three men looked at one another with bewildered looks. "W...Who w... were t...they?" Matsu uttered.

Takeo and Masaru simply stared back at him and shrugged their shoulders.

From their partially concealed location behind a beam, Isamu and the other man watched the card game already in progress. They saw Akio and the crewman standing near the action as first one, then another of the conspirators placed their bet and picked the winning card. The current victim predictably took his turn and lost. Today the starting ante was five yen. Isamu and the older man watched as the victim picked the jack of spades.

Before he had a chance to try again, the crewman stepped up with a ten-yen note. "I'll play," he said. "I think I have it figured out."

Orochi looked up at him from his seat on an upturned bucket. "Who are you?" he asked. "I haven't seen you around here before." Then he looked over at Akio, who was standing beside the stranger. "Is he with you?" he asked. "You've been here before. Is he with you?"

"Yes, I brought him," Akio said, trying not to show his growing fear. "He's a friend of mine. I was telling him about the game, and he wanted to try it, too."

"You didn't have very good luck, as I recall," Orochi said. "I remember you from before Honolulu." Then he scanned the dark corner of the ship, looking for anything out of place. Catching a glimpse of Isamu and his companion several meters away, his gaze lingered momentarily on the two men. The companion pulled a cigarette from one of his pockets and offered one to Isamu.

Orochi turned back to face the crewman. "How come I haven't seen you before?" he repeated. After this many days at sea, I've seen almost everyone on steerage deck."

Isamu felt his body begin to warm. Orochi had never questioned players before. He turned to his companion and shrugged his shoulders with a grimace across his face. Then he turned quickly back to Orochi.

"I boarded in Honolulu," the crewman replied nonchalantly. "I was tired for the first two days, so haven't been away from my bunk very much. Today is the first day I've been out."

Orochi moved his gaze to Akio and then back again. "Can you afford to play? Some passengers, especially down here, don't have a lot of money to spend. I'd hate to cause a hardship in case your luck runs bad."

"Yes, I've been working in Honolulu for a year. I was a foreman in the cane fields, so I made good money. I can afford to play."

"You know how the game is played?" he asked.

"Yes, I think so," the crewman replied. "All I have to do is watch the cards and pick out the queen after you lay them down."

"That's all there is to it," Orochi replied. "It's as easy as that. You'd be surprised how many people don't pay attention. They let themselves get all worked up and forget to pay attention. Are you sure you want to play? We can start with two yen, if you want to see how it works."

"No, let's start with five," the crewman said. "I think I have it figured out."

Orochi smiled at the newcomer and motioned for him to come closer. He methodically shuffled the three cards, then showed them face up for all to see before turning them over and laying them gently down on the makeshift table.

Isamu's hopes remained alive as he watched Orochi ceremoniously turn over the queen of hearts. He was playing exactly to his script. Let the victim win the first hand, then up the ante.

Orochi moaned in agony as he displayed the queen, and handed five yen over to the crewman. "See, I told you. It is just a matter of paying attention. It's so easy to win I don't know why I keep playing it myself. I'll be broke if we don't get to San Francisco soon," he said. Then he looked directly at the crewman and pleaded, "Could you give a poor old war casualty like myself a chance to win back his five yen? Looks like I'm going to need it by the time we get to California."

The crewman looked at the small group gathered around the makeshift table and then at Orochi. "I suppose that's only fair. I wouldn't want you to disembark with empty pockets." The entire group chuckled about that. "Do you want to go for ten?"

"Oh no, I wouldn't dare go for ten. Not with my luck today. Five is enough."

Orochi mixed the three cards as he looked around the table, first at the crewman, seated across from him, and then his cronies, scattered behind. Not a trace of recognition did he show, when he scanned the faces of his three gullible conspirators. All four of them were too engrossed in watching the cards to return his gaze. But before he laid them on the table, something caught his eye and he turned quickly to the dark corner where Isamu stood with his companion.

Isamu froze when he saw Orochi watching them a second time. In a purely instinctive reaction, he jerked his head toward his companion as quickly as he could. When his companion saw what was happening, he calmly turned toward Isamu, laughed as if Isamu had just told him the best joke of his life, then took a slow drag on the remains of his still burning cigarette.

It caught Isamu so off guard that he chuckled himself, at seeing the worldly gentleman next to him laugh so easily at nothing at all.

Seeing the younger man's strange reaction a moment before, Orochi tensed and momentarily stopped mixing the cards. When the four men around the table saw his hands come to a stop, they looked up in search of an answer. Orochi was staring at something off in the corner.

The crewman sucked in a breath when he looked for himself. Orochi had spotted his companion. He tried to stay calm, but he felt his face starting to flush. He turned back to face Orochi, who was still looking at the two men in the shadows.

When the older man laughed and put a cigarette in his mouth, Orochi continued to stare. But when the younger man smiled and laughed in return, Orochi slowly started to mix the cards again, and then looked down at the wooden crate. He carefully mixed the three cards and displayed them for all to see before laying them down, one by one.

Isamu had not seen this tactic before. He expected Orochi to double the bet. Surely Orochi was not on to them. This was their only chance. The captain would never allow a second time, especially if this first one did not reveal any cheating. He turned to his companion and once again, shrugged his shoulders and grimaced. He turned back to the game with a dreaded feeling.

The Difficult Years of Toshi Ozawa

For the second time, the crewman laid his five yen on the table, next to what should be the queen of hearts. And for the second time, Orochi slowly lifted the card and displayed, for all the group to see, the queen of hearts.

Isamu's heart sank. Color drained from his face as he turned to his companion in the dark corner of the ship. "I can't believe it," he whispered to the distinguished-looking man. "This has never happened before. He always wins the second hand."

The companion faced Isamu and said, simply, "Let's see what happens next."

Orochi nearly collapsed as the card displayed the queen. "Uwa! He gasped. I can't believe it. I knew I shouldn't have agreed to another game. When my luck changes, it changes for good. Congratulations, 'Honolulu,' he said to the crewman. "You must have brought some good luck from the cane fields. I'm glad you didn't play yesterday or the day before. I would be broke for sure. Please don't come back tomorrow," he said playfully. "I can't afford your company." Then he laughed in a feigned and forceful voice.

He slowly handed the crewman the second five yen note. Then he began to gather his cards and rise from his seat on the bucket. Just as he stood, he reached in his pocket and pulled out ten yen. "I know this is probably the dumbest thing I've ever done, but what do you say to one more game, for ten yen? That would let me break even for the day. What do you say?"

Isamu was riveted to the game with his eyes but could make out only bits of the conversation, due to their distance away. When Orochi stood, he thought the game was over, and along with it, their only chance to catch him cheating. And if he wasn't cheating at the card game, what chance was there of the captain searching his lockers? That too, must have been a simple misunderstanding of some kind.

He turned to look at his companion, who smiled back in return. He didn't seem the least bit concerned.

Isamu watched as Orochi sat back down and looked over at the crewman. Then he saw a crooked smile move slowly across his face. This was something new, and Isamu could not ignore the feeling. Something was wrong. Something was definitely wrong.

For the third time, Orochi mixed the three cards and laid them methodically on the wooden table. With only slight deliberation the crewman laid ten yen next to the card on his right, which should easily have been the queen.

But when Orochi raised it to show his opponent and the group, it was clearly the jack of spades.

Isamu took his eyes off the game just long enough to look at the man standing next to him. The man turned to him and smiled. He did not seem alarmed. When Isamu returned his gaze to the game, Orochi was surprisingly calm. He turned to the crewman, sitting across from him, and graciously pulled the ten yen to himself.

"Finally, my luck has turned," he sighed with great fanfare. "I can afford to eat when we get to San Francisco." He paused and complimented the crewman. "You are a worthy opponent," he said. "You really had me worried today. I don't think I've played anyone as good as you. You had me worried."

"Thank you," the crewman answered in a neutral voice. Then he began to stand, as if to walk away.

"Wait!" Orochi said. "I always like to give an honest man a chance to redeem himself. What do you say to one more hand? Now that I have my ten yen again, what do you say we play one last hand, for…say, twenty yen? What do you say?"

The crewman remained standing for a moment trying to decide. He had not been given specific instructions about how long to keep playing. He'd been told the game would be interrupted before it actually came to an end, and he had already played three hands. No one had intervened. They had given him forty yen to play, so apparently it was okay to continue. He sat back down at the flimsy table.

"Twenty yen?" he said, as he settled himself.

"Yes, twenty yen, and this will be our last game, win or lose."

Orochi, now for the fourth time, mixed the three cards and displayed them for all to see: jack, king, queen. Then closed them together and laid them down, one by one, on the wobbly table.

The crewman picked the third card. The one on his left as he faced the three cards. The card on Orochi's right, as he sat across the weathered wood. It should have been the queen. But Orochi, with practiced fanfare, slowly lifted the card to display the jack of diamonds.

As the now familiar imitation smile filled his face, he reached out to retrieve the twenty yen lying next to the missing queen. But before he had the note tucked safely in his pocket, Isamu's companion walked briskly to the group of players and announced:

"Under orders of the Captain of the *S.S. Coptic,* I command all of you to remain as you are. Do not move. Do not try to leave. You..." he pointed to Orochi, "are under house arrest for illicit gambling on board this vessel, which is forbidden."

He pointed to the other three conspirators. "The three of you are also under house arrest for enticement and participation in illegal gaming on board the vessel."

Orochi stood in protest. "Surely, sir, you cannot deprive a few hard-working passengers a brief respite from the boredom of days below deck, with hardly enough sunlight or fresh air to keep us alive. What's the harm in having a little fun at a game of chance among friends?"

The man looked squarely at Orochi in the eyes and replied, "I agree that a little harmless fun between friends at a game of chance does not demand the involvement of the ship's captain. However, in this case, it is neither harmless nor a game of chance.

"The captain of a ship such as the *Coptic* has seen more games of chance than you have likely dreamed of. And he could tell you as we speak that your sleight-of-hand is obvious even from ten meters distant. The captain has received reports of your behavior since the beginning of the voyage. He has all the evidence he needs to order your arrest and incarceration for the remainder of the voyage.

"As for your accomplices, it has been their unfortunate circumstance to fall under your influence. They might well be honorable men if not for your persuasion of easy money."

The man then lifted his arm and, with a quick motion of his hand, signaled what must have been a half-dozen men who seemed to appear from nowhere, and converge on the three partners.

"Take them away," he said. "Put them in the brig until further notice."

Then he looked at Orochi while the others looked at one another in disbelief.

"You said we were safe," one of the men shouted at Orochi. "You said nothing could happen to us," he continued. Before they could even think about running, had there been a place to run, the crewmember's helpers were upon them, placing shackles around their wrists.

To Orochi, the man said, with a voice of calm authority. "And you, Orochi, I have more to say to you."

Orochi stared at the man with a look of mystified disbelief.

"Yes, I know who you are, Orochi Mizuno. Any passenger brought to the *Coptic* by the *Kempeitai* is bound to have the full attention of the ship's captain. But, a more serious matter has been brought to his attention."

He raised his arm a second time, and with the same quick rotation of an extended finger, another half-dozen men appeared from beyond the shadows, to surround Orochi.

"I would like for you to lead us to your storage locker. We think it might be interesting to see what we find inside."

Orochi smiled with relief. "Of course. I have nothing to hide. Whatever you've been told is nothing but lies," he sneered.

Surrounded by the men, Orochi headed for his locker. Isamu and the older man fell in behind.

The small band marched down the portside aisle and came to a halt in front of the locker Isamu knew to be Orochi's.

"Is this your locker?" The older man asked,

"Yes," he snarled. "But look all you want; you won't find anything that doesn't belong to me."

"Hand me the key," the man ordered.

Orochi tried to hide the look of sudden alarm when he thought about the key. He had taken to carrying only the master key in his pocket so he would not have to fumble with finding the right one in the middle of the night.

The man held out his hand. "Hand me the key to the padlock, please."

Beginning to perspire, Orochi had no other choice. He reached in his pocket and pulled out the single key. He handed it to the man, trying to display a look of confidence.

The man took the key, placed it in the lock, and turned it, allowing the latch to open. He then removed the padlock and stepped back. "Please empty the contents of the locker for us," he said to Orochi.

"What is it, exactly, that you expect to find? Everything here belongs to me. I don't know how many times I have to tell you that."

The man cast a look at Orochi, which convinced him he had better do as instructed. He carefully reached in and pulled one small valise from the locker. He set it on the floor between them.

"This is your only possession?" asked the man.

Orochi nodded.

"Please open it for me," he said.

"That is my private property," Orochi whined. "You have no right to inspect my private property."

The man looked at one of his helpers and nodded toward the valise.

The helper stepped forward and bent down to the parcel. He lifted the small tab at the end of its long zipper and proceeded to pull it to the opposite end. That done, he grasped the sides of the bag, one with each hand, and spread them open as far as they would go. The contents came easily into view. A kimono, a tunic, and a second pair of shoes. Little else.

"See, I told you so!" snarled Orochi. "Are you satisfied now?"

The older man looked at his helper once more. Whether previously rehearsed or simply from working together for most of their lives, Orochi could not guess. But either way, the result was the same. The helper bent down and searched the sides of the valise. Just as he expected, inside the lining was a barely visible pocket. He slipped his hand into it, and when he pulled it out, held up for all to see. His hand was filled with money.

From where he stood, Isamu could identify what might be as much as fifty or even a hundred yen. Folded together as they were, only an actual tally would reveal its worth.

"Does this belong to you as well?" the older man asked.

"Yes, how many times do I have to tell you? That is my grubstake for getting started in San Francisco. Are you satisfied now?"

"You are certain this is your money alone?" The man repeated. "No part of it belongs to anyone other than yourself?"

"For the last time. Yes!" he exclaimed. "No one else but me. Now am I free to go?"

"Not quite," the older man replied. "When you boarded, you were brought here by your father and an officer of the *Kempeitai*; is that correct?"

Alarmed the man would know his history, his face began to pale. "How I boarded is none of your business, and besides, what difference would that make?" he retorted.

"It is my business, because the captain of the ship has made it my business. And it makes a difference because, according to the boarding documents signed by your father and the officer, you were given the choice of prison or deportation. And to be eligible for deportation to America, you are required to have at least twenty-five yen on your person.

"The documents clearly state you were given twenty-five yen at the boarding ramp to meet that requirement. Your comrades confirmed that you had no money, thus forcing them to contribute on your behalf. Therefore, it is relevant because if it is your money, as you have indicated, then I am curious as to how the twenty-five yen you came on board with, somehow multiplied by threefold."

Orochi stuttered, trying to think of a plausible explanation. "I had some money they didn't know about," he stammered.

"So, either you lied to your father and an officer of the military, or you are lying to me. Either way, it is not behavior the captain will accept on board his ship."

"Do you have any other lockers for us to see?" The man continued. "Are you sure this is your only one?"

Orochi nodded vigorously. "Yes, this is my only locker. Why would I have another locker when I have barely enough to put in one?"

Still holding the key Orochi had given him, he stepped forward to the locker next to Orochi's.

"Wouldn't it be a coincidence if this key happened to open the locker next to yours?" the older man asked Orochi.

Orochi was too shocked to reply. He stared into his now-empty locker with a vacant look.

The man inserted the key in the lock and, with a simple turn, released the latch. Facing Orochi, he met his eyes. No words were needed. Orochi exhaled as his color continued to fade.

But the man was not done yet. He held up the key for Orochi to plainly see, then inserted it into the padlock of the locker directly above the last. Turning the key, it too, unlatched the lock.

"Do we even need to look in these two lockers, Mr. Mizuno? Is it possible they contain the results of your midnight raids?"

Orochi knew it was over. The two lockers were filled with booty from a hundred other passengers taken since the second night of the voyage. That, plus his cash from the card games, would be enough to keep him locked up for longer than he cared to imagine.

When he considered a return to prison, something inside him snapped. His brain refused to comprehend the obvious. There was no place to hide. It was nothing but instinct and adrenaline that made him run.

In an instant, one quick and unexpected motion, Orochi pushed the two crewmen closest to him in the direction of Isamu and the older man. It was enough to give him the smallest head start, and he ran toward the front of the ship, away from the man and his crewmen.

He had seen life vests hanging at any number of locations along the railing on the main deck, and they were only one day away from San Francisco. It would be better than a trip to prison. He would take his chances.

Running at full force toward the forward stairwell on the starboard side, he amazed himself at how agile he was, considering his bad leg. Matsu, Takeo, and Tomoki were still standing at the bottom of the stairwell waiting for news of the impending raid when they spotted Orochi coming toward them on the run. Then, only meters behind, they saw several men who looked like passengers chasing after him. Near the end of the pack came Isamu and the older man.

Whether his instincts were good or bad will long be debated, but Matsu followed his without thinking, and stood to block the stairwell opening from the fast-approaching Orochi. When still several meters away, Orochi stopped momentarily, stooped down to his right leg, fumbled with the material of his pants, and emerged with a knife. Its ominous blade gleamed even in the dim half-light of the lower deck.

Holding it prominently in front of him, he resumed his gait, waving the knife at Matsu in a dangerous and menacing arc. Only at the very last second did Matsu yield his position and let Orochi pass. But as soon as he had, Matsu turned and followed in close pursuit up the steps and out to the upper deck. He had to shield his eyes from the sun it was such contrast to the dreary deck below.

Orochi, on the other hand, seemed not to care when he knocked a first-class passenger to the deck; nothing less than what they deserved, he felt. He headed instinctively toward the outer railing, then kept running as he tried in vain to remember where he'd seen the vests. *They are never there when you need them,* he silently cursed to himself.

Matsu, after a moment for his eyes to adjust to the bright sky above, watched Orochi as he raced along the rail, headed toward the bow of the ship.

Orochi was in the lesser position, though it had not occurred to him. He did not know where he was going, and he was searching for a life vest as he ran. In addition, even though he cared little about running into or even knocking down an innocent bystander, the sheer act of doing so slowed his escape.

Matsu, on the other hand, was only concerned about catching Orochi, who was in his sight the entire time. While Orochi had to change course or push people out of the way, Matsu had only to keep his eye on the prize.

Passengers enjoying a late afternoon stroll around the deck scrambled when they witnessed the confrontation now developing along the forward rail. Lounge chairs emptied of sunbathers and book-readers alike, as the noise and commotion erupted.

An elderly man speaking with his wife dropped his walking cane on the deck as he hobbled along in slow motion. In a flash, Matsu reached down and grabbed the cane from the deck. Now he had a semblance of protection.

Closing in, he lashed the cane at Orochi from left to right in powerful swinging strokes. Orochi could not get close enough to use his knife, with Matsu fending him off by the distance of the cane. Slowly, Matsu drove Orochi closer and closer toward the rail.

Twenty meters below, the clear blue water of the Pacific stretched for miles in every direction.

Orochi was cornered. He looked down over the railing. There was a narrow ledge five meters below. It marked the floor line of the steerage deck. The upper deck was built slightly narrower than the lower deck for better stability. It was his only choice. As Matsu held his ground and waited for the others to catch up to him, Orochi climbed over the rail.

Matsu froze in his tracks, the cane still in hand above his head and ready for a decisive blow. Orochi looked at Matsu with coal-black eyes, spewing only hate and venom. Matsu felt a moment of pity as he watched in disbelief, the actions of the crazed man before him.

Matsu saw Orochi look past him to the fast-approaching crewmen. His face reflected the horror and futility of his situation. With one last look at Matsu, Orochi let go of the railing, aiming for the ledge below.

Lost from view, Matsu rushed to the rail and looked down.

Orochi was falling along the side of the ship from main to steerage. His feet struck the ledge, but it was less than a meter wide. He landed close to the wall and struggled to keep his balance, but because of the distance, was forced to buckle his knees to absorb the fall. In doing so, the force of his torso pushed him away.

Matsu watched in vain as Orochi's hands scoured the wall in search of something to grab. There were no windows on steerage deck, no need for fancywork on the outside walls, nothing there for a falling man to grasp, even to save his life.

Although the outcome was never really in doubt, the sea and the *Coptic* had one last surprise for Orochi. The wind had freshened and altered direction at just the time of Orochi's last deal of the cards. Now, thirty minutes later, the sea was adjusting its surface in a timely confusion of wave patterns. The bow of the *Coptic* rose to ride a crest just as a second and competing wave pushed the bow ever so slightly off to port.

Matsu felt the collision but held on to the railing with one hand, while the other remained firmly ensconced around the handle of the gentleman's cane. When he looked down again, Orochi was gone from view. Matsu hurriedly looked around for a life vest, then called out for one.

One of the men chasing Orochi, a man who seemed familiar with the ship, ran from view momentarily, then returned with several under his arm. He rushed to the rail and threw them over, one by one.

The older man, still standing close to Isamu, suddenly excused himself. "I need to get word to the bridge," he said, and hurried away.

Only a few minutes passed until everyone on deck felt the change in speed of the *S.S. Coptic*. It had slowed its pace. They felt the change of course as well. The few experienced mariners on board rightly deduced they were commencing a man-overboard drill, by slowing and turning a narrow circle around the last known location of the victim.

There were several hours of daylight left, which worked in their favor. The captain maneuvered the large vessel into a series of concentric patterns, even though he well understood the odds of finding a man overboard were not good. The sea continued to swell.

The captain ordered a lookout at the crow's nest atop the mast. On the second pass, they sighted three life vests, each one still empty. They remained for three more circles until at last, the captain ordered the navigator to resume their course.

Orochi might well have intended suicide, given his state of mind and the situation he was in. Had he lived, his next ten years or more would have been in prison. *How does a man get to that state of affairs?* the captain wondered.

Later that same afternoon, a notice appeared at several locations on steerage deck.

NOTICE

Several alert passengers and crew today recovered a cache of stolen property illegally taken from certain steerage passengers during the voyage. All steerage passengers should inspect their lockers and luggage, whether secured by lock or not.

Report all missing property to the ships' store, on steerage deck by noon tomorrow for possible recovery.

Certain currency has also been recovered, believed to have been obtained through an illicit game of chance known as 'find the lady.' If you were a victim of this game, register in the ships' store by noon tomorrow for possible recovery.

The mess hall was abuzz that evening, with a hundred different conversations linked to the unexpected news. Isamu and his decidedly amateurish band of five shared a bench for the first time in days. It was finally safe to be seen together. They smiled with relief as the reality set in. They even laughed together as they heard speculation from nearby diners regarding the heist.

"I knew there was something fishy about that game," said one, with obvious authority.

"When I felt the ship slow up, I thought it was because we were ahead of schedule," offered another.

"I heard the locker was filled with gold bullion. The man who told me saw it with his own eyes," chirped another.

"You should have seen the look on that man's face when he ran up the stairs," said another. "He looked like a man possessed. He took his own life, I'm sure of it. I could tell by the look in his eyes."

The remark Matsu liked best, however, was the one most filled with truth.

"That man who caught up to him on deck was the bravest man I ever saw. He didn't let a knife stop him. He headed right up the stairs after him, bare-handed. I wish I could have seen what happened up there. I heard someone handed him a cane.

And that's the only weapon he had against a madman with a knife. He's a hero, all right. And good riddance to the crook if you ask me."

All five of them smiled when they heard it. Four of them nodded in agreement.

**

The following afternoon, Isamu and his group of five were requested to meet with the captain at three o'clock. Their crewmember friend retrieved them from steerage deck and led them up the stairs to the main deck, then through a corridor to another stairwell, and up another flight of stairs. They had not seen this hallway before.

At the top of the steps, he led them into a large cabin with windows on all sides. In the center was a beautiful wooden wheel nearly two meters in diameter, surrounded by more dials and gauges than they had ever seen. Off to the side was a work table, on top of which were spread a series of maps and charts that none of the five could interpret, not even Isamu, with his limited experience in the fishing boats.

Presiding over the several smartly uniformed crewmen in the room was, of course, the captain. Isamu skipped a breath when he looked at the man. Then his face turned red with shame. This was the older man from yesterday. The man who organized the raid. And the man Isamu had first met briefly back in Yokohama when he needed somewhere private to retrieve his money belt. He was horrified to realize he had not recognized the man.

"Welcome, gentlemen," the captain said.

Looking directly at Isamu, he continued. "Isamu, we meet again. When we met in Yokohama, it did not occur to me I would be seeing you again. As much as I'd like, I seldom have an opportunity to meet with passengers from steerage. Don't tell anyone I said this, but the company wants me to spend my available time with the wealthy people on main deck. I guess they think they're more likely to make a second voyage," he said. "I want to congratulate all of you, first of all, for noticing something amiss on your deck, and secondly, for doing something about it. If more people in this world would make an effort to right what is wrong, we would be living in a better world."

All five of them began to blush at such kind words from a man of his distinction.

"Our crew members at the ship's store have done everything possible to restore property to its rightful owner. Together, we are hopeful that almost everything will be returned. Orochi did leave the ship while in Honolulu, and it's possible he sold some of his plunder while there. That could explain why he had more than twenty-five yen in his valise. But the fact remains: he was certainly fleecing his unsuspecting victims in the card games.

"His co-conspirators have confessed to helping him, and the better news is that they have agreed to confirm which of the victims are legitimate. As you might imagine, there are still people among us who want to make easy money. They thought all they had to do was register, and we'd hand money over to them. That is not going to happen. We know three of your group were victims. We know you are aware of several others. The co-conspirators can fill in the gaps for us. We'll ask them individually, just between us, and if all three agree, we'll return the loss. If they don't agree, then we won't. If, at the end of it, there are one or two who we think have merit, we will ask your advice.

"Unfortunately, Orochi probably had twenty or thirty yen in his possession when he…left the ship. If there is not enough money to reimburse everyone, we will adjust each person downward accordingly. It is certainly better than where they were before you intervened.

"On behalf of the *Occidental and Oriental Steamship Company*, it has been our privilege to share this voyage with you. I wish you every success in your new life in San Francisco. Remember carefully the lessons you have learned on board the *Coptic*. There are always people eager to take what does not belong to them. They have no scruples and no concern for the hardship they cause their fellow human beings. And sadly, friends, San Francisco will be no better than the *Coptic*."

The captain then turned to the giant windows facing the bow, checked the compass heading, then turned to one of the several open charts atop the table.

It did not take them long to understand, the meeting was adjourned.

Isamu turned toward the door as the others stepped in behind.

"One more thing," the captain said. "Tomorrow afternoon, we should see the California coastline. If you're interested, I'll have a crewman issue main deck passes for you. It is pretty exciting to watch it come into view."

Five solemn faces changed to smiles.

CHAPTER 40
FIRST VIEW

JUNE 23, 1899 – APPROACHING SAN FRANCISCO

The minute Isamu and his four friends received their deck passes from a crew member, they scurried to the nearest stairwell like schoolboys heading to the creek on a hot summer day. They bounded up the steps two, three at a time, stopping briefly before opening the door for the first time ever, during main deck hours.

Actually, there were two exceptions. Matsu had pursued the scoundrel, Orochi, up these stairs and out among the 'privileged,' the day before. On that occasion, he was far too focused on his prey to notice the disapproving eyes and frequent vocal judgments directed at the 'riff-raff' so expected of steerage passengers. And Isamu followed behind, alongside the distinguished older man who turned out to be the captain of the ship.

Today was different. Raised in a culture of almost pretentious formality and self-dignity, the five men intuitively knew the importance of assimilating themselves into the upper-class populace beyond the door. There was nothing they could do about the absence of a proper walking cane or a fine silk obi, but they could certainly conduct themselves as proper gentlemen.

Matsu opened the door wide and held it as his friends walked through into the morning sunshine. The sun was higher now than at any time they'd been allowed on deck. The heat felt instantly good on their faces, and together with the steady breeze provided by their forward movement, created a sensation they could not describe. Only Masaru failed to contain his emotion. His smile increased with every step he took. He led them to the furthermost point on the starboard bow. They would be the first to spot California.

When they reached the rail, lined up in a row, they looked around. No other passengers had claimed the space. Surely they were just as eager to see America come into view. The five young men squinted into the eastern sun. Isamu shaded his eyes with the palm of his hand. Together, they scanned the horizon in a wide sweep, from port to starboard. And together they saw nothing but ocean, for as far as they could see, nothing there but water.

Then Isamu laughed. When the others looked at him, he exclaimed, "We must be four hundred kilometers away from California. No wonder we can't see land. Unless your eyes are more powerful than mine," he chided.

"No wonder no one else is watching," Akio replied.

"We're just ahead of everyone else," Takeo proclaimed. "Maybe that's an omen of things to come in San Francisco. We're going to be more successful than everyone else around."

"We're unstoppable," Akio chimed in.

Isamu looked at Matsu, then at the others. "I guess we are," he said.

Matsu nodded at first. Then he took a deep, long breath and said, "Y...Yes, we are. We're unstoppable."

They were quiet for several minutes, dreaming of success in a new land, remembering families far away, even remorse for the unfortunate demise of Orochi, who no doubt deserved his fate. Then Isamu spoke up.

"Matsu, did you just say what I thought you did? All those words and only one tiny stutter. Have you been practicing your speech?"

Matsu flushed at the complement. Nodding, he said "Y...Yes. But I also pretend I'm s...singing."

***

Lunchtime was hours away. Even without the sight of land, they could not bear to return to steerage since now they had received a waiver. Isamu and Matsu walked together in the clockwise pattern they had started on the second day. It felt good to feel safe walking together again, now that Orochi was gone. They no longer worried about who might be watching.

The others stayed at the railing for some time, simply staring at the open water. When Isamu and Matsu came by on their first lap of the ship, the three other men were gone.

Free again to practice their speaking exercises, Isamu rehearsed his English. "Good morning," he greeted every approaching passenger as they walked. He nearly tripped in response to the single passenger who replied, "Good morning to you." When he restored his stride alongside Matsu, he smiled. His English must be at least somewhat credible.

For Matsu, the exercise was breathing, relaxing, choosing his words in advance. By their third lap, it occurred to him to try speaking Isamu's English phrases instead of the Japanese he'd been using. After all, he would be living in America, as well.

What a contrast the two of them made, as they walked lap after lap around the *Coptic's* main deck. Amongst the staid and reserved, mostly elderly couples walking silently with faces fixed, and eyes staring but not seeing, these two young men walked the deck filled with excitement in their eyes and a bounce in their step, thoroughly engrossed in learning something new.

Word came down from the bridge the *Coptic* would pass through the 'golden gate' tomorrow at noon. Steerage passengers were to remain on their deck until released by the captain. Their daily visit to main deck would not be possible due to crew preparations for docking. They would be called after the main-deck passengers had disembarked. Steerage passengers would miss the event. Everyone but them.

The five barely slept. As soon as they awoke, they selected their finest kimonos, combed their hair the best they could without a mirror, clutched their precious passes tightly, and climbed the stairwell, too excited to eat. Carefully opening the door at the top of the stairs, they expected to find the deck crowded with passengers. Instead, there was open space all around. The sun was still low on the horizon, and the air was cool. Above them, a cloudless sky blended into the Pacific water, off in the distant horizon.

"We must be about fifty kilometers away," Isamu said. "We should be able to see land before long." It was something not to be missed.

"Why are there so few passengers here to watch?" Akio asked.

"Are we sure this is the right day?" Takeo added. "Maybe the captain said tomorrow."

They made their way to the bow, staking a claim at the rail, but still no land in sight. Not in any direction. Isamu had never been this far from land during all his time in the fishing boat, so he could not be sure how far a person could see into the distance. He presumed the curvature of the earth must play a role. And, of course, the height of the landfall. He knew there were mountains in California, but not their location or their height. There was nothing to do but wait and watch.

Conversation was absent or brief for the next two hours. Their hearts beat high in their chests. Their minds once again alternated between thoughts of home and dreams of the future. Would they be successful in their new life? Would they see their families again? Did they have enough money to see them through until they found work?

So lost in reverie they were, that when a small anomaly appeared on the distant horizon, they wondered how long it had been there before they noticed.

Pointing excitedly, as though it were necessary to point out the direction in which they were headed, Masaru exclaimed while trying not to shout, "Look! Isn't that land on the horizon?"

The others stared intently in the direction his arm was extended, in spite of its absurdity.

"Sure enough," Takeo answered. "I can see something. It's dark and almost fuzzy compared to the rest of the horizon."

"It's not very high," Akio added. "Does anyone know if there are mountains near San Francisco?"

Only now did Isamu come to wish he had asked Fr. Katz more about the topography of San Francisco. He knew the city included hills, but he had not mentioned anything one way or the other about mountains. He had talked mostly about the bay. He decided to write to Fr. Katz as soon as he settled. He could not wait to tell him all the things he'd seen already, and they had not yet arrived.

Another hour went by. The sun was now well off the horizon, but not high enough to warm the ocean air. Leaning on the forward rail, nothing prevented the oncoming breeze from beating their faces directly, as the *Coptic* steamed toward its destination at a steady twenty knots. In the excitement, they hadn't minded at first, but now they were starting to chill.

"I can't wait for the sun to get higher," Akio said. His voice was shaking from the cold.

"My hands are getting cold," Masaru replied.

"Mine, too," Isamu added. "Why don't I go to the mess and get us five cups of tea while we wait? I see several passengers walking around with cups. It must be acceptable to bring them out on deck."

"I'll c...come with you," Matsu offered. "Will you s...save our p...places?" he asked, looking at the others.

"For a hot cup of tea, I'd not only save your place; I'd bring you one of those empty lounge chairs," Akio said.

Matsu laughed at his remark. It felt good to be so close to the end of their journey. He turned to head for the stairwell when Isamu touched his arm, then held up the main deck pass. "Let's try their mess hall," he said. "They seem to have cups we can take with us. Looking closely at his pass, he said, "I don't see anything on here to indicate we're steerage passengers. The pass simply says 'M.'"

Matsu nodded with a smile.

They headed to mid-ship and found the corridor that led to the captain's bridge two days before. "I think I saw the mess hall through one of the doors on our way to meet with the captain," Isamu said.

Sure enough, just before the stairs leading up to the bridge, there was an open door exposing a number of tables and booths displaying linen napkins, sparkling water glasses, and beautiful porcelain cups and bowls. Not only were there chopsticks, but also western-style eating utensils in gleaming silver.

Timidly, Isamu led the way. Scanning the large room filled with light from windows on two sides, he spotted what appeared to be a serving line along the rear. He looked at Matsu for moral support, then straightened his back, squared his shoulders, and headed toward it. Stealing glances as best he could, he exhaled when he saw a large porcelain pot at one end, surrounded by a sea of cups. They walked directly to the station.

The waiter standing guard at the porcelain pot bowed politely when they stopped in front of him.

"We would like five cups of tea for the deck," Isamu said.

"As you wish," the man replied. Instead of the fine matching cups laid out before him, he reached to a shelf below and retrieved five metal cups. "These are safer for outside use," he offered quietly. Then he methodically filled each cup to the exact same level and turned the handles toward Isamu and Matsu. "Do you wish for them to be delivered?" he asked as though from a script.

Isamu was so surprised at the question that it took a moment to answer.

"No, thank you. My friend and I can deliver them." Then he bowed to the man, whose turn it was to be surprised. Main deck passengers never bowed to a server. But thinking about it now, he wondered why.

Their friends were waiting at the railing when the cups of steaming tea arrived. They could barely wait to wrap their hands around the warm metal cups. It felt so good they waited a few minutes before actually taking a sip.

"H…Have you s…seen anything y…yet?" Matsu asked excitedly.

"Nothing has changed," Akio replied. "It seems to be getting closer, but we still can't make out the shoreline."

One hour passed. Another hour passed. The men, still looking at the eastern horizon, noticed an increase in activity behind them. Isamu turned around to find the deck populated with a number of passengers—far more than when he'd gone to the mess hall for tea.

"We must be getting close," he said. "Look how many others are starting to come on deck. It's a good thing we came early, even if we did have to stand here for hours."

Another hour passed before Akio raised his arm and pointed to the horizon. "I see something!" he said. "I definitely see something. It looks like the top of a mountain, sticking up above a cloud."

The others stared intently at the horizon, some fifteen kilometers ahead of them.

"I see it," Tomoki exclaimed.

"Me too," Takeo replied. "But it's not a very big mountain."

At that moment, a passerby, a middle-aged man with the appearance of a successful businessman, said to them, "That's not really a mountain; what you're seeing is a layer of fog. It covers San Francisco most mornings until the sun burns it off. We should have a splendid view as we pass the 'golden gate' into San Francisco Bay."

As the *Coptic* drew close and the fog began to lift, so did the spirits of the five young men. They held fast to the railing as more and more main-deck passengers began to crowd around them in search of a clear view of the coming coastline.

Isamu watched with wide eyes and deep breaths as other ships, sailing boats, and fishing boats headed in and out of the narrow channel into the bay. He puzzled at how the shoreline north of the channel had many trees, while to the south there were fewer trees and more shrubs and grass.

The coast itself, while rugged, was not like the rocky fjords of Kamaishi. What cliffs there were, were smaller here, the ground more barren. *Not as beautiful as the coast at home*, he thought. And for a moment, the only thing he could see was the view from their house overlooking Kamaishi Bay. He wondered if his mother was watching it now, thinking about her son so far away. He looked down at the deck and blinked away a tear.

Gulls and other seabirds appeared from nowhere to follow the *Coptic*, another sign they were close to land. Most circled lazily above, hoping for an easy meal, stirred up by the relentless propellers of the ship. A few of the more adventurous landed atop a lifeboat or vent tube for a closer look at the incoming strangers.

"Look," Takeo cried, "a welcome committee," as he pointed to a pair of seagulls gliding just above the bow.

Isamu watched as a pilot boat pulled alongside the ship and a uniformed man deftly climbed the rope ladder thrown over *Coptic's* rail. Once on board, the man headed directly to the bridge without the need for guidance. Apparently, he had boarded this ship before. The pilot boat then slipped away from the *Coptic* and was on its way to its next assignment, with only a few alert passengers aware of its brief presence.

And then, almost before they realized, the *Coptic* was sailing through the 'gate' and slowing her speed. They entered San Francisco Bay. The *Coptic* throttled back to a steady pace that seemed like a crawl after days at sea. Now the five wished they had staked their claim on the starboard bow instead of port, for a better view of San Francisco.

Across the bay was another city. A passerby called it Oakland. Toshi had never heard of Oakland. Once through the gate, the ship began its turn to starboard for its final destination. Pier thirty-eight, Isamu thought, but could not be sure.

And suddenly, far too soon, it was over. The *S.S. Coptic* tied securely to its berth in San Francisco, California, United States of America, five thousand miles from home.

Looking around, trying desperately to imprint the scene in his memory forever, Isamu again thought of his family. Not just his mother, but everyone and everything he'd left behind. "Lord, help me," he prayed to himself. "I am afraid. Please guide me. Amen."

CHAPTER 41
Epilogue

JUNE 24, 1899 – SAN FRANCISCO, CALIFORNIA

When he opened his eyes again, he was aware of noise coming from every direction—people shouting and waving, people fighting their way to the departure gangway. It seemed like every passenger was afraid they would be last. In what he considered a deeply ingrained behavior, it became man against man, woman against woman, and family against family. The innate desire to be first in line was on full display.

Knowing they could not disembark until all main deck passengers were off, Isamu and Matsu contented themselves with staring at the wharf and its surroundings. The first of many realities set in when he could find no signs written in Japanese. Nearly everyone still on board was speaking Japanese, but there were no other indications of the language to be found. He swallowed hard with a dry mouth. He searched for a street sign he could decipher with his hundred-word English vocabulary. His heart quickened when he saw the word *California*. And again, when he saw the word *Front*. With time, maybe he could learn them all.

He thought of the priest who would be there to meet him. And then a moment of panic. *What was his name?* Fr. Katz had repeated his name until it was second nature to him. But now, when it counted, he had forgotten it. It was written down in one of his tablets. He would need to retrieve it before they walked down the gangplank. *How embarrassing,* he thought, *the only person in America who knew he was coming, and now to forget his name.* Isamu momentarily regretted his decision to come. *But it's too late now,* he told himself.

It was after three o'clock when Isamu and Matsu reached the disembarkation station. A doctor from the county health department checked their temperatures, peered closely into their eyes and ears, and checked more places than the two men thought necessary, looking for skin anomalies. After passing their exams, they proceeded to the next station for final approval to step foot in America.

It should have been a routine inspection, and would have been for the two, had Matsu not struggled with a stuttering speech impediment. Neither Matsu nor Isamu knew if the ailment would prevent him from legal entry. They only knew that America did not want persons of low character, poor health, or other deformities, thus adding to an ever-expanding list of indigents residing in San Francisco.

The official, seated at a small table near the gangway, stared closely at the names on the manifest. The second man, a large American in a blue uniform, with long blonde hair and a mustache to match, held a paper with details regarding each passenger. A Japanese interpreter sat next to him. In watching those who preceded them in line, the two realized it contained their answers when boarding the ship. Basic things, like name, occupation, and so on. They relaxed a little. They had nothing to hide.

Isamu went first. The questions were routine. Isamu then prepared to answer the questions on Matsu's behalf, as he had done at boarding. But when the uniformed man turned and asked the first question, "What is your name?" Matsu extended his left arm out with palm up to Isamu, as a signal for him to refrain. Matsu would answer himself. He had listened intently to the questions as they were repeated to each man in the line ahead, and knew them from memory.

"M.. My name is Matsu Konishi. I am twenty-five years old. I am a f…fisherman and a c…carpenter. I have at least t…t… twenty-five yen as required." He tilted his head toward Isamu and continued, "W…We are m…meeting Fr. Ramm from St. Mary's C…C…Church."

The Difficult Years of Toshi Ozawa

They stood at the top of the gangplank and scanned the crowd for a man wearing the familiar black robe of a Catholic priest. That's the only way they knew to identify Fr. Ramm. That, and that he was in middle age. Thirties most likely, or maybe early forties, according to Fr. Katz. What they saw was a sea of humanity of every size and shape. Mixed among them were carts, bicycles, dogs, cats, and, of course, birds flying low in search of food.

Passengers behind them shouted to keep moving, an unnecessary endeavor since the crowd proceeded to push them forward, anyway. With luggage in both hands, they had little choice but to shuffle down the plank and into the crowd. Instinctively, Matsu took the lead. His tall frame enabled him to see above most of the disembarking Japanese. The scattering of Americans, he found, were generally taller. But there were few of them at this pier. Everyone meeting a friend or family member at this pier was Japanese.

The two made their way through the throng of people, toward a row of buildings at the edge of the wharf. Their only objective was to find enough space to put down their luggage and watch for the priest. Having missed their midday meal, they were hungry, and getting tired.

The upper-deck passengers had mostly dispersed by now. Carts and wagons, loaded with luggage of every kind, were seen heading up Townsend Street, then north on Second Street to one of the nearby hotels, or Japantown, to visit friends or family members. Passengers followed close by, in two-wheeled taxis.

Even steerage passengers were beginning to thin from the dock, which provided an opportunity for the two men to spot an outdoor dining table where two other men were just about to leave. Rushing over to it with luggage in hand, they bowed to the men as a signal they would like to occupy their newly vacated table.

Just having a place to sit was enough to relieve their aching backs. They had been standing since early morning, and not until now did they realize how tired they truly were. Isamu scanned the small courtyard in search of someone to take their order. Seeing no one, he left Matsu at the table and went inside the hut to find someone. He saw an elderly man far in the back who was working intently over a wood-burning stove. Nearer the front, a woman about the same age worked diligently over a tub, washing pans and cups.

Isamu waited for what seemed a courteous amount of time before speaking. "Hello," he said, to the one nearest him. When she did not acknowledge him, he repeated, but louder this time. "Hello."

This time the woman looked up and then shouted something back to the man at the rear of the hut. Isamu waited and watched as the man lifted a pot from the stove and placed it safely away from the heat. Then he hurried toward the front of the hut, to within a meter or two from Isamu, where he stopped and said, "So sorry, didn't see you come in. What can I get for you?" Isamu noticed several beads of sweat running down his forehead.

Isamu stared back at the man as his mind went blank. Whatever he said were not words Isamu had memorized.

"What can I get for you?" The man repeated.

"Good afternoon," Isamu replied. That's all he could think of to say. Then, realizing how foolish it must have sounded, he added, "Can you tell me directions to the wharf?"

The man looked at him with a blank face and then switched to Japanese. "What can I get for you?"

Isamu sighed with a combination of relief and disappointment. It was turning out just as he predicted. When he actually needed to use English, his mind went blank.

Finally, with the man still looking at him, Isamu replied in Japanese, "My friend and I would each like a cup of tea and something to eat...something 'American' to eat. What do you suggest for our first American meal?"

The man thought for a moment and then broke into a smile. "I have just the thing for you. It tastes good, is quick to make, and easy to eat. Very popular with Americans. It's called a 'hot dog'."

Isamu scrunched up his face. "Hot dog?" he repeated. "I don't think I want dog meat. What else do you suggest?"

The man laughed. "Oh, it's not made from dogs. That is only the name of it. How it got that name, I do not know. It is a small round tube of ground up meat, between two halves of a small loaf of bread. Try one and see for yourself. It is the only 'American' choice on our menu today. Everything else is Japanese." He laughed again. "Usually, I get requests from 'Americans' asking for something Japanese. Not today. You are other way around."

Isamu smiled at the man. He was drawn to his obvious work ethic and humble sincerity. "My friend and I would each like to order your best hot tea and one American hot dog. We are seated at one of your tables out front. Should I come back when they're ready?"

"No, no... I'll bring them to you. Go enjoy the fresh air and afternoon sun. It will be cool when the sun goes down. I'll bring your order very soon." He bowed quickly and hurried to his stove.

"I ordered us something American," Toshi said. "He will bring it out when it's ready. He said it is very popular with Americans. It's called a hot dog, but it's not really a dog. I can't wait to try it."

He had barely seated himself when the man came from the hut carrying two cups of tea. Isamu could see the steam rising above them as he set them carefully on the table in front of them. "Our very best tea," he assured Isamu. "We only buy tea from our backward neighbor," then he leaned in to the two men and lowered his voice to just above a whisper, "China," he continued. "Very despicable neighbor, but they grow the best tea trees in the world. *Thea Sinensis*, I think. Regardless, they make the best tea leaves, and I select them personally from a shop in Chinatown. You try it. See if I'm telling the truth." He smiled again, then hurried back into the hut.

The two barely had time to sample their first sip when the man returned. This time, he carried something in each hand, which they could not see because of what appeared to be remnants of newspaper wrapped completely around the treasure.

With great fanfare and a smile to match, he set one of the treasures carefully down in front of each man, next to their cups of tea. "No chopsticks needed," he said. "Only hands. Some Americans like to add vegetables or spices, like tomato sauce or pickles. I'll bring them if you like. Others say no, just eat it like it comes, with the special tiny bread loaf."

The two men timidly removed the paper wrapping to reveal a miniature loaf of bread, inside of which was a cylinder-shaped tube of brownish-red meat, about the diameter of their thumb, but longer. With the man standing next to them in obvious anticipation, they had little choice but to pick up the loaf, which they found to be the perfect size to grab with one hand, but perhaps even better with two. It seemed rather primitive, however, to deliver food directly to your mouth without the refinement of chopsticks. Or, as they would have to learn in America, the strange metal tools.

Recognizing their hesitation, the man at the table encouraged them. "Yes," he said. "Yes, that's how they eat them in America. Bite a piece off the end, and there you have it. You can lay the hot dog back down on your newspaper while you chew if you want. Some people do, some don't; they just hold onto it between bites. That's what makes it so easy. Especially popular at American baseball games…make sure you see a baseball game while you're in America."

Having taken their first bites, they could relax enough to consider whether they liked them or not. This was something completely foreign to anything they had ever eaten before. Not wanting to disappoint the man, they both smiled and nodded their heads as he watched them eat two more bites. "If you want anything more, I'm right inside," he said. Then he returned to the hut.

More relaxed now, with the man not standing there to watch, Isamu and Matsu took time to examine their meals. At first, they were not impressed. It was far from their usual meal of rice or fish. But after the third bite, it started to taste a little better. They liked the warmth of the outside loaf. They liked the convenience of it. However, the convenience also created a downside. One tended to eat it too quickly. Part of the pleasure of dining was to take one's time and savor every bite. Chopsticks encouraged the practice. It was hard to cram one's mouth with food with two tiny sticks of wood. The utensils Americans used to eat with, looked prone to the same disadvantage. *Did everything in America revolve around speed?*

After finishing their hot dogs, they sat back in their outdoor chairs and reveled in a long, slow sip of Chinese tea. The man was right. This was the best cup of tea Isamu had tasted since leaving Kamaishi. Maybe ever. He decided to tell his parents about it in his first letter.

With food in their stomachs and the lingering smell of the exceptionally delightful tea, the two men renewed their attention to the wharf around them. As they scanned the diminishing crowd while watching for a faceless man in priest's attire, the significance settled on them both.

Isamu looked at Matsu with a smile that filled his face, and exclaimed, "We did it. Can you believe it? We came to America." Looking at their table of rumpled newsprint and two porcelain cups, he continued, "Our first meal in America… American hot dog. I can't wait to tell my family all about it."

Matsu nodded.

As he scanned for the priest, he noticed for the first time, a hut next to the teahouse with wooden racks out front, under a covered awning. A sign hung from the awning, with both Japanese and English letters. A single word appeared in each language…Souvenirs.

"Would you keep watching for Fr. Ramm?" Isamu asked Matsu. "I want to look inside that shop to see what they have. Maybe I'll find something to send home to my family."

Matsu nodded again.

Isamu walked the short distance to the souvenir hut, and Matsu watched as he looked intently at the two wooden racks. He observed as Isamu selected several items from the racks and moved inside the hut to pay for his selections.

Isamu had no more than stepped inside the hut when Matsu spotted a middle-aged Caucasian man dressed in a black robe, hurrying toward the *S.S. Coptic*. At his side was a Caucasian boy about ten years old. Matsu jerked a look toward the souvenir hut, but Isamu was not in sight. With no other choice coming to mind, Matsu simply stood and shouted toward the man. "Fr. Ramm?"

The black-robed man faltered and turned his head, but not seeing Matsu, he resumed his pace toward the *Coptic*. Matsu shouted a second time, this time with increased volume and a hint of alarm. "Fr. Ramm!" he shouted. He waved his arm as well.

This time, both the man and the boy stopped and turned. Ironically, it was the boy, much shorter than the priest, who saw Matsu first. Matsu watched as the boy tugged at the man's robe and pointed to Matsu.

Upon seeing him, they turned and changed course directly toward Matsu and the small teahouse. When close enough to hear, the man said, "Isamu?"

Matsu shook his head. He pulled both hands to his chest and said, "Matsu." Then he pointed to the souvenir hut and said, "Isamu."

Then, to his relief, the boy approached Matsu and said in Japanese, "I am Francisco. People call me Cisco for short. I speak Japanese for Fr. Ramm. He does not speak the language, so I translate for him."

"Isamu is in the h...hut next d...door, he should be right b...back," explained Matsu. "M...My name is Matsu, and we m...met during the v...voyage. He asked me to w...wa...watch for you in c...case he was inside the h...hut," Matsu continued. Then he turned to the priest and bowed with respect. Cisco relayed the message to his companion. The priest seemed surprised but returned the greeting.

Matsu watched the empty doorway nervously, hoping to see Isamu's face appear. Trying to make polite conversation with a stranger in a foreign country, caused perspiration to form on his forehead. Droplets ran down his cheeks.

Finally, Isamu broke through the nearby doorway holding his purchase in hand, and as soon as he spotted the familiar black robe standing near Matsu, waved his arm high in the air and rushed to meet them.

He nodded a look of appreciation to Matsu for finding him, then stopped short of the priest by one or two meters. It did not yet occur to him the ten-year-old standing nearby was with him.

Isamu had been rehearsing this for weeks. "Fr. Ramm?" Isamu asked in English.

The priest nodded and replied, "Isamu?"

Fr. Ramm was shorter than Isamu expected and rather small in stature. In American terminology, Isamu guessed him to be about five and one-half feet tall, smaller than the university football hero Fr. Katz had proclaimed him to be. As Isamu studied his face, a single word came to mind... determined. It was a handsome face, but his eyes were the defining factor. Deep and dark, Isamu felt as if they could see right through him. His demeanor seemed perpetually serious. Unlike Fr. Katz, who seemed on the verge of a smile at every moment, Fr. Ramm seemed more like he was late for saving his next wayward soul.

"Yes, I am Isamu Ozawa." He continued in memorized English. Then he tilted his head toward Matsu. "And this is my friend, Matsu Konishi. Thank you for coming to meet us. Fr. Katz sends prayers and peace from Kamaishi."

Fr. Ramm then extended an arm toward his young companion. "This is my friend, Francisco. He helps me with the Japanese language."

Isamu listened with a look of panic beginning to form on his face. Those were words he had not memorized. When Isamu made no reply, the priest looked at the boy and said something more, which Isamu did not understand. The boy quickly repeated his greeting in Japanese to Isamu and Matsu. "He said my name is Francisco, and that most people call me Cisco. I help him with the Japanese language. Do you speak English?"

Isamu answered in Japanese, "I am learning English, but there are a lot of words I do not know. There was no one for me to practice with."

Cisco explained his answer to Fr. Ramm. The priest spoke to the boy in English, who then passed it to Isamu in Japanese. "That is good to know. For now, we will use Francisco. He can show you where to continue your lessons in English. Do you have all your belongings? I have arranged a place for you to stay. I didn't know you were coming with a friend, but hopefully they can squeeze him in...at least for now."

As Cisco relayed the message, Isamu remembered they had yet to pay the teahouse for their tea and hotdog.

Looking at Cisco, Isamu said, "I have to pay for our meal first, then we can go."

He rushed inside the shop, looking for the owner. It took longer than expected because the man wanted to know how they liked their meal, then apologized for it taking so long. He was always short of help, he lamented. People would accept the job only to leave when a better one came along. Isamu wanted to ask more about it, but he could not keep the priest waiting.

Once outside, he gathered up his luggage, as did Matsu, and they fell in line behind Fr. Ramm and Cisco. He led them to King Street and then right on Second Street for several blocks to a very wide street, which Cisco pointed out was Market Street.

They crossed over it, and Isamu was surprised to find that all the streets on the other side followed a different pattern. They ran at a forty-five degree angle from the streets they had just marched along. *How will we ever find our way around?* he wondered, *when streets follow one pattern here and another pattern there.*

They marched on, the priest in his distinguishing black cassock, Francisco at his heels and half his size, followed by Isamu with a valise in each hand, and then by Matsu, easily a head taller and fifty pounds heavier than Isamu or the priest, bringing up the rear with his solitary bag.

The thing that amazed Isamu most, however, was that no one seemed to notice. The streets and walkways were busy with people of all kinds. Many were Japanese, obviously just arrived, by the looks of their luggage. Some were Chinese. Some were Mexican. A few were dressed like royalty, intrigued by the shop windows, or simply out for an afternoon stroll. Others seemed not to have bathed for days, with faces covered by whiskers that reached their chests.

Isamu noticed that Fr. Ramm seemed to speed up as they passed certain storefronts, and finally he noticed the pattern, the ones where young women were anxious to hold the door open for them. At first, he felt sorry for them, seemingly unable to afford a complete wardrobe. *Jobs must be hard to find,* he thought. These poor women are relegated to such menial tasks in an effort to clothe themselves.

Onward they marched, along Montgomery Street, north until they reached a street sign Isamu recognized: California. They turned left on California, as Fr. Ramm explained through his interpreter, Cisco, they would be living among several other Japanese at the edge of what was called Chinatown.

"Chinatown is where nearly all Chinese live," Cisco explained. "But a lot of Japanese also live there. They prefer to be together so they have someone they can talk to. Also, it's easier to find work in their own neighborhood. Unless you speak English, it will be difficult to find any kind of work that requires communication. That's why some Japanese take to the country and work on farms. They don't need much talking while tending the fields. Some find jobs in laundries or Japanese teahouses. Some find work as fishermen," he added. "But there is much competition for jobs."

All this was coming from Cisco himself. It was obvious he had accompanied Fr. Ramm many times before, and had the welcome story memorized.

"Fr. Ramm said you must stay away from the 'Barbary Coast' in Chinatown. It is home for the devil himself," he said. "He wants you to promise to stay away. If he learns you have visited there, he will write to your parents."

Cisco said this with a firm face. It was not meant as a joke.

"Fr. Ramm has written to parents," he then added as reinforcement.

At Dupont Street, Fr. Ramm pointed out the large building on their right. "That is the old St. Mary's church," Cisco said as the priest pointed. "It is not the church he's assigned to; it is where mostly Caucasians and a few Japanese attend mass. You will be welcome there. It is a good and welcoming parish. Fr. Ramm is assigned to a newer church, which is called the Cathedral of St. Mary of the Assumption. It's located several blocks from here at Van Ness and Geary Streets. Of course, you're welcome there as well. It is not as convenient, but you may want to visit it occasionally. It is where your friend Fr. Katz was assigned until he went to Kamaishi," he added.

They turned right on Stockton Street and followed a handful of other Japanese carrying luggage, like themselves, to a nondescript doorway beneath a sign that read:

ROOMS – DAILY – WEEKLY – MONTHLY.

Cisco led the way through the doorway and to a small counter, behind which stood an elderly Japanese woman. He pointed to the two strangers standing by Fr. Ramm and then spoke to the woman in Japanese, explaining the presence of the extra person. Eventually, the woman, after making eye contact with Fr. Ramm, nodded her head and smiled at Cisco. She handed him a key and, with a tilt of the head, authorized him to lead them up the stairs to what would become their home for an unknown period of time.

The small room was on the third floor. It had a window overlooking Stockton Street, which was more than they had hoped for. But there was only one small bed. There was a washbasin next to the window and a small wardrobe for storing their clothing. Cisco showed them a toilet at the end of the hall. It was shared by all the third-floor residents. The room was five yen per week. But because of Matsu, they could split the cost. Meals could be had for an additional two yen per person. The charge included two meals per day, morning and evening. The typical meal was rice, eggs, or vegetables, sometimes fish, plus bread and tea.

"You are expected to pay in advance," Cisco continued in Japanese. "She will be expecting two weeks payment on our way out. Once you find a job, she will accept payment in either yen or dollars," he added.

Isamu pulled his secret money belt from under his clothing and pulled out his share of the nine yen total. He was down to twenty-seven. Finding work would be his first priority. He and Matsu followed Fr. Ramm and Cisco down to the front desk to make their payment. Fr. Ramm borrowed paper and a pencil from the woman and wrote down the address of St. Mary's of the Assumption.

The lady opened the door to a small closet behind the desk and retrieved a sleeping mat. It would be their second bed.

"Tomorrow is Sunday. Cisco can come for you Monday morning after breakfast if you want, and help you look for work. You will find his service very helpful. I live next to the church. Send for me or come to see me if you find yourselves in need. I'm sorry I do not have time to care for everyone personally. But as a friend of Fr. Katz, I am at your service if you need me." He smiled politely as Cisco repeated the message to them.

Then he and his young helper turned and exited to Stockton Street. They walked South on Stockton as far as Geary, where they turned right until it reached Van Ness. Shadows were already forming from the tall steeple above the cathedral.

Their first day in America had come to a close for Isamu and Matsu.

But a whole new life was about to begin.

If you enjoyed *The Difficult Years of Toshi Ozawa*, please leave a review to help others find it. Better yet, tell a friend.

To learn the fate of Isamu in San Francisco, please continue his journey with the next book of the *Kamaishi Heritage* series, *Isamu's American Dream*.

To receive notification on release of each new book, please *follow the author* wherever you buy books, or contact the author at dddavenport.author@gmail.com

AUTHOR'S NOTES

Cholera struck Kamaishi in 1882, taking more than three hundred lives. English physician John Snow determined that the disease was transmitted through contaminated water almost thirty years before, but I could only speculate regarding how much of that knowledge would have reached Kamaishi. Japan was a closed nation until the Meiji Revolution in 1866-1869. I could find no documented source of the outbreak, but it might well have been introduced to the village by a traveling stranger. Saburo Kondo seemed the proper candidate, given the tragic death of Suki, the girl he had placed at the silk factory some years before.

Once exposed to the lives of the young girls at the silk factory, Toshi and Haruki could not abandon them. They had a chance to return to the iron foundry, but even bandits, stubborn mules, and freezing nights on the ocean would not deter them from providing food to the silk factory kitchen.

I was surprised and fascinated to learn Kamaishi had experienced a devasting tsunami in 1896. More than 27,000 people were killed. As told in the story, the fishing fleet was out for the night, and amazingly, did not feel the earthquake or its resulting tsunami. Only when they returned the following morning did they discover the disaster. Sadly, it took the life of Fr. Henri Lispard. His body was later recovered from the sea.

The tsunami hit Kamaishi in the late evening of June 15. The village had been celebrating the return of soldiers from the first Sino-Japanese war, and many of the revelers were partying on or near the beach. The tsunami traveled far up the river valley, and it would have made little difference for those living in the village. Those who lived on the ridges of the peninsulas were safe from the wall of water, but of course, their lives were forever changed.

The *S.S. Coptic* sailed from Yokohama and Honolulu on the dates described. I was able to find references regarding the ship using a helpful research tool, *newspapers.com*. I could not determine the cost of a fare, however, and as with most of the references to prices and wages, I had to improvise with what seemed plausible.

In addition to Fr. Lispard, other actual people who lived during the period were Fr. Charles Ramm, the priest who met Toshi and Matsu at the wharf in San Francisco, and Bishop Beguinot, of France. Whether the bishop had any connection to Fr. Lispard is doubtful. The only link I could find is that they were both from France.

The idea for rebuilding St. Mary's church with a window facing the sun came from a visit to Ave Maria Catholic Church in Ave Maria, Florida. It seemed exactly like something Toshi would do, and Fr. Lispard provided the seed on their last visit together.

THANK YOU to:

My mother, Mary Esther Davenport, who taught in country schools throughout her long career, and always championed proper use of the language.

My English and Writing teachers along the way, including Dr. Jean Pettit at UNK, Jack E. Nellson at Shelton Public High School, and Liz Kay, at MCC in Omaha.

Kirsten Bublitz, who inspired me to write this book, having written two of her own before she graduated college at UNA, and to her mother and family who went out of their way to help support this project.

To my friends, when asked how the book was coming, listened patiently through a longer response than they thought actually necessary.

To Petra Jacobsen, my pen pal research assistant, for her help in language translation with the Kamaishi Iron Museum as well as her first-hand accounts from Japan.

To my Beta readers at *fiverr.com*. The story was greatly improved because of their candid suggestions.

Robert Marshall

Sasha Pinto-Jayawardena

Cover art - depicting Fr. Lispard at the Ozawa family teahouse:

Rob Williams

Books by D.D. Davenport

Kamaishi Heritage Book 1 – The Mostly Happy Life of Toshi Ozawa

Kamaishi Heritage Book 2 – The Difficult Years of Toshi Ozawa

Kamaishi Heritage Book 3 – Isamu's American Dream

Soon to be released

Kamaishi Heritage Book 4 – Isamu's Broken Dream

About the Author.

Don was born in Custer County, Nebraska, attended public schools in Callaway, and later graduated from Shelton High School and the University of Nebraska at Kearney. A lifelong learner, he also attended the University of Nebraska at Omaha and the Metropolitan Community College of Omaha.

During his career as an IT specialist, Don commuted for extended periods to Worcester, MA, Houston, and San Antonio, TX. He currently resides in Omaha with his wife, Marian.

The story of Toshi's family was seven years in the making. It is a story of inspiration that reflects the difficulties each of us encounters at times in our lives.

You can reach the author at:

dddavenport.author@gmail.com

for comments or to request discussion questions for any book in the series.

To learn more about events which inspired *The Kamaishi Heritage Series*, please consider the following publications.

Inventing Japan, by Ian Buruma

Factory Girls, by E. Patricia Tsurumi

The Ghost Map, by Steven Johnson

History of California, by Matt Clayton

Califia, by Rick Walker

The Age of Gold, by H.W. Brands

Historic San Francisco, by Rand Richards

San Francisco's Japantown, by The Japantown Task Force, Inc.

The Barbary Plague, by Marilyn Chase

Divine Lola, by Cristina Morato

The San Francisco Earthquake, by Gordon Thomas and Max Morgan-Witts

1929, by M.L. Gardner

A Rabble of Dead Money, by Charles R. Morris

Looking like the Enemy, by Mary Matsuda Gruenewald

Cho's Story, by Choichi Shimizu

Someone Else's Shoes, by Jojo Moyes

From Bugle Boy to Battleship, by Lloyd Glick

USS Indiana BB-1, by U.W. Navy Fact File Battleship

Farewell to Manzanar, by Jeanne Wakatsuki Houston & James D. Houston

Book Club Discussion Questions

1. Which character(s) from the story did you like best? Why?
2. Did you know cholera was transmitted by drinking water contaminated by the feces of an infected person?
3. Did you know that three to five million people worldwide are still affected by cholera every year? What are some ways this could be reduced?
4. Did you know that Christianity was banned in Japan for two hundred years prior to the Meiji Revolution?
5. The author's notes indicate more than 27,000 lives were lost in the 1896 tsunami. Do you think that was more or less than the number taken in the 2011 tsunami?
6. Share with one another what you think it must have felt like for Haruki to lose his daughter and grandson to the tsunami.
7. Do the recent natural disasters in America and around the world (tornadoes, hurricanes, and wildfires) help you comprehend what it must have been like to survive the tsunami?
8. Did the story help you to consider the hardships of migrating to a country where you didn't know the language or the culture? Think about your ancestors. Would it have been more difficult for them than for immigrants today?
9. Have you ever sailed on a large ship such as the *S.S. Coptic*? Did it bring back any memories for you?
10. Have you ever been to San Francisco or viewed its shoreline or skyline from a distance? Have you crossed over the Golden Gate Bridge? Share your experience.

Made in the USA
Las Vegas, NV
19 March 2025